ALIEN™

CULT

THE COMPLETE ALIEN™ LIBRARY FROM TITAN BOOKS

The Official Movie Novelizations
by Alan Dean Foster
Alien, Aliens™, Alien 3, Alien: Covenant, Alien: Covenant Origins
Alien: Resurrection by A.C. Crispin
Alien 3: The Unproduced Screenplay by William Gibson & Pat Cadigan

Alien
Out of the Shadows by Tim Lebbon
Sea of Sorrows by James A. Moore
River of Pain by Christopher Golden
The Cold Forge by Alex White
Isolation by Keith R.A. DeCandido
Prototype by Tim Waggoner
Into Charybdis by Alex White
Colony War by David Barnett
Inferno's Fall by Philippa Ballantine
Enemy of My Enemy by Mary SanGiovanni
Uncivil War by Brendan Deneen
Seventh Circle by Philippa Ballantine and Clara Carija
Perfect Organisms by Shaun Hamill
Cult by Gavin G. Smith

The Complete Alien Collection
The Shadow Archive
Symphony of Death

The Rage War
by Tim Lebbon
Predator™: Incursion, Alien: Invasion
Alien vs. Predator™: Armageddon

Aliens
Bug Hunt edited by Jonathan Maberry
Phalanx by Scott Sigler
Infiltrator by Weston Ochse
Vasquez by V. Castro
Bishop by T. R. Napper

The Complete Aliens Collection
Living Nightmares

The Complete Aliens Omnibus
Volumes 1–7

Predator
If It Bleeds edited by Bryan Thomas Schmidt
The Predator by Christopher Golden & Mark Morris
The Predator: Hunters and Hunted by James A. Moore
Stalking Shadows by James A. Moore & Mark Morris
Eyes of the Demon edited by Bryan Thomas Schmidt
The Complete Predator Omnibus by Nathan Archer & Sandy Scofield

Non-Fiction
AVP: Alien vs. Predator by Alec Gillis & Tom Woodruff, Jr.
Aliens vs. Predator Requiem: Inside The Monster Shop by Alec Gillis & Tom Woodruff, Jr.
Alien: The Illustrated Story by Archie Goodwin & Walter Simonson
The Art of Alien: Isolation by Andy McVittie
Alien: The Archive
Alien: The Weyland-Yutani Report by S.D. Perry
Aliens: The Set Photography by Simon Ward
Alien: The Coloring Book
The Art and Making of Alien: Covenant by Simon Ward
Alien Covenant: David's Drawings by Dane Hallett & Matt Hatton
The Predator: The Art and Making of the Film by James Nolan
The Making of Alien by J.W. Rinzler
Alien: The Blueprints by Graham Langridge
Alien: 40 Years 40 Artists
Alien: The Official Cookbook by Chris-Rachael Oseland
Aliens: Artbook by Printed In Blood

Aliens vs. Predators
Ultimate Prey edited by Jonathan Maberry & Bryan Thomas Schmidt
Rift War by Weston Ochse & Yvonne Navarro
The Complete Aliens vs. Predator Omnibus by Steve Perry & S.D. Perry

ALIEN™

CULT

A NOVEL BY GAVIN G. SMITH

TITAN BOOKS

ALIEN™: CULT
Print edition ISBN: 9781785651960
E-book edition ISBN: 9781785651984

Published by Titan Books
A division of Titan Publishing Group Ltd
144 Southwark Street, London SE1 0UP
www.titanbooks.com

First edition: November 2025
10 9 8 7 6 5 4 3 2 1

A CIP catalogue record for this title is available from the British Library.

EU RP (for authorities only)
eucomply OÜ, Pärnu mnt. 139b-14, 11317 Tallinn, Estonia
hello@eucompliancepartner.com, +3375690241

Printed and bound by CPI Group (UK) Ltd, Croydon CR0 4YY.

To Andrew, Ceri, Kiera,
Trev and Yvonne, for reasons.

PART I

1

Tyler felt the swamp water seep into his boots. He tightened his grip on his service weapon, his sidearm slick from the thick humid air and his own sweat. The night vision element of the tactical lenses clipped to his glasses had turned the wooded Missouri swamp land into a ghost world of twisted and gnarled hickory trees, wearing Spanish moss like a funerary veil. The bare bones of the rewilded military base were still just about visible, lumps of concrete encrusted with lichen and cracked by tree roots. The old motor pool was a largely intact concrete bunker rising out of the swamp water, a low hill covered in the fecund plant life but with oddly angular sides and leaking man made light and sound.

Ahead of him Tyler could make out the back of one of the Bureau's elite Hostage Rescue Team members. She wore servo-assisted armor, the words FBI stenciled across her back, pulse carbine at the ready. Despite her bulk she was somehow moving quietly. Tyler didn't feel stealthy. His own breath was deafening in his ears and he seemed to slip or stumble every other step. He didn't need to look behind him to know that Serena was following him, nearly silently.

The music was grating on him. It sounded like a looped nursery rhyme over a discordant industrial beat, with an incongruously light and fast bassline woven into the track. He could feel his heart trying to match the drumbeat. His excitement came with a thrill of guilt. He knew that there would be no hostages for HRT to rescue. Credence Greco had worked too hard to remain off grid, leaving such a small footprint that even AI-augmented analytics and surveillance had been little help in tracking him. Tyler knew that the families of those that had been taken were living in false hope.

Tyler had been searching for Greco for months. The break had finally come when speaking to the survivor of an earlier attempted abduction. She had been able to describe the old base. Finding the survivor had taken the time but Greco had messed up. It must have been early in his career as a monster. He had struck too close to his lair.

A flickering strobe light then a staccato thunder, and Tyler felt things passing him at velocity. Serena pulled him down from behind. It took him a moment for his brain to unpack what was happening. They were taking fire. The HRT agent ahead of them staggered, but then her pulse carbine was at her shoulder. A different frequency of strobic light: flickering lightning accompanied by the screaming of pulse-accelerated bullets. Tyler couldn't see what she was firing at, but whatever was firing at them stopped. He wondered if Greco was already dead.

"Sentry weapons..." *someone said over comms. It meant Greco could still be alive.*

"Red Actual to Blue and Red teams, breach, breach, breach." This over the comms from the HRT's Special Agent in Charge.

The HRT agent in front of Tyler increased her pace. All attempts at stealth now abandoned, Tyler staggered after her as fast as he could, trying not to faceplant in one of the many pools of stagnant water.

He caught a glimpse of the sentry weapon as he ran past it. It was a scratchbuilt job, a civilian rifle designed for hunters modified for full auto with an extended magazine, mounted on a mechanized tripod and augmented with a motion detector. It was just so much scrap now. Not for the first time Tyler wondered at the Venn diagram overlap between serial killers and DIY enthusiasts.

Tyler scrambled and slipped up the moss-covered concrete slope to the bunker's side door, following the HRT agent. Serena was little more than a fleeting shape in the darkness, always just behind him, ready to assist.

Tyler held back as three more members of HRT's Blue team materialized out of the dark undergrowth. Tyler felt entirely ineffectual standing there with only his sidearm: but then, HRT had only allowed him and Serena along as a courtesy. Serena, unarmed, was at his side now.

More fire and thunder. An underslung breaching shotgun hit one of the hinges with a solid lockbuster slug, then the other hinge and finally the door's lock. Metal screamed as a power-assisted boot kicked the door in and Blue team filed in. As Tyler moved after them, he heard multiple breaching charges go off at the main doors as Red team effected an explosive entry. Like Tyler, nobody here had any illusions as to whether Greco's victims were still alive.

He clambered over the metal door, near bent in two, into the bunker and put his back against the wall. He was trying to catch his breath, breathing harder than even his current level of exertion warranted. Serena stood by him, scanning the area around them.

Tyler heard more gunfire: strobic light animated the shadows. He was standing at the end of rows of shelves filled with years of accumulated junk, all of it coated in moss and mold.

Movement to his left. He swung round, bringing his sidearm up. The flashlight mounted under the weapon illuminated the figure in his night vision. He almost squeezed the trigger. Then Serena was next to him, pushing the weapon down. For a moment he thought that he had almost made a terrible mistake. One of Greco's victims was alive. Then he saw the wires sprouting from the man's head, the crudely implanted servos on his joints, the only partially successful embalming. Tyler slumped against the wall and forced himself to look away, but he could still see the crudely animated body.

Somebody was shouting to cease fire over the comms, panic in their voice. It was his voice. Then the HRT agents realized what was happening, the source of the movement all around them.

***

An agent was curled up in his armor, hugging his knees, sobbing, another one comforting him. A third spitting vomit from her mouth.

Serena led Tyler through the old, overgrown motor pool. The HRT agents glared at him as if it were his fault, as though he had brought them here, and he had. It didn't matter. He couldn't really feel anything.

Greco was small, dirty and unkempt. Two of the armored agents pushed him onto his knees between them. Tyler stood over him. Greco's tear-filled, wide eyes looked somehow innocent.

"I'm sorry," he said, "I was lonely."

Tyler thought of the expanding web of grief growing exponentially out from this inadequate man's fantasies.

Serena, always Serena, pulled the sidearm from Tyler's fingers and stopped him from doing something really stupid.

Tyler woke up in the hypersleep chamber screaming and clawing at the glass. The hatch slid open and Serena was standing over him.

The city's starscrapers were a field of glass spikes reaching up to a washed-out night sky. The passenger shuttle's torch was just about bright enough that it could be picked out against the indeterminate glow of the light pollution. The southern polar city grasped the shuttle's bulk as it sank between the spires towards the aerospace port. A patina of executive comfort grew like a fungus over the port's vast, labyrinthian industrial superstructure. Engines on a heavy burn made their last few directional adjustments as the passenger shuttle was engulfed in a bath of its own exhaust. Flames licked out from the raised shuttle port's exhaust venting. The landing pad sank on vast shock-absorbing coils as the shuttle touched down.

Thick umbilicals snaked through the smoke, plugging into the ship to provide fuel, oxygen and other essentials while sucking out waste. Moments later the passenger bridge concertinaed out to mate with the shuttle and the hierarchical disembarkation process began.

Tyler had been awake, in theory, for the better part of twelve hours. He was, however, nursing his lag, his hypersleep hangover. He half welcomed the numbness that came with it. It left him with a definite sense of dislocation, awake but asleep, as though he were haunting himself. He was aware that he had dreamed the entire month he had been in hypersleep and that those dreams had been unpleasant. He had a strong suspicion as to the content of the dreams. With an entire month to sleep since they had left Gateway Station, it was inevitable that sooner or later his subconscious was going to cycle back to that swamp in Missouri. He was thankful that he couldn't remember the actual dreams. That he remembered the sensation but not the content only heightened his feeling of dislocation, however.

"Special Agent Matterton?"

Tyler looked around the luggage reclamation area, a huge concrete hall with a vaulted ceiling, as though seeing it for the first time. He located the source of the voice: Serena. His partner. She was white, dark-haired, and her medium build belied her speed and power. Serena had been designed, apparently, to look professional but unassuming, unthreatening but not unpleasant to look at. In terms of unassuming the designers had outright failed. In terms of being not unpleasant to look at, they had underestimated the aesthetics of professional competence. That she was a packaged product, made Tyler all the more uncomfortable. He did his best to forget it. Maybe that was the problem.

"Serena, we're off duty. Can you please call me Tyler?" he asked again.

"Protocol," she said by way of explanation. "I believe our luggage has found us and our liaison is waiting beyond customs."

Somewhere else he would have perhaps asked if the local authorities could fast-track them, but here on Alexandria Colony everything had a cost. Even professional courtesy.

Their autonomous luggage caught up with them. Tyler watched Serena walk away from him. He was in too much of a twilight state to sort through his thoughts, so he just followed her. It was easier. She was never not going to know the correct thing to do, after all.

The pickup area was mostly full of liveried drivers. The Buchanan-Memorial aerospace port was close to the city's financial district. It was a place for commercial rather than tourist travelers. Tyler tried looking for Jean in the crowd but things weren't entirely making sense yet.

"There," Serena said, pointing to a figure in a rumpled temperature-regulated business suit, leaning against a pillar in such a way as to cause ripples in the holographic advertising.

Detective Second Class Jean Hoyle didn't look much different to how she had looked when they had attended the academy back on Earth together. It was in and around her eyes that he did see a change, however. Even through his fugue he could make out all the new lines. They had both been pushed hard as cadets at Quantico but even at their most sleep-deprived, he had never seen her look so weary. Jean had quit the Bureau for the lure of significant money with Hume City Serious Crimes back when the Core Systems, particularly Alexandria Colony, had been aggressively headhunting from some of Earth's more prestigious law enforcement agencies.

"You look like shit," Jean told him.

Tyler managed a smile.

"Hey Jean, this is my partner, Serena."

Jean turned to look at Serena.

"Hey," she finally said.

"Detective Hoyle." Serena nodded.

Jean turned from Serena as though dismissing her.

"Tired?" she asked.

"I've just slept for a month," Tyler said.

"That's what I thought. Want to get a beer? I'll take you to your hotel later."

Tyler didn't want a beer. He didn't particularly like drinking. He was, however, aware of its importance in forming and furthering productive relationships with fellow law enforcement professionals. Besides, he wanted to catch up with an old friend.

"Sure," he said.

Tyler was impressed with the gyrocar despite himself. They lifted off from the top level of the AS port's parking structure. Lines projected on the screen offered flight paths that would keep them well away from the port's airspace and the exhaust venting from shuttles landing and taking off. Around them all was steel and mirrored glass. Tyler felt the same way about

Hume City's financial district as he felt about almost every financial district he'd ever visited: the glass and steel towers were clearly supposed to inspire awe, but it was always a sterile awe.

"Yours?" he asked, nodding at the gyrocar. It looked more than a little worn around the edges. On the other hand, it was an gyrocar.

"Came with the job," she told him, concentrating on pressing buttons, adjusting controls with one hand, the other working the steering wheel-like yoke. She flew the gyrocar over the edge of the parking structure. Tyler could make out the aerospace port's ground traffic on the raised roadways that grew from the huge structure. He saw bridges for the high-speed passenger maglev lines and the heavier, slower cargo-carrying ground trains. Between the port and the surrounding glass and steel was a chasm where the light from the surrounding buildings and roads faded into darkness. There wasn't much in the way of air traffic moving in the chasm, though as Tyler's eyes adjusted, he was pretty sure that he could make out light further down in the murk.

"The port's one of the old atmosphere processors, isn't it?" he said, then frowned. He was surprised that the gyrocar was sinking down into the chasm.

"Yeah, WY realized in the sixties that if they were going to spend so much on the processors it made sense that they should be repurposed. I've seen super malls, entertainment complexes, and giant apartment blocks, but they're good as aerospace ports because they're solid enough to take the load and most of them already had a few heavy lift platforms."

Having drifted past the main passenger concourse level, the light grew dimmer and dimmer. The lower levels of the aerospace port's surrounding towers were caked in a thick layer of grime. Past the raised roadways and rail bridges that fed the cargo port, the only thing to see was blinking collision lighting on the superstructure.

"Where are we going for a beer?" Tyler asked. "Hades?"

Jean laughed without humor. She hadn't switched on the gyrocar's running lights but now, through the grimy steel supports of the superstructure, Tyler could see other lights far below. Garish neon, flashing in greens, pinks, blues, and a lot of red. The gyrocar was slowly spiraling down between the supports as Jean relied heavily on the collision sensors to pilot the vehicle. Tyler could make out the neighborhood now. It looked like a mixture of stage one colony pre-fabs, some stacked eight or more stories high, and more permanent, poured concrete, stage two type buildings. It could have been some kind of living history exhibition except everything was caked in soot from the aerospace port's exhaust discharge: on every building was a grimy, garish, blinking neon sign collectively offering everything from gambling to cheap booze to pit fighting—some even openly advertising narcotics.

Tyler glanced back at Serena, her face illuminated by the neon as she looked around.

Jean switched the gyrocar's running lights back on and took the vehicle over the crawling ground traffic of the main drag. Tyler could see drug dealers, barkers for the clubs, what he suspected were gang members, sex workers of every gender, and their pimps, all working their grift on the crowded sidewalks. The rest of the people on the street had to be the clientele, the marks, the victims and johns. Even from the vantage point of the gyrocar the visitors to this place, this neon Hades, had the look of people from better neighborhoods, slumming for illicit pleasures. All of them, natives and vice tourists alike, stepping over the omnipresent homeless.

Tyler wasn't sure what most people thought when they saw a place like this. Some sympathy, others disgust, some were perhaps intrigued or even fascinated, some angry; any combination of those feelings was possible. What Tyler thought, however, was that this place was a prime hunting ground for a predator. He was starting to develop an inkling of why Jean had brought him here.

As they flew over the street a Hume City PD cruiser crawled by underneath, going in the other direction. Nobody on the street paid the police any notice. A few faces looked up at the gyrocar but nobody showed them untoward attention. The steel blue light of the gyrocar's headlights picked out the hydrocarbon rain from another shuttle landing.

"Put this on," Jean told him, handing him a filter mask. He affixed it over his mouth and nose. Jean was doing the same thing even as she steered the gyrocar over a four-story poured concrete tenement building. She took the gyrocar down between a stacked container motel and the tenement. Green and blinking red neon leaked into the alley, illuminating the filth.

The gyrocar's gullwing door slid up as the vehicle slipped down between the two buildings. Tyler saw more than he wanted through the 'motel's' windows. Then he felt the atmosphere seep into the gyrocar. The air had a physical presence: gritty, thick and membranous. It had an unpleasantly warm and humid quality, formed of something more toxic than mere moisture.

Tyler felt the gyrocar touch down.

"Welcome to the Exhaust Town Strip," Jean told him as her own door slid up and she climbed out.

Jean had parked the gyrocar with its rear facing the main street, which Tyler guessed was the Strip. She opened the trunk. There were a number of beers in a cooler. Then she extruded a straw from the top of a bottle and fed it into an aperture in her mask.

Tyler reached into the smoking moisture of the cooler and retrieved a beer for himself to show good form. He went to extrude the beer's straw and then stopped.

"We're standing in a crime scene, aren't we?" he said.

"The whole of the Strip is one big crime scene," she told him. He couldn't quite make out her demeanor here. She seemed bitter. Tyler wasn't sure if it was aimed at him or not.

"A murder scene?"

"It's certainly statistically likely. Your synth going to stay in the car?"

"She's not 'my' anything. Her name's Serena and I'd rather you used the term *artificial person*."

Jean didn't say anything. She just looked at him. Was it obvious? Had he made too much of defending Serena?

"I live there," Jean said pointing at the tenement and then sucked some beer through the lid-straw. "On the top floor, but it's still Exhaust Town. I have to pay one of the local gangs to protect the car." She patted the gyrocar.

Tyler frowned. It didn't really make any sense.

"I thought you came here for the money."

"The key phrase is on-target-earnings."

"And you've not been meeting the targets?" he asked.

Jean just took another sip of the beer. Tyler did the same and tried not to grimace. He still didn't like the taste, and the atmosphere of Exhaust Town just made it worse.

"To earn you need to make high-profile cases but all the cherry cases go to those with the rank. They'll throw you scraps if you do their legwork for them but that's about it. Rank, and the profile of the case, dictate access to forensics, analytics, manpower and every other resource. You can pay for it out of your own pocket but who has the money?" She didn't look at him as she said it. Perhaps she was fearing an 'I-told-you-so' from him. It wasn't really how he worked: besides, Tyler wasn't sure that HCPD had done anything other than formalise what were practically unwritten laws back in the United Americas. He'd heard colleagues say that people got the law enforcement that they paid for more than once.

"So, what am I doing here?" he said instead.

"A lot of the people who live down here, particularly off the Strip, aren't criminals. They're just working stiffs, mainly for the AS port, but they're poor and have no safety net. On the Strip, however, people go missing all the time. The gangs kill each other, others get trafficked up-town, junkies OD or kill each other over drugs, or they lose their place in the food chain, and sometimes people just get in the wrong car. Nobody gives a fuck." Jean paused. Tyler just waited. Jean's mask covered much of her face: with her head down, her hair covered the rest. Once again, he reminded himself that he didn't like beer by taking a sip. "I've been hearing things for the last few months. People are going missing in greater than usual numbers and the street bosses don't know who's doing it." She pointed down the alley. "A woman used to sleep in this alley. Her name was Maggie. A bottom feeder—her words—homeless, substance abuse issues with no real way to feed them, twenty-five and looked twice that, used up. We get to talking. She imparts some wisdom occasionally. She's telling me about the disappearances, but I've also had it confirmed from a couple of other sources. Then nine days ago she's nowhere, gone. I look. I talk to people. Nothing."

"Homelessness is a high-risk situation."

Both of them turned to look at Serena who was standing in the particulate rain that glittered in the neon.

"She's right," Jean admitted. "Except the people I'm speaking to are spooked."

"You think she found something out and whomever is behind the disappearances took her out?" Tyler asked.

Jean gave this some thought.

"No, I just think she rolled double-one on increasingly loaded dice. Like your syn... like Serena said, it's high risk. I just think her snake eyes came in the shape of whomever is responsible for these disappearances."

"And nobody in the PD is taking an interest?" Tyler asked, already knowing the answer.

"There's no financial impetus to investigate something like this. Nobody wants to take too close a look at where people who disappear from the Strip end up. It all ultimately heads uptown." She gestured all around her. "The Strip is just one big pool of victims. The majority of their predators are probably untouchable.

There's the occasional sweep when someone of sufficient influence gets rolled, or they catch an STD off a partner who's stepped out, and that's about it."

It was grim but Tyler had heard similar stories. It was what happened when you didn't regulate areas like this, when you don't enforce the law: drugs, trafficking, slavery, murder. He found himself glancing back at Serena, still perfectly still.

"What do you think is happening, detective?" Serena asked.

Jean looked surprised that Serena had addressed her.

"Some predator is taking them and using them to live out whatever fantasy he's running in his misfiring mind," she finally said. "It's the only thing that the street couldn't account for."

"What's your interest?" Serena asked.

Jean turned her head, sharply, to glare at Serena, whose expression remained completely passive.

"She means—" Tyler started.

"I know what she means," Jean snapped. "You get that people are going missing? That a crime is being committed? That there's probably a predator preying on these people?"

"I understand that," Serena said, "though I am unable to empathize with the victims as you might. I also understand that you are incentivized, financially and in terms of prestige and status, for bringing in big cases."

"You want to know if I'm doing it for the good or the glory?" Jean asked. Serena nodded. Jean looked away from her. "A little of column A and a little of column B."

Serena nodded again as though satisfied that she had learned everything she needed to know.

"Look," Jean said. She was looking straight at Tyler now. "I'm compromised. I went for the cash and it didn't work out the way I'd hoped. I get that." She inclined her head towards the main strip. "But people end up here because of poor decisions, bad luck and sometimes just circumstances completely out of their control. Someone has to speak for them."

It sounded as though she was trying to convince herself.

"So, we will have no remit. No access to forensics and no resources," Serena confirmed.

"We?" Tyler asked, trying to focus again.

"This is within our remit for inter-agency cooperation. It is perhaps stretching parameters a little, but as long as we are only advising..." Serena explained.

"It's worse than that," Jean said. "Nobody's doing any kind of organized AV monitoring or recording down here and nobody will talk to us."

"We'll have to do this the old-fashioned way then," Tyler said.

2

"I'm afraid I have to ask you a personal question about Detective Hoyle."

It was not something that Tyler had expected to hear from Serena as she did his tie for him. He knew how to put a tie on. He did so every day, but it always looked better when Serena did it and his big presentation to HCPD on the Greco case was today.

"It's unusual for you to take an interest in my personal life." *Not that he particularly had one*, Tyler thought. They were stood in the center of their comfortably appointed hotel room. One wall was a floor-to-ceiling window that looked out over the city's spires, under the pale sky, to the temperate desert of the polar cap. Jean had been impressed by the room, understandable having seen the area that she lived in. That said the, the room was easily the size of Tyler's own apartment back in Virginia. Jean had told him that how well guests were treated by HCPD was based on algorithmic predictions of their future usefulness. It appeared that HCPD felt he had great things in his future.

"It may have bearing on the case if we are to work with Detective Hoyle and may have to be logged in terms of human resources guidelines," Serena told him as she slid the tie up and checked her handiwork.

"You want to know if we were ever involved?" Tyler asked, wondering why this conversation was so awkward. Serena simply nodded. "We were friends. We had similar backgrounds. The academy was very challenging. Our friendship came with certain… benefits but we were never in a relationship. We found…" Words abandoned him as he watched Serena's face, looking for some response from her, some reaction, seeing nothing. Expectation and judgement were almost conspicuous by their absence in her expression.

"Solace?" Serena suggested.

He opened his mouth to tell her that it was nothing so intense but the door chimed. He turned to get it at the same time she did but then stopped. Instead, he just watched the economy of Serena's movement as she went to the door and let Jean in.

Tyler realized that Jean had asked him a question.

"I'm sorry, what?" he said, broken from his reverie.

Jean looked between him and Serena.

"I said, are you ready?"

***

They were riding the hotel elevator up to the conference center in the hotel's upper levels. Tyler looked down the vast open central well to the lobby. An artificial stepped waterfall took up the opposite wall, cascading into the hotel's leisure pool far below.

"Where does she sleep?" Jean asked him. Her tone was neutral but there was just the trace of a smile at the corner of her mouth.

"She can hear you," Tyler said. Jean was stood on one side of him, Serena the other.

"But there's only one bed," Jean persisted.

"I do not require sleep. I can recharge in almost any position. Last night I sat in an armchair and caught up with some work while Special Agent Matterton slept," Serena told Jean.

Tyler found himself feeling more and more uncomfortable. Neither Serena's helpful matter-of-fact tone nor the smirk on Jean's face were doing anything to alleviate that feeling.

"Watching you sleep, isn't that a bit creepy?" Jean asked.

Tyler turned to face her.

"Je... Detective Hoyle, you work with artificial people in HCPD as well. Is there a particular reason why you're pursuing this line of questioning?"

The smirk had gone.

"Detective Hoyle?" Jean asked.

"Cut it out, Jean," Tyler warned.

She leaned to one side to look at Serena directly. "Did I offend you?"

"I think your questions were a passive-aggressive bid to elicit a response by implying impropriety," Serena replied.

"Wow," Jean said turning around to face the door as they arrived at their floor. "Nobody has a sense of humor anymore."

Tyler gave the presentation in one of the hotel's many luxuriously appointed conference rooms. The attendees, mostly high-ranking officers in HCPD's Serious Crimes division, helped themselves to the complimentary breakfast and champagne, while Tyler talked them through the investigation of thirty-five abductions, all of which had resulted in the victims being murdered.

His presentation was accompanied by holographic material, mostly stills taken after HRT's raid. The three-dimensional images were a haunting entity in his periphery that he dared not look at directly. Tyler made it through the questions, though Serena fielded a number of them. The niceties, the so-called networking, was always the most difficult part. His one consolation was that he had clearly not made a good enough impression for them to try and head-hunt him on the spot. So far.

He saw Jean heading towards him across the light and airy conference area, which had an even better panoramic view of the polar cap than Tyler's hotel room. The conference area had seemed like such an incongruous place for him to give this presentation. Jean was accompanied by a solidly built blond man, who could have been anything from thirty to fifty years old. He wore a tailored suit that Tyler suspected cost more than his car back on Earth.

"Special Agent Matterton, this is my boss, Lieutenant Havern," Jean told him.

"Jeff, please," the lieutenant said offering his hand.

"Tyler." He took the proffered hand. It was exactly the kind of grip that Tyler had come to expect. At a guess, 'Jeff, Please' had read somewhere that it was designed to project dominance.

"Interesting case. Must have been harrowing work," Jeff Please said. Tyler opened his mouth to say something but the HCPD lieutenant ploughed on. "I was impressed with Detective Hoyle's initiative in suggesting that we invite you here." The backhanded compliment was clear. Tyler could almost hear Jean grind her teeth. "There's something you left out of your presentation."

"What's that?" Tyler asked.

"What were your thoughts on how to monetize the case?"

Tyler stared at him for moment or two.

"Excuse me?" he finally managed.

Someone was flicking through the images on the holo-projector.

"I mean it seems that the case was ripe for merch. I mean, animatronic action figures of the victims alone."

In the air above the center of the conference table was an image of Greco's workshop. Half-filled body bags arranged in neat rows on the filthy concrete.

"No, I mean *excuse me*," Tyler said. He turned and strode to the door of the conference room. He waited until the doors had closed behind him and then bolted for the closest bathroom.

Jean found him sat on the floor of the cubicle practically wrapped around the bowl. Tyler had heard the door to the bathroom open. Heard her heels on the tile floor and had unlocked the cubicle before she even knocked. She handed him a handful of paper towels.

"I have some breath mints as well," she told him.

He just nodded his thanks.

"How many times have you given that presentation?"

He held up four fingers as he spat bile into the bowl.

"Every time?"

He just nodded.

"I helped process the crime scene, we ran the Bloodhound PUPS, recorded everything. I even helped talk Technical Support through shutting down the... remote control OS. I mean they were losing it. I can do these things, step back, intellectualize, disassociate enough to get the job done," Tyler told her. He left out that he had only been able to help process the scene with the help of Bureau-approved amphetamines. He also left out that after he had made it back to his room in the Kansas City field office, he had broken down on the floor in a crying jag that had lasted until he'd crashed and finally passed out.

"We can all do it until we can't," Jean said. "It's gotta leak out somewhere."

Tyler wiped his mouth with one of the towels and looked around at the gleaming white tiles. It may have been one of the cleanest bathrooms he'd ever been in.

"What sort of question was that?" He still couldn't quite believe he'd heard it right.

"Welcome to the ICSC," she said, meaning the Independent Core System Colonies. She offered him some gum. He didn't immediately take it, though he wasn't enjoying the aftertaste of bile.

"What was that about this morning, in the lift?" he asked.

"I was just messing with you, Tyler. You used to have a sense of humor," Jean said.

"Did I?' he asked, more than a little surprised.

Jean laughed.

"Maybe not," she conceded.

"I think you were the only one having fun."

Jean straightened up, still leaning against the cubicle's partition.

"Girl's gotta get her kicks. I don't think your synth minded."

"Jean!" Tyler warned.

"For fuck's sake, artificial person then."

"I prefer partner."

Jean just looked at him.

"Where is she?" Tyler asked.

Jean laughed without humor.

"Oh, she's still back there talking up a storm. The brass loved her."

It was difficult for Tyler to imagine Serena 'talking up a storm'. He took the proffered gum and pushed himself to his feet.

"You good?" Jean asked.

He shook his head.

"Want to go get lunch?"

"No."

"Want to go and work a case with no resources or backup?"

"Sure," he said.

Tyler was thankful that Jean was using the gyrocar's running lights this time as they descended back into chasm beneath the Buchanan Memorial aerospace port.

Now able to get a better look at it, he could see that the framework of the old atmosphere processor that the aerospace port was built on formed a kind of skeletal tent over Exhaust Town. The Strip had presumably been operating since the early days of the colony, before its independence and the formation of the ICSC. Tyler guessed that it was still allowed to exist because nobody really wanted the land and because it was deemed to serve a purpose: entertainment, dumping zone, hunting ground.

"Can we set up our own surveillance?" Serena asked from the backseat.

"We do it every time there's a sweep. The gangs and the other more organized criminals run countermeasures. It might be worth a try but I suspect it'll be found and it'll just make it more difficult to get them to cooperate," Jean told them both.

"What's our in?" Tyler asked. His nose was practically pressed against the hardened plastic of the passenger-seat window. In the surrounding gloom, Exhaust Town's neon and holographic signage reminded him of deep-sea bioluminescence.

"The main thing we've got going for us is that what we're trying to do works in their favor: a predator in their midst is ultimately bad for business. They don't like us and certainly can't be seen to cooperate, but it's in the best interests of their bottom line to help us." Jean looked at the feed from the gyrocar's undercarriage cameras as she brought it to land curbside on the strip.

Helping drug dealers, thieves, pimps and traffickers because someone was predating on their people, on their customer base, didn't sit well with Tyler. It wasn't just their best hope; however, it was probably their only hope.

"Have we considered that it's more than one person doing this?" Serena asked.

"I've not ruled anything out," Jean said.

Tyler had considered this as well but something about it felt like a solo predator. Where this feeling came from, he couldn't say. He guarded against these hunches: they knew so little about the situation. Intuition to try and connect disparate information was one thing but this was just guessing, building erroneous preconceptions.

"What's first?"

Jean engaged the gyrocar's wheels and it became a ground car. They were now very much cruising the Strip in all its degrading filth and splendor.

He watched people from uptown buy drugs and engage with the sex workers. Some couldn't make eye contact with the dealers, others were all fake bonhomie, bravado and still others took what Tyler thought of as an emotionless retail approach. In their nice suits and designer P-Dats, he wondered if the Strip's customers thought of themselves as 'good' people? Did they see the people who served their appetites as scum? Where they heedless to the fact that the Strip was supply and demand in action? That it existed because of them. He watched as a pickpocket 'dipped' a P-Dat from some executive's purse.

There was something hungry about the visitors to the Strip, the clientele of the unregulated bars and clubs, the audiences at the pit-fight clubs and strip joints, an eel-like quality to their eyes. Everything here was transactional in the meanest sense and every small piece of disciplinary violence he witnessed made him flinch. He could understand a functionalist justification for the existence of a place to purchase drugs and engage in other vices but this wasn't it. This served no-one but the violent parasites. This was a suppurating wound.

Jean pulled up to the mouth of an alleyway between a pit-fighting emporium and a 'restaurant' called The Mystery Meat. A lean-to shack had grown between the two buildings like a cyst. There was something odd about its construction: something that Tyler couldn't quite put his finger on.

Tyler and Jean masked up and the three of them climbed out of the gyrocar and into the carbon rain. Jean led the way, pushing the lean-to's surprisingly sturdy door open. Tyler followed, pausing only long enough to let a kid, who couldn't have been older than ten, sprint past him and disappear into the sidewalk's throngs. He guessed the kid had been disturbed by Jean's presence as a representative of the HCPD.

Inside Tyler found himself looking around at ribs of a metal cage that formed the lean-to's hidden skeleton.

"It's a Faraday cage," Serena said, "though I don't think it's a very good one."

"It's good enough," said the woman behind the chunk of salvaged plastic that passed for a counter. She looked to be in her mid-twenties, but could've been younger. Exhaust Town aged people. She wore a shapeless overall, tools in the various pockets, over a filthy gray T-shirt.

"This is Cinders," Jean said leaning on the counter. It seemed a cruel nickname given the burn scars on the woman's face.

"And what does Cinders do?" Tyler asked, still looking around the lean-to.

"I run a lost and found service," Cinders told him, her expression the kind of wary neutral that many criminals adopted when talking to law enforcement.

Tyler nodded.

"What she means is that she runs a gang of pickpockets who steal P-Dats and deliver them to her. She advertises them as 'found', for a finder's fee—"

"Hey, this is the ICSC, everything has a cost—" Cinders interjected.

"But not before she cracks the P-Dats, extracts all

the data, and sells it on the open-market. Anything particularly juicy she sells onto pro-blackmailers. When she does return the P-Dats to their rightful owners, they're full of intrusion malware," Jean continued. Now the Faraday cage made sense. It would block signals from the stolen P-Dats to the various 'find-my-device' services.

"Scurrilous slander," Cinders protested.

"But, the absolute best thing about Cinders is that she hates doing prison time so much that she will cooperate with community policing efforts."

Cinders was glaring at Jean, her eyes little more than slits.

"You're going to get me killed," she hissed.

"I'm here to do you a favor," Jean told her. "Have you seen Maggie?"

Cinders shook her head.

"Cinders, Maggie was good to you, looked out for you when you were coming up," Jean said.

Now Cinders glared at the detective.

"Don't tell me who Maggie was," she said with some force.

"What happens if you speak to us?" Tyler asked.

Cinders just stared at him like he was a moron.

"I don't care what she said," Cinders nodded towards Jean. "We don't talk to cops down here."

"We're not police," Tyler said gesturing between him and Serena.

"Bullshit," Cinders said.

"They're off-world," Jean said. "No jurisdiction here."

"Like that helps me."

"We know someone is taking people," Serena said. "That puts you at risk and it's bad for business."

Cinders just laughed once, utterly devoid of humor. She pointed through the door they had entered by.

"Think anyone out there cares about that? If there's a killer preying on us that's just part of the excitement, the spice of their slum tourism. If anything, business is booming."

This didn't surprise Tyler. It was another mark against his faith in humanity but it didn't surprise him.

"Maggie was my friend as well," Jean said quietly. Tyler wasn't sure if it was true or Jean was just trying to manipulate the data thief. He hoped the former.

Cinder pulled her lips back, showing brownish-yellow teeth, but then shook her head.

"You used her, like you're trying to use me. How do I know it wasn't something that she told you that got her killed?"

"Who do you think is taking people?" Serena asked, taking Tyler by surprise.

Cinders gave the question some thought, clearly also surprised to be asked her opinion about anything.

"I think it's someone who maybe thinks they're cleaning up the streets, maybe getting rid of all us lowlifes."

"A vigilante?" Tyler asked. Cinders nodded. "Any particular reason you think this?" he added.

Cinders shrugged.

"Maybe they got into trouble coming down here, or just can't cope with their own desires? I think when rich people hate themselves, they take it out on others," she said.

Tyler guessed that by 'rich' she meant anyone who didn't have to live in Exhaust Town. It was insightful but it didn't feel right to Tyler. If it was a vigilante they would be looking to make a statement. Bodies would've been found by now. If they were taking people, it was more likely it was because they were using their victims to live out their fantasies.

"Found anything on the P-Dats?" Jean asked. The data thief shook her head. "Cinders?"

"If I'd found anything it would've been dealt with already," she snapped.

"Because people are looking for whoever's doing this?" Tyler asked.

Cinders didn't answer. He guessed this was the kind of thing that she could get killed for.

"Who's he taking?" Jean asked.

"Anyone with an asphalt bed, people fucked up on drugs or blind drunk on vat hootch, hookers, and at least one of Big Malky's fighters."

"This fighter—was he in a bad way?" Tyler asked. "Like punch drunk?"

Now Jean was looking his way, still leaning on the counter.

"He was fucked up. I heard that he'd had one too many fights that day and then bit off more than he could chew by getting in the pit with some jarhead on furlough."

"They were all vulnerable," Jean said.

Tyler nodded. Their predator was batting a hundred because they knew the area and picked their targets carefully. They were an opportunist, but it was opportunism backed by knowledge and presumably enough prep to be able to capitalize on such an opportunity.

"And nobody cares about them," Cinders said quietly. "Nobody who matters anyway."

"How many?" Jean asked.

"I don't know."

"Cinders," Jean warned.

"Really! I don't fucking know!"

Tyler glanced at Serena. Reading micro-expressions to gain insight into interrogees wasn't an exact science, but it could certainly provide some useful information.

"But you know something," Serena said.

Cinder looked down, refusing to meet anyone's eyes.

"Is somebody keeping count?" Jean asked. Cinders didn't look up, didn't say anything. "Cinders," Jean said, more quietly this time. "Is The Bish keeping count?"

Now she looked up.

"Please." She sounded close to tears. "I need you to go now."

Tyler opened his mouth to ask something else but Jean caught his eye and shook her head.

Jean used the car's siren and lights to clear a space before coming in to land next to a battered boardwalk built from construction scaffolding. They were in front of a club that Tyler suspected was supposed to be reminiscent of a saloon from America's nineteenth century. It was built out of a stacked network of truly ancient shipping containers. The containers were covered in electrostatically adhered grime. The particulate pollution was shaped and formed to accentuate the retro look. The neon sign announced that the establishment was called Jack It All In; the advertising hologram was an obscene rendering of the name.

The three of them got out of the car and climbed the steps through a forest of glares emanating from those working the boardwalk.

The door to Jack It All In was an airlock painted up to look like old saloon swing-doors. The décor was so on-the-nose that Tyler half expected the victim of a barroom brawl to come flying out of the red-lit window. There were two security personnel on the door. A man and a woman, their supplement-enhanced bulks clad in paramilitary black chic and civilian body armor.

The male had an oversized P-Dat slate, the female a shotgun. Jean stopped in front of them and looked at them expectantly. Tyler sighed. He knew where this was going.

"Yes?" the male doorman asked through his mask.

"You new?" Jean asked. She used her P-Dat, clipped to her belt, to project a hologram of her badge.

"So?" he asked.

"Tell The Bish that Detective Hoyle needs to speak to him," Jean said. She spoke clearly and slowly as if talking to a moron. Tyler couldn't see what getting the doorman's back up would accomplish.

"No," the doorman told her.

"You get that I'm police, right?" Jean said.

"I get that you live down here. We," he used his thumb to point between himself and the other guard, "don't even live down here. You've got no juice, you're a bottom feeder."

Hologrammatic drops rained down about them. Tyler didn't want to think too much about what they were supposed to represent. The doorman's words were harsh. Tyler only just caught the incremental slump of Jean's shoulders. Then she straightened up and opened her mouth, an angry retort on her lips.

"Tell The Bish we know he's keeping count," Serena said.

Both Jean and Tyler turned to look at her.

The doorman looked momentarily unsure.

"Please," Serena added.

The doorman took a moment and then turned away from them. Tyler noticed the other guard shift her grip on the shotgun. Jean turned to look at her. The doorman had his head cocked as though listening to someone, frowning, not liking what he was hearing.

Something made Tyler turn and look around him. As he did, the lounging gang-members, the corner boys and girls, the pros and the casual pedestrians all averted their eyes. They had all been enjoying watching this micro-street drama unfolding.

Tyler looked out into the sluggish worm of traffic making its way down the Strip, wondering if the predator they were looking for was watching them right there and then. Finally, he turned back towards the door, tuning back into the conversation.

"—hand in your weapon," the doorman finished.

"An HCPD detective never—"

"Detective," Tyler said.

Jean turned towards him and he just looked at her. Finally, she nodded. The airlock door swung open. All three of them stepped in. The door closed behind them and the scrubbers started cycling in fresher bottled air.

Jean turned on him.

"Don't ever undermine my authority again!" she snapped at him. "I have to live down here with these street creatures. One slip and I'm carrion."

Tyler nodded. He could see her point: this constant,

exhausting jockeying for a position in the food chain was one of the reasons he couldn't be a cop. He didn't have time for street politics. He needed the fastest route to the information. He needed to find the solution.

"And what was that?" Jean demanded turning on Serena. "You playing hunches, synth?"

Serena remained impassive. Tyler opened his mouth to defend his partner but Serena then did a pretty reasonable impression of clearing her throat and nodded up at the security lens in the corner of the airlock.

The internal door opened, flooding the airlock with red light.

The western décor on the inside had clearly seen better days but Tyler suspected that the Jack It All In was something of an Exhaust Town institution. Dancers of various genders moved, with little enthusiasm, on the catwalk for the early afternoon customers, tokens clutched in their fists. The customers were almost as unenthusiastic as the dancers. The three of them followed a waiter through the saloon/club as one of the dancers doubled over, wracked by a hacking coughing fit. Nobody reacted.

The waiter led them to a private booth and pulled the threadworn curtain to one side. Sat at the table, his arms over the back of the semi-circular seat, was a gray-haired, craggy-faced individual. Despite his obvious age he looked lean and hard. He wore a black waistcoat over a dress shirt and a bolo tie around his neck. A pair of revolvers rode his hips; twin semi-automatics hung in shoulder holsters.

Tyler assumed this was The Bish. He reminded Tyler of someone, but he couldn't quite think who. Tyler couldn't get a read on him at all, his face completely neutral as he looked at the three of them.

The music quietened.

"Detective," The Bish said, his voice like gravel. Then he pointed at Tyler.

"Special Agent Matterton," Tyler told him.

"FBI?" The Bish asked. Tyler nodded. "Are you here officially?"

"I'm officially here in an advisory capacity." Which was almost true.

"ViCAP?" he asked. He meant the FBI's Violent Criminal Apprehension Program, the unit in the FBI responsible for the analysis and investigation of serial violent and sexual crimes.

"ECU," Tyler told him. They were attached to the Critical Incident Group, the same division as ViCAP.

There was a soft chuckle, utterly devoid of humor, from The Bish.

"The Esoteric Crimes Unit. Crimes involving exotic technology and possible first contact situations, the weird murders. Don't you know that all murder is mundane? Banal? That's the sad part."

"We just work cases," Tyler said, trying to keep

the defensiveness out of his tone. He had heard this before. Some considered the ECU a joke unit. Many thought that much of what the ECU were tasked with was already covered by other parts of the FBI, like Behavioral Analysis, and the rest of their responsibilities were just pure fantasy.

The Bish seemed to lose interest in him. He turned to Serena.

"Sister," he said.

"You are a Hyperdyne Systems Model 341-B," Serena said matter-of-factly and as soon as she said it, Tyler saw it.

"What happened to your face?" Tyler couldn't help himself. He'd never seen an artificial person look so old.

"Wind shear," The Bish told him.

"The harshness of the environment will have broken down some of the components of this model's synthetic skin. Without treatment it resembles something similar to the aging process." Serena explained. And then to The Bish: "Someone has broken your program."

The Bish's smile was completely devoid of emotion.

"I have been emancipated." He made an expansive gesture. Tyler wondered if that comment had been aimed at him.

"Cut the crap, Bish," Jean said. "We know you've been keeping count."

The Bish turned his head slowly to look at her. Now

the 'keeping count' made sense to Tyler. The Bish couldn't help but collate and sort anything he heard. This artificial person shot-caller would be the closest they could get to an actual database on the murders. It would all be hearsay, street talk, but beggars couldn't be choosers.

"It's in your best interests to cooperate," Tyler told him.

The Bish turned to look at him.

"It's your people being killed," Tyler added.

"My people, Bureau man?" The Bish said. "The people, the humans that I control are to me what she is to you." He pointed at Serena.

Serena didn't react.

Jean was looking at Tyler now.

He felt sick.

"How many?" Tyler asked.

The Bish looked at him for what seemed like too long.

"Twelve, as far as I can tell. Started four months ago. Two weeks between the first and second disappearance, a week between the second and third, then getting shorter each time. Just two days between the last disappearance and the previous."

Tyler glanced at Serena, but she didn't waste time with a meaningless expression. She would know what he knew, and doubtless Jean did as well. The increase in pace suggested a loss of control—though that was at odds with how careful this predator had been. The worrying part was that this often pointed to an inevitably violent crescendo. It had happened with the British serial killer Joachim Hanald, the so-called Beast of Basinggrad, in the 2020s and with the still as-yet-unidentified Gateway Charlie.

"Have you discerned similarities?" Tyler asked.

"In the victims?" The Bish asked. Tyler nodded. "They were already victims before he got to them. I will interlink what I have collated to my sweet sister here," The Bish added, nodding towards Serena.

For an artificial person, cracked programming or not, Tyler had decided that The Bish was an asshole.

Serena concentrated as she received the information from The Bish, doubtlessly scrubbing it for malware.

"We good?" Tyler asked Serena. He didn't want to spend any more time in the artificial gangster's presence.

The Bish smiled like a shark.

Serena turned to look at Tyler and Jean.

"Someone survived an abduction attempt."

3

For a city with such high rent, Jean's apartment was of a reasonable size, presumably because of its location. Everything looked old and worn but serviceable. Jean had turned the place into a decent home. There were just a few giveaways about its location like the incredibly secure metal door with multiple locks and the semi-pornographic neon ghosts polluting the apartment's light from the nearby animated holographic signage. The apartment was on the top floor corner of the tenement, overlooking both the alley where Jean parked the company car, and the Strip itself.

"I have taken the information that The Bish collated and used it to make something that resembles a victim and crime scene database." Serena was standing in the corner of the apartment. Pinks, greens, and reds from the Strips' never-ending light show washed over her. She had made a map of Exhaust Town appear on the apartment's wall screen. There were twelve dots on it, each with a line connecting to a mugshot-style image with a name. "We only have the victims' street-names to go on and the images are based on The Bish's memory, but I think we can assume that they're fairly representative, cracked programming notwithstanding."

Tyler stood in the center of the apartment on an old rug just looking at the map. Twelve names, twelve faces, twelve people. The best that they could hope for was that their lives had been irrevocably interrupted by someone's fantasies, but more likely they had suffered and were now dead.

"Sit down," Jean called from the open plan apartment's kitchen area. She was making coffee. Tyler did as he was bid. Serena did not. "I'm guessing the positions on the maps are where they were last seen?"

"Yes," Serena said. "As far as I can tell, The Bish had his people collect the info. I don't think he wanted to conduct an investigation himself but I do think he was intending on turning it over to the first members of law enforcement who expressed an interest. That said, we can't rely on this information. It's secondhand and the witnesses are unreliable for a number of reasons. I've uploaded everything he gave us to your P-Dats."

Tyler kept staring at the map. He wasn't trying to memorize the details; that would come later. He was trying to commit twelve names to his memory. Street-names would not be enough: he would need to know their real names. Someone had to remember them, after all.

"Anything stick out to you?" Jean asked, handing Tyler a coffee and sitting down next to him on the threadbare sofa.

"Nothing we haven't already discussed. The victimology is opportunistic. They are targeting the vulnerable. There are elements of organized killing—"

"If the perpetrator is killing them," Serena pointed out.

Jean and Tyler just looked at her. In his gut, Tyler knew they were dead, but Serena was right to remind them to only act on the information they had.

"—in their patience," he continued, "but they're picking up pace, becoming more disorganized. Almost a spree."

"Quantity, not quality," Jean said and then sipped her coffee. "The thing I don't get is that Exhaust Town's not a big place. Somebody must've seen something."

"Undoubtedly, but without surveillance footage or the resources to canvas we are unlikely to find them," Serena pointed out.

"Did The Bish… do I have to keep calling him that?" Tyler asked.

"Synth gangster?" Jean suggested.

"Did he provide the name of the witnesses for the victims' last known sightings?" Tyler was pretty sure that he knew the answer to this.

"No," Serena told him. It made sense. The Bish wouldn't have wanted law enforcement interrupting business on the Strip any more than was strictly necessary. "Nor did he mention any affiliations. In answer to Detective Hoyle's question," Serena pointed at the map, "while these are not necessarily where our victims disappeared from, we can infer that our perpetrator knows the area well and was not taking them publicly from the main Strip."

"Infer?" Jean asked.

"It seemed quicker than saying I abductively reasoned it with my metaheuristic problem-solving capabilities," Serena said.

Jean laughed. Tyler wondered if they were bonding.

"Some john must've seen something," Tyler mused.

"Probably," Jean said, "but nobody outside Exhaust Town even knows about this."

"Your superiors are not aware?" Serena asked.

"Trust me, they don't care," Jean said focusing on the map.

Serena and Tyler exchanged a look.

"And as the model 341-B mentioned, the time between abductions is lessening," Serena told them.

"Because it's either coming to some kind of conclusion..." Tyler said.

"Or they're losing control," Jean added. "Unless it's cyclical, but I don't want to think about a dormancy period right now."

"If they are losing control, it would explain the thirteenth abduction attempt," Serena said.

"Where was that?" Jean asked, scanning the screen.

Tyler stood up and moved to the window. He looked down at the street. He took a sip of coffee. Bitter. They weren't dealing with a master criminal here. Their predator had some discipline, a degree of patience, but he didn't have the skillset of a monster like Greco. Tyler knew that if anyone had spent any effort at all in trying to catch this guy then they would have. He turned back to look at the screen. A new face had appeared. That of a young man, his features suggesting Asian descent. He had long straight black hair and was beautiful enough that Tyler suspected he was relatively new to the Strip. This place hadn't used him up just yet. Or at least not at the time his image had been recorded.

"Jaran," Tyler said, reading his name, trying to commit it to memory. Then he looked at the last known location: the alley directly opposite where he was standing. He turned away from the screen and looked out the window and across the street. "Jesus." Tyler just shook his head. "Is it worth sending Bloodhounds into the alley?" Bloodhounds were evidence-collecting drones, a repurposing of Parameter Uplink Spectrographs developed for colonial surveying and mapping work.

"We'd get fifteen thousand different flavors of DNA. Half in blood, half in semen," Jean said. She was staring at the screen. Tyler followed her eyes to the image of the tenth victim, a scarred woman who looked to be in her late thirties or early forties but was probably much younger. Maggie. No surname, just like the rest. Jean's informant. Her friend?

"I concur with Detective Hoyle's sentiment, if not her exaggeration," Serena added.

"Good of you," Jean muttered. She didn't look away from Maggie's image.

"Model 341-B say who Jaran worked for?" Tyler asked. Saying the model number hadn't felt right either, like a slap in Serena's face. Not that she showed any reaction.

"No," Serena said.

"I know him," Jean said. Serena and Tyler both turned to look at her. "I mean, I don't know him. I know the crew he runs with."

"You think you can find him?" Tyler asked.

"I think I can find his piece of shit pimp. Look, I know we need to go over all of this..." she gestured at the screen.

"But we can't let this run cold," Tyler said, then he made the mistake of looking in the wrong direction. He could see through some of the windows of the container stack hotel opposite. It seemed like the place was so cheap it couldn't even afford air scrubbers. All the 'guests' in their rent-by-the-hour rooms were still wearing their filter masks.

"Serena?" Tyler asked.

"Please go. There is work that I can be doing here," she said.

Jean and Tyler made for the door, Jean throwing him the pollution mac she'd loaned him. The raincoat-like garment was designed to protect his clothes from the worst of the air pollution but he still smelled like an exhaust.

"We can walk," Jean said stepping out onto the road and holding a hand up to stop the traffic as she crossed the street. Tyler followed. Despite the obvious irritation on the face of some of the drivers, nobody leaned on their horns because they didn't want to draw attention to themselves.

They reached the throngs on the pavement on the opposite side of the street. Jean had apparently reached a natural equilibrium with the area, the crowd on the street seeming to part for her as she slipped through. Tyler felt as though he was constantly going against the flow, buffeted by the tide of pedestrians. As he passed red-lit windows, he noticed that it was now night, in the city above. With the night had come the tourists and office workers. There was the veneer of a party atmosphere smeared across all the transactional desperation.

"If we hadn't taken an interest, would they have just

gone on killing?" Tyler asked Jean as he sidestepped a group of USASF support crew on shore leave.

"Until they melted down, or made a mistake and got caught by the local fauna," Jean replied without looking in his direction. "If it got bad enough then some of the pimps and local gangs might have pooled resources to hire a private detective."

"But this is still HCPD's job, right?" Tyler asked. He understood the ultra-capitalist ethos but there still had to be some kind of order, or so he thought.

"Don't think of us as police," Jean said, ahead of him now and still not looking in his direction. "Think of us as private security." This last was said so quietly that he almost missed it.

Ahead of them they could see a small group standing curbside next to a heavily customized ground car. Two of the figures looked to be security, bulked up on boosted muscle and wearing black hoodies. The other male was thinner, wore a leather effect pollution mac, had long stringy, lank hair and a scrabbly beard. His twitchy movement suggested some kind of relationship with an amphetamine analogue. He was leaning against the car talking to a long-haired young woman wearing a miniskirt, knee-length boots over stockings and a tight top. As they approached, Tyler saw the thin man pass the girl something. She smiled up at him as though it was true love.

Jean reached under her mac, unclipped her backup

piece from her belt and handed it to Tyler, along with two spare magazines.

"Jean..." Tyler said ineffectually as he clipped the compact pistol and spare magazines to his belt, increasing his own pace to keep up.

"Hey, Roach," Jean said pushing past the surprised heavies.

The thin guy, Roach, only had a moment to register surprise as Jean pushed her thumb and forefinger into his eyes, her thenar tissue pushing up hard against his nose. His mask was pushed up and he began to hack and cough as breathing became an issue. He resisted, trying to pull away. With her other hand gripping the back of his head she changed the direction of the force she was exerting, dragging him away from the curb and through the protesting crowd. The young woman he'd just handed something to staggered as Roach was torn away from her. Jean shoved him through the streetside chairs and tables, to the sound of more protests, before finally ramming him against the wall of the bar.

The two heavies started to move.

"Don't move!" Tyler shouted, not stopping.

They ignored him. Tyler sped up, grabbed the closest one around his face from behind, kicked out his knee and then pulled hard, stepping out of the way of his falling bulk. The other heavy was turning, reaching for something under his hoodie. Whatever he was taking for muscle growth wasn't doing anything for his speed. Before the heavy could draw his weapon, Tyler had his borrowed gun out of its holster and leveled at him.

"Don't," Tyler warned, stepping out of the reach of the one he'd just put on the floor, cursing that he hadn't time to check the weapon's safety mechanism. The heavy that had been reaching for his own weapon became very still.

"You on the ground. Stop moving or I will shoot you in the face," Tyler said.

Jean was grinding the back of Roach's head against the wall in a way that Tyler couldn't approve of. The pimp continued to cough, clawing ineffectually at her.

"Both of you are going to put your weapons on the ground and move away from them, okay?" Tyler told the two heavies. Despite the adrenaline surging through his system, he was managing to keep his voice even and his hand steady. None of the onlookers were moving away from the situation despite the drawn weapon. It was just another piece of improvisational street theatre for them.

"You crazy? You can't come down here," the one still standing said, his hand remained on the weapon under his hoodie.

"What do you want to do here?" Tyler asked. "You pull on me, I'm out of choices." He was desperate to reach the man, just for a moment.

The heavy nodded and very slowly pulled a handgun out of his waistband, placed it on the ground and stepped away from it.

"And you," Tyler told the one on the ground.

"Fuck you, bitch!" he spat.

"Do you want to die on this dirty street?" Tyler asked. He didn't want to shoot. He had no idea of his legal standing here, but he suspected it wasn't good. On the other hand, he suspected justice was a bidding war on Alexandria. He tried to ignore the sound of Roach's pain and distress.

"Dude," the still standing heavy told his friend. The man on the ground pushed a firearm out from under him.

"Back! Back!" Tyler told the thickening, encircling crowd of bystanders, using all the authority he could muster. "Both of you on your knees, lace your fingers behind your head." They moved with a tired familiarity. They knew the drill. He secured both their weapons.

"We good back there?" Jean asked.

Tyler opened his mouth to reply.

"Hey, you're hurting him! Let him go!" It was the woman.

Tyler's heart sank.

"Get out of here," he told her.

"He's my man. She can't do that. It's police brutality."

"Honey," Jean said, not turning around. "I get a

bonus for every complaint." She kneed Roach in the groin, and let him sink to the ground and then kneed him in the face, breaking his nose and battering the back of his head off the wall. There was a kind of sympathetic exhalation from the crowd. They were still just enjoying the show, but that could change at any moment.

"Detective," Tyler said.

Jean sighed. Roach had managed to pull his mask back on but it was full of blood.

"Fine." She removed her cuffs from the holder on her belt and threw them to Tyler. "Cuff them to the car."

She grabbed Roach by the hair and dragged him into the alley.

Tyler cuffed the two heavies together around the open window of the customized ground car and then followed Jean into the alley.

"Don't hurt him," the young woman told him as he passed.

Roach was on his feet now, leaning against the alley wall, the bottom part of his face covered in blood from his busted nose.

"Th' fuck, Hoyle!" he snapped and spat out more bloody mucus into his filter mask. "Fuck me up in front of my people!"

Jean was stood a little way from the pimp, arms crossed. She looked at Tyler as he joined her. He gave her a look to say: *What was that*? She just shrugged.

"You hook your people on drops, brand them, I put my hands on you," Jean told the pimp. "To my boss it just looks like I'm doing my job. Where's Jaran?"

"What do you want… Agh!"

Jean had pressed Roach's filter mask against his broken nose.

Tyler was shaking his head.

"Quit it!" said Roach. "He's all fucked up, isn't he? Got himself bit, didn't he?"

"Bit?" Tyler asked. Judging by her expression it wasn't what Jean had expected to hear either.

Roach was nodding enthusiastically, eager for Jean to stop hurting him.

"Some twist tore off the bottom part of his face, went through bone, man, no joke!"

It didn't sound right. It took a lot of pressure to go through bone. Tyler put it down to exaggeration, or perhaps Jaran had been attacked by something like a bolt cutter.

"Where is he now?" Jean demanded.

Roach looked wide-eyed and desperate, like he was afraid to tell Jean the answer.

"How hard do you want me to ask, Roach?"

"I don't know. He was my best earner, he was still pretty up until he got bit but nobody was going to pay for that horror show, were they?"

Tyler saw Jean's features harden. That was when he saw it, when he realized just how much this place affected her, how much she needed to stop this predator, regardless of her career. But this wasn't the way to go about it.

"What did you do?" It was practically a hiss but her voice still carried.

"Nothing!" Roach protested. The pimp must have heard it in Jean's voice as well. He sounded scared.

"Where is he?" Tyler asked, trying to forestall more violence.

"I don't know!" Roach told them. "I had to let him go."

"You piece of shit," Jean muttered.

"Hey, I'm not a charity!" Defiance was creeping back into his voice. "I even gave him a bit of cash, y'know, like a golden handshake."

"You're a prince amongst kings," Jean muttered.

"Any idea where he could've gone?" Tyler asked, wondering if you could fall much further than the Strip.

"Wherever dropheads go, man." Roach was looking at Tyler to save him from Jean now. It made Tyler feel dirty.

"He was still doing drops?" Jean asked, her voice low and full of menace.

Roach risked looking at her.

"He was in a lot of pain. No lie, this guy fucked him up bad. He was running across the strip with half his face hanging off." It was the closest thing to empathy that Tyler had heard from Roach's mouth. There was something else too. Fear, and not of Jean: of whomever had bitten Jaran.

"You could have sprung for reconstruction," Jean said. "Even a lowlife wannabe hustler like you could spring for a basic package. Better than nothing."

Roach's eyes dropped.

"Sunk cost fallacy," he mumbled. Jean nodded as if she understood, only Tyler noticed her hand moving under her mac. He recognized the movement. She had just pushed down the loop on her holster, freeing her weapon.

"Detective…" Tyler said.

"Hey, I could have sold him for organs. I know people." The defiance was back: if Roach had thought to demonstrate what a good guy he was, he may have found the wrong audience.

Tyler started to move as Jean drew her service weapon but couldn't reach her in time. It seemed to happen in slow motion. Jean pistol-whipped the pimp. His mask flew off and he spat blood and teeth. He hit the ground coughing and panicking as he tried to draw in the fumes that passed for air in Exhaust Town. The pimp started to panic. Jean had grabbed the front of his jacket, her service weapon raised again, when Tyler finally reached her and pulled her away from Roach.

"Get the fuck off me!" Jean snapped.

Tyler stepped back arms raised. What she'd said earlier came back to him: *We can all do it until we can't. It's gotta' leak out somewhere.*

The pimp crawled across the filthy alley and retrieved his mask, holding it over his mouth and nose, desperately trying to draw in breath.

"We can't do that," he said.

"This isn't Earth and I'm not the FBI. This isn't illegal," she said gesturing at Roach, who was spitting out blood before pulling his mask back on. Blood was dripping off her service weapon. She had taken her frustration out on Roach, now he'd take out his shame and humiliation on someone he considered beneath him, and on and on.

"I don't care," Tyler said. "This happens again and I walk and you're on your own."

She closed the distance to him. Tyler almost made to defend himself.

"You want this guy as badly as I do," she said.

"Not like this," he said quietly.

"Fucking boy scout," she spat.

Any confrontation risked further escalation but he knew that this had to be sorted now if they were going to work together. What had Hume City done to her?

"It matters how we do this," he told her. "You know that."

Tyler watched the tension seep from her face. Then he realized that he had been holding his breath.

She leaned against the wall and sagged, almost doubling over. Tyler wondered if she was going to throw up.

Roach had climbed to his feet.

"Go," Tyler told him. "Get out of here."

He didn't need to be told twice. He bolted.

Tyler moved over to Jean and put his hand on her shoulder.

The gyrocar struggled as Jean piloted it through the gritty sky, visibility limited by the heavy carbon rain. She had been quiet during the walk back to the gyrocar and the subsequent flight over Exhaust Town. Tyler hadn't said anything. What was there to say?

She was keeping the gyrocar under the aerospace port's superstructure lattice, flying low over the roofs of the tenements and container hotels. Again, Tyler found himself struggling to ignore the insight he was getting into the lives of the people of Exhaust Town. Ahead of him, through the airborne grime, he could see the dark hulking shape of some kind of structure. Jean flicked a switch and the gyrocar's spotlight cut through the murk to play over the filth-encrusted shape.

"Is that a ship?" he asked.

"It's the first colony ship," Jean told him. "The USCSS *Concordat*. There was a plan to turn it into a museum, conference space, hotel and leisure complex, but Hume City built up too quickly around it."

They were making towards a long, angular shape. Large chunks of it were missing: he guessed parts of it had been recycled or repurposed. He saw the old hulk's exposed interior structure, tented over with flapping tarpaulin. He even saw what looked like the glow of camp fires. He was surprised there was enough oxygen for combustion down here.

"It's called something else now," she told him. "Heaven."

The Heaven moniker stretched irony to the limit. The whole ship was a drop gallery, filled with red-eyed drop zombies coughing up blood into their filter masks. It was clearly Exhaust Town's end of the line. After the Strip chewed you up, this was where you got spat out.

"There's no point in asking anyone anything, they're on a different planet," Jean said, resignation in her tone.

"Look for a face injury?" Tyler asked.

Jean nodded.

"We should probably stick together," he added.

Other than the scenes of ritualistic murders, Heaven was one of the more soul-destroying places Tyler had ever been. It was a shanty town in the gutted, skeletonized remains of the spacecraft that had brought the first humans to Alexandria. He moved between the shelters made from scavenged materials and tarpaulin tents, shining the steel blue light in the faces of the barely conscious. Few of the drop zombies could even muster up muttered complaints. Tyler couldn't shake the feeling he was violating their privacy somehow, interrupting an intimate moment in their relationship with their drug of choice. The particulate fall looked like snow in the blue light. The shuffling drop heads became twisted, shadow giants projected on the superstructure in the beam of the flashlights.

Tyler and Jean moved from level to level, risking some pretty shaky makeshift mezzanine platforms. He tried to ignore the small darting shapes of neglected children playing a purposeful game of hide-and-seek with Jean and himself. Despite their age, the kids would have been drilled to avoid anyone with even a sniff of authority about them. Jean didn't say much, even when their flashlight illuminated drop-heads as they were using, holding pipettes above already ravaged eyes as they held their breath.

They got lucky. It didn't feel particularly lucky, but they found Jaran as he was returning from Exhaust Town, in the desperate minutes between scoring and dropping. Gaunt as he was, wrapped in rags, Tyler could still see his beauty in the top part of his face. The bottom part, under his ill-fitting mask, was covered in a filthy gauze from someone's rudimentary idea of medical care.

"Jaran?" Jean said.

Tyler wouldn't have recognized him from the picture. He suspected that Jaran's face wound was infected. It was easy to understand why he wanted a few hours narcotically free from pain.

Jaran just looked up at them both and swayed a little. His body language suggested that he wanted to bolt but Tyler suspected that he didn't have the energy.

"We just want to talk. Nobody's going to take your stash. There's maybe even a few DRs in it for you," Tyler said.

Jaran put his back to a support strut, slid down it and started sobbing. Tyler wasn't sure if he was crying for all that had happened to him, or just because his drop was delayed. Tyler knelt down next to him.

"Jaran, can you understand me?" he asked.

Jaran nodded his head.

"Can you talk?"

He shook his head.

Jean stood over Tyler, checking all around them.

"May I look at your wound?"

Jaran shook his head as vigorously as he could manage.

"Jaran, please. It may help us catch the person who did this to you."

Jaran shrugged. Tyler understood. The matter was indifferent to him now: the damage was already done.

"Jaran, I'm going to have to take a look at the wound, okay?"

Jaran just looked at him as Tyler reached for the gauze. He'd never felt more like a sadist. Jaran's eyes narrowed and more tears squeezed out as Tyler pulled the gauze aside. There was some resistance where the gauze had adhered to the flesh. Tyler tried not to show any response but he could taste bile again for the second time that day. Roach hadn't been lying. Where Jaran's lower jaw should be, there were only two chunks of bone separated by a gap of infected flesh. He was astonished that Jaran could function at all. The wound was all wrong, somehow. A human wasn't physically capable of something like this.

He was aware of Jean shifting behind him, but she remained quiet. Tyler took out his P-Dat and used it to photograph the wound. He interlinked the images to Serena and left Jaran to rearrange the gauze dressing as he saw fit.

"Jaran, the person who did this to you, was he male?" Nod. "Young?" Another nod. "Twenties?" Another nod. "White?" Nod. "Blond?" Shake of head. Then he touched his own lank hair and shook his finger at Tyler. "No hair?" Nod. "Shaved?" Nod. "Did you see the color of his eyes?" Shake of the head. "Was he in a vehicle?" Nod. "A car?" Shake. "An SUV?" Hesitation and then a shake. "Pickup?" Shake. "Van?" Nod.

"Give him your P-Dat," Jean said, exasperation seeping through her filter mask.

Tyler knew he should have thought of it himself. It

was the sort of thing that Serena would have suggested immediately. He opened a note application on his P-Dat and offered it to Jaran. Jaran didn't take it. He just stared at it instead.

"Shit," Jean muttered.

"You can't read or write, can you?" Tyler asked. He would have been appalled at this on the most backward planet. There was no excuse in a Core System world as wealthy as Alexandria.

Jaran rubbed his thumb, fore and index fingers together.

"Parents couldn't afford schooling. Thank goodness he was pretty so he had something to offer the economy," Jean muttered.

Jaran's head dropped and he started to sob again. Tyler turned to look at Jean. She held her hands up.

Jaran pulled a pipette out from within his ragged clothes. Tyler gently took hold of his hand, making Jaran jump.

"I'm sorry," Tyler said. "Just a little longer, I promise."

Jaran stared at him with badly bloodshot eyes, then shook his head.

"We could try and get you medical help."

Jaran just looked up at Jean.

"No, we can't," Jean said quietly. "Neither of us can afford it and nobody else would pay."

Tyler squeezed his eyes shut.

"I'm sorry," he told the other man.

Jaran watched him for a moment or two longer and then nodded as though he believed Tyler. He touched Tyler on the side of his face almost tenderly. Then he used both hands to gesture at his own neck.

"There was something wrong with his neck?" Tyler asked. Jaran nodded. Then he moved his hand further away from his neck.

"It was too big?" Jean said, sounding confused but Jaran nodded again. Then he pointed at his own jaw and made a similar gesture.

"His jaw was wrong as well?"

Jaran nodded. Then he made a talking gesture with one hand, whilst tilting the other hand from side-to-side.

"Something wrong with his voice?" Tyler asked.

Jaran nodded. Finally, he held his hand up next to his face, then he shot it forward and made snapping gestures.

It took Tyler a moment to work through the charade, but finally he got there.

"He was modded, wasn't he?" Tyler said.

Jean was looking at him.

Jaran nodded.

4

The gyrocar flew over the roots of the starscrapers. They were away from the carbon rain of the aerospace port but little light made it down this far. Here the foundations of the steel and glass towers had an organic look to them, an intertwining lattice of root structures to counteract the height and mass of the city's towers. As the gyrocar swept through the gloom it was repeatedly pinged by various automated security systems. They only had clearance to fly here by dint of Jean's position as a member of the HCPD. He saw a number of the roots shifting, like snakes coiling over and around each other, as they adjusted the weight distribution of their starscraper. It was easy to believe that they were alone on this planet. Though Tyler only had to look up at the raised roadways, maglev rails and air traffic overhead for evidence to the contrary.

In the distance the sky lightened. A false dawn effect

created by neighborhoods of smaller, older buildings that let in more light. That was where they were heading. Anthem was an old warehouse district that had been abandoned by the development of a more heavily automated, modular container facility built into the aerospace port's superstructure.

"I'm interested to know what your partner's contributing," Jean said before taking a sip from the bulb of coffee she'd bought from a street dispenser and grimacing.

Tyler was studying his P-Dat. He pressed the holographic display and a strange shape was projected from the device. Jean glanced over at it. It looked like a rod with an irregular cube shape at one end formed of discrete sections.

"This," Tyler said, frowning.

"What is it?" Jean asked.

Tyler animated the hologram. Suddenly the irregular cube split open into two sets of metal teeth and shot forward as the rod extended hydraulically and then snapped shut again.

"Jesus!" Jean said. "What is that? A secondary cybernetic mouth?"

"Serena modeled it based on the photos of Jaran's wounds. It's extremely speculative, but she reckons it's something like this."

"Who does that to themselves?" Jean wondered aloud. Tyler guessed she meant implanting something like that into their mouth. Though Tyler knew something of the transgressive nature of the modder sub-culture, having worked cases connected to illegal cybernetics.

"Things like that legal here?" he asked.

"Regulated, mostly for medical use, though some wealthy types favor the hard tech approach to transhumanism. This street stuff—DIY augments—not so much, but it only gets enforced when it gets enforced."

They flew out of the starscrapers' roots, crossing a terminator of light into a street grid of warehouses, bypassed by the newer raised roads above. The warehouses had been extensively redecorated: everything from all-encompassing graffiti murals, to scrap metal sculptures, to rewilding. As far as Tyler could tell, when the corps had moved out the squatters had moved in. Anthem now belonged to an uneasy alliance of criminals, artists, and other general non-conformist and so-called counterculture types.

Under normal circumstances Tyler would have had a degree of contempt for them. It wasn't that he disliked art, quite the contrary: it was the refusal to contribute. For better or for worse they all lived in a society, after all. That said, on Alexandria, in the ICSC, if all society wanted to do was take and take, he guessed he understood their wish to opt out. Though to his mind, change was better than the abrogation of responsibilities.

"Serena is turning everything we got from The Bish into something that resembles a case file. We'll be thankful for the work she's putting in when it's time to prosecute." He wondered if he sounded too defensive.

Jean landed the gyrocar on waste ground outside a crumbling warehouse that had held on to its original industrial aesthetic. As they came in to land a number of people, some with odd protrusions under their clothes, put their heads down and moved away.

Jean turned to look at him.

"Tyler, are you fucking your 'artificial person'?"

"She's my partner, and no. That would be an immoral abuse of power, against Bureau regulations and illegal," he snapped.

"And because it's like fucking the office coffee machine?"

His head whipped around to glare at Jean. She had an expression of concern on her face. It was clear that she had just been looking for some kind of reaction and he'd given it to her.

"Jesus Christ, Tyler," she said and climbed out of the gyrocar.

There were narrow windows high up on the warehouse wall. Some of them still had a few glass bricks in them. An intermittent blue light swept across the window slits. He could hear a harsh industrial beat and electronic music, devoid of any acoustic warmth, emanating from within.

"Who is this?" Tyler asked, still not able to look at Jean as they made for the warehouse.

"He calls himself Luscious. There are other modder street surgeons, but he's the best, for a given price, and most well-known. If he didn't do that mouth, then he knows who did."

They were almost at the sliding metal door and again Tyler caught flashes of the blue light.

"Can we do this my way?" Tyler asked as they tried to shift the door, but it wouldn't budge.

"Sure," Jean said, reaching under her mac to push the loop down on her holster, freeing her service weapon. Tyler still had Jean's backup. "He does illegal surgery for a living. If he cooperates with us the best that happens to him is that he loses his customers. More likely some cybered-up snowball will just off him. What's your leverage?" She squeezed through the gap in the door.

Tyler had to admit that she had made a very valid point, as he squeezed through after her. But there were lines he felt he shouldn't cross, whether it was legal here or not. Besides, what would Serena think?

Inside, the volume of the harsh discordant 'music' was its very own type of sonic hell. The blue light was a spotlight atop one of four scaffolding towers. Just as Tyler could make out the shadow of a figure behind the spot, the light was turned on him and Jean. Tyler had to shade his eyes with his hand.

"HCPD, get that out of my face!" Jean called but the light didn't shift away from them: instead, it followed them across the warehouse. Tyler was a little worried that Jean might try and shoot out the spotlight.

They were making for a large square area surrounded by transparent plastic sheets, hung from poles that ran between the scaffolding towers. Despite the bright light, Tyler was aware of figures in the periphery of the warehouse walking quickly towards the various exits. One of them looked towards Tyler as they reached a side door, eyes glowing red with artificial light.

Jean pushed angrily through one of the curtains, the movement of the plastic sheet doing strange things to the beam of the spotlight. Tyler followed, allowing him to better make out the heavily jury-rigged medpod that looked as though it had been forcibly mated with a 3D printer. A figure stood next to the machine, illuminated by the pod's inner light. Tyler could see the silhouette of someone inside the machine. There was a strange smell in the air that Tyler couldn't quite place.

"Luscious, I swear to the gods that I will put a bullet through that light," Jean told the figure.

There was a gesture from Luscious and the spotlight was taken out of their faces. Now Tyler could see the figure in the pod properly. There were no eyes in her sockets. Instead, protruding needles were knitting her new ones, layer by layer. Tyler looked away. He was pretty sure that the figure behind the spotlight was armed. Chrome glinted around their chin.

"Jean," Tyler said. A warning.

"I got it." She had seen the figure as well.

Tyler moved to one side so he could get a better look at Luscious but also keep an eye on the figure on the tower. His hand moved towards his weapon.

"Detective Hoyle, you find me in the midst of committing a crime that I don't wish to pay the consequences for. Can we come to some arrangement?" Luscious wore a simple but elegant suit. It took a moment for Tyler to realize that his almost goggle-like sunglasses were actually fused to the modder surgeon's face. His head was shaved and numerous jack ports sprouted from the irritated flesh. Several had jacks in them, connecting Luscious to the pod and other nearby machinery. Closer now, Tyler could make out figures cascading down the inside of Luscious's goggles, some kind of unnecessarily visible heads-up-display. Much of what Tyler could see seemed to be cybernetics-for-cybernetics' sake, machine-flesh fusion for fashion not function.

"And what happens if I decide that you have to take responsibility for your actions?" Jean asked him.

Luscious didn't move, didn't say anything. Figures cascaded down the inside of his eye-augments. Tyler guessed the carrot was a semi or even completely legal bribe, and the stick was the weapon in the hands of the woman in the tower.

Jean gestured to Tyler that Luscious was all his.

Tyler produced his P-Dat with his left hand, his right still near Jean's compact backup piece at his waist. He activated the holographic display. Luscious moved his head slightly to look at the animated image and then inclined his head to look at Tyler, who saw himself reflected in the modder surgeon's goggles. He said nothing.

"Your work?" Tyler asked.

Luscious did not reply. Tyler had the feeling he was communicating with someone else. He followed the cable from one of the head-jacks to a P-Dat.

"Really? A full brain-computer interface just to interlink?" Tyler asked as he turned to look up at the woman in the scaffolding tower again. The needles in the medpod were still moving rapidly in the periphery of his vision.

Luscious sighed and turned to Jean, whose arms were crossed now.

"I would prefer to keep our relationship entirely transactional, Detective Hoyle," he said.

Jean gestured for him to speak to Tyler.

Luscious turned slowly back to face Tyler.

"We don't care about your modding," Tyler said. "What you do with your own flesh and that of other consenting adults is up to you."

Luscious nodded as though it was the first sensible thing he had heard since they had entered the warehouse.

"But the person you made this for has hurt a lot of people. He is using it as a weapon."

Tyler detected a slight expression of distaste on Luscious' features, probably due to the inelegant use of his tech rather than out of empathy for the victims.

"If, and I do mean if, I made that particular item, I am neither morally nor legally responsible for the use it has been put to. It looks like a simple mouth prosthetic, perhaps made for someone who has lost their teeth."

"Mounted on a miniature hydraulic ram, with enough power to bite through bone?" Jean said. Again, Tyler thought he saw the trace of a grimace from Luscious. "What did he want to eat? Lug nuts?"

"And yes, if you made an illegal weapon, regardless of the intent, and it was used in the commission of the crime, then you will be charged as accomplice," Tyler said.

"And the crimes this guy has committed are the worst ones we have laws for. This isn't something we can ignore even if we wanted to." Jean told the modder.

"And we don't want to," Tyler added.

"It's almost like actions have consequences," Jean said looking down at the woman in the medpod. As she did so, Luscious glanced up at the woman with the gun behind the spotlight. "Don't be stupid, Luscious. You might get one of us but the other puts you down, and even if they don't it's not like the HCPD are going to run out of cops."

Luscious took a long deep breath.

Tyler realized the smell was a mixture of ozone and the mealy smell of an old-school butchers.

"What do you want?" he finally said.

"You made it?" Jean asked.

He nodded.

"Who for?" Tyler asked, trying not to betray the excitement he felt.

"I don't know, it's not like I ask for ID. He was in his late twenties, early thirties, no hair, not on his head or his body, even eyebrows. He didn't speak much, paid in hard currency. Full jaw reconstruction, the mechanism for the ram fused into his throat. It was ugly, like UPP architecture ugly, but the customer is always right."

"Seen him before?"

"Yes."

"This is like drawing teeth, Luscious. The sooner we get what we want, the sooner you can go back to jacking off over your surgical fetish," Jean told him. "Where have you seen him? He part of the scene?" Tyler guessed she meant the body mod scene.

Luscious shook his head, rattling the cables plugged into it.

"No, he'd had work done before. An endocrine shunt, neural sheathing, sub-dermal plating. His rib cage looked like an exoskeleton."

Tyler didn't like the sound of any of that. The illegal body mod cases he had worked before allowed him some notion of the effects of the modifications that Luscious had described. The shunt stimulated hormone production to increase strength. The neural sheathing decreased the electrical resistance of, and some electrochemical interference to, the recipient's nerves, making them faster. The subdermal plating was effectively armor. There were serious mid-to-long-term side effects for all three procedures but Tyler suspected the person they were after wasn't planning for the future.

"Wonderful," Jean said.

"You have an image?" Tyler asked.

"I don't keep any images post-op," Luscious told them. He wasn't as still as he had been. He was more jittery, clearly uncomfortable. "People trust me."

"Luscious…" Jean said.

"Yes, you do," Tyler said. He was sure that Luscious was the type that liked trophies.

Luscious's head jerked around to look at Tyler.

"If I did, I would be ruined the moment I shared one with the police," he spat, but his defiance was performative. He was rattled.

"Your people want nothing to do with this guy," Jean told him.

"Luscious…" The voice, although not raised, carried. It was clear and beautiful and very much synthesized. It came from the woman with the gun atop the scaffolding tower.

Tyler turned to look up at her. She was still only a metal shadow, cold smoke rising from the venting medipod drifted across the spotlight's beam.

Luscious closed his eyes and concentrated.

Tyler's P-Dat received several image files. The device's countermeasures began automatically checking them.

"This… man you're searching for…" Luscious began hesitantly. "We are all transgressive with the flesh we were blessed or cursed with. We are enthusiastic adherents to transhuman manifest destiny but him… well, he doesn't want to be human anymore."

Tyler stared at the image of their as-yet-unnamed suspect. His exposed flesh was very pale, as though it had been bleached. His eyes were a solid mass of black: undoubtedly a cosmetic mod. His body was shrouded in a long, thick, black pollution mac, but in the grainy footage that Luscious had provided their suspect moved with an economic grace that Tyler instinctively connected to predatory insects. The still images showed a before and after. In the after images his throat and part of his neck were covered by protruding, overlapping plates of black ceramic armor. In some of the shots their suspect was stripped to the waist. It seemed the paleness of his skin was universal: Tyler now understood what Luscious had meant about the suspect's subdermal armor. It did look like an exoskeleton. Tyler hit a few more keys on his P-Dat and projected the image of the suspect's head and shoulders into flickering low-res 3D. There wasn't quite enough information to go on for a high-quality hologram.

Jean glanced over at the suspect's images. She tapped destination data into the gyrocar and then flicked on the autopilot. Now she turned to look at the image proper.

"I'm assuming you don't recognize him?" Tyler said.

"I don't," Jean said after a moment's hesitation, "which is kinda odd. You'd think that a guy like that would stick out."

"I've sent the images to Serena but asked her to hold off doing anything with them."

Jean nodded.

"Which begs the question: what now?" he asked her. They were coasting over the root system again, through the ghost town of the starscrapers' lower levels. He nodded at the image. "This is our best lead. Quickest way to find him without a name or DNA is an image search." They had enquired from Luscious about the possibility of residual DNA but he had assured them that he was quite conscientious in ensuring that no traces of his clients remained. It made sense. Had he not been careful with his client's genetic privacy, he would not have remained in business very long.

"We need the HCPD files?" she asked.

"We do," Tyler said. "There's no way this guy isn't on file. I mean the way he looks alone. He's living in a complex fantasy world, something that's well developed. He's practiced: it has to have leaked out well before now." He pointed at the image. "This guy did not spring fully clothed from the head of Zeus."

Jean made a face.

"Sorry," he added.

"Unless he's from off-world," Jean said, "or he's changed his appearance so much that facial recognition no longer works."

Both were good points, though they would be using the before image to look for him, not the post throat/ mouth reconstruction image.

"The moment we do a search in the HCPD files it'll get flagged," Jean said quietly, not looking at him. "The case gets taken away from me."

Tyler didn't say anything for a moment.

"I get that," he finally said, "and I know it's not a selfish thing to want to bring it home, but what's our priority here?"

Jean shook her head, her face twisting. "Don't patronize me, Tyler, I know what the priority is. It's… fuck!" she slammed her fist down on the mock-leather of the central console. "It's not the kudos. It's…" She turned to look at him. "I keep being told I've got to pay my dues. Okay fine, but I'm twice the detective that most of them are. This is going to sound arrogant, but how many people fucking die because I'm paying my dues?"

"It doesn't sound arrogant," he said, trying to

reassure her. He understood the requirement for a command structure but to him a good leader was someone who knew how to use the best tool for the job, regardless of seniority and politics. Anything else was just a waste of time. In situations like this Jean was right: it was potentially a waste of life.

"This seem like a hard case to you?" she asked. He thought about the months he'd spent chasing Greco. He shook his head. "No, of course not. Less than twenty-four hours and we've got a solid lead. Not because you're the great Agent Matterton who captured the famous Wire Head Killer but because we did something old-fashioned. We fucking looked."

Tyler just nodded.

"I just want to be in a position where I can..." She lapsed into silence.

"Do some good?"

She was shaking her head.

"Don't judge me, Mr High-and-Mighty G-man. It shouldn't be mutually exclusive to take down bad guys and make some bank."

Tyler was reasonably sure he hadn't been judging her. He suspected she was judging herself and pretty harshly.

"So maybe just give me a moment," she added.

He sat quietly. Ahead he could make out the skeletal metal tent that was the atmosphere processor-cum-Buchanan-Memorial Aerospace port. He watched a high-speed passenger maglev train shoot by overhead on its raised monorail.

"I'll get Serena to do the net search. She's run the images and the footage that Luscious gave us through image enhancement and sent it to both of us."

"I'll run it through HCPD," Jean said, her tone weary with resignation. She picked up her P-Dat.

Jean had been quiet most of the way back to her apartment despite Tyler's inadequate attempts to make conversation. They had reached the door to the apartment when her P-Dat started bleeping. Jean took it out of the pocket of her pollution mac, looked at the screen then showed it to Tyler. Their image search through HCPD files had turned up nothing. He wasn't in the system. Tyler couldn't believe he'd called it that wrong. The method of picking the victims alone showed a degree of sophistication that only came with practice and rehearsal.

"He must be from off-world," Tyler said. He didn't like the idea of having to send it out. Even waiting for replies from planets in the core systems could take months, let alone the colonies.

Jean didn't say anything. She just touched her P-Dat to the armored door of her apartment and it clicked open.

"I may have found him," Serena said a few moments later as Tyler and Jean emerged from the hall. Serena was standing in front of the screen. She had superimposed two headshots over the rest of the murder board. One image was of their suspect. The other was of a blandly attractive man in his mid-to-late twenties, with floppy light brown hair and a wide smile on his face. It looked like a promo shot.

"That doesn't even look a little bit like our suspect," Jean said, giving words to Tyler's thoughts.

"The facial recognition software looks at the structure of the face, not the cosmetics," Serena told them, then concentrated. The software took a latticed 3D model of the promo shot's bone structure and superimposed it on the image of their suspect. That was when Tyler saw it.

"Jesus," Jean breathed.

"It's a ninety-two-point-three-two-seven percentile match. Nobody else came close," Serena said.

"Who is he?" Tyler asked.

A bio with the same picture appeared on the screen. Tyler and Jean both started reading.

"He's a professional dreamer?" Jean said incredulously. Commercial dreamers created extensive dreamscapes that could be played back to less 'skilled' dreamers in hypersleep transit. "And he's native." She added, glancing over at Tyler.

"Perhaps semi-professional would be a more apt description," Serena suggested.

Tyler was reading Darius Snell's credits. He had never heard of any of the commercial dream productions that Snell had been involved in, but then he had never used commercial dreams for entertainment in hypersleep. He had been thinking of doing so on the way back to Gateway to drown out the noise of his own subconscious.

"A series of well-received indie projects," Serena said.

"But never made the big time," Jean added, still reading. "Wait, are these pornographic dreams?"

"Yes," Serena said.

Snell wouldn't have been the first commercial dreamer to turn to pornography when his career hadn't quite gone as planned.

Jean was tapping away on her P-Dat.

"Okay, according to his tax returns he worked as a commercial dreamer for three years, then fifteen months ago, everything stops—"

"Off-world," Tyler suggested.

"He starts paying taxes again six months ago," Jean continued.

"Disappearances start two months later," Tyler said. "An address?"

Jean scrolled through the info on her P-Dat with a furrowed brow.

"Got an address in Randton, blue-collar suburb on the south-eastern outskirts of the city." She continued reading through the info. "Parents' house."

Tyler pointed at the bleached white ghoul on the screen.

"That guy lives with his parents?" Tyler asked. "Something's not right here."

The words *Priority Override* appeared on the screen in Jean's apartment. Suddenly the whole screen was taken up with Lieutenant Havern's wholesome smiling face.

"Jean," he said as though he were delighted to be speaking to her. "Who is Darius Snell? You working a hobby case?"

"Uh… yes boss—"

"Jean, c'mon, let's keep it casual. Jeff, please."

Tyler could see Jean struggling not to grimace. This level of fake bonhomie was actually quite uncomfortable to witness.

"Serial kidnapping in the Strip. Twelve vics in the last four months," she told him.

He frowned.

"Low priority crimes against low priority people, Jean. C'mon you know that."

"Yes, sir, I mean, Jeff."

"Anything salacious, something that might get us newscast time?"

Tyler tried to keep the distaste he felt off his face. He failed. He was conscious of Jeff-please's eyes flickering his way.

"Um… the suspect's a major league weirdo, into extreme body modding. I think that there's a pretty solid PR angle for helping the less fortunate—"

"Fortune's got nothing to do with it, Jean, you know that. Might be able to do something with the body modding aspect though. Is it sexy, Jean? Have you brought me something sexy?"

"Em, what?" Jean asked. She looked as though she genuinely didn't know how to answer the question.

"I mean, what's he doing with the vics?"

"We don't know," Jean said, her features hardening. "Nothing good."

"Okay, well, look. Send everything over to my assistant. I'll have her look it over and see if anything stands up and salutes, if you know what I mean," Jeff told her.

"Not really, sir," Jean said through gritted teeth.

"Look, Jean, I appreciate the initiative you've shown here, even if you did need a bit of help." Then he was speaking to Tyler: "Agent Matterton, it's good of you to step in here but the HCPD can handle its own business." Any warmth, fake or not, had disappeared from Jeff's eyes. This was the lieutenant pissing down Tyler's leg to mark his territory.

"We..." Tyler started but Jeff just plunged on.

"Anything comes of it, Jean, and I'll bear you in mind, but if I can be honest, I think you have been living down there too long. Jeff out." His image disappeared from the screen and the two side-by-side images of Darius Snell superimposed over the murder board reappeared.

"What a tool," Serena said. Tyler's head whipped around to stare at his partner. He had never heard her say anything of that ilk before about anyone—and she had met some pretty repugnant murderers. He had previously believed her to be incapable of such a thing. She looked genuinely irritated by her encounter with Jeff-please. "Shall I send everything over?" Tyler was surprised that she had asked Jean.

Jean sat down hard on the sofa and nodded to Serena. She looked close to tears. Serena looked to Tyler as well. He wanted to say no. He wanted to run it down himself. Pay a visit to the parents with Jean, but she had to live here and he had zero authority. He nodded to Serena. He felt dirty.

"This happen before?" he asked her.

Jean just looked up at him. He was wrong. She didn't look as though she were about to cry. She looked too weary for tears.

Serena sent the entire case file to Jeff, Please's assistant for review.

"I think you might both enjoy a drink," Serena said.

Tyler appreciated the precision with which Serena used words, but he didn't see either Jean or himself enjoying anything for a little while yet.

For all that Tyler didn't enjoy drinking, Serena had been right. He did want a drink. He suspected that the whisky Jean had collected for them from a street kiosk might have been a bit too much for someone unused to spirits but he quite liked it, despite the burn.

Tyler and Jean were both sat on the patched sofa staring at nothing. Neither of them really saying anything. Serena stood in front of the wall screen, which still displayed the murder board.

Serena was staring at a small window on the wall screen. Images were rapidly cycling through the window. Tyler had been aware of it for some time now but had only just focused in. Jean appeared to notice as well.

"Serena, what are you watching?" Jean asked.

Tyler frowned leaning over to get a better view past Serena. His partner appeared to be speed-watching footage of drunk people on their nights out.

"I am reviewing Interlink-posted, P-Dat party footage shot in the Strip," Serena told them both.

"Oh okay," Jean said and then looked at Tyler and mouthed the words: *What-the-fuck*?

"What are you looking for?" he finally managed to ask.

"Vans," Serena said.

Tyler's eyes widened.

"That's genius," Jean said and then turned to Tyler, "I'm starting to see the secret of your success."

It was said in jest but Tyler had to agree. He lacked the frame of reference to think of it, it was so out of the box.

Serena concentrated and the screen began to fill with images of vehicles that could conceivably be thought of as vans. The more that appeared, the smaller each of the images got.

"There are a lot of them," Serena told them. "Did you have a chance to have a look at Mr Snell's employment record when he reappeared on Alexandria?"

"Yeah," Jean said, "he was doing scut work for some material fabrication outfit, Resinable Printing, on the outskirts of the AS port." Jean inclined her head in the general direction of Hume-Memorial above them. "I figured that it would have given him an opportunity to check out his hunting ground but they closed down—"

"A little over four months ago," Serena finished.

"Fuck!" Jean screamed. "I should've have seen it. I would have gotten there eventually."

"You were distracted," Serena pointed out.

"By Hurricane Havern," Jean snapped, more at herself than anyone else.

Tyler was thinking.

"There's no room," he said. Jean and Serena turned to look at him. "At Snell's parents' house. He has to be taking his victims somewhere else."

Serena concentrated for a moment and the images of thousands of vans disappeared to be replaced by three still images from self-shot party clips. Each showed a different angle of a white van on a nearby street, seen through a bar or club window, or glimpsed from the sidewalk as partiers moved through the throngs. The lettering on the side spelled out *Resinable Printing*.

5

Serena and Tyler climbed into the gyrocar as Jean shared Resinable Printing's address to the gyrocar's navigation system from her P-Dat. Tyler took off his filter mask as the gull-wing door clicked into place. The Strip's neon was a dirty smear in the heavy carbon rain.

As Jean prepared for take-off, a sex worker crossed the mouth of the alley. She wasn't wearing a filter mask. Turning to look at the gyrocar as it started to rise, Tyler recognized her as a cracked Serena model. He had to force himself not to turn and look at his partner in the back seat as he tried to suppress his thoughts.

High above them, the aerospace port's exhaust conduits vented fire into the grimy air.

Resinable Printing existed as a business in the lower levels of one of the older starscrapers that surrounded the AS port. Below the raised roads and the high-speed passenger maglev line was a street carved through the middle of the huge tower. Shopfronts lined either side but few of them had active holographic signage. A heavy ground train line ran through the center of the street. The gyrocar came in over the spiral ramp from the raised road above. Jean wove the vehicle amongst the support pillars and over a goods train crawling along the rails like some carboniferous millipede.

"Looks deserted," Tyler said. The shopfront was blank, the holographic projectors inert.

Jean brought the gyrocar down in a flurry of loose trash; presumably the neighborhood couldn't afford a street cleaning service. They were on the other side of the tracks from Resinable Printing, having used the train as cover.

"Are we legally permitted to enter the premises?" Serena asked.

"I'm checking now," Jean said tapping away on her P-Dat. "There's an automated risk assessment based on the likelihood of legal action. It's dependent on who owns the building and their clout." She concentrated on the screen. "Okay, we're good to go." Jean reached for the driver's door handle.

"Detective Hoyle, could you interlink the permission to me?" Serena asked.

Jean stopped and then turned to look at Serena. Tyler could see that Jean wanted to say something. Whatever it was she thought better of it and instead tapped a couple of keys.

"Happy?" she asked.

Serena nodded.

Masks went on and the gyrocar's doors swung up.

They crossed the tracks in the wake of the freight train. Jean had the crowbar she had taken from the trunk of the gyrocar.

"Are we calling Havern?" Tyler asked. He was starting to feel apprehensive. He couldn't stop picturing Jaran's face.

"He's on do-not-disturb so I've left him a message, couched in suitably humble terms." This last was said bitterly.

They reached the shop front. A concertinaed roller door took up the majority of the frontage. There was a smaller door next to the roller. Tyler checked up and down the almost-empty street. It was late. Though Hume City had the reputation of being open for business 24/7, everywhere looked to be either closed or in the process of closing down.

"Rent increase," Jean said. "I'm guessing the area's about to be gentrified." She didn't even try the door, instead she put the crowbar into the frame. "Serena?"

Jean gave the crowbar a solid yank at the same time as Serena gave the door a kick. It flew inwards. Jean shoved the crowbar through her belt and drew her service weapon. She looked at Tyler.

"Oh yeah, right," he said and drew the compact that Jean had loaned him.

Jean entered first, sweeping left and then right, the illuminator mounted under the barrel of the pistol shining a cold blue beam of light over the shop's darkened interior.

Tyler followed Jean, using his P-Dat for light, weapon at the ready. Serena was last in. Straight away he knew that something was wrong. He saw a sparse and utilitarian interior, open-plan, presumably to allow for sizeable printed objects to be moved around. There were a number of automated cargo trolleys, lying inert, close to a cargo lift. There was a bench counter with a number of monitors on it, all of them dark. Tyler assumed, judging by the cargo elevator, that the printers were downstairs.

It was what was on the walls that really caught his attention, however. The images looked as though they had been painted on with tar, but there was still just about enough detail to discern distinct shapes. As far as Tyler could make out, the images on three of the walls depicted crowds of people, the features on their hairless heads completely blank. They were standing amongst the skeletal ruins of a city, staring eyelessly at some huge, multilimbed figure crouched on a mountain of skulls on the fourth wall. Tyler was sure that the figure was female, though it was so inhuman that he couldn't explain why he thought this. It reminded him, perhaps unfairly, of some of the more stylistic representations he had seen of the death goddess Kali.

"That's not at all disconcerting," Jean muttered.

Tyler knew that the images may be completely unconnected to their case, he still found them more than a little unnerving.

"There is music coming from below," Serena announced.

Jean led the way down the stairs, weapon at the ready. Tyler covered her. Serena looked as though she was going for a casual stroll as she quietly scanned the room. The 'music' was a discordant nerve-shredding barrage on the senses, with sampled screams woven into the cacophony. The stairwell stank of chemicals, with an undercurrent of something else, something mealy, like animal feed.

Tyler couldn't hear the noise of 3D fabricators over the sound of the music but he could feel their thrum through the floor. Jean reached the door and motioned that they were going through. Tyler nodded. Jean turned the handle. A wall of sound hit them when she opened the door. Tyler followed Jean in.

It was dark except for the illuminator on Jean's service weapon and the light on Tyler's P-Dat. Tyler couldn't make sense of the environment they found themselves in. It was as though they had stepped into the tortured hellscape of another planet.

Tyler whipped one way and then the other, trying to understand. He could feel the printers but saw nothing that looked like man-made machinery. All he could see was contoured dark organic-looking structures flowing into each other everywhere he looked. It was as though he was inside some kind of esoteric hive. As the thought occurred to him, a semi-hysterical giggle threatened to escape from his lips.

"It's resin!" Serena had to shout to be heard over the noise. The music was somehow becoming diegetic to the environment in Tyler's mind. He glanced back. His partner had snapped off some of the material and was rubbing it between her thumb and forefinger. He wanted to tell her not to touch anything.

"There's someone here! On me!" Jean shouted.

Tyler looked back to find Jean moving quickly towards an anomaly in the surrounding material. He moved after her. In the steel blue light of Jean's illuminator, he could make out a human torso protruding from the resin. It didn't make any sense. Closing with the figure he was able to make out some details in the bouncing light. He recognized one of the victims, though he couldn't remember her name: his mind was trying to process too much information. Her legs and arms were embedded in the resin.

For a moment he wondered if Snell was creating some kind of murderous art installation, then Tyler saw the distended, liquid-filled sac that had been fused to the flesh of her stomach. He could make out the outline of a dark, inhuman shape in the sac. As he moved closer, he saw a medical monitor bracelet on the woman's wrist. Electrodes had been adhered to her skin all over her visible body. Closer still and Tyler could make out a hanger for multiple medical drips lodged between her back and the contoured, biological-looking resin sculpt. It was as though the drip had been hidden so as not to spoil the aesthetic with human technology. Then he saw the tubes running from the drips to various catheters lodged in her flesh.

Jean reached her first and started checking for vitals. As soon as she touched her neck, the woman looked up.

"Help me," she begged.

Tyler saw Jean's eyes go wide. She staggered back.

"Detective…" Serena tried to warn her.

Jean stepped back onto the distended sack and it rolled under her. She lost her footing and landed on the sack, bursting it.

Tyler was already bringing his weapon up as the segmented, insectile creature spilled out of the sack in a deluge of viscous fluid. Tyler saw two muzzle flashes, heard two gunshots over the screaming, and only then realized he'd fired his weapon twice.

Jean was scrambling backwards away from the creature. Then, realizing, she had dropped her service weapon, leaned forward and grabbed it, levelling the weapon at the alien creature.

"It's dead!" Serena shouted.

"What the fuck is that!" Jean demanded, her voice tainted with near-panic.

It had a tapered body, a rounded, bullet-shaped head, two partially formed pincers, and two equally partially formed, fins on its back. It had more crab-like legs than Tyler was prepared to deal with at the moment and a wicked looking stinger. It looked familiar, like something he'd seen on some kind of media in the past but he was operating on a semi-instinctual level at the moment, struggling to access long-term memory.

"It's a scorpionid!" Serena shouted over the discordant noise. "A desert arthropod carnivore from Tanakan! It looks only partially formed! I think our suspect was trying to incubate it in a living host!"

The word 'suspect' sounded so innocuous for what was unfolding in front of Tyler's eyes.

"Why?" Jean demanded. She sounded very close to losing it.

"Insufficient information, Detective!" Serena said crouching down next to the unmoving creature. "If I was given to speculation, I would assume an aberrant personality disorder of some kind mixed with a complex fantasy life." There was something predatory in the way that Serena examined the creature. "I think it was dead before Agent Matterton shot it!"

Jean had managed to stand up, fluid dripping from her.

Tyler was aware of movement behind him. He swung back to the woman embedded in the resin. Her lips were moving but he couldn't hear her over the noise. He forced himself not to look at where the punctured and drained sack was fused with human flesh. She was either praying or pleading for release.

Then something occurred to him. There had been more than one victim. He lifted his weapon and the P-Dat and started shining it around. He found them quickly enough. More of the missing people. Some moving, others just hanging limp in the resin. All in similar states to the first victim.

"We can't handle this! We need tactical and paramedics!" Tyler shouted.

"Agreed!" Jean shouted back. "I wish we could turn that fucking noise off!"

"Why don't we stay, and you go upstairs and call for backup?" Tyler shouted. He wanted to leave too, but it made sense for Jean to call: she was the only one with the authority to request backup. One of them needed to stay in case their suspect was down here, amongst this twisted, pseudo-organic hellscape. His hope was that Jeff, Please had got Snell at his parents' house but Tyler couldn't quite square what Snell had turned himself into, what he had done down here, with someone who went back to Mommy and Daddy after a long hard day of kidnapping and mutilation.

Jean just nodded.

Something landed behind Jean with such grace and economy of movement that Tyler didn't immediately register its presence. The figure straightened up behind Jean and she still hadn't noticed.

"Detective!" Serena cried, already moving.

Jean spun around, bringing her service weapon up. Tyler saw her squeeze the trigger. Nothing happened. The gun was batted out of Jean's hand, and sent spinning. The powerfully built figure, dressed in black, lifted Jean into the air. The pale flesh around the figure's mouth split open and a gleaming stainless steel secondary mouth shot out towards Jean's face. A splash of blood hit Serena as she closed with the figure. Serena grabbed Jean with one hand and pushed the attacker with the other. Jean hit the floor. Powerful synthetic muscles made the bulky figure stagger back, albeit not very far.

Tyler came around the side of Serena, firing rapidly. The bulky figure staggered back in the flare of the muzzle flashes but didn't go down. Tyler was aware of Jean, limp, lying on the resinous floor, a blood-covered Serena standing over her protectively, as he continued firing with increasing desperation.

The compact pistol's magazine ran dry.

The figure turned and ran.

Tyler hit the release, flicking the empty magazine out and reloading the pistol. It was the last magazine he had.

Serena was already kneeling over Jean examining the bloody mess that used to be the detective's face.

"Go!" Serena shouted at him.

Tyler scrambled after the figure, stumbling across the uneven, printed hellscape. He had only caught a glimpse of their attacker. He had worn a black skin-tight suit that looked exoskeletal under a long black coat. His head was devoid of hair, chalk white; his eyes were black pools, and of course his throat and mouth showed signs of significant reconstruction. There was no doubt it was Snell.

Tyler ran past Snell's victims embedded in the resin, most unmoving, a few reaching out for him, their lips forming words unheard over the cacophony.

Snell disappeared into a narrow passage in the resin. Tyler followed. For a moment it didn't make any sense for there to be something as mundane as an open emergency exit and flight of concrete steps at the end of the contoured resin passage. Tyler caught a glimpse of Snell's boots near the top of the stairs, then they disappeared from view.

Tyler reached the top of the stairs moments later and looked around. The bulky figure of Snell was sprinting along the street in the direction of the aerospace port.

Tyler ran after him. A heavy ground train was rolling down the tracks in the center of the street.

"Police! Stop or I will fire!" Tyler shouted. Snell ignored him. Tyler decided not to waste his breath on further words. Snell was pulling away from him, his augmentations making the difference. Tyler already had the coppery taste of blood in his throat as he gave chase. He hoped help was on its way.

Close to the edge of the street Snell ran across the road to a chain-link gate topped with razor wire. He gave the gate a hefty kick and then disappeared from view. It took Tyler a few moments to get there but he followed. Past the gate were metal steps down to a maintenance catwalk that ran under the ground train bridge.

As he clambered down the steps, Tyler felt the catwalk shake from Snell's heavy, booted footfalls. He had Snell cornered now. Aerospace ports had extremely high security. Snell would run out of places to hide and the port's security contractors would quickly pick him up on their internal surveillance cameras, then they would be after him as well.

As he ran across the catwalk there was a burst of flame off to his right from the exhaust venting as a shuttle took off from one of the launch pads.

Tyler started to cough as he ran, struggling to breathe from the air quality as well as the exertion. As he fumbled to put his mask on while running, he could see Snell increasing the distance between them. Mask in place, the sound of his own gasping breath loud in his ears, Tyler pushed on.

Snell reached the steps at the other end of the catwalk and thundered up them.

Tyler reached them moments later. He accidentally glanced down into the murk under the port, and just for a moment found himself vertiginously aware that he could fall from here all the way down to Exhaust Town. He forced himself up the steps. The chain-link gate ahead of him had been kicked so hard it was almost bent in half.

Tyler found himself on another external walkway running along the edge of the converted atmosphere processor. He checked either way, the walkway disappearing into the smog. He even checked over the edge to see if Snell had tried climbing down. The depth of the chasm running between the AS port and the surrounding starscrapers rushed up, overwhelming him, and he staggered back from the edge, leaning against the port's grimy superstructure as he controlled his breathing.

Tyler had lost Snell. He knew he had to get in contact with HCPD and see if they could patch him through to port security. He just couldn't shake the feeling that it was going to be a bureaucratic nightmare involving a credit check, and frankly he didn't have the time.

He caught movement in his periphery. Whipping

around, he saw a figure disappearing into one of the clouds. Tyler started running. The smog was lit up briefly from within by a flashing red light designed to warn local air traffic and Tyler caught a glimpse of the figure, then it was gone.

Tyler ran into the cloud and was enveloped by the smog, barely able to see more than a few feet in front of him. He almost collided with a solid security gate constructed of thick metal, surrounded by a web of razor wire designed to stop people from climbing around it. Tyler could just about make out the locking mechanism: it was sophisticated and very heavy duty. Exactly the sort of high security he had expected from an AS port, except that the gate was open.

There was another gout of flame, close enough for Tyler to feel the heat. The gate was here to keep people away from the port's exhaust system.

As the flame subsided, a bulky, shadowy figure detached itself from a nearby niche in the wall and loomed out of the murk over Tyler. Too late, he tried to bring his weapon up. A hand caught his wrist. It had the grip of a power loader. Another hand grabbed him around the neck and picked him up. He caught a glimpse of a long black coat, ghoulish chalk-white flesh and black pools where eyes should be and then he was flung over the railing and into the chasm.

The world tilted around him. The port's super-structure, the starscrapers, the chasm spun through his vision. He was no longer holding the gun as fingers of fragile flesh searched for purchase on old, pitted and unyielding metal. His left hand managed to find grip and he swung into the superstructure hard. It felt like his shoulder had been wrenched out of its socket. He hung there. Flame vented above him: he was aware of someone looking down at him, then they were gone.

He couldn't move. Fear had overtaken rational thought. At some level he knew he was going to hang there until he lost his grip and plummeted to his death, perhaps splattering himself across the Strip on impact.

Then he heard a voice inside his head explaining to him, calmly and rationally, why he had to move. Why he had to climb.

He screamed as he pulled himself up, agony shooting through the wrenched shoulder. His right hand found purchase and he let go with his left, not sure if he would be able to rely on it to take his weight again, but knowing that it would have to.

His feet found purchase. That made things easier. He made his way back up towards the metal railing, inch-by-agonizing-terrifying-inch. He finally pulled himself over the railing and collapsed onto the catwalk. As he lay their dry sobbing, shaking like a leaf, his adrenaline now in charge of his body's biochemistry, it felt like the climb had taken an age but he knew that only a few short moments had passed. The other realization he came to was that the person that had thrown him over the railing, despite their similarity, hadn't been Snell. There was an accomplice.

Tyler pushed himself to his feet, more than a little shaky on his legs, and staggered in the same direction he had been heading previously. He reached the exhaust vent. It was part of a network of conduits that ran between the various shuttle pads. The reinforced concrete was still radiating heat from the last take-off.

He risked a peek round the corner.

There were three of them. One lying on the floor of the exhaust vent: Snell. Two other figures, identical to Snell, were standing over his unmoving body. Tyler had only risked a glance around the corner but in that moment, he'd seen the two standing figures react to his movement. He closed his eyes, leaning against the corner.

What are you doing? he asked himself.

He texted his whereabouts and the situation to Serena, not calling her because she would tell him to hold back. But he couldn't. Snell was within his reach but he was out of plays. His best hope was to keep them talking until backup arrived.

He came round the corner his hand in the air.

"My name is Special Agent Tyler Matterton. I'm with the FBI and I'm currently working with the HCPD." He pointed at Snell's inert shape. "That man is wanted in connection with a series of kidnappings."

The two standing figures just watched him, their

expressions completely blank. They gave no indication they had even understood his words.

Tyler moved forwards. Now he had a better look at them he could see that they weren't quite identical to Snell. For a start their throat and lower mouth hadn't been reconstructed. Tyler wasn't sure what else it was about them that was different: their exoskeleton-style bodysuits looked similar, as did the black pollution-macs they wore over them, the same chalk-white skin, lack of hair, the same powerful build. Somehow, however, the two newcomers felt purer, as though they were the real deal and Snell was aspiring to be like them.

"So, we're all going to go the precinct house to sort this out," Tyler pointed at Snell, "but he is coming with me. Understand?"

Nothing.

Tyler moved carefully towards them.

They just stared at him.

He could see himself reflected in the black pools of their eyes as he approached.

He heard the roar first. The structure shaking underfoot. Then he felt the warm wind howling through the exhaust vent. Then he saw the hot red glow.

Tyler turned and ran. He felt his back blistering from the heat as he did so. Reaching the mouth of the vent he threw himself to one side onto the catwalk. He hit metal hard, screaming, on fire.

PART II

6

TWO MONTHS LATER

Colonial Marshal Cassandra Stock went down on one knee in the dusty scrub and examined the dust storm shelter's air intake. The intake had been squashed flat against the earth.

"Yep," she said. "you'll need a new dust filter as well." She stood up but remained slightly bent, her fist in the small of her back out of deference to the pain in her spine. She was stood with Harvey, the rancher, by the entrance ramp to the shelter. There were still patches of late fall snow dotting the ground. Though it wasn't the snow that was worrying Harvey. It was the inevitable winter dust storms that clogged the airways of his herd of buffalo hybrids and suffocated them, unless he could get them into the subterranean shelter.

Cass forced herself to straighten up, trying to ignore

the pain in her back and in her knees, trying to appear steadier on her feet than she felt. Fifty-some years of abusing her body, one way or another, was starting to take its toll. She looked back along the dirt track that ran from the ranch house, a little distance away, to the raised ridge of the highway that bisected the plains. Cass could just about make out the white peaks of the distant Telemark Range over the northern horizon.

"You had me drive out half a day from Steer City to see this?" she asked.

Harvey had maybe ten or fifteen years on her. The skin was all but hanging off his frame, his face droopier than a sad bloodhound's, but she knew he had the dirt of this land in every pore. She looked around at the other four air intakes on the shelter. They'd all been squashed flat as well. He didn't deserve this.

"I figured you could use some of your investigative skills," Harvey said. He'd just rode in off the plain to meet her and was still holding the reins of his favorite horse, King. The horse, snorted and pawed at the cold ground.

"Well, Harvey, as you know I'm not a detective..." she started. He nodded, perhaps agreeing a little too quickly. "But I think someone run over your air filters, maybe with a truck."

Harvey nodded as though mulling this over.

"My tax dollars at work," he finally said. He just sounded sad.

"Hear anything?" she asked.

"Sure," he said. "Heard it, saw it, put a bullet through one of the big-assed lights mounted on top of the Daihotai tractor they were driving. I mean, they were good enough to cover up the Chisholm Meats logo on the side at least."

"Didn't want to make it too easy for us, I guess," Cass opined. "Get any footage?"

"No. Because the time before the last time they came onto my land to sabotage something, they took a laser to the security cameras, and who can afford to replace them?"

Cass felt for Harvey, she really did. His kids had seen there was no future on Gamma Leporis 3 and had left. Too much work and not enough money had put his wife, Marjorie, in the ground not two years hence. But Harvey had to know that there was nothing she could do.

She looked up into the white sky, a few flakes of snow were falling lazily towards her. The third sun in the Gamma Leporis trinary system, the one GL3 orbited, was a ball of cold light only a few shades from the color of the sky itself. The second sun was an even smaller, paler ball that she had to look hard to see. The primary sun in the system would be the brightest star in the sky when night fell. The wind blew, kicking up dust and biting at her bones like a cemetery dog.

"What exactly do you want me to do?" she asked Harvey.

"Seems to me a while back, I saw some media or another where the police took casts of tracks, went looking for bullet holes in tractor lights, maybe fragments of damaged air intakes in tyres, things like that."

"You saw that?"

"Yes, ma'am."

"On a media?"

"Uh huh."

"Well, see, those kinds of media, do you think they maybe give people the wrong idea, maybe unrealistically raise their expectations?"

Harvey just looked at her. King snorted again, shaking his head as though making his opinion on the matter known.

"Maybe in you, Marshal," he said bitterly.

She looked away. Let the wind blow grit into her eyes.

"Oh hell, Cass, that wasn't fair," he said a moment or two later. "I didn't mean it."

She turned back to see that he actually had his hat in his hands.

"Yeah, you did and you're right. Now put your damn hat back on before you catch a cold."

Harvey put his hat back on.

Cass walked over to her prairie rover and leaned against it.

"You know how this would play out, right?" she asked.

He just nodded.

She would go over to the closest Chisholm Meats station up at Coldstream. The station boss would speak to her and be very sorry he couldn't let her inspect the vehicles without a warrant. She might get a warrant, or she might not, depending on which judge she was able to speak to. In the meantime, any damage would have been fixed, any evidence cleaned away. None of that mattered, anyhow, because everyone was on station at the time whatever happened, happened, and everyone was everyone else's alibi. She knew it and Harvey knew it. Colonial marshals were supposed to have some pretty wide-ranging powers out here on the Frontier. Funny how those powers always ended up stymied in the face of Big Agri.

"Know the thing that really gets me?" he finally said. "I'm gone. I can't compete on scale. I can't sell my stock for enough to make back my costs. So that's it. They'll give me cents-on-the-dollar for the land, less for the stock, assuming I can get them to town before the first storm, otherwise they're just rotting on the plain." His fists were clenched. "What a fucking waste."

To the uninitiated it might have looked like his heart was breaking but Cass knew Harvey. His heart had been broken some two years gone now.

He looked up at her. Angry now. Eyes red.

"So, you want to know what I want from you? I want a good reason not to take my rifle and ride over to that station and go to work." He pointed north, roughly in the direction of Coldstream Station.

She met his eyes, struggling to come up with a good reason. When you took everything from someone, you couldn't be surprised when they decided that they had nothing to lose.

"They'd kill you, and if they didn't then I'd have to arrest you, and I don't want to do that."

"Not hurting your feelings ain't a good enough reason, Cass. Maybe they'd be doing me a favor."

She had nothing.

Harvey looked down as though he was ashamed.

"I'm sorry, I shouldn't have used that language."

Cass couldn't quite believe what she'd just heard. She let out an involuntary laugh. His head snapped up as though she were laughing at him.

"Harvey, it's okay. I was a marine, I heard much worse."

He just nodded.

"Tell me you can't do anything," he said pointing at the air filters.

"I can't do anything, Harvey, I'm sorry. I wish I could."

He nodded.

"And I know you've tried in the past, which isn't nothing." He thought for a moment. "Can I get a rebate on my taxes?

"If it were up to me." Cass was smiling despite herself.

"Follow me up to the house, I'll fix you some coffee and you can use the facilities before you head back. Least I can do for dragging you all the way out here on this fool's errand."

The thing was it shouldn't have been a fool's errand. It was her actual job.

In the end Harvey made her some lunch. She had stayed longer than she had intended to. He didn't have anyone to talk to now except King and the few remaining drones he was running. She was only just passing Coldstream Station as evening fell, still two hours back to Steer City. She had been able to see the lights of the Chisholm Meat operation from some distance. The meat company lit their land with drones, so they could move their huge genetically engineered cattle at night.

The prairie was lit up like a Core System sports stadium. She could make out some of the 'cowboys' rounding up stragglers on their fancy hover ATVs. How was Harvey supposed to compete with that? It hadn't always been this way. In the early days of the colony there had been more than enough room for small ranches to survive, if not thrive. So perhaps Old Harvey's ranch wasn't economically viable any more. Didn't mean that Chisholm Meats had to be assholes about it.

Cass had thought about going into the station, speaking to the foreman and telling them to leave Harvey alone. Except it might just encourage them to take further action against him. It shamed her that not least of her worries about warning off the foreman was that Chisholm Meats were more than capable of making her life legally difficult with the Colonial Administration. She couldn't shake the feeling that fifteen, maybe even ten years ago, she would have taken the turning, driven up to the cattle station and had words. She felt like a coward as she drove past the gate.

With the Telemark Mountains to her east and the Jöhannsen Range to her west, Cass was now close enough to see the torch of the Friday night heavy lift shuttle decelerating towards Steer City's shuttle port. She couldn't see the town itself yet, nestled as it was in the flat basin at the mouth of the Wyrm Pass that ran between the two ranges. The sky had cleared. Gamma Leporis's primary was now a bright star in the black sky. She could feel the drop in temperature that had come with the setting of the secondary and tertiary suns. It was going to be a cold night.

The rover was enveloped in a dust cloud as Cass pulled out to overtake a Chisholm Meats land train. She watched the long line of refrigerated trailers pulling butchered carcasses for fancy Core System markets and restaurants, as well as frozen, genetically engineered calf embryos for export all over the Frontier.

Cass was using the rover's sensors to navigate round the lengthy land train, as visibility was effectively zero in its dusty wake. It had come from Coldstream. She gave the huge vehicle the finger in an utterly pointless act of defiance. By the time she finally managed to overtake the land train's two drive units and the wipers had cleared the thick dust off the rover's windscreen, Cass could see the lights of Steer City. The tallest structure was the newly landed heavy lift shuttle. It dominated the skyline, lit up like a cathedral.

Port Street, Steer City's main drag, was a dust-mud bog. Most of the main streets radiated out from the shuttle port like spokes on a wheel. The actual paved roads were only for the one-way in and out routes taken by the land trains. She could see one of the long cargo vehicles up at the port. It drove through a cut-out part of the shuttle, where internal automation would lift the modular containers from the back of the land train and stack them in the shuttle's cargo bay.

Cass drove past the old slaughterhouse and genetics facility. It had a different purpose now. The town was a mixture of settlement-stage prefabs, with later buildings of native stone and lumber from introduced species. The lights of bars, eateries, honkytonks, and other entertainment establishments of an even less savory nature jostled for port-workers, ranch hands, and tourists' attention. The Colonial Marshal's office was on Port Street. It was less distance to drag drunk-ass cowboys.

When Cass pulled up outside of the office, the rover was bathed in the white light coming from the marshal's logo on the sign. She had just removed the Traylor Model 15 shotgun from its rack on the roll bar when she heard the raised voices. Cass sagged even before she risked a look.

On the other side of the road three ranch hands, all of whom she recognized from Coldstream Station, were hassling two of the Bio-Transcendents.

"Right outside the shop," Cass muttered, referring to the marshal office. She glanced through the window but couldn't see any of her deputies. Cass worked the charging handle on the semi-automatic shotgun, ejecting two red cartridges and replacing them with two white ones from the buttstock ammunition sleeve.

Cass swung down from the rover and into the mud, feeling herself sink in, cursing her poor timing. Her shift had ended more than two hours ago. She made her way across the street, through that peculiarly Gamma Leporis 3 experience that was cold wet dust, or airborne mud as she had long since come to think of it, towards the inevitable confrontation.

As she waded through the mud, she saw the biggest of the cowboys—she was pretty sure he was called Teddy—shove one of the Bio-Transcendents. The thing was neither of the Bio-Ts, a male and female, were that much smaller than Teddy. Their ripped physiques were accentuated by the exoskeleton-like muscle suits they wore. Their clothes, along with their freaky black eyes, lack of hair and chalk-white skin that glowed like a beacon in the wash of neon bar lights, made the Bio-Ts stick out like the proverbial. Cass understood their freedom of religion, their freedom of expression, it would just have been better, however, if they didn't look so goddamned weird compared to everyone else. It was asking for trouble, and variations of this scene played out daily. She was just so done with it all. Weirdos or not, the Bio-Ts deserved equal protection under the law and she just wished that everyone could leave everyone else in piece.

She reached the steps to the boardwalk just as Teddy spat at the male Bio-T. The Bio-T didn't flinch as spittle and chaw ran down the bleached skin of his face.

"Like that?" Teddy asked. One of his friends, Lance maybe, was chortling along at this high comedy. The third cowboy, a smaller, wiry-looking guy whose name Cass didn't know, looked uncomfortable with how things were playing out. All three of them were armed. Cass had tried repeatedly to get a no-carry city ordinance passed but the Colonial Administration kept vetoing it. As a result, the single biggest cause of violent death in Steer City was escalating drunken arguments, situations which could have otherwise been resolved with a bar brawl and a night in the cells, or the hospital.

"Now why don't you get down and lick the shit off my boots?" Teddy asked the male Bio-T. He tried pushing the pale, hairless man down but the Bio-T didn't budge. Nor did he say anything. Neither of them made any attempt to defend themselves. Both silent and impassive. They always were. That didn't much help their standing in town either.

"Alright boys, you've had your fun, move on and let these people get on about their business." Cass said as she climbed up onto the board walk.

Teddy turned around to face her. His bulk eclipsing the neon lights of the bar behind him. He stank of booze. Big, drunk and armed. Cass's favorite combination of asshole.

"You taking these freaks, side, Marshal?" Teddy demanded. He sounded genuinely aggrieved.

"Strictly speaking you've just assaulted this gentlemen, so it's not so much me taking their side as me taking the side of the law on account of it being my job. That said..." she turned to the Bio-T, "you gonna press charges?"

"I just spat some chaw in his face." Teddy made it sound as though he had the God-given right to go around spitting in people's faces and anything else was an attack on his civil liberties.

The Bio-T said nothing.

"What I figured," Cass said before turning back

to the three Coldstream Station cowboys. "So at the moment what I've got you for is disturbing the peace—"

"We weren't disturbing no—" Lance began.

"—being a public nuisance, acting like assholes and genuinely chapping my tired ass after a long shitty day."

"Is being an asshole a crime?" It was the wiry one who'd spoken. The one whose name she didn't know. He seemed less drunk and genuinely interested in the answer.

"For the purposes of this conversation, yes," Cass told him. "Now, gentlemen, do you want to sleep it off in the cells or in your bunkhouse?"

The Bio-Ts just stood there, unmoving, giving no sign that they were aware of the events unfolding around them.

"The fuck are you going to do about it?" Teddy demanded, taking another few steps forward to loom over her in a distinctly threatening manner.

"Do you know what a force multiplier is, Teddy?" Cass asked.

"Huh?"

She hit him in the nose with the butt of her shotgun. There was an explosion of blood as the offending nose was spread across Teddy's face. Cass took a couple of steps back and leveled the shotgun at Teddy's groin and squeezed the trigger. He hit the ground, hard.

Lance was going for his gun. Cass moved to one side, shifting her aim. She squeezed the trigger, again, unloading it into Lance's face, turning it red. The cowboy's hands went to the bloody mess as he hit the ground screaming.

The third cowboy, the, wiry one, was trying to get his sidearm from its holster but he was more drunk than he had initially appeared.

"Don't!" Cass snapped.

He froze. Then slowly raised his hands. He looked almost as white as the Bio-Ts.

"You killed them," the third cowboy said, appalled. "They were just having some fun."

"Get on!" Cass snapped at the two Bio-Ts. They continued on their way as though nothing had happened, making their way back to the old slaughter-house/genetics facility they had turned into their church.

Teddy started crawling around the floor, making a mewling sound. There was sobbing from Lance behind his hands, blood leaking through his fingers as he clutched his face.

"Prairie salt," Cass told the third cowboy, "hand loaded. Just really rapid exfoliation."

She was being flip. She'd be lucky if she hadn't blinded Lance. Still, she'd given them the opportunity to be reasonable. Now would come the inevitable whining about the consequences.

***

Cass had the wiry guy drag the mewling Teddy across the muddy street, up the steps onto the boardwalk and into the marshal's station.

Deputy Sorgram was waiting for Cass as she guided Lance into their offices. The deputy was leaning on the desk closest to the door. He was in his mid-thirties, medium build, average height with a short beard that he'd grown in bid to offset his otherwise completely non-descript appearance. Deputies Williams and Amsa were sat at their workstations.

Sorgram pointed at Teddy.

"He's just covered in shit."

Cass's turned her head to regard her second-in-command.

"Three of them, each of them twice my bodyweight and half my age, didn't think to give me some backup?"

Sorgram pointed at the wiry cowboy that Cass hadn't shot.

"He can't be more than half your weight again," the deputy pointed out.

Cass just stared at him.

"Jesus, Marshal, they were just hassling a couple of weirdos. It didn't occur to us that you were going to start a gunfight." Sorgram hadn't moved from where he was leaning against the desk, his arms crossed.

Cass was divesting herself of the guns that she'd

confiscated from the three cowboys. The wiry guy was just standing around looking awkward. Lance was staggering around a little; Teddy had his hands on his bloody groin, whimpering.

"After I'd got three armed suspects subdued you didn't think to cross the street help me disarm them, get them in cuffs? Or were you too busy calling the foreman up at Coldstream?" She wasn't even terribly angry. They'd had variations of this argument many times before. They were just going through the motions.

"Like you said, you had them subdued, figured you had it under control. Particularly as you started it."

"I..." Words abandoned her. "Think you can manage to book them, put them in the cells, or do you want to check with Chisholm first, make sure it's okay with them?"

Sorgram glared at her.

"Remind me again, when are you retiring?"

"Half-past-I-don't-give-a-shit. Just do it."

Sorgram still didn't move.

"What am I booking them for? Being on the receiving end of excessive force or just getting shot without a license?"

"Disturbing the peace, creating a public nuisance, threatening a marshal, resisting an arrest. Y'know, all the things you just watched them do."

He straightened up.

"Well, hell, Marshal, I'm not sure I saw any of that."

Cass looked at him, eyes narrowing.

"Either do it, or leave your star on the desk and fuck off." Every day was another knife fight. The two junior deputies just watching them. The thing was, she knew it wouldn't make any difference. None of it would stick to the three cowboys. It never did. There's a good chance she'd get an official reprimand: it might even affect her pension, or bring forward her retirement date. The best she could hope was for Teddy, Lance and the other guy to have a deeply uncomfortable night in the cells. When she was gone and Sorgram was in charge, then Steer City would finally become a company town in totality.

"Erm, should I call one of the paramedics?" Deputy Amsa asked, her features obscured by the harsh light of her monitor.

"No," Cass said.

"Yes," Sorgram said.

Cass sighed. More than anything she just felt tired. She just wanted to roll into retirement. Instead, even doing the basics of her job had become a constant uphill struggle. The problem was Sorgram was right, in this case. If she'd done any real harm to either Teddy or Lance then there would be hell to pay.

Cass looked at Amsa and nodded.

Sorgram gestured for the wiry guy to drag Teddy towards the cell as the deputy tried to guide Lance.

"Wait!" Cass snapped. "You guys know anything about some rowdies taking one of those big Daihotai eight-wheelers you boys use over to Harvey Jermaine's place last night? Did some damage to his dust shelter?"

"Anything happened to that old man, chances are he had it coming," the wiry cowboy sneered.

"C'mon," Sorgram snapped, pushing the cowboy towards the cells, presumably before he could say something that incriminated their mutual employer.

Cass watched the wiry cowboy guide Lance towards the stairs down to the cells. What she couldn't work out was how one working person had been taught to have so much contempt for another working person. When had that happened?

She turned to Williams and Amsa. She had no idea if either of them, or indeed both, were on the take yet. Had Sorgram corrupted them already? She knew that he was much easier to get along with than she was.

"Can you girls book 'em? Lock up their guns? I'll do the rest of the paperwork in the morning?"

Amsa just nodded.

"How are our friends?" Cass asked.

"Back in the Stagecoach," Amsa told her, meaning the Stagecoach Hotel.

Two newcomers had piqued Cass's interest when they had arrived on the last Halfday shuttle. A heavy-set bearded man and a wiry woman that Cass was convinced was ex-military.

Amsa rolled back some of the footage of the couple taken by Steer City's many security cameras. It showed the couple wandering all over town. The woman occasionally glanced up at the cameras. Some of the footage was just the woman on her own.

"They showed particular interest in anything?" Cass asked, leaning into her deputy's workspace to study the screen. The couple in question had not done anything to warrant suspicion: she just couldn't shake the feeling that the woman was conducting a reconnaissance.

Amsa used the touchscreen to freeze an image. It showed the woman, hood up, shades on, looking at her P-Dat.

"Us," Amsa told her. The image was taken outside from earlier in the day. Cass suspected that the woman had been recording the comings-and-goings of the marshal's office.

"She wants to know what the opposition is like," Cass muttered.

Williams was hovering over her as Cass straightened up.

"Marshal," she said, "there's two people from the FBI here to see you."

"What?" Cass hadn't meant to snap, but it was just about the last thing she had expected to hear.

"They're in your office." Williams told her.

They were at least sat in the chairs on the right side of her desk. The special agent was a good-looking Black guy. Cass suspected she had at least twenty years on him. Even the Feds looked like kids to her these days. He made his newly bought outdoor clothes and boots look like a uniform. Even his high-back-and-sides haircut looked regulation, somehow.

The agent's 'partner' was an android. She had that same non-threatening, easy-on-the-eyes efficient look that all artificial people seemed to have. Cass had only seen one of this particular model before, working as a secretary for a Chisholm board member. She guessed this one was programmed specifically to offer investigative support.

Both the agent and the android stood up and turned around as she entered. The agent offered his hand. Cass noticed burn scars peaking over the collar of his shirt.

"Marshal," the agent said by way of a greeting. "I'm special Agent Tyler Matterton; this is my partner, Serena. We'd like to talk to you about the Church of Biological Transcendence."

7

Tyler hadn't been impressed when Marshal Stock told them that her shift had finished two-and-half hours ago and that if they wanted to talk to her then they would have to do so while she ate. It was how they found themselves in a bar/restaurant called The Old Pioneer Saloon. The marshal had described it as the best place to get a steak and whisky that she could afford and if they were lucky, they'd get a booth where they could just about hear each other talk. She ordered a whisky with a beer chaser as the waiter showed them to their table.

"I mean I know what I'm having," the marshal said as they slid into the booth. "Steak and potatoes. I'd recommend them."

The waiter looked at Tyler expectantly. He hadn't even seen a menu.

"Salad?" he asked.

"It's a steak salad," said the waiter, whose name badge said *Marv.*

"Could I get it without the steak?" Tyler asked.

"I'd have to charge you the same. It's a lot of money for just lettuce and some dressing."

"Just the salad," Tyler said, hoping that was an end to the conversation.

"And you, miss?" Marv asked Serena.

Serena opened her mouth to say something, but the marshal beat her to it.

"She's a synth, Marv."

Marv looked as though he didn't quite know what to say.

"She prefers 'artificial person'," Tyler said.

Marv was looking positively uncomfortable now.

The marshal relaxed back into the curving bench seat. Something in her manner reminded Tyler of The Bish. Like the android pimp, a revolver rode her hip, though only the one.

"She prefer speaking for herself as well?" the marshal asked, somewhat hypocritically, Tyler thought. Then she turned to Serena. "No offense meant, Ms."

"None taken, Marshal, and as Special Agent Matterton said, it is a preference."

The marshal was looking at Serena as though she was weighing her up.

"Thank you, Marv," the marshal said without taking her eyes off Serena. The waiter practically fled.

"You a vegetarian?" the marshal asked, still not taking her eyes off of Serena.

"I am. That a problem?" Tyler asked. Something about the marshal's attitude was grating on him. Now she turned to look at him.

"Not for me. I just think you might find that this a hard planet to be a vegetarian on."

Tyler looked around. The Old Pioneer Saloon was packed, but then it was a Saturday night and he had heard that on some Frontier worlds the arrival of even a twice-weekly shuttle was something worth celebrating. Most of the tables were full, either with young families or groups of friends and co-workers. Beer and whisky were flowing freely, and plates stacked with meat and carbohydrates were being delivered to tables by waiters that moved through the crowd with the skill of ballet dancers. Country music played loud enough to be heard, but not loud enough to drown out conversation, not on their table anyway.

The water Tyler had ordered, along with a whisky and a beer, turned up on the table as if by magic. The marshal shot the whisky, head back, eyes closed as she savored the taste. Her head rocked forward again and she opened her eyes.

"Don't drink either?"

"Not on duty," Tyler told her. He hadn't meant it to sound as judgmental as it had.

The marshal narrowed her eyes.

"Well, I'm off duty. Want to talk to me on duty, I'm back at midday tomorrow. Besides..." The marshal went quiet. Clearly, she had thought the better of whatever she had been about to say.

"Problems in your house?" Tyler asked.

The marshal regarded him for a few moments before answering.

"You're me, how do you answer that?"

It was a good point.

"What'd you see?" the marshal asked.

Tyler just looked at Serena.

"We saw nothing," Serena said. "We heard your two junior deputies requesting permission to provide you with backup, while your senior deputy refused them permission and implied that it would be detrimental to their future career prospects if they disobeyed him."

"Goddamnit." It was said so quietly that Tyler practically had to read the marshal's lips. He took a good look at her now. He knew she was in her early fifties but she looked older. She had a spare, lean frame, leathery skin and craggy features. She looked tough but more than anything she looked done.

"We're here because I'm tired, hungry and I want a drink. If what you've got to talk to me about is in any way sensitive then it's best we talk here."

This admission sounded as though it had cost the marshal.

"I would be happy to testify in any disciplinary

action you bring against Senior Deputy Sorgram," Serena offered.

The marshal just shook her head. Tyler couldn't shake the feeling that it wasn't the way that she handled things. It was an old-school attitude that he had encountered before. To Tyler's mind it just meant that the bad apples were able to operate with impunity, their corruption infecting others.

Tyler's burns started to throb despite Serena having attended to them just before descent. The pain would come later.

"Do you know who Darius Snell is, Marshal?" Tyler asked.

It took a moment but then the marshal shrugged.

"Would it surprise you to hear that he had lived in Steer City?"

"I'm guessing he is, or was, one of the Bio-Ts. They change their name when they join their church. Stop trying to trip me up and get to the point." There was no irritation in her words, just weariness. Tyler assumed that Bio-T was the local name for a member of the Church of Biotechnological Transcendence.

"He was responsible for sixteen kidnappings, six of his victims ended up dead, three are still missing. The rest required serious medical intervention. At the very least they will need significant mental health care for the rest of their life." Tyler left out that most of them wouldn't receive that mental health care because they couldn't afford it. In addition, the lifesaving procedures they had received to undo Snell's horrific modifications meant that they would be in medical debt for the rest of their lives.

"Jesus," the marshal said and then very quickly took a large mouthful of beer. "You get him?"

"We believe he's dead," Serena told her.

"He's dead," Tyler agreed, "turned to carbon by a shuttle's torch."

"Your burns?"

Tyler nodded. He couldn't help but pull the collar of his shirt up. In hypersleep he had still, somehow, been able to feel pain from the burns even as he repeatedly dreamed Snell's entire back catalogue of commercial dreams.

"Case file?" the marshal asked.

Tyler tapped away at the screen on his P-Dat and brought the file up. The marshal held up her ruggedized P-Dat and Tyler touched it with his own to facilitate the file transfer.

"Get a dust-case for your P-Dat and everything else you own as-soon-as," the marshal told him as she opened the file.

Marv appeared at their table carrying their food orders. Tyler found himself looking at a pile of refried beans in the center of half a lettuce covered in blue cheese dressing.

"For the protein," Marv told him helpfully.

Tyler just nodded. The marshal had a smile on her face now.

"Marshal," Tyler said after Marv had left them. The marshal was removing a fork and steak knife from a cloth napkin. "You haven't asked where this all went down."

Again, the marshal spent a moment or two just looking at Tyler before she answered.

"I figured with the FBI involvement it happened on Earth or its environs. You both have Core Systems written all over you. Besides," she tapped her P-Dat, "I also figure you'll mention it in here."

"Alexandria," Tyler told her.

"Special Agent Matterton, are you trying to catch me out again?"

Tyler didn't answer.

The marshal turned to look at Serena. She said nothing as well. Tyler suspected that the marshal was a pretty good poker player, but she would know that Serena would be capable of analyzing every micro-expression that passed across the marshal's craggy features.

The marshal held up her P-Dat.

"I'm gonna eat my food, probably order another shot and a brew, and then we can talk but only if you stop playing games, understand me?"

It was fair, but Tyler was sure that the marshal knew more than she was letting on. A shared glance with Serena confirmed his suspicions. She had seen it as well.

"Alexandria's a little out of your jurisdiction. That's ICSC, isn't it? Corp space." The marshal hadn't looked up from the screen of her P-Dat.

"We were consulting," Tyler said.

The marshal smiled to herself as she started reading.

"Well, there goes my appetite," Marshal Stock said and put her fork and knife down next to her half-eaten plate of steak and potatoes. She knocked back her second bourbon of the night and picked up her glass of beer. She pointed at the P-Dat and then took a sip. "That report's been cleaned up a lot but that's a sloppy investigation, even by our backward-assed standards."

"Events happened quickly. We were playing catch-up. It wasn't my finest hour but Serena did what she could with what we had for the report," Tyler told the marshal.

The marshal nodded and picked up her P-Dat again and started writing a message.

"Marshal?" Serena asked.

"So, you think that Snell was a Bio-T. Went back home and started kidnapping people to use as incubators for Tanakan scorpionids, for reasons best known only to the head full of rabid squirrels that passed for his mind. Then the Bio-Ts sent two of their own to take care of him?" The Marshal asked. Tyler nodded. "And they were so fanatical that they would rather turn themselves into so much carbon than get arrested?"

"That's about the size of it," Tyler said. "We can trace the two Bio-Ts from Anchorpoint Station to Alexandria."

"But not from here?" the marshal said, finishing her message and sending it. "Not surprising. We can keep track of stock well enough but this is a cargo port. Nobody really gives a shit about passengers. I shouldn't imagine Anchorpoint is all that different. That said, these Bio-Ts stick out like a vegetarian in a steak house." There was a very brief pause to see if Tyler was biting. He wasn't. "I've asked a friend of mine at the port if any Bio-Ts took passage in the time frame we're looking at."

It was a start.

"Now why did Detective Hume's gun jam?" the marshal asked.

The question took Tyler by surprise. It was clear that it was a test. How much was he prepared to share with her?

Serena opened her mouth to answer, but Tyler held his hand up to stop her. Coming from her it was programming; coming from him it was trust, even if she was withholding herself.

"Jean's an old academy buddy, a good cop—" Tyler started.

"But?"

"She pistol-whipped a pimp. A bit of his flesh got stuck in the slide, her weapon couldn't cycle."

The marshal sucked in air between her teeth.

"She packing some carbon-fibre, ceramic, nine-millimeter piece-of-shit?" she asked. Tyler nodded. He had been as well for what it was worth. "See, you going to pistol-whip some asshole pimp, you want steel in your hand." She tapped the solid-looking .357 Magnum in the leather cross-draw holster on her left hip. "Your report said that she got bit?" the marshal asked. Again, Tyler nodded. "She gonna be okay?"

"Three reconstructive surgeries, one more to go. But she survived," Tyler told her. He liked that the marshal had asked. HCPD medical just about covered the operations, though Jean would have some excess to pay off despite it happening in the line of duty.

"The lock?" the marshal asked. "Even here it's pretty tricky to get into the port's exhaust venting."

"Lock hacker," Serena told the marshal.

Stock gave this some thought.

"Ain't common here. Common in the Core Systems?" she asked.

Tyler couldn't shake the feeling that she knew the answer.

"It's heavily restricted tech," Serena replied, "even on Alexandria."

"Because you can use it to get into high security areas like shuttle ports and even through airlocks. With a lock hacker that sophisticated you could cause havoc," Tyler said.

"So, assuming it was a pair of our homegrown

religious types, what were they doing with tech that restricted?" the marshal asked rhetorically.

Tyler was starting to suspect that she was genuinely interested. It gave him a degree of hope that she might still be prepared to put the work in.

"Snell tries to make it as a commercial dreamer, fails. Comes here, of all places, to seek enlightenment at the ass-end of the Frontier." The marshal tapped at the P-Dat's screen. "What's the report not telling me? How'd the Bio-Ts recruit him?"

"He was head-hunted by a recruitment agency on Alexandria. Part of the recruitment process included a battery of psychometric testing," Serena told the marshal.

The marshal stared at her.

"You're kidding—that's legal?" she asked.

"The church is incorporated," Serena told the marshal. "They have filed a number of genetech patents."

"So that's why they're here," the marshal said. "Always wondered."

Tyler knew that the laws on genetic engineering were extremely lax on Gamma Leporis 3 because of the cattle industry. It was an ideal place for a gene-hacking cult.

"The recruitment agency immediately lawyered up, but we got the feeling that the head-hunting, the psychometric questions, were all designed to find and recruit people who were susceptible to manipulation and control," Tyler explained.

"And he was an unhappy young man because his chosen career wasn't going well?" the marshal asked.

"There's probably a number of factors but yes, that would certainly seem to be the case. Snell was despondent; he felt like a failure; felt like something was missing."

The marshal thought about it for a moment and then shook her head.

"Now they've got recruitment agencies doing their dirty work for them, that's something. That means there's money behind this."

Tyler shrugged.

"We interviewed his parents," Serena said. She left out that they had to wait until the parents had gotten over the trauma of being SWATted by Jeff-please. "They told us that he was unhappy before he left for Gamma Leporis 3, but when he returned there had been a complete change in his personality. He was a different person and they eventually had to ask him to leave."

"So, whatever got in his head to drive him nuts happened here?" the marshal asked.

Tyler couldn't quite put his finger on it but there was something guarded in her expression.

"Again, we can't know for sure but if that level of dysfunction was present in his psyche before he joined the Bio-Ts then it was pretty well buried," Tyler told her.

"You don't think the commercial dreaming had

anything to do with it? I mean it's an odd thing to invite complete strangers into your psyche."

"I reviewed everything he ever made. There's a wistfulness to it, a longing, even in the pornography. If there's even the tiniest trace of someone capable of such objectification of their fellow humans as to use them as incubators, I didn't see it, and I've been trained to look for it."

"But people don't change that much," the marshal said. "I mean, I've only had very basic training in psychology, but we're talking a pretty significant break with reality, right? Either there'd have to be some kind or warning signs or—"

"Something very significant happened here," Tyler finished.

"And we didn't notice?" It sounded like the marshal was asking herself the question. Whatever the marshal was holding back was really troubling her. It was as though she didn't want this to have happened on her watch. Tyler knew there would be a time when he and Serena would have to push on this but it wasn't now. Not if they wanted her cooperation.

"I don't know that much about the Bio-Ts," the marshal told them. "What I do know is that they're a transhumanist cult. So, I can maybe understand that he wanted to become something else, to transform. But the incubation? The resin sculpting?" The marshal turned in her seat and looked out the window in the direction of the church's building as though it could offer some insight.

"The most obvious explanation is that he was acting out the cult's belief system," Serena said, "their mythology."

"It was as though he was trying to fake being one of them," Tyler added. "The contact lenses, bleaching his skin, implants. Whereas the two I saw..." He wasn't quite sure where he was going with that. Again, the marshal was just watching him. "Is there anything else you can tell us?"

The marshal shrugged.

"They keep themselves to themselves, don't even speak, except for Dawkins."

"Dawkins?" Tyler asked.

"He's their spokesperson. For someone investigating this, you sure don't have much."

"Well, marshal, to be honest we were hoping for a bit more cooperation from your office," Tyler told her.

"I'm here, aren't I?" Again, she sounded defensive.

"We sent a request for information ahead of us," Serena said.

The marshal opened her mouth to say something and then closed it again. It was clear that she hadn't seen the request.

"Snell's parents told us they couldn't understand a lot of what he said, that he was raving. He did, however, make frequent mention of a goddess," Serena told Stock.

"Gotta say that doesn't really sound like our Bio-Ts. I always had the impression that they were the try-too-hard types, all that live-up-to-your-potential bullshit," the marshal told them.

All three were leaning in over the table, food, drink and noise momentarily forgotten.

"Do you know anything else about them, marshal?" Tyler asked.

Stock gave the question some thought. She swallowed down another mouthful of beer before answering.

"Not much. They came to town about three years ago and took over the old Chisholm Meats' slaughterhouse and genetics facility. Refitted it, brought in a lot of off-world lab equipment. People don't like the way they look and, like I said, they never talk. If I'm honest, however, other than people's reaction to them, they're probably the least amount of trouble in town. The ranch hands, port crews, off-duty marines, all of them are a much bigger pain in my ass. I just thought people didn't like them because they were different."

Tyler saw a brief glow from the marshal's P-Dat. Stock turned it over and read the message.

"That's my friend at the port. As far as he's aware no Bio-T has taken a shuttle off-world in the last six months. He's in a good position to know but he asked around as well. Doesn't mean it didn't happen, just didn't happen openly."

"Thank you, marshal," Serena said.

Tyler nodded. They would have to take the marshal's information at face value for the time being.

"Is a federal agent as an eye-witness enough to get a warrant to enter their premises?" Tyler asked. He didn't take his eyes off the marshal but he could feel Serena looking at him.

The marshal frowned.

"It's pretty weak," she said, "But nobody likes them and every lawyer works for Chisholm, so as long as you're not messing with the meat, I think it's a fair-to-even chance."

"We would not wish to do anything untoward," Serena said. Tyler was pretty sure that it had to have taken every last bit of her diplomacy programming not to use the word 'illegal' rather than 'untoward'.

"Honey," the marshal said and then belched loudly, "'Scuse me, it's still law. Frontier law but still law." She knocked back the rest of the beer and stood up, putting her hat on. "Send over an official request, and I'll see which of the judges I want to try."

"Thank you, marshal," Tyler said.

"Got a place to stay?" she asked.

"We came straight to you when we landed." Tyler could practically hear the marshal thinking *Lucky me.*

"Stay here. It's noisy but you're less likely to get a bullet through the floorboard and it won't morally compromise your position as a federal agent."

The marshal turned to leave, then stopped.

"Also, can you re-send the inter-agency cooperation request? We must have missed that."

"Of course, marshal," Tyler said. He watched the marshal weave her way through the crowd, exchanging words with a number of people as she passed them. Tyler could feel Serena looking at him again.

They had gotten a strange look as they checked in. Tyler guessed they weren't used to a human checking in with an artificial person. He didn't care. He felt as tired as the marshal had looked, six weeks of hypersleep notwithstanding. Not that the hypersleep had been particularly restful. Anytime he wasn't mainlining indie or porn dreamscapes, he was back in the hellscape under Resinable Printing. One way or another he had been living inside Snell's head in his dreams. Except it seemed like there were two very different heads involved.

The room was basic but it had a comfortable rustic-looking wooden framed bed, a place to put his luggage, and a bathroom. He could hear the bar/restaurant below. It was rowdier now. The families had gone home. The music was louder, and it sounded as though the dancing had started.

Serena was sat in the room's one arm chair. Tyler was lying on the bed.

"What do you think?" he asked her.

"It is by no means a certainty, but analysis of her micro-expressions suggests that Marshal Stock knew who Snell was and knows more about him than she was prepared to tell us," Serena said.

"Agreed."

"It could simply mean that she doesn't trust us yet," Serena pointed out. It was a good supposition. The marshal had no real reason to trust them.

"Did you buy how little she knew about the Bio-Ts?" Tyler asked.

"I did. Secrecy is part of the makeup of such an organization. If, however, they had the means to move off-world, unnoticed, and to procure a sufficiently sophisticated lock hacker—"

"Then they have some juice behind them."

"I could look into that."

Tyler watched her for a moment or two.

"Agent Matterton?" Serena asked.

"Yes, do that, and please, Tyler when we're alone."

Now it was Serena's turn to just look at him.

"Tyler," she said as though tasting the word, "I am surprised," Serena was clearly picking her words carefully, "at our presence here."

"Why? We have jurisdiction, it's interstellar, the genetech connection puts it well within ECU's remit."

"And you have discretion to pursue cases that come within that remit," Serena said. "I'm just unclear what the crime is here. The murder-suicide happened out of our jurisdiction on an ICSC world and the links to Gamma Leporis 3 are quite circumstantial. I suspect that had this gone to review—"

"It will be reviewed. You sent the report in yourself. If we waited until we heard back..." The degree of discretion an individual agent was granted when away from a field office was a necessity because of communication times across interstellar distances.

"Agent... Tyler... you have suffered trauma—"

"That you have the training to help me work through."

"Programming," Serena said softly.

"What?" Tyler asked. He couldn't quite keep a trace or irritation out of his tone. He felt like the discussion had just veered wildly off topic.

"I have the programming to provide a degree of field counselling. It is not a long-term solution, particularly not in light of the physical and psychological trauma that you were subject to on Alexandria. Nor do I think you have fully processed the Greco case."

"Processed?" Tyler demanded. "Should we be able to process something like that?" It was such a sterile non-word for the things he had seen, experienced.

"And you can become obsessive—"

"I'm supposed to be obsessive, to not stop. How can you just... Those people trapped in the resin, what Snell did. We can't just ignore how he got so far removed from..." He was sat up on the bed now. It took him a moment to realize how foolish he was being. Serena couldn't be expected to feel the same way he did about what they had experienced. She couldn't really be expected to feel at all.

"Is it the puzzle or the need for someone to pay?" Serena asked.

Tyler stopped.

"Is this the field counselling?" It was practically a growl.

"I have clearly upset you," Serena said.

"You haven't, the situation has. I'm supposed to be upset. These things are upsetting. Look, I'm sorry. Yes, I'm motivated. Yes, I'm having bad dreams, but we can continue to work through it here and I'll return to the program when we get home, but this needs doing, Serena. You must see that."

She didn't say anything. She just looked at him. He tried not to think about how the expression of concern on her face was just her algorithms going through the motions.

He closed his eyes and took a deep breath.

"As regards Snell," he said opening his eyes, "what was your reading of her emotional state when we did bring him up?"

"I saw micro-expressions that I would associate with guilt," Serena said. Her words seemed loaded but then Tyler knew that wasn't something that she did. "I will re-send the inter-agency request for cooperation direct to the marshal."

"Thank you," Tyler said lying back on the bed, feeling like shit.

Tyler was embedded deep in the resin everything was fire.

He sat bolt upright in the bed screaming. A figure stood over him. One of them, come for him. No. Just Serena. It may have been some psychosomatic dream residue, but his back was agony.

"Shhh," Serena said.

"My back..." he managed. The pain was such that his eyes were watering.

"Roll onto your front," she told him, and he did as he was bid.

Serena applied the soothing gel to his burns.

8

Sleep hadn't come easy to Cass. She had found what Matterton and Serena had to tell her about Snell extremely disturbing, not least because Cass knew that she was in part responsible. She was pretty sure that she had done a good job of hiding it except for the fact that Serena was a walking, talking FBI lie detector. Reading micro-expressions might not have been admissible in court, but they must suspect that she knew more than she was telling.

The threadbare carpet of her apartment was cold underfoot when she finally gave up on sleep and got up. Winter was definitely on its way. It would let itself be known when it came howling across the plains carrying great clouds of dust with it. Her spartan apartment was above the marshal's office. Somehow, she couldn't imagine Sorgram living here when she retired. He had a nice place on the edge of town. He barely even bothered to hide where the money had come from. Still at least it sounded quiet downstairs but then it was still early on a Sunday morning.

Cass busied herself making coffee and eggs. For her, coffee was like steak, whisky and firearms—so intrinsic to her life that it was something she tried never to skimp on. As comforting breakfast smells started to permeate the small apartment, she found herself looking out over the rooftops of Steer City. In the center of town, the shuttle still dominated the surrounding buildings. Umbilicals were feeding the vessel the fuel, water and air it would need for its return journey to the Meat Locker, the orbital station where interstellar shipping docked high above GL3. Beyond the hard lines of the shuttle, the distant mountains looked like escape to the marshal.

Why didn't you tell them about Snell? she asked herself. She had always carried her own water, both as a marshal and as a marine before that. Had she wanted to give herself space to formulate the best way to present what had actually happened? If so, it was a weasel response. She had to face up to the fact that she was at least partially responsible for the murder of six people, possibly more, and the kidnapping and torture of at least nine others.

She checked her P-Dat. Agent Matterton had sent over his part of the search warrant request. Cass suspected that Serena had done her best to smarten it up but it was thin. She started to add her own words to the form. She decided to send it to Judge Heiden, the judge she suspected was in Chisholm Meats' pocket. Cass was used to going to Judge Khan whenever she was going against the meat company and she didn't want to wear that relationship out. Besides, the meat company was no friend to the Bio-Ts.

At around 11.15am she heard the VTOL go by overhead. By 11.30 she could hear raised voices downstairs. She had derived a degree of petty pleasure in ignoring messages from Sorgram demanding that she come down. If he wanted to wear the big hat, he was going to have to learn to take responsibility. She had showered instead. The shower and the coffee she'd been mainlining all morning had made her feel almost human. She took a deep breath, tried to marshal her last remaining reserve of tolerance, put on her hat and headed downstairs.

Cass heard Charters before she saw her.

"Deputies, we're not having a conversation. There's me giving you an instruction and you doing your very best to follow it. Do I make myself clear?"

"See I keep telling them this, not like they listen," Cass said as she walked into the office.

Regina Charters was holding court from the center of the office. She may have dressed prairie, in her designer suit, Stetson and boots, undoubtedly made from the hide of an endangered species, but her accent, bearing and unassailable sense of entitlement marked her as a product of the English upper classes. She was the general counsel for Chisholm Meats, their legal attack dog.

Charters' security was so unobtrusive that Cass almost hadn't noticed him, which suggested at least a degree of competence. He was a wiry man, with a receding hairline, dressed in jeans and a jacket that Cass suspected was armored. The bodyguard at least had the good manners to take his hat off inside. He was leaning against a desk, trying to stay out of everyone's way while enjoying a good view of the door and everyone else in the room.

The secretary wore a skirt suit almost as impressive as Charters'. All the more interesting because the secretary was a synthetic. Another Serena. Cass didn't know that much about artificial people but she guessed the Serena model had to be top-of-the-line for Chisholm to have bought Charters one.

All eyes were looking in Cass's direction now.

"Where the hell have you been?" Sorgram demanded.

"Showering," Cass offered. "Us gals have to look our best. Wouldn't you agree, Regina?"

Cass could feel the other woman's eyes boring into her.

"It's Miss Charters, and that's the reason I've been kept waiting?" she demanded.

Cass sighed and moved over to the office coffee machine. It wasn't nearly as good as the one she had upstairs, but she had the feeling that it was going to be a long day.

"It wasn't like we were closed. What was it that my competent staff couldn't help you with?" she asked as she poured herself another cup of coffee. At this rate she wasn't going to be able to stray too far from a bathroom.

"I understand that you assaulted three of our employees yesterday and then held them without due cause," Charters said.

Cass turned to lean against the counter.

"Then you're laboring under a misapprehension. Glad we could clear things up."

"Don't you start—" Charters began.

"Regina, the performative assholery may intimidate your subordinates, but it won't wash here. Now do you want to horse trade or talk shit, because I can just go back to bed. Your men assaulted a citizen—"

"Some freak."

"Doesn't matter."

"And they just spat at him."

"I'll tell you what, you let Deputy Sorgram over there, spit in your face and I'll take that off the charges?"

Sorgram glared at her but Deputy Amsa let out

a snort of laughter, her hand flying to her mouth. Williams was grinning and even Charter's security guy had the trace of a smile on his lips.

"No?" Cass asked. "I gave them the chance to walk away. They responded with verbal abuse and threatening behavior…"

"So you shot them?" Charters demanded.

"With non-lethal rounds. When did cowboys become such pussies? The amount of violence was appropriate to the threat they presented but your boys can argue how they're the real victims in front of the judge, if you like."

Charters crossed her arms.

"We will of course be pursuing a complaint against you for excessive force."

"That's your prerogative, and I'm sure that Deputy Sorgram would be just plain delighted to take the details of your complaint. Now, you can bitch, moan and file all you want, but I have every right to hold them three boys. However, I don't have the cell space, don't want to feed them out of our dwindling coffee budget and don't much enjoy their company. I'll release them into your custody," and she pointed at Charters, "and I do mean yours, Regina, if you provide me with a written, legally binding guarantee that they show up to be arraigned when the judge gets back to town. It's either that or I call Colonel Thakore and have them put up in Camp Rodriguez until their arraignment. What's it to be?"

Charters gave her a look that could have cooled a wild fire.

"Fine," she finally said, her tone matching her expression.

"Deputy Sorgram, go and get those three boys from their cell," Cass said.

Sorgram hesitated but then disappeared down the stairs to the holding area.

He came back into the office with the three very hungover-looking cowboys. Cass looked up from the agreement Charters' secretary had just texted her. The wiry cowboy whose name she still didn't know and Lance were both glaring at her, though Lance was only doing it with one eye. The other was covered in bandages.

Teddy, however, stopped in front of her, his hat in his hands.

"Ma'am, I just wanted to apologize for my behavior yesterday. I was drunk, which ain't an excuse but that wasn't how I was raised."

"Quiet," Charters hissed.

Cass nodded, accepting the apology.

"Out, now," Charters snapped. Teddy didn't move, though he didn't look happy.

"How're your balls, son?" the marshal asked. Teddy grimaced. "Go on, get on now."

Teddy practically fled, Charters glaring after him. She made to follow.

"Regina," Cass said. The general counsel turned to look at her. "Your people need to stay away from the Jermaine Ranch, understand me?"

"That sounds dangerously close to slander—"

"I mean it, Regina. I'm going to be spending some time down there. Anyone comes on his property with ill intent, we're within our rights to shoot and I'm a good shot."

Regina just swung around and marched out the door. Her security man nodded to them all, as though he was having a lovely time, and then followed his boss, putting his hat on as he stepped out onto the boardwalk. It was only when Charters' secretary stood up to leave that Cass really became aware of the artificial person's presence again, she'd been so still.

Cass looked down at her P-Dat as she trudged along the muddy board walk. She'd received a text from Judge Heiden. She read it, then tapped out her own text to Agent Matterton. An icy cold rain was falling from an angry, dark sky. Head down, Cass pulled her duster tight around her. Not for the first time she found herself wondering why she hadn't requested assignment on a world with a sub-tropical climate.

Plain Living was a long log building that sold everything from boots to saddles. Cass had always loved the smell of leather in there. It was her go-to place for ammunition and any gunsmithing she couldn't handle herself. The original shop had been one of the settlement-era pre-fabs. It was still attached to the log building that housed the shop now. Ben, the owner, had sound-proofed the pre-fab, dropped a piece of discarded shuttle-hull at one end and converted it into a firing range.

"Hey Ben," she said as she stepped in, wiped her boots on the mat and tried to shake the worst of the cold rain off her hat and duster.

"Marshal," Ben said, smiling though his thick white beard.

"You seen two lost-looking, Core Systems feds?" she asked.

He chuckled and used his thumb to gesture toward the range.

"Yeah?" she asked. I mean it was good, in a way. Shooting was a perishable skill after all. "You sell them anything?"

"Compact backup piece off the FBI's approved list, ankle holster, magazine pouch for the other ankle. I told him he'd be better off with the snub-nosed version of your three-fifty-seven."

"Heavy on the ankles, 'less you're athletic like I am," Cass said, though she felt that anyone who wanted to wear an ankle holster in this town didn't understand how mud worked.

"He buy anything else?" she asked.

"Extended magazines for his service weapon, belt clips for same, one of the folding knives that Stevie makes over at the forge—"

"Good knives, got two myself."

"Indeed, and a one of those extendable stun batons," Ben finished.

"The Buffalo Persuaders?"

Ben nodded.

"Your man figuring on doing some gunfighting while he's in town?" There was just a trace of concern in the shop keeper's voice.

"Give me a box of the usual and a pair of ear defenders," Cass told him. It sounded like Matterton was gearing up to re-fight the whole Tientsin campaign on his own.

Cass pulled on the ear defenders and stepped into the range. Matterton was stood at the table, his service weapon held in both hands as he fired rapid three-round-bursts down range, shredding the target. Cass watched. Matterton emptied the magazine from the pistol and reloaded rapidly, taking the new, extended magazine from a clip on his belt. A new target slid in place and he started firing again. Matterton's grouping was okay, but he was relying too much on rate-of-fire, the sheer amount of lead in the air. It wasn't that he was a bad shot, but like a lot of shooters he was in too much of a hurry. It was a habit that the USCMC's scout sniper school had gone to some lengths to cure her of.

Matterton emptied that magazine, cleared and checked his weapon and then put it down on the table next to the Compact and took his ear defenders off. Serena leaned into him and said something. Matterton turned to look at the marshal as she joined them at the table.

"Been shopping?" she asked. Matterton nodded. "Worried about something?" He didn't answer. Cass was reading between the lines, but the pair that had killed Snell and almost killed Matterton must have given the special agent a fright. Understandable. The thing was, gun company advertising notwithstanding, the absolute worst time to buy a gun was when you were frightened. The psychology was all wrong. "Mind if I shoot?"

"Go ahead."

Cass and Matterton both pulled their ear defenders back on. Serena apparently didn't need any.

Cass drew the Hancock .357 Magnum from its holster and took her time, firing all seven shots. She reloaded from one of the speed loaders on her belt and fired another seven rounds, and then another seven. Finally, she flicked the Hancock's cylinder open, removed the spent casings and set the revolver down.

"You're pretty good with that," he said. "I guess you have to be when you've only got seven rounds."

"It's a primitive world, you want a primitive gun," she said quietly, then turning towards him. "Don't use gun oil here. The dust'll just stick to it, clump up and you'll get jams. You want a light synthetic grease and you really need to work it in. Ben'll see you right."

"Okay," Matterton said. "Not that I don't appreciate it but is there a reason…?"

Then she remembered.

"Judge says no search warrant. Insufficient grounds," she told them both.

"It's probably for the best," Serena said. She was right: a good lawyer could have made anything they found inadmissible.

"What now?" Cass asked.

"We go and speak to Dawkins. We tell him that we're doing background on Snell, not investigating their cult," Matterton suggested.

"Just go and ask for their cooperation, huh?" Cass asked.

Matterton nodded.

It was still cold, wet and dark outside as they made their way up the boardwalk. Port Street looked more like a muddy stream than a road. An eight-wheeled tractor was pulling a prairie rover out from where it had gotten bogged down in the street. Hover ATV's bobbed past the mud-covered vehicles, their quad impellers a blur.

The Church of Biotechnological Transcendence was by far the largest structure on Port Street, though it was actually two buildings. The old Chisholm Meats slaughterhouse on the west side of the street was connected to the genetics facility on the east side of the street, by a covered bridge. Faceless and institutional, both buildings had the look of windowless warehouses.

As they approached the church, Cass found herself hoping that Matterton had a plan. She had dealt with the cult spokesperson before. He was no fool and if they went in there half-assed, they would be telling him more then he'd be telling them. As this thought occurred, Cass looked up, intent on sharing it with Matterton but instead saw her favorite couple, apparently out for a walk in the freezing rain, heading towards them on the boardwalk.

The big barrel-chested guy with the bushy black beard, seemed to be trying a bit too hard to not get noticed. His companion: the smaller woman with the pinched face, was acting much more casually. Cass couldn't shake the feeling that they were both working.

The couple paid no attention to Cass, Matterton and Serena as they passed them. Cass stopped and turned around to look at them once they had gone by.

"Problem?" Matterton asked.

"I don't know," the marshal said. She removed her P-Dat and interlinked a message to Williams. She knew where they were staying, now she wanted to know what their names were and what they said they were doing on GL3.

***

It had taken some time standing at the video intercom outside the old slaughterhouse to get a response. The icy rain, and biting wind hadn't gotten any warmer. The rain felt gritty, which suggested that a storm was on its way, despite all the moisture in the freezing air.

"Yes, how may I help you?"

Cass recognized Dawkins' smooth easy tone.

"Mr Dawkins, its Marshal Stock, here," Cass said leaning into the intercom's lens, Tyler and Serena standing behind her. "I've got two federal agents with me. We'd like to talk to you."

"How intriguing, please come in."

The huge metal door, original to the structure, started to slide open with a horrific grinding noise. The three of them moved to the opening and Dawkins was there to meet them. He was a small, trim man with short blonde curly hair, dressed dapperly in white. The near constant smile on his face gave him a somewhat cherubic expression. On the few occasions Cass had met him, Dawkins had reminded her of an artificial person, though he clearly wasn't one.

"Please come in out of the cold," Dawkins said, "I apologize for the delay in answering, they had to come and find me. Perhaps a restorative tea?"

Cass could remember when the vast cavernous space they found themselves in had contained pens full of cattle. Now it was like stepping onto another world, leaving the mundane reality of Steer City behind them. Even the sound of Port Street cut out as the thick metal door ground shut behind them.

The light inside was subdued, almost as if it was being sucked into the textured, black metal ribs that now formed the walls. It felt like being inside something organic, a gullet or the stomach of some vast beast. Dominating the space, however, was a huge floor-to-ceiling head, sculpted from the same black metal as the ribbed walls. The head appeared to be that of a hairless man, but on closer inspection the physiology of the face—the raised brow ridges, the high nose bridge made the face look subtly inhuman. Cass had never liked this place. Though at least it didn't smell of cow shit anymore.

"No thank you," the marshal said as nobody else had answered.

Serena was looking all around, recording it all. Matterton looked rooted to the spot, staring at the statue of the giant head, his eyes wide as though he was about to bolt. Cass cursed herself. She should have warned him, told him what to expect, but it was so difficult to explain. She knew that Tyler would be looking at the face and seeing the faces of the Bio-Ts that had almost killed him back on Alexandria. Assuming it had been Bio-Ts. To the special agent the statue had to represent what Darius Snell had aspired to become. Yes, Cass decided, she definitely should have said something.

"Which agency?" Dawkins asked.

Tyler didn't look as though he was in a position to answer. Cass opened her mouth to do so but Serena beat her to it.

"We're with the FBI," she told Dawkins. "The Esoteric Crime Unit."

Cass might have kept that last tidbit to herself, she decided.

"How interesting. Um, Agent... are you alright?" Dawkins asked Matterton.

The administrator's voice seemed to break the FBI agent out of his reverie.

"Special Agent Matterton," he finally said. He offered his hand to Dawkins. The administrator kept his hands to himself.

"I'm terribly sorry, I don't mean to be rude but contamination is an issue for us."

"Biological or social?" Serena asked.

Dawkins just smiled. Matterton moved past the administrator and pointed at the head.

"I've seen this before," he said.

"You have?" Dawkins said, unable to keep the surprise out of his voice.

"Yes, in Italy," Matterton continued.

"On Earth?" Cass asked, a little confused.

"Everything about it is designed to make us feel small, afraid." He gestured all around. "This is fascist architecture." Recovered now. Matterton seemed pleased with his observation.

"Oh." Dawkins on the other hand sounded a little disappointed in the FBI agent. "I've always found it inspiring."

"What does it represent?" Serena asked. Cass suspected that if this wasn't rehearsed, then it was at least a routine the two of them used when talking to persons-of-interest in the past.

"The Arcturians called them the Star Teachers. Have you perhaps read the works of Doctors Shaw and Holloway?" Dawkins asked.

Cass had never even heard of them.

"I have actually," Matterton said.

Dawkins looked impressed, though Cass suspected that was for their benefit.

"Shaw and Holloway posited that humanity had a progenitor species, whom they called the Engineers," Dawkins explained.

"In defiance of the laws of God and man," Matterton added.

"How come I've never heard of them?" Cass asked. She'd never had cause to dig into the beliefs of the Bio-Ts too deeply before.

"Because their work was suppressed," Dawkins said.

"Suppressed or nonsense?" Matterton asked. "It flew in the face of hundreds of years of well-established scientific thought on evolution."

"And yet you're aware of it," Dawkins pointed out.

"My job involves a degree of knowledge around fringe faiths."

"Faith?"

"You call yourself a church," Cass interjected. The four of them were just standing in the cavernous space. The acoustics of the ribbed metal interior were doing strange things to their voices.

"My understanding is that the appellation of church should not be taken completely seriously. If the knowledge of the Arcturians and the works of Shaw and Holloway are unofficial scripture, then they are useful only as inspirational, and perhaps aspirational, parables," Dawkins explained.

His explanation posed more questions than it answered.

"Your understanding?" Serena asked.

"Yes, I'm not an adherent, merely an employee. I handle the mundane day-to-day operations, while the adherents do all the real work."

Cass supposed that adherent sounded better than cultist.

"Which is?" Matterton asked.

Dawkins smiled again.

"Special Agent Matterton, you'll forgive me, but this sounds a little like an interrogation. May I ask what this is about?"

Cass exchanged a look with Matterton.

"Darius Snell," Matterton finally said.

The smile left Dawkins' face.

"Yes, a troubled young man. I take it by your presence something serious has happened? Is he okay?"

"He's dead," Matterton said.

"Oh my goodness," Dawkins said. His serene demeanor had disappeared. Cass wondered how much of it was performative, what Serena was making of it all. "He was... fragile. The church never should have taken him on. They look for the best of the best, people strong of body and mind. One of the many reasons that, while I approve of their mission, I could never be an adherent. I fear that poor Darius must have gamed the psychometric testing somehow."

"What is your mission?" Cass asked.

Dawkins opened his mouth and then closed it again.

"Mr Dawkins?" Serena prompted.

"As you can imagine, we do proprietary genetic research here. I am bound by some very strongly worded NDAs and more to the point, as I said, I believe in the work we're doing here."

"If you're withholding—" Matterton started.

"Please," Dawkins said holding up his hands. "Let's not bandy around legal threats. I will help you as much as possible. Anything I can't tell you directly I will provide guidance for the legal steps you will need to take to further your investigation. I feel it's very important that we help as much as possible. It's clear that we failed that poor boy."

It was not what Cass had expected to hear at all. Nor Matterton, judging by the expression on his face.

"Thank you," Serena said. "The church's mission?"

Dawkins appeared lost in thought.

"The quick answer," he finally said, "is that the church seeks to break the Twenty Parsec Limit. It has been almost eighty years since the failure of the *Covenant* and *Affiance* colony missions. Since then, with the exception of Hyperdyne's mining venture in the Hyades Cluster, humanity has remained trapped within twenty parsecs of Sol. The Church believes that this is the result of blinkered thinking and that it is leading to the stagnation of the human race."

"What does that have to do with gene-hacking?" Cass asked.

A pained expression crossed Dawkins' face.

"Marshal, please," he said. "Thanks to sensible laws governing research on Gamma Leporis 3, we are engaged in genetic engineering research."

"Of the human form?" Serena asked.

"It's liberation biotechnology. Regardless of what you may think of Shaw and Holloway's theories, what is clear is that the Arcturians were in contact with an advanced species, a species that thought nothing of the Twenty Parsec Limit. For humanity to break that limit, it requires a shift in approach. We believe the human form, the human mind, needs to change. That is what the adherents are working on. That is about as much as I can tell you. The specifics of our research being, of course, confidential."

"And the adherents do the work?" Serena persisted. She sounded confused in the way that artificial people rarely were.

"Yes," Dawkins said.

"Snell had no initial knowledge of genetics," Matterton pointed out.

Again, Dawkins looked troubled.

"There's a degree of on-the-job training and, I shouldn't tell you this, but imagine what sufficiently advanced applications of biotechnology do to our ability to process and apply knowledge and skills."

"You mean all the muscle-bound bald guys wandering around Steer City are science geeks as well?" Cass asked.

"I perhaps wouldn't have put it that way myself, Marshal, but yes."

"But Snell couldn't make the cut?" Matterton asked.

"Nor could I, Agent Matterton." Dawkins sighed. "I understand how we look to the outside."

"Not helped by your refusal to engage," Cass pointed out.

"That is also true and your even-handed, if sometimes idiosyncratic, application of the law in keeping our adherents safe has not gone unnoticed Marshal. You have my thanks."

Cass inclined her head.

"When did you last see Snell?" Matterton asked. He was practically standing behind Dawkins now.

"He went missing, disappeared without a trace, nine, maybe ten months ago. I can check my records for a precise date and send it over to you."

"About nine months ago there was maybe a week or so where there were a lot of your people on the streets," Cass said, though she was pretty sure she knew why.

Dawkins turned to look at her, the smile gone.

"Well of course, Marshal, we were very worried about him." He took a deep breath, looking as though he was trying to come to a decision. "As I said, I understand how we seem to the outside. Goodness knows, there are elements of our organization that I wish were different—"

"What elements?" Matterton asked. He had moved past Dawkins to look up at the huge sculpted metal head again. Cass didn't like looking at it herself. She didn't like the intensity of its sightless gaze.

Dawkins turned to face Matterton, but the agent had his back to him. Cass was aware of Serena moving so she could get a better view of Dawkins' features, presumably to read his expressions. It was like a subtle dance.

"I… question some of the more theatrical aspects of our operation, even though I understand that there are standards that must be set in order to bring about the changes that we feel must happen."

"Who sets these standards?" Cass asked.

"The community," Dawkins said turning to face her now.

"Why?" Matterton asked.

"A prophylactic separation from your culture and society," he told them.

"Purity?" Matterton asked, still looking at the statue.

"I can't imagine why anyone would think you were a cult," Cass muttered.

"I feel the tone of this conversation is becoming more adversarial. Perhaps we should suspend it, and renew when the Church's lawyers have been contacted?" Dawkins suggested.

"If you were so worried by Snell's disappearance, why didn't you come to me?" Cass asked.

"It wasn't a matter for law enforcement," Dawkins said. Suddenly he didn't look quite so comfortable.

"A missing person?" Cass asked.

"We just thought he'd gone home," Dawkins said. He wasn't wrong.

"Did he leave a note?" Cass persisted. Dawkins didn't answer. "So, for all you knew he was dead in a shallow grave out on the plains?"

"I suspect I will not be thanked for saying so, but I think we made a lot of errors as regards young Mr Snell. I am really not comfortable discussing this any further without—"

"Darius Snell kidnapped sixteen people, that we are aware of. Six of his victims died whilst he held them captive, three are still missing but presumed dead," Serena told him.

Dawkins turned to face her. Even side-on Cass could see he that he looked appalled.

"I..." he started opening and closing his mouth.

"This is the first you've heard of it?" Matterton asked.

"Yes. I mean... that's awful. We suspected that he wasn't well but... I mean, something like that. How could we know?" Dawkins managed.

"He had extensively redecorated the chamber where he kept his captives," Matterton said. To Cass's ears it was starting to sound more like a traditional interrogation. The FBI agent gestured all around him. "It looked very much like this place."

Dawkins just stared at him.

"I mean, I'm not sure what you're implying," he finally said.

"Do you engage in any kind of goddess worship here?" Cass asked.

Dawkins didn't say anything for a moment or two.

"I'm sorry, that's not what we do... why would you ask that?"

"His parents said that when he returned, he talked of a goddess and had bad dreams, the wake-up-screaming-covered-in-flop-sweat kind of bad dreams," Matterton told him.

"You can't think that's anything to do with what we do here," Dawkins protested.

"I'm still not entirely sure what you do here," Matterton said. "The actual process, I mean."

"We certainly don't worship a goddess." It was the closest he'd come to raising his voice.

"So, it would surprise you if I told you two people, who looked exactly like your adherents, were responsible for Snell's death in the exhaust vent of an aerospace port? They killed themselves in the process and nearly killed me," Matterton said.

Dawkins blanched.

"Agent Matterton, despite what your attackers may have looked like, I can assure you that it has nothing to do with us. None of our people have been off-world, in well over a year." He sounded as though he couldn't quite believe what he was hearing.

"Convenient that they chose an exhaust vent. Can't find evidence of gene-hacking at the autopsy if the body's just so much carbon," Cass pointed out.

"Marshal! I must protest, I do not like these insinuations at all." He gestured towards the door that had started to grind open, seemingly of its own accord. "I must ask you to leave. Should you wish us to answer any further questions I insist you make an appointment. I assure you that we will have legal representation present."

9

"Well?" the marshal asked as they made their way along the slippery boardwalk. It was still raining. Tyler was starting to suspect he would never be warm or dry again.

"It wasn't quite what I was expecting," Tyler said. Dawkins had been almost solicitous in his helpfulness, initially, at least. He glanced over at Serena. Unaffected by the cold, her only need to wear outdoor clothes was to better blend in.

"An analysis of his micro-expressions suggests that he was being as honest as he was able to be in the situation. The only possible exception was when Marshal Stock asked him about goddess worship," she told them.

Tyler screwed up his face against the cold rain.

"Really? He came across as on the level," Tyler said.

"His expressions were inconclusive."

Either Dawkins was kept in the dark by his bosses, or he was a world-class actor. The Bio-Ts were dangerous: Tyler had the burns to prove it.

He turned to the marshal for her opinion as she came to a halt, looking at her P-Dat.

"Something wrong?" Tyler asked.

The marshal looked at him.

"You enjoying the weather?" she asked.

He just stared at her.

"It is inclement," Serena offered.

"No," Tyler finally said.

"So, you wouldn't, for example, just wander around town for the hell of it?" the marshal asked.

Tyler didn't bother to answer, hoping that the marshal would eventually get to her point.

She showed Tyler and Serena the screen of her P-Dat. It was quartered, each window was a feed from a different security camera on one of the town's main throughfares. They were all running footage of the couple that they had passed on the way to the church from various different angles. They appeared to be aimlessly wandering, but on a closer inspection it became clear that they were paying attention to something.

"They casing some place?" Tyler asked. The marshal made a non-committal sound. "Any banks on that street?"

"That is Jersey Street," Serena stated.

"It is," the marshal agreed and pointed east. "Next street over. The old genetics facility backs onto it."

***

"I am concerned that this is not within our remit," Serena said as they waded through a muddy alleyway, an old pre-fab on one side and a newer wooden building on the other.

Tyler marveled how it always seemed to be freezing on GL3 but never froze. His new boots sank into the mud once more.

"The marshal deputized us," Tyler pointed out.

"The marshal made the sign of the cross over you. It's not the same thing," Serena replied.

"They could be connected to our investigation."

"They could be tourists from another cold and wet climate," Serena said as they reached the end of the alleyway and climbed onto the Jersey Street boardwalk.

The couple were heading towards them. The man's head was down, the woman's was on the proverbial swivel. She saw them both immediately. She must have read intent in Tyler's posture, as she stopped. The man did the same a moment later. They exchanged a word and turned the other way.

Tyler and Serena picked up their pace.

The couple took a few steps forward and then stopped again as the marshal stepped out on to the boardwalk ahead of them.

The woman's hand moved towards her hip.

"No!" Tyler said, his own hand now on his service

weapon. He was aware of Serena's questioning glance in his direction.

"We don't want that," Stock called to them.

The burly man said something to his companion. The wiry woman moved her hand away from her hip. He kept his hand on his gun, just in case, and moved towards the couple with Serena. The marshal was closing in on them as well.

"We just want to talk," Stock was saying as Tyler reached them. He didn't want to talk. He wanted to jam the stun rod into the woman. Somehow, she was managing to both look relaxed and coiled like a wound spring, like the promise of imminent violence. The woman glanced behind her at Tyler and Serena.

Tyler realized he was jacked up. Heart hammering in his chest.

The bearded man looked at his companion and she just shrugged.

"Okay, let's talk," he said.

"Not her," the woman said nodding towards Serena.

They were in a fifth-floor room of the Stagecoach Hotel, which as far as Tyler could tell was one of the taller buildings in Steer City. It was a much nicer hotel than the one Serena and he were staying in but that was the private sector for you. The room was on the east side of Port Street: the corner bay window provided a commanding view of the town. He could see the shuttle on its pad to the north of them. To the south he had an excellent view of the old slaughterhouse and a partial view of most of the top of the Church's genetics facility. There was an inert but sizeable roll-screen monitor adhered to the wall.

Tyler was stood by the window. The marshal was leaning on the wall close to the door. Opposite the marshal, the woman was leaning against the other wall. Having removed her coat, her holstered sidearm was now obvious. The bearded man was sat on the bed, his back against the headboard, seemingly relaxed.

"Lace," the marshal said pointing at the woman, "Harris," now she pointed at the man. "At least those are the names you're using."

"Other way around," the man said. "I'm Lace." He was American, East Coast, somewhere urban, though the outdoors clothes he wore looked old, worn and he seemed very comfortable in them.

The woman moved to the table, next to the window and switched on a device that looked like a tripod-mounted portable speaker. Tyler registered a sonic change in the atmosphere without actually hearing it. It was uncomfortable. He guessed it was some kind of white noise anti-surveillance device.

"You an ex-Marine Commando?" the marshal asked the woman. Harris shrugged, but it seemed like an affirmative. Tyler knew that the Royal Marine

Commandos were the Three World Empire's equivalent of the Colonial Marines. "SBS?" the marshal continued. Harris didn't respond at all. Instead, she moved to where she could keep an eye on everyone. Tyler wasn't sure what the SBS was but guessed by the context that they were a special forces unit within the Royal Marines, presumably the equivalent to the USCMC's Raider Regiment. He was glad that they hadn't started a gunfight out in the street with Harris.

"What are you doing here?" Tyler asked.

Nobody said anything.

Cold gritty rain pelted the glass in the window.

"I'm a psychologist specializing in—"

"Cults," Tyler finished for him. "Gosh, what a coincidence. There happens to be one here in town."

The marshal pointed at Lace. "You're a cult deprogrammer," then she pointed at Harris, "and you're a merc. Which means some rich kid has gone and joined the Bio-Ts, right?" Stock did not sound at all happy.

"My colleague prefers 'extraction specialist'," Lace said from the bed.

"I bet she does, she also talk for herself?"

Lace shrugged.

"When I have to," Harris said. Her accent was British, but one of those thick regional accents that Tyler didn't know enough to able to identify. There was a twang to it, however, that he associated with someone who'd grown up on a colony.

"I see why you didn't want my partner here," Tyler said. Serena hadn't been happy, but Tyler managed to talk her into returning to their hotel to continue work on the cult's finances. Though she would only get so far without actual access to their accounts.

"This is off the record," Lace said.

"You get that we're peace officers," Stock asked, pointing between herself and Tyler. "Despite what you may've heard, not everything's for sale here."

Lace held his hands up in a placatory gesture.

"We know, Marshal. That's not what we're getting at," Lace said.

"And if it was, we wouldn't have invited your boy scout friend here," Harris added. Unnecessary, Tyler thought.

"So, I look around your room I'm not going to find some military-grade weaponry? And you're not planning on turning my town into a warzone, kidnapping someone and deprogramming them for their Core Systems Mommy and Daddy, right?"

Lace took a deep breath.

Tyler heard and then felt thunder. He turned back to the window and saw thick clouds of smoke coming from the shuttle pad. Moments later the heavy-lift shuttle rose out of the cloud, accelerating towards orbit. It reminded him of seeing a shuttle's exhaust up close on Alexandria. His back hurt.

"...It's not about deprogramming. That's not how the

human mind, works," Lace was saying as Tyler tuned back into the conversation. "We're talking about helping a recruit come to terms with having been in an abusive co-dependent relationship, about trying to disassemble the mythological trap he's been living in—"

"Who are you after?" Tyler interrupted.

Lace and Harris exchanged a look.

"His name is Matthew Fitzgerald. His parents are both senior Seegson execs, board level," Lace told them.

Tyler glanced back, the only evidence of the shuttle was the contrail cutting through the murk.

"Be nice if all those poor fuckers had megacorp board members for parents," the marshal was muttering.

Tyler turned back to Lace again.

"What do you want us to do?" Tyler almost demanded. "Even if we wanted to, we can't help you kidnap someone... and I don't want to." This wasn't entirely true.

"Look, we're with you," Lace said. "If we can do this legally and above board, help some others who aren't rich kids, then all the better. It's a risk for us speaking to you as well."

"I didn't think we'd given you a choice," Stock said.

"Just so we're clear, this is happening," Harris told them. "We've done our homework: even with Mr FBI here and his synth friend, you do not have the resources to stop us."

The room went very quiet. The only sound was Lace

sighing. It sounded like posturing to Tyler. He couldn't see the play. Though Harris had sounded very self-assured.

"Excuse me?" the marshal finally said, her voice low, dangerous. Tyler felt like putting his hand on his gun again.

"I'm not looking to fight, Marshal, but I think we all need to know where we stand," Harris explained.

Lace gave his partner a look and produced a P-Dat from the pocket of his puffer vest.

"How about you stand in one of the cells underneath my shop?" the marshal suggested. It didn't sound unreasonable to Tyler.

"On what charge?" Harris asked, the tone of her voice not changing.

The roll screen monitor adhered to the wall had come to life as Lace tapped away at his P-Dat.

"Conspiracy to kidnap, I'm betting illegal weapons charges, hell, suspicion of urban terrorism, and being a tedious limey asshole, take your pick." The marshal had pushed herself off the wall.

The screen was dividing up into picture and bios. The pictures were all of young, physically fit, people. A mixture of genders and ethnicities, Tyler noticed.

"…I will shoot you—"

"Marshal," Tyler said.

"—in the face right now and throw your stupid ass out into the—"

"Marshal!"

Stock's head whipped round to look at him. Both her professionalism and capability had not just been questioned but insulted. Harris might be ex-3WE special forces, but the marshal was no pushover herself. He got it, but they were getting nowhere with this. Tyler just pointed at the wall screen.

"What's that?" the marshal asked.

"A bit of 'you show me yours and I show you mine,'" Lace told her. "According to some of the people at the shuttle port, the Bio-Ts have had something like a hundred recruits in the last year."

Tyler turned to look at the marshal.

"We started investigating them in earnest this morning," she said defensively, then muttered, "that's not a hundred people."

"Before we set off, we tried to work out who the Bio-Ts had recruited. We managed to find thirty-two recruits."

"Well, look at you with your access to Core System networks," the marshal muttered.

"You did your homework," Tyler said. "Any connection beyond the obvious."

"A degree of disenfranchisement," Lace told them. He sounded distracted as he tapped away on his P-Dat again.

The pictures of the thirty shrank and shifted to the left side of the screen. Twelve larger images appeared the exoskeleton-style clothes, white skin and black eyes of the hairless Bio-Ts. Initially Tyler thought that they all looked the same, other than gender, but as he studied them, he saw that each of them were individuals. It was clear that these images had come from surveillance pics taken surreptitiously in the street. Two of the pics, however, looked like stills from security camera footage.

"Where are the rest of them?" Tyler asked. He could see where this was going. Judging by the stricken expression on her face, Stock did as well. This had happened on her watch after all.

"These are the Bio-Ts that we've seen on the street since we arrived here—" Lace began.

"Four days ago," the marshal said.

"We're also in the process of reviewing all the security footage from the last year," Lace continued.

"How the hell did you get that?" Stock demanded. Lace just looked at her. Tyler was starting to feel sorry for the marshal. These two private contractors were making them both look like fools. Lace may well have been a specialist in cult psychology, but it was clear that both he and Harris were very experienced investigators.

"We haven't finished our image search through your footage, but we only found two more Bio-Ts that we hadn't already seen in the street since we got here. And that's not all." Lace tapped away at his P-Dat again. An image from the thirty-two, a dark-haired white girl in her late teens or early twenties, and one of the Bio-Ts, a female, filled the screen. Contoured grids appeared over both faces, comparing them: 72.2 percent similarity between the two faces. Tyler had already seen it. The bridge of her nose was different and her brow was much heavier but Tyler could see it was the same person.

"That's the only match you found?" Tyler said.

"So where are the other thirty-one recruits?" the marshal asked.

"There could be as many as eighty-eight unaccounted for," Lace said quietly. "Maybe more: the hundred was a rough figure."

"I didn't..." the marshal started. She looked like she wanted to be sick.

"You weren't meant to," Harris said. "You're just supposed to see them on the street."

"Because they all look the same," Tyler said quietly.

"Ever wondered what they were doing?" Harris asked the marshal.

"Wh-what?" the marshal asked.

"I've been following them around for the last few days," Harris told them. "They just go for a lovely walk."

The marshal stared at her.

"Why?" she finally managed.

"If I was to guess I would say it's for your benefit, boss," Harris said.

Stock swallowed.

"Mine?"

Then Tyler got it.

"Not just yours, the community's. To be seen. So you have no idea how many there are. You just think that they're all coming here and making themselves into lookalikes of Dawkins' Star Teachers," he said. Lace nodded along with him. "So, what happened to everyone else?"

Harris and Lace exchanged a look, then Harris crossed to the window and pushed the curtain back further to allow for a better view of the roof of the genetics facility. He pointed at a capped tube rising from a network of pipes.

"Know what that is?" Harris asked.

"A chimney," the marshal said, unable to keep the irritation out of her voice.

"For an incinerator," Tyler added.

"A Lasalle Bionational Asclepius 4TS medical incinerator, to be precise," Lace told them.

"And it runs every night," Harris added, letting the curtain drop back in place. Something about the way she said it chilled Tyler.

"Surely it's more likely that they're all living there behind closed doors. Have you checked the amount of food going in?" Tyler asked.

"Not yet," Lace said.

"All their deliveries come off the shuttle from Anchorpoint," Stock said. "They're sealed but sizeable. It takes a truck to deliver them from the port. They come once a month."

"Never thought to check?" Harris asked the marshal. It was clear that she was bad cop to Lace's good cop.

Stock glared at the extractor.

"On what pretext? We can't all just go around breaking into shit!"

Harris held her hands up.

"You may well be right, Agent Matterton," Lace said. "They may all be living in there. I hope that's the case but I suspect, like me, you've dealt with apocalyptic cults. You know how these things can end."

"Not like the FB of I have a particularly good track record with such organizations," Harris pointed out.

Tyler turned to look at her.

"Any reason you're trying to needle us?" he asked.

Harris opened her mouth to say something, then seemed to think the better of it.

"Force of habit," she finally said. "Our worst-case scenario is that they're doing some kind of biotech process on them that's dangerous enough to have a high mortality rate. That bodes ill for our target."

Tyler turned to Lace.

"You got any legal standing in this?"

The cult specialist shrugged.

"Got papers that say I'm the Fitzgerald's legal proxy, but anything I do with that means having to go through lawyers and there's about five on this rock. Three work for Chisholm and the other two are shit."

"And we've only got two judges," Stock said. She

looked pale but had gotten a hold of herself. "What do you want from us? All you've got is some extremely compelling info but nothing you could build a case on."

"Cooperation," Lace said.

"We can't help you do what you're here to do," Tyler told him. Stock's expression didn't suggest that she completely agreed with that as a sentiment.

"We're not asking you to," Lace assured him.

"You've been inside, you've spoken to Dawkins. You let us debrief you, we hand over everything we've learned since we got here," Harris told them.

It was tempting. Very tempting. Lace and Harris had made him feel like a fool, and probably made the marshal feel worse. If he hadn't been back-footed the entire time, then Serena would have been able to do likewise and perhaps even found enough grounds to take action against the Bio-Ts. Whatever the reasons, they had information he needed. The problem was, sharing information with criminals, intent on committing criminal acts, wasn't a good look for an FBI agent.

On the other hand, something that Lace had said was starting to resonate.

"You're the Fitzgeralds' legal proxy?" he asked. Lace nodded. "You think the kid's still alive?"

Harris regarded him for a moment.

"He does," she nodded towards Lace. "I don't."

"I hope he's alive," Lace said. "I hope they all are."

There was something in his voice. This wasn't just a job for him.

"Is one day going to make a difference?" Tyler asked.

"Well, he's either dead or he isn't. Be pretty unlucky if he gets slotted tonight," Harris said. It didn't look as though Lace liked his partner's thinking, but he kept quiet.

"Tomorrow, you make a big noise about Fitzgerald. Call the two lawyers, send a message to lawyers on Anchorpoint."

"That blows us," Harris said.

"You're in a town of six thousand people," Stock said. "People know you're here."

"And another two thousand tourists," Harris pointed out.

"We use that as a pretext, for a welfare check," Tyler finished.

Lace and Harris shared another, longer look.

"They might just kill him," Lace said.

"And gain what?" Tyler asked. "Dawkins' game is to appear as cooperative as possible while giving away as little as possible."

"I don't like it," Harris said. "I mean, how does it help us."

"They say no, we learn something," Tyler said.

"And they know we're coming," Harris countered.

"Do you think their degree of alertness can get any higher, within the timescale we're talking about?"

"Yeah, I do."

"They say yes, we learn more. They say no, it's more suspicious behavior, better legal grounds for the Fitzgerald's legal proxy. We might then have enough to act."

"I don't see this being resolved legally," Harris told them.

"Well, how about this," the marshal said, "we're going to do it anyway. Do you want our help or not?"

"We're very persuasive," Tyler added.

Harris muttered something that sounded a little like 'fucking pigs'.

"'Scuse me?" Stock demanded.

Harris opened her mouth to retort but Lace got their first.

"If you're going back in there, look for an authority figure—someone with charisma. Someone has to be selling them on this," he told them.

Despite the supposed durability of the clothes he had purchased for the trip, Tyler was still cold and wet by the time he got back to the room. Serena looked up from the armchair as he entered. Tyler tried to wipe away the gritty feeling on his exposed skin, to little effect.

"I reviewed the information that Lace and Harris provided," Serena told him. They had reluctantly turned over their information to Tyler and Stock, despite not getting quite the result they had hoped for.

Tyler had sent it on to Serena. "It is cause for concern."

Tyler nodded as he divested himself of his wet outer layers.

"They are intending on committing a criminal act," Serena said after a moment or two. He hadn't told her exactly who Lace and Harris were but she would have had little problem inferring it from the information they had provided. "Any association with them will jeopardize our investigation, such as it is."

Tyler looked over at her.

"Such as it is?" he asked.

"I have made my position clear. Any association with mercenaries compromises us."

"Kind of you to say 'us.'" He considered them partners. He wasn't sure how Serena thought of their working relationship. She didn't answer. "Did you discover anything?"

"Not much, I'm afraid. They bought the slaughterhouse and genetics facility from Lasalle Bionational—"

"I though the facility had belonged to Chisholm Meats?"

"Chisholm Meats is a subsidiary of Lasalle Bionational," Serena told him. "The church's funding is off-world, and comes in regularly."

"They're well-funded?"

"And seemingly with no questions asked, as far as I can tell. Without a court order there's only so much I could discover."

"And?" he pressed. Tyler knew Serena well enough that her metaheuristics had taken her into the realm of speculation. She did not like to share such speculations until she had more information.

"They may be financed through a slush fund."

Tyler gave this some thought.

"That suggests external funding from either a government or a corporation, but why would either fund a cult?" he mused.

"Because it's deniable," she suggested.

"And because you can get willing cult members to do things that lab rats won't?"

Tyler moved across the room and sat on the corner of the bed closest to Serena.

"Tell me there's not something wrong here."

"I believe there's something wrong here," she said, "but we cannot take shortcuts, Agent Matterton."

She was right. Law enforcement had to hold themselves to high standards: cities burned when they didn't. He didn't usually need Serena to remind him of his duty. Was the marshal starting to rub off on him?

"Tyler, do you wish to talk?"

It was written all over his face that he wanted to talk. Just not what she wanted to talk about. She wanted to provide him with on-the-job counselling as part of her programming. The wretched thing of it was that he had considered accepting just for the contact.

10

Tyler spent the following morning poring over the information that Lace and Harris had given them while trying to ignore Serena's disapproval. With the marshal's permission, Serena had set up her own image search through the town's security footage history as they couldn't use Lace and Harris's illegally obtained footage.

They were both still in their hotel room and Tyler was feeling a little trapped. It had stopped raining and the mist that had rolled in off the plains earlier in the morning was starting to clear, teasing what might actually pass for a nice day on GL3. He was stood by the window looking down on a near empty Port Street, the occasional pedestrian a ghost in the thinning mist.

He was waiting to see if Lace's legal shenanigans would get a reaction. Harris was maintaining observation on the old slaughterhouse, but Tyler suspected that any response would be internal, unseen. If Harris and Lace had tapped the church's comms, they would keep such information to themselves. Evidentiary, such a violation of the church's privacy would have been fruit of the poisoned tree. That said, Tyler would have liked to have known where the church's funding was coming from.

"We can't be sure this will even get back to the church," Serena said.

"Even if Dawkins does let us in, I can't see him letting you in. Not a second time," Tyler said.

"I'm going to try and recreate as much of Lace and Harris's investigation as I can," she told him. "I will start by speaking to the marshal's contact at the spaceport. Then I will see how much of the information they gathered in the Core Systems was done so legally."

Tyler wasn't sure if he was imagining a tone in her voice. He knew agents who treated their artificial person partners as labor-saving devices, but that wasn't how he thought of Serena. At times like this, however, it did feel like she did all the grunt work and he got all the glory.

"At least the marshal has filed your deputization," Serena added.

Tyler checked his P-Dat. No messages. If there had been a response from the church to Lace's efforts this morning then it had gone unnoticed by the mercenaries and the marshal.

***

"Special Agent Matterton, Marshal, I feel I made myself very clear during our last meeting. I have made our legal representation aware of the situation and they will be in contact in due course." Dawkins' voice was coming from the intercom. He did not sound happy.

Tyler was stood outside the old slaughterhouse with the marshal. It might not have been raining but it was still cold, despite the threat of the system's third sun finally breaking through the mist.

"We understand your position, Mr Dawkins. We're here regarding a separate matter," the marshal told the intercom.

"Would you care to enlighten me?" Dawkins asked.

Stock just looked at Tyler. The day was already trying her patience. Tyler wondered how much coffee she'd had that morning.

"Dawkins, I'm not going to force my way in. I already know all the secrets of your reception area, and it's too cold to stand out here shouting at the wall. You'll have to take my word for it that it's in your best interest to talk to us."

This time they did not have to wait as long before the door ground open. A less-than-pleased Dawkins was standing there with one of the male Bio-Ts. Tyler had to force himself not to flinch. They had a definite presence that he hadn't had time to fully appreciate the last time he had met one. He found himself staring up that black-clad, white-faced figure. His physicality was intimidating, the musculature was all wrong, the eyes pitiless voids. This was a violation of the human form. A clear attempt at intimidation. It was working.

"Muscle?" Stock asked.

"The adherent is just here as a comfort. You've seen church members around town. You know that we're pacifists."

"May we step in?" Tyler asked.

"Can I assume that you do not have any kind of warrant?" Dawkins asked in return.

The Bio-T shifted slightly. It took everything Tyler had not to take a step back.

Stock sighed.

"We can shout your business on the street if you'd prefer," the marshal told the church administrator.

Dawkins stepped to one side and gestured for them to enter.

Tyler tried to step in without getting too close to the Bio-T but without looking as though he was trying to avoid the huge figure. He was extremely conscious of the door grinding shut behind him. The lighting had changed in the old slaughterhouse. Still subdued, the huge metal head was now underlit, which had given it a halo. Glancing between them, Tyler had the sense that the Bio-T was religious iconography given flesh and form. Even as he rejected it, Tyler could understand Dawkins' sense of awe towards the huge metal bust.

"I'm sorry, Marshal, your last visit rattled me somewhat and, as I'm sure you can imagine, caused something of a stir in the community."

The marshal looked up at the Bio-T.

"Oh yeah, he looks stirred."

The Bio-T gave no indication that he'd even heard the marshal.

"You have to admit, your accusations—"

"We didn't make any accusations," Tyler said.

Dawkins pursed his lips.

"*Insinuations* were quite outlandish."

Stock just looked up at the Bio-T.

"Well, I'm afraid I bear more bad news," Stock told the administrator.

Tyler was looking around. Harris had practically given him a checklist, though he had in no way agreed to follow through with it. He was looking for ways in and out of the re-purposed slaughterhouse, as well as the whereabouts of any security cameras. He was seeing neither at the moment.

"Marshal, I should really prefer to let our legal—"

"Mr Dawkins, what I'm doing here is trying to forestall the need to get your lawyers involved. I'll admit, I've no idea what this is all about," she looked around the head chamber, "and we fear what we don't understand but despite how strange y'all look," Tyler was wondering if she was perhaps laying it on a bit thick, "you're the least of the pains in my ass in this town."

Dawkins smiled despite himself.

"That was not the tone and tenor of our last conversation," he pointed out.

"That was my fault," Tyler said, distracted as he continued to look around.

"I was just trying to do my job, and I have to cooperate with federal agencies," Stock added.

"And your presence here, Agent Matterton," Dawkins said.

"Purely observing," Tyler told him. It was bullshit. He knew it, Stock knew it, Dawkins certainly knew it, and depending on their level of awareness, the Bio-T probably knew it as well.

"What can we do for you, Marshal?" Dawkins asked. "Again."

"I've been asked, by the CA, to perform a welfare check on one of your adherents," the marshal told Dawkins. The CA was the Colonial Administration, Stock's bosses.

"Which we're under no legal obligation to concede to," Dawkins pointed out.

Tyler knew where the bridge to the genetics facility was on the outside of the building. He just couldn't find a corresponding entrance, or even stairs on the interior, which meant a concealed exit somewhere on the Port Street facing wall.

"That's correct, you're not. Going back to the CA and telling them that you refused to cooperate kicks it up a notch, though. The proxies will either accuse you of holding their client's kid against their will, or claim diminished responsibility. Then I have to come back in here with a court order and deputies, and won't be able to take no for an answer."

"And I get what I want," Tyler said. At this point, it was obvious that he was casing the place. He felt eyes on him. Not eyes, voids where eyes should be. Tyler could see himself reflected in the black pits that passed for their eyes. He looked small in the reflections.

"Most of our adherents sever relations with their family as they move beyond them, evolutionarily speaking—"

"Wow," Tyler said. He couldn't help himself. "That how you feel?" he asked the Bio-T. It was like talking to alabaster.

"Many families are unable to come to terms with this. Some may even resort to extra-legal methods, kidnapping, attempting to brainwash their own relatives. If the church agrees to your request, can you provide us with assurances that, should we be targeted with any such illegalities, we can rely on the protection of the law?"

"I'm not perfect, but everyone receives the same treatment," Stock told the administrator.

"Very well," Dawkins said.

"You haven't asked us who, yet," Tyler pointed out.

Dawkins turned to look at him. Despite his normally

solicitous manner, Tyler could see a hint of distaste in the administrator's expression.

"Agent Matterton, I appreciate that you feel that you're doing your job but the constant attempts to trip me up are somewhat tedious and do you discredit." Dawkins turned back to Stock, an eyebrow raised in question.

"Malcolm Fitzgerald," Stock said, her own expression guarded.

Tyler and the marshal knew that there was no way that Dawkins would allow them to meet with any of the Bio-Ts unless it was staged. Dawkins had known who they were here to see. The decision to allow them access had been decided before they had arrived. The administrator had put up just enough of a fight to make it seem real. Serena had run Dawkins' background, but there was very little on him on GL3. He was clearly from the Core Systems, probably Earth. Serena had sent a request for a background check to Earth, but it could only travel as fast as ships and relays carried it. It would be weeks, more likely months, before they heard anything back, and that response could well be the Bureau recalling him. Tyler couldn't help but wonder if, before he had gone to work for the church, the smooth-talking Dawkins had in fact been an actor, or perhaps a long-con operator. They did, after all, have similar skill sets.

"Ah, Brother Dak," Dawkins said.

"These guys have names?" Tyler said to himself. Dawkins' just looked at him.

"What's your name, big fella?" Stock asked the Bio-T. Nothing.

"This way, please," Dawkins said gesturing to the external wall. The wall's sculpted metal was moving, but some optical illusion quality of the architecture made it look as though the ribs were flexing, breathing. It was only when he got closer that Tyler saw the spiral staircase of skeletonized metal that had extruded from the wall. Stock and Tyler exchanged a glance.

"This is some next-level rich person bullshit," the marshal muttered under her breath.

A panel of metal rib-work had concertinaed up, at the top of the spiral staircase, to allow ingress to the covered bridge over Port Street. The banality of the bridge's architecture was almost a culture shock after the slaughterhouse. Dawkins walked in front of them, the Bio-T behind, as one of the eight-wheeled tractor units rumbled through the mud beneath the bridge. Tyler knew that this was the furthest that the marshal had ever penetrated the Bio-Ts' facility. Maybe it was the furthest anyone outside of the church had made it.

Looking out of the windows on either side, Tyler got a much better idea of the size of the genetics facility. It was considerably larger than the slaughterhouse, which was probably little more than a reception area for the church. He also noted the three-hundred-and-sixty-degree camera bubble on the ceiling in the center of the bridge.

At the other end was a heavy, hermetically sealed door. As they reached it, Dawkins paused and let out a performative sigh.

"Problem?" the marshal asked. Her thumbs hooked in her belt.

"I'm sorry, Marshal," Dawkins said. He put his hand on a palmprint reader. Waited. And then typed a long code into a keypad, ensuring that his body obscured their view of the process. Then he turned the handle and stepped over the lip of the doorway.

Tyler followed suit, to be greeted with a lot of white tile, stainless steel and thick plexiglass. They were in a wide-open space that looked much like any other industrial laboratory that Tyler had ever seen, though the scale of it certainly confirmed that the church wasn't lacking for funding.

Tyler saw much of what he expected to: various microscopes, centrifuges, glass-fronted fridges and smoky freezers full of test tubes. There were work stations with full modular computing suites that included high-resolution holographic projectors. A number of free-standing cubicles looked to contain hermetically sealed work areas or sub-labs, at least one of which was set up like an operating theatre. There were a number of other areas in the larger open-plan lab that looked as though they could also be used to perform medical procedures.

At the top of the metal stairway, they were level with a rail-mounted roof crane. A maintenance catwalk ran alongside the length of the rail. Tyler guessed it was a holdover from when they had to move around sedated, genetically-modified cattle. The crane still looked very functional, however.

Against the opposite wall was a mezzanine, on which there were a number of office suites and a glass-fronted conference area, all of which had a commanding view of the lab space.

In the north wall was a thick, sliding external door, with a very sturdy-looking locking system. The door was large enough that it could easily accommodate a semi.

Dominating the space, however, was a piece of equipment that Tyler didn't recognize. Close to the external door at the north end of the cavernous genetics facility, on a raised platform, was a was a huge, stainless steel sphere. Heavy gauge cables and insulated pipes ran into the device.

"What's that?" Tyler asked as he followed Dawkins down the metal stairs, grateful that the marshal was between him and the Bio-T.

"Bio-reactor," Dawkins told him.

"Never seen one that size. Shape is odd too—they're usually cylindrical," Tyler said.

"You'll forgive me if I'm not drawn on that, Agent Matterton."

"Bio-reactors supposed to be refrigerated?" Stock asked, surprising Tyler, perhaps unfairly. Dawkins didn't respond to that either.

"Where is everyone?" Tyler asked.

There were only two other people in the vast lab.

"We cleared the lab," Dawkins told them. Deeper inside his own facility, the church's administrator was considerably less verbose.

"Did you know we were coming?" the marshal asked, doing a good job of making it sound completely innocent. They passed one of the other two people in there. A Bio-T, naked, lying face down on some kind of ergonomic surgical couch. The chalk-white skin of their back was being rapidly and repeatedly penetrated by a bank of needles all moving in synchronicity, like some industrial sewing machine.

They approached the other figure, whom Tyler assumed was Fitzgerald, or, apparently, Brother Dak. He was standing in one of the areas that looked as though it was set up for medical procedures. Tyler barely recognized him from the picture Lace and Harris had shown them. He was stripped to his waist. There was something off about his musculature and the structure of his ribs, something faintly inhuman that Tyler couldn't quite put his finger on. His skin was white and he was hairless, but only one of his eyes was a black pit. The other looked like a normal, and very green, human eye. He had a syringe full of a viscous blue liquid in one hand. He was very clearly well on his way to becoming a Bio-T.

"Malcolm Fitzgerald?" Stock asked.

Fitzgerald looked down at the marshal with his mismatched eyes. Tyler didn't like it. The incongruity was worse than the two black pits.

"Brother Dak," Dawkins admonished.

"Okay, enough." There was an edge in Stock's voice now. "Your family has asked us to perform a welfare check, to ensure that everything's okay here, that you're okay."

The marshal's words sounded so inadequate in their present situation.

Fitzgerald looked at Dawkins as though asking for permission. Stock followed the look.

"It's okay, Brother Dak, the community guidelines allow for verbal communication in certain extreme situations."

Fitzgerald took a deep breath.

"Feels wrong," he said. His voice was deep, the voice of someone who talked rarely. "I..." he paused as though searching for the words. "I don't have a family."

Tyler was watching Fitzgerald carefully but couldn't get a read on him. Even Serena would have struggled.

Stock turned to Dawkins.

"So, here's the thing. Normally when we do this we speak to the person involved alone in case they're being coerced. Now I don't think that's what's happening here, but if I can't talk to Mr Fitzgerald—"

"Brother Dak." There was a firmness in Dawkins' tone that Tyler hadn't heard before.

The marshal practically flinched.

"—then I can't report that all's well in the Church of Biotechnological Transcendence."

"Very well," Dawkins said, turning and moving away from them with his Bio-T escort.

"We don't have much time," the marshal said quietly, urgently, "we need to know what's going on here."

Fitzgerald just looked at him.

"What have they done to you all? Where are the others?" Tyler asked.

"Are they holding you or anyone else against their will? Are they forcing you to do things? Experimenting on you?" Stock added.

Fitzgerald looked past them.

"We're finished," he called to Dawkins.

Tyler just stared at him. Part of him couldn't quite believe that someone could embrace this situation. Another part of him knew better, however. Humans could talk themselves into anything.

Dawkins' steps on the guttered tiles sounded deafening, though Tyler couldn't hear the Bio-T's movements.

Then the mask fell. Tyler saw not just fear but abject terror on Fitzgerald's barely human face, in his one good eye. Then, just as quickly as it was there, it was gone.

Dawkins was nearly upon them.

Fitzgerald lifted the syringe towards his eye.

Tyler stepped forward to stop him. Stock grabbed his wrist. A tiny shake of her head.

Tyler could see the conjunctiva membrane flex inwards, then the needle broke through and the syringe emptied its contents into Fitzgerald's eye.

"I think we're done here, Marshal, Agent Matterton. I believe Brother Dak has made his position clear. Anything more and I suspect it would border on harassment—in our lawyers' eyes of course, not mine."

Fitzgerald's face was an impassive mask now. His eye turned black as they watched. Tyler felt as though he was witness to the final part of the transformation of Fitzgerald into Dak.

Somewhere at the back of his mind he registered the sound of a door sliding open. Tyler had to will himself to look away from Fitzgerald/Dak. Serena was standing in an open door under the mezzanine. She was wearing a lab coat, carrying a P-Dat slate, a variable micro and macroscopic lens rig over her eyes. She was the same model but a different artificial person. Past her he could just about make out the area she was coming from. He saw what looked like egg-shaped hypersleep pods. The pods seemed to fit the same, organic-looking design ethos as the old slaughterhouse.

Tyler fell into the shadow as the Bio-T stepped between him and the open door. Dawkins was moving with some speed towards said door. Tyler stepped to the side and saw the artificial person look up as Dawkins approached. She stepped back inside the room she had just come from. The Bio-T shifted and blocked his view again.

"Really?" Tyler asked the Bio-T. There was no response. He heard the door slide shut. Tyler was pretty sure that this hadn't been part of the script. "What's that room for?" Tyler said moving around the Bio-T again as Dawkins returned to them.

"Marshal, Agent Matterton, we acceded to your request," Dawkins said, his arms open as though to hurry them out.

"I thought you said the adherents do all the work," the marshal said. "That was a syn… an artificial person."

"Please leave."

"You've had more than a hundred recruits this year alone, where are they all?" Tyler asked. "Are you freezing them?"

"Marshal, we've asked you to leave. At this moment you're trespassing."

"Sue us," the marshal said. "Answer the question."

"Are you refusing to leave the premises?" Dawkins asked. He sounded calm, but Tyler suspected that Serena would've had a field day with his micro-expressions. This wasn't going Dawkins' way now. The risk the church had taken by allowing them access hadn't paid off. This would be the last time they cooperated.

"I think it's a reasonable question," Stock said, "one that nobody who was legit would struggle to answer."

It was only because he was so strongly keyed to the Bio-T that Tyler noticed the slight shift in position. Suddenly adrenaline coursed through his body. They were in danger.

"Marshal," he said, trying to keep his voice steady.

She turned to him, a question in her eyes.

"I think we've got everything we need."

Stock looked as though she was ready to argue. Tyler was willing her to understand.

"We'll show ourselves out," the marshal said.

"I think not," Dawkins said and gestured towards the stairs.

Being escorted out by Dawkins and the Bio-T, Tyler felt like he was the one doing the perp-walk. All the way across the lab and up the stairs to the bridge Tyler could feel the pits of Fitzgerald/Dak's eyes on his back.

"Well, that was some happy horseshit," the marshal spat.

They were back out on Port Street walking past the Stagecoach. Tyler glanced up, half expecting to see Lace or Harris in the corner window of their hotel room.

"It was certainly a well-orchestrated bit of theatre," Tyler said, "until it wasn't."

"Goddamned side show. See the hypersleep pods?"

Tyler nodded. Other than Fitzgerald being alive it was the most positive takeaway of the whole debacle. Hopefully it meant that the church's recruits weren't all dead.

"You saw it, right?" Tyler asked as they made their way back towards the marshal station. In the cold light of day, he was questioning himself.

"That kid was terrified."

Tyler nodded, relieved that the marshal had seen it as well. They had a lot of rumor and innuendo but still nothing solid. They wouldn't be able to get a search warrant or subpoena financial records based on a facial expression. Tyler was worried that, more and more, his thoughts were turning towards Lace and Harris' methods.

"There's something else," Stock said. "Whatever else he is, Dawkins is a true believer."

"You make him as the charismatic leader?" Tyler asked.

"He comes across more as middle management."

Tyler had to agree. Which left the question, who was pulling the strings? Though one other thing had come from their visit: Tyler was pretty sure that he'd seen a way in.

11

Deputy Amsa called Cass over to her monitor when all five of the ranch hands poured out of the Heartbreaker Saloon as a Bio-T walked by. The wiry cowboy Cass had arrested the other day, whose name she still hadn't been bothered to learn, and Lance, one eye still bandaged, were both there. Lance was doing a lot of the talking. By the time Cass had reached Amsa's workspace the cowboys had surrounded the Bio-T, who had come to a halt and was just looking ahead impassively, ignoring them, which of course just made them angrier.

"Every goddamned week," Cass muttered under her breath. Though the last incident had only been the day before yesterday. She grabbed her duster and hat on the way to the door.

"Want me to come with?" Amsa asked.

"No, I need you here on the cameras. Where's Sorgram?"

Amsa shrugged. It seemed her senior deputy was AWOL again.

"Okay, tell Sorgram to meet me outside the Heartbreaker. He'll ignore you, but tell him anyway," Cass said pausing by the door, pulling her duster on. "Then I want you to contact Special Agent Matterton, let him know that there's something going on with the Bio-Ts on Guernsey Street."

"You want him to back you up?" Amsa asked.

"No, just thought he might be interested because of the Bio-T connection. Share the camera link with him."

Amsa nodded and Cass was out into the cold, dry, dusty air. She waded across the muddy street, making for the boardwalk on the other side of Port Street, putting the earpiece in for her P-Dat and connecting through to Deputy Amsa as she did so.

"What's going on, Deputy?" she asked as she reached the boardwalk and started to run, not for the first time thinking about how undignified it was to have to run at her age.

"Lot of talking," Amsa told her, *"Though one of them, the guy with the bandaged eye, Lance? He's just started up his ATV."*

Shit! She cut through an alleyway to cross Jersey Street, huffing through the mud, and then down another alleyway at which point she could hear raised voices.

"I take it they're all armed," she asked Amsa.

"At least four of them have sidearms," her deputy told

her, she decided to assume the fifth was carrying as well, *"of the three ATVs I can see, two have sheaths for longarms."* Which meant rifles or shotguns. As she reached Guernsey Street, Cass was regretting not bringing her own shotgun with her.

"Two of them are tying the ends of their lassos to ATVs," Amsa updated her, but Cass could see it. She was on the opposite side of the street, south of the Heartbreaker. Lance and another were sat on their ATVs, as they bobbed up and down on spinning impellers. The wiry cowboy and a cowgirl were spinning lassos above their heads on either side of the massive Bio-T. Seemingly unperturbed, the Bio-T was nevertheless looking between the two lassoists. The fifth Coldstream ranch-hand was just watching, laughing, hand on the butt of the holstered automatic riding his hip. There were a number of people standing in the open doorway of the Heartbreaker, watching, letting in the cold air and dust. A small crowd was gathering on the other side of the street. Cass moved towards the crowd, aware of the fifth cowboy noticing her and saying something to Lance.

The lassos were thrown. The first slid down past the Bio-T's shoulders. The Bio-T slipped his hands out before the cowgirl tightened the lasso around his waist. The second lasso was tightened around his neck.

Lance turned around to glare at the marshal with his one good eye.

"Move on, now!" the marshal told the small crowd that had gathered on her side of the street.

"Let them watch the fun!" Lance called from his ATV.

There was some grumbling from the crowd. After all, everyone enjoyed a good mud-drag.

"Get!" Cass snapped as she moved closer to one of the thick support posts that held up the boardwalk's covering. It had started to snow gently.

"Stay out of this, Marshal!" Lance called.

Cass turned to face him.

"Not, how this works," she called back. "Get your ropes and head on back to the station."

Lance looked down, as though he was giving her words some deep consideration. Then his head twitched back up, anger evident in his expression.

"Why is it you always side with these freaks against your own?" he demanded.

"They start trying to drag you through the mud behind an ATV and I'll come down on them just as hard."

Cass did not like the way this was playing out. Lance was clearly drunk. Mean drunk. She suspected they had spent the last few hours getting good and liquored and talking themselves into this nonsense.

Lance slid off the ATV into the mud of Guernsey Street and waded towards her.

"Maybe I should rope you behind one of the

ATVs?" he said before pointing at his bandaged eye and playing to the crowd. "She did this to me, with a fucking shotgun, just for having some fun with one of these freaks!"

There was a ripple of noise from those still on the boardwalk. Cass felt like knocking him in the dirt and dragging him to a cell, but she needed to de-escalate.

"Lance, you know that I can't just let you go dragging people through the streets, but you can let him go and head back. Nobody needs to go to jail."

"There's five of us, Marshal, what are you going to do about it?"

"Only two more than last time." She could see where this was going. Lance didn't think he could back down now. "I don't want this," she told them. It was a stupid reason to have to kill someone over, worse still to die for.

Lance went for his gun. Cass's .357 Magnum slid out of its holster. Her first shot was hurried, from the hip, catching Lance in the leg, tearing it out from under him, sending him sprawling face down in the mud.

The cowboy on the ATV was going for the scabbarded longarm.

The cowgirl had let go of her lasso and was reaching for her gun.

The other lassoist, the wiry cowboy she had arrested with Lance the day before yesterday, was standing stock-still, eyes wide.

The fifth cowboy, the one who'd just been watching, the one who already had his hand on his gun, was drawing. Cass shot at him first, moving for what little cover the support post provided as she did so. She felt the recoil, saw the tongue of fire and the cowboy staggering back.

The small crowd in the Heartbreaker's doorway were diving for cover.

Cass fired again.

The cowboy stumbled backwards across Heartbreaker's threshold before going down.

Cass shifted aim. The cowgirl's gun was almost level with her but Cass forced herself to take the moment she needed. Her finger squeezed the trigger. The cowgirl spun away from her, hit.

Cass shifted aim again: the cowboy on the second ATV had wrestled a shotgun out of its scabbard. She saw the tongue of flame from the shotgun's barrel. Wood exploded from the post next to her, splinters and stray buckshot opening up her face. Cass returned fire and he was thrown back across his ATV.

Cass shifted aim back to the cowgirl, who was still moving. Still trying to bring the gun up. Cass fired again and the cowgirl went down and was still. It felt like an execution.

Back to the ATV rider. Another shot. The shotgun discharged into the air as the rider slid off the ATV, head first into the mud.

Movement in her periphery. Enraged screaming punctuated with gunfire. Lance was somehow back up on his feet, covered in mud, firing again and again. The air exploded from her lungs as she took a jackhammer to her chest, staggering back, the world tipping as her legs slipped out from under her and her face hit the cold, muddy boardwalk. Lance was wading towards her, firing. She clawed at her belt for a speed loader with one hand, the other flipping the .357's cylinder open, letting seven spent cartridges tumble to the wood. It was no good. Lance had her dead. She found herself looking down the barrel of his semi-automatic as he took his time, wishing she had the breath for a curse.

More gunfire. A three-round burst, then another and another, Lance stumbling in the mud like a drunk trying to dance. Matterton on the other side of the street, the V of the muzzle flare from his service weapon's gas venting, as he fired yet another burst. Lance went down. Then Matterton was covering the wiry cowboy.

"Hands behind your head! Do it now!"

The terrified cowboy did as he was told. Matterton kept his pistol as far from the cowboy as he could as he disarmed him.

The Bio-T was still standing there in the midst of it all, completely passive, as though a gunfight hadn't just taken place all around him.

"Lace your fingers together and get down on your knees!" There was authority in Matterton's voice but, as Cass found herself able to breathe again, she could hear the tension in the special agent's words. The fear. She would have felt it too if Lance and his friends had given her the time.

"Lay still, Marshal." Serena was suddenly crouched by her side.

Cass ignored her and sat up, letting out a cry of pain. Her side felt like one big bruise. Luckily, her body armor had taken the worst of it.

"Marshal—" Serena began.

"I'm fine," she muttered and then cried out again as she hauled herself to her feet. The side of her face was wet. Serena straightened up next to her.

The wiry cowboy was on his knees now. Matterton had stepped back, his gun still trained on him.

Serena saw it before Cass did. The artificial person took off at a run, heading across the muddy street towards her partner. The Bio-T was moving. With speed that belied his impressive bulk, the Bio-T grabbed the surrendering cowboy by the back of his head. The huge alabaster hand fitted comfortably around the cowboy's skull. In one easy fluid movement the Bio-T rammed the cowboy's face against the side of the Heartbreaker with enough force to crack some of the logs that formed the saloon's wall. The cowboy's head was crushed like an egg, the nearly headless corpse leaving a trail of blood, skull fragments and brain matter as it slid bonelessly to the boardwalk.

It happened so quickly that Matterton was still looking at where the cowboy had been a moment before.

Cass still had her Hancock in hand. The cylinder open. Speedloader in her other hand.

The Bio-T turned towards Matterton.

Cass reloaded rapidly, flipped the cylinder shut.

Matterton looked up at the Bio-T.

Cass brought the revolver up and levelled it at the Bio-T.

"Don't you do it!" she yelled. She would not fuck around. All seven pills were heading his way if she even thought the Bio-T was about to move on Matterton.

Serena reached the other side of the street, seemingly having run across the top of the mud. She interposed herself between Matterton and the Bio-T. It may have been her programming but it looked like something else to Cass.

Serena's sudden proximity seemed to wake Matterton up. He moved back, Serena keeping pace, his service weapon moving to cover the Bio-T.

"Do not move!" he screamed.

The Bio-T just stared at Matterton.

Now Cass had the leisure to examine her own fear. She had no idea how many rounds Matterton had left in his weapon. She knew that whatever else they were, the Bio-Ts were human, made of flesh and bone, but somehow it didn't feel like they had enough firepower to take him down.

Movement in her periphery. She risked a glance but the Hancock never wavered. Dawkins running along the boardwalk on the other side of Guernsey Street.

"Don't shoot!" the church administrator called.

"Stay where you are, Dawkins!" Cass shouted back. "Put your hands in the air and keep them where I can see them. I even think you're fucking around you get shot, understood?"

Dawkins had already come to a halt. Now he raised his hands.

Cass risked a glance at Matterton. He looked shit-scared. A reasonable but unfortunate response. Scared people made mistakes.

"Dawkins. We're arresting your boy here—" Cass told him.

"It was self-defense—" Dawkins started.

"Dawkins!" Cass snapped. The church administrator shut up. "This is happening. If you have any influence with him, then you'll get him to cooperate. This doesn't have to be any worse than it already is."

"Get down on your knees, hands behind your head, lace your fingers together!" Matterton told the Bio-T.

The Bio-T didn't move.

Cass could feel her own stinging sweat running into the shot and splinter wounds on the left side of her face.

"This goes south, it's on you, Dawkins," Cass called. "He doesn't do what he's told, I'm erring on the side of caution."

"I can't let you take him into custody, marshal," Dawkins said. "His body contains propriety technology."

"You kidding me?" Matterton said loud enough for Cass to hear. She could hear the tension in his voice but she didn't want to take her eyes off the Bio-T.

"His choices are cell or morgue," Cass told the administrator.

It went very quiet in the street.

Cass almost shot the Bio-T as he went down on his knees and laced his fingers behind his hairless head. If a signal had passed between Dawkins and the Bio-T, Cass hadn't seen it. She advanced across the street, keeping the .357 leveled. She came to a halt in the mud, hopefully far enough away that the Bio-T couldn't reach her before she extensively shot him if his surrender was a ruse.

Serena walked behind the marshal so as not to cross anyone's field of fire. Then she moved behind the Bio-T. There was no resistance as she put him in smartcuffs, his left hand still dripping. Even then Cass struggled to heave a sigh of relief. She certainly didn't holster her weapon.

"Five dead in the fucking street!"

Sorgram was in her face the moment they pushed the unresisting Bio-T into the shop. It was too much for Cass. Tension became rage. Her right hand, that was still holding the Hancock, was swinging before she'd even registered it as a conscious act. She caught him on the side of his face with enough force to send him sprawling across a desk. She was on him before he could get back up, her left hand grabbing the front of his body armor, pushing him back down again. She kept her right hand, holding the now bloodied Hancock, behind her back in a bid to resist temptation.

"From now on I know where you are every fucking second of your shift! I call, you answer, understand me?" she screamed in his face.

"You're done," he told her. He was probably right.

"Until then you either do what I tell you, or leave your badge and gun and get the fuck out."

She let him up. Aware that she looked like a bloodied, muddied and insane savage to the deputy's eyes. Cass was shaking from the soup of adrenaline, fury and fear coursing through her.

"You think you can—" Sorgram started.

"Hey!" It was Matterton. "Read the room."

Sorgram looked around. Deputy Amsa was looking at him appalled. Serena was staring at him as well.

"I'm reporting this," he said.

"Just put the prisoner in a cell," Cass said more quietly now.

Sorgram looked as though he was about to argue but then thought the better of it.

"I'll help you," Serena told the senior deputy.

"I suppose asking you if you're alright is redundant," Matterton said after Serena and Sorgram had taken the Bio-T downstairs.

Cass held up her bloodied revolver.

"See," she said.

Matterton looked confused for a moment, then remembered their conversation about the correct kind of firearm with which to pistol-whip an asshole.

"He never knows when to shut up," Amsa said looking at the open door to the stairwell down to the cells. "Williams is on her way back, she cut her patrol short but she's still at least three hours out. We can stay on with the night shift."

"No, it's fine, I'll brief them when they come in. I'll be upstairs but on call. No drinking tonight though, you're on call as well," Cass said, hypocritically—she knew she was having a drink tonight.

Amsa nodded.

Cass slumped against one of the supports and stared at nothing.

"Marshal, may I examine your wounds?" Serena asked, shaking Cass out of her fugue, as the artificial person and Sorgram came back into the office.

"Sorgram, take a shotgun and go and stand outside the cell. He starts doing anything odd you shout for backup and call me in that order. Looks like he's somehow about to get out of his cell, you shoot him and keep firing until he's dead," Cass said, ignoring Serena.

"Are you out of your—"

Cass advanced on him. She still had her bloody gun in hand. He actually flinched away from her. Cass knew how it looked.

"Badge and gun, or go and do what I fucking told you to." She was so through having to argue every single thing with this whiny little bitch.

Sorgram threw his hands up before grabbing a shotgun from the rack and picking up one of the office chairs.

"I know you heard me say stand," Cass growled.

Sorgram looked as though he was about to argue again but something in the set of Cass's bloodstained face must have put him off. He put the chair down and went back down the stairs.

"Do you know when's a good time to argue with your boss?" Cass asked the air. Only now could she feel the tension starting to drain from her. Her chest was really hurting, so was her face.

"Anytime but immediately after a gunfight?" Amsa suggested.

Cass waved a finger at the deputy.

"Clever girl, you'll go far in law enforcement." Cass realized she was babbling at about the same time as her legs went out from under her. Serena reached her before she hit the floor.

* * *

Cass awoke lying on her own bed in the flat above the marshal's station. Her face had been cleaned and dressed. She checked her chest. It was basically one big bruise. Then she remembered pistol-whipping Sorgram. She clearly hadn't been thinking straight but it was still a deeply satisfying memory. She knew that she had screwed herself, however. She was gone as soon as the paperwork cleared and with good reason. She'd be lucky to keep her pension. She'd played right into Sorgram's hands and those of his puppet master at Chisholm, who was almost certainly Regina Charters. Cass only hoped she'd loosened a few of Sorgram's teeth.

"You've really done it this time," Cass told herself. She knew she could make excuses. Her blood had been up, she'd had tension piled on tension, not to mention getting shot and nearly killed. She could not, however, justify striking a subordinate, even one that was as big an asshole as Sorgram was. She had been doing this, working as a marshal, ever since she had left the marines. This case, however, this thing with the Bio-Ts was getting to her. She wasn't even particularly sure why, beyond the strong feeling that things were not only bad but really, really bad, and it had all happened on her watch.

She needed a drink.

She heard movement in the other room. Looking around she saw her pants over the chair in the corner and her Hancock on the bedside table.

Matterton raised his hands up when Cass emerged from her bedroom, gun in hand.

"Serena took your pants off, I wasn't even in the room," he said. He was sat at the kitchen table, drinking some of her fine coffee. His service weapon was disassembled on a mat in front of him as he cleaned it.

Cass put the gun down on the table. She got her gun cleaning kit from the shelf under the gunrack, then got the good bourbon and two glasses from the cupboard.

"Drinking and gun maintenance, this should go well," Matterton muttered as she poured three fingers into each tumbler, before sitting down opposite him.

"Thank you," she said, raising a glass. She was pretty sure he had saved her life, turning up when he had.

He put the brush down, picked the tumbler up and clinked her glass. He at least had the manners to take a sip before putting the tumbler back down on the table. Cass enjoyed his whisky face. It was clear that he didn't drink the hard stuff frequently. She took a sip herself. It hurt because everything did right now.

Cass opened up the gun cleaning kit and set it out, putting the Hancock on the mat. She had already checked. It was unloaded. She guessed Serena had seen to that as well.

"Serena said that your ribs are bruised, not broken. She dressed your face as well. Though she thought you might get a scar."

Another one, Cass thought.

"She gave you a phyto shot to speed up healing and naproleve for the pain," he continued.

"Yeah, that's wearing off."

"She didn't give you very much."

It was probably for the best, Cass decided. She didn't need any more habits. She shot the rest of her bourbon.

"Must've figured me for a self-medicator," Cass said as she poured herself another bourbon. "What's the story with you two, anyway?"

He looked up at her.

"She's my partner."

"Partner? She's an artificial person. Aren't they—"

"What? A piece of equipment? A slave?" His tone was steady, devoid of emotion. The way he was reassembling his service weapon wasn't, however.

"I was going to say a resource."

Matterton looked up at her.

"But you tell me she's your partner, she's your partner. I'm on your side. I owe you."

He checked the action on his service weapon's slide and then put it down. Grimacing as he took another sip of whiskey.

"Is it that obvious?" This time he didn't look at her.

"I mean... only to the people that've seen you in her company. I take it the FB of I have some pretty stringent regulations about that kind of fraternization."

Now he did look up at her again.

"That's not the point. She's not free."

Cass didn't say anything. She just started to clean her own weapon as Matterton finished reassembling his gun in silence. He slid the magazine home, chambered a round, checked the safety and slid the weapon into his holster. Then he rewarded himself by finishing his bourbon. Glancing over at him Cass saw that his whiskey face wasn't going anywhere soon and that his hand was shaking.

"First gunfight?" she asked him.

"First time they fired back."

Cass chuckled.

"I mean, a one-sided gunfight is pretty much as good as it gets."

"The first time I was firing at Snell," he told her, helping himself to some more of the bourbon. Only spilling a little. "Sometimes I wake up screaming. I fear sleep. I mean, I've worked some pretty bad cases but a few stick, y'know?"

She nodded, though it was what she'd seen, what she'd done in the Dog War that had stuck with her. Most of the murders they had on GL3 were pretty mundane. Until today anyway.

"First Greco, then Snell, nearly getting thrown off an old atmosphere processor. Does it get easier?"

Cass had no idea what or who Greco was.

"Wounds become so much scar tissue," she told him. "It doesn't so much get easier as fade. It'll still sneak up on you sometimes." What she was telling him wasn't particularly comforting, but she couldn't quite bring herself to lie to him.

"Thank you," he said.

She put the Hancock down and studied him for a moment or two. He looked drawn. Worn. As though he'd aged in the two days she had known him. Cass almost laughed. It seemed she had that effect on people.

"What are you doing here?" she finally said.

He didn't say anything for a while. "I need to know."

"Sometimes bad things just happen. He could have just been insane." She had to push down the guilt. Try and keep a poker face.

"You know there's something very wrong here, don't you?" As he said it their eyes met.

She did know. She had known it for a long time, long before Snell, and she had done nothing because it was too big, too difficult, too well insulated to even try. Except those were all excuses.

"I helped Snell escape," she told him.

12

Tyler stared at the marshal. Serena had been sure that Stock had been hiding something about Snell but the extent of it still came as a surprise.

"When were you going to tell us?" Tyler finally managed.

"When I decided I could trust you."

"As opposed to a professional courtesy to fellow law enforcement officers?"

Stock didn't answer for a moment or two.

"No excuses," she finally said.

Tyler nodded, his eyes lidded, trying to keep his expression as neutral as possible. He wasn't sure how he felt, but anger was a good start. The marshal had played a part in the events that led to the deaths of at least six people, Tyler's own near-death experience and the traumatizing of many others.

"Want to tell me about it?" he asked, his voice taut.

"Am I being interrogated?"

Tyler didn't say anything.

Stock just shrugged. Then she started talking.

"So maybe nine, ten months ago I'm walking home and I'm seeing a lot more Bio-Ts on the street than normal. They're acting casual, but it's like they're looking for something."

"Snell?"

The marshal nodded.

"I found him under the boardwalk near the office. I had him crawl round the back and I let him up into my apartment. He was soaked to the skin, shaking so badly he could barely talk." The marshal poured herself some more whiskey.

"If they were looking for him, that suggests that he was being held against his will," Tyler said, a hint of anger in his voice.

She let out a sigh.

"We travelled that road. I got him warm, got him fed, managed to calm him down a bit but he was shit-scared—I mean, fucking terrified. Over the next few days, I managed to get bits and pieces from him. He kept on saying that it was him, not them. That he wasn't good enough, strong enough. He wouldn't say anything that would incriminate them at all but he begged me not to tell them where he was."

"Did he say anything about a goddess?" Tyler asked, remembering what Snell's parents had told him.

Stock shook her head. She wasn't looking at him.

"No, but he had bad dreams: soak-the-sheets, wake-up-screaming dreams." Something about the way she said it made Tyler think that the marshal understood those kinds of dreams.

"Did you report it?" Matterton all but demanded.

"To whom, for what?" the marshal asked, then she looked up at him. "You may well be the first FBI agent ever to visit Gamma Leporis 3. I am the law for this entire planet and I've got twelve deputies. Six in the office and the rest roving. That's it. He gave me nothing and I tried. Believe me, I tried."

"Tried?" Tyler asked, a little heat creeping back into his voice. "Six people are dead, marshal, three more missing, probably dead, and at least seven other people have had their lives irrevocably damaged."

Stock held his look.

"If I'd had the slightest hint… That boy was broken, non-functioning and he was with me for weeks until I could sneak him onto the shuttle."

"Who paid for his passage to Alexandria?"

"I did."

Matterton pinched the bridge of his nose. Maybe he shouldn't have had the bourbon. He wasn't a drinker, though he was starting to understand the appeal.

"If I'd known I would have taken him out onto the prairie and put two in the back of his head myself," Stock said.

He believed her. It didn't help.

"There's something else," she said. Tyler steeled himself. "I couldn't shake the feeling that it wasn't them he was afraid of—the Bio-Ts I mean."

"Then what?" Matterton asked.

"I don't know," Stock said. "But whoever it was, they were in his head."

On the table the marshal's P-Dat vibrated. Tyler saw the relief on Stock's face for the interruption. That was wiped away when she read the message.

"'The fuck?" Stock said as she walked into the marshal's office, Tyler behind her.

There was a deputy on duty that Tyler didn't recognize. Sorgram was still there and he didn't look happy. The shotgun he'd taken to guard the cells was lying across his desk. There was a fit-looking man in his early sixties sat in the marshal's chair. He wore a Western-style suit, a bolo tie, even metal collar tips on his shirt. He had a silvery goatee and a matching full head of hair, his hat on the desk.

"Cut him loose," the man said. It took Tyler to realize that the newcomer meant the Bio-T.

"I don't even know where to start with this," the marshal said.

"There's no starting, cut him loose."

"It's not your call," the marshal told the newcomer.

"Leaving aside he killed a man in cold blood in the middle of a street full of witnesses—"

"And on camera," Sorgram added, surprising Tyler and the marshal.

"Shut up," the man told Sorgram. "This isn't open for discussion. Cut him loose. Do it now, or I'll have your deputies here arrest you and then cut him loose anyway."

"On what grounds?" Tyler demanded.

"False imprisonment."

"Who the fuck are you?" Tyler rarely swore but he was struggling with what he was hearing, right now.

"Special Agent Matterton, Judge Khan. The one judge on this dustball that I didn't think was corrupt," the marshal told him.

Khan was out of his seat, finger pointing at her.

"You started a gunfight, killed five people—"

"Three. Agent Matterton killed one and the Bio-T killed the other," the marshal corrected.

"In self-defense," the judge said. "He had a reason to fear for his life."

"He stood there in the middle of a bullet storm without flinching!" the marshal pointed down towards the cells. "That guy wouldn't know fear if it was butt-fucking him with a live bear! He killed a surrendering suspect after the fight!"

"You'll never make it stick," Khan said, crossing his arms.

Tyler was struggling to believe what he was hearing.

Serena stood at the top of the stairs to the basement cells. She was so unobtrusive that Tyler couldn't be sure how long she had been there.

"Never make it..." Stock managed. "Leaving aside... y'know, all the fucking evidence, that's the Colonial Attorney's call not to prosecute, not yours."

"He agrees."

The marshal stared at the judge, not trusting herself to speak.

Tyler stepped forward as well.

"Judge, I'm a federal agent. I witnessed the suspect kill that man in cold blood, after he had surrendered. You're not releasing him."

The judge turned to look at him.

"This isn't your jurisdiction," he told Tyler.

"Public corruption comes under the FBI's remit."

As he said it Tyler saw the reaction. A momentary flinch. The beaded sweat on the judge's forehead. He was scared.

"Judge, under the Colonial Criminal Code, Section—" Serena started.

"Enough!" the judge roared with a voice that could silence a courtroom. "This isn't a debate. And thank you, young woman, I happen to have practiced colonial law for twenty-five years before I became a judge."

"Keep practicing," the marshal muttered. "She's an artificial person in the employ of the FBI. I think she understands colonial law pretty good."

The judge blanched but recovered quickly.

"This is happening." The judge turned to Sorgram. "Release the prisoner. Anyone tries to stop you, arrest them for obstruction."

"I'll obstruct your bowels with the tip of my boot," the marshal muttered.

The deputy that Tyler didn't know stifled a laugh.

Sorgram looked between the marshal and the judge.

"Don't you fucking dare," the marshal growled.

Tyler struggled to believe that Sorgram was more afraid of the judge than Stock, particularly after today. Nevertheless, Sorgam was moving towards the stairs to the cells. Tyler stepped in front of him and looked at Serena.

"Have I grounds to arrest him?" Tyler asked, meaning the judge.

"Does he have a court order?" Serena asked.

"Yes," the marshal said. Tyler assumed that it had been the court order that marshal had received via interlink upstairs.

"And it's been signed off by the Colonial Attorney's office as well," the judge pointed out.

"Then you can initiate an investigation, which should be simple enough as this is an easily provable and egregious act of public corruption," Serena told him. "But you do not have the grounds to arrest him at this moment."

The judge swallowed hard. He looked sick.

"What've they got on you?" the marshal asked.

The judge didn't say anything. He just looked at Sorgram. Clearly not happy, the senior deputy headed downstairs.

Tyler moved away from the stairs, Serena joining him, an expression of concern on her face. The marshal picked up the shotgun from Sorgram's desk and checked the chamber.

"What do you think you're doing?" the judge demanded.

"I saw this guy turn a man's head to paste in cold blood today," the marshal told him.

A shadow fell across the office as the Bio-T reached the top of the stairs. His hands, one still encrusted in gore, remained secured behind his back.

The judge stumbled into the corner of the office at the sight of the pale giant.

"Who's got the code for the smart cuffs?" the judge asked, his voice faltering.

"I do," Serena said.

"Release him," the judge ordered.

"Send the judge the code, he can release the suspect when he's outside the station," Tyler said. He still couldn't quite believe what he was seeing.

The judge nodded.

"Go on now," a very nervous Sorgram said.

The Bio-T just looked down at the deputy. Sorgram looked close to soiling himself. In spite of everything,

Tyler sympathized with Sorgram at that moment. The sheer, imposing physicality of the Bio-T in this enclosed space was more than a little disconcerting. It was like being locked in a cage with an apex predator. The Bio-T crossed the station and shouldered his way out the door as Serena interlinked the smart cuffs release code to the judge.

The judge made as to follow.

"Tell me, judge," the marshal started, her head down, holding the shotgun at port with one hand. The judge stopped by the door. She looked up at him. "If he crushes your head, is that self-defense as well?"

The judge just walked out of the station.

Stock turned on Sorgram.

"What did you do?" she demanded.

"It wasn't me, I swear!" Sorgram said. Tyler believed him.

Something inside Tyler broke. He made for the door. Serena moved to join him.

"Stay here," he snapped at her.

It was snowing outside: the dust in the cold air made Tyler cough. He could see an gyrocar heading away from the marshal's station and assumed that was the judge. The recently released Bio-T was nowhere to be seen, already swallowed by the snow.

Tyler pulled his coat around him and headed south

down Port Street away from the snow-obscured lights of the shuttle port. Pushing against the stinging wind, he walked down the frozen mud-covered boardwalk to the Stagecoach Hotel.

Inside, he headed up to Lace and Harris's room and knocked on the door. There was some movement inside and muffled, urgent conversation. He knocked again. The door opened a crack and Lace peered out.

"Agent Tyler," the cult psychologist said, "'fraid we're a little busy at the moment."

"I have a way in," he told Lace.

Lace just stared at him.

"Let him in," Harris said from inside the room.

Lace stepped to one side and opened the door. Harris was dressed in a dark gray one-piece. She wore lightweight body armor over the top of it. There was all manner of equipment laid out on the bed, some of which, including the EM assault carbine, was less than legal.

"Well?" Harris asked.

"I've been inside the genetics facility. I think I know where Fitzgerald will be," Tyler told her.

"Think?" Harris asked.

"Got anything better?"

"Draw a plan for me?" Harris asked.

Tyler nodded.

Lace was stood behind him, by the door, arms crossed over his barrel chest.

"We still need a place to stow Fitzgerald until we can get him off world," the cult psychologist said.

Tyler looked back at Lace.

"Ask the marshal."

Harris shook her head.

"I don't know, Special Agent Matterton. So far this cooperation has been very one-sided and we're about to be doing some serious crime here."

"I think she'll help now," Tyler told the extractor.

"Why the change of heart?" Lace asked.

Tyler didn't say anything. It was difficult to explain why he was prepared to piss his career away, but out here, what did it matter? Perhaps he had always been naïve but laws had to count for something. Here they were meaningless. Maybe it was the same everywhere else, just better hidden. He understood the inequal way in which the law was enforced, but if you could just kill someone out in the open, in front of a street full of witnesses, and then walk away, then what was even the point?

"You said you had a way in," Harris said when it became apparent that Tyler wasn't going to answer Lace's question.

Tyler just nodded.

Harris finally looked at him, an expectant expression on her face.

"One condition," he said. Harris raised an eyebrow. "I come with you."

"I don't think that's a very good idea," Lace said.

"This requires a certain skill set," Harris told him.

"I've worked surveillance, done sneak-and-peaks," Tyler said.

Harris was just watching him as if she knew that what he'd just said was only half true. He had never done any physical penetration work, or even had the training.

"It's a full package, take it or leave it," Tyler told them.

"Sold," Harris said, finally. "Hold me up, I leave you behind. Get in my way and I kill you."

Tyler stared at her. Then he nodded.

This was a mistake. Tyler was in well over his head. He could still taste the marshal's bourbon. He hadn't been drunk by a long shot but he was pretty sure that his decision making had been compromised. He was surprised that neither Harris or Lace had noticed. Maybe they had.

Tyler was lying flat on the roof of the Church of Biotechnological Transcendence's genetic facility. Harris had provided him with a stealth suit of photoreactive material, after making it clear that he had to do whatever she told him to do, when she told him to do it. As far as he could tell, Harris's infiltration plan involved using the stealth suits to try and fool the church's roof cameras. This meant crossing the roof slowly enough to minimize the chance of anyone watching the camera feed, human or otherwise, picking up on the movement. She had told him however slow he felt he was crawling, he was almost certainly going too fast. It felt like he had been lying on the roof of the church for hours, the cold concrete sucking heat from him as ice crawled through his flesh.

Harris had reached the roof's central camera bubble. She had crawled over the hardwired cable and was drilling into it with the goal of splicing the cable and using the penetration software on her P-Dat to ride the signal and spoof all the facility's cameras at source. It was not an easy hack: it took both significant skill and resources. It would appear that Harris's military occupational specialty had been comtech.

Tyler had used Harris and Lace's imaging software to draw the plans for the facility as best he remembered them. He had told them about the chamber of strangely designed hypersleep pods. Most importantly, he had told them about roof egress from the maintenance catwalk that ran along the ceiling mounted crane. It perhaps hadn't been as much as they had hoped, but it was better than what they themselves had.

Harris rose up from the roof, tucking tools back into various pouches under her stealth suit. She stretched and flexed her fingers before finally pulling up the photoreactive veil to reveal her face. She beckoned Tyler to join her. He had to force his cold and aching body to do as he was bid, reaching Harris as she pressed a lock-hacker against the concealed door. Then they both waited. Finally, she bent down and checked the device. Seemingly happy, she stowed the lock-hacker and pulled on the door, gently. It clicked open. Harris hesitated: after all, neither of them could be sure that they weren't walking into a sentry gun.

Harris readied her carbine, a compact Belgian-made weapon. The carbine worked on a similar principle to the phased plasma pulse rifles that all branches of the UA armed forces used, but fired smaller caliber projectiles and had an adjustable velocity. Tyler reached for his own weapon, but she shook her head. It seemed Harris was the only person Harris trusted with a weapon.

The extractor pulled the door all the way open and stepped down inside. Tyler followed.

The genetic facility's night-time lighting was a subdued ultraviolet. They were on a flight of skeletonized steel stairs. It creaked as Tyler put weight on it. To his ears the creak sounded like a scream echoing through the cavernous facility. Harris turned to look at him. He mouthed an apology, for all the good it would do.

The stairs, the catwalk and the roof crane's infrastructure all obscured the view of the facility. Tyler pulled the door to the roof closed behind them as quietly as he could manage and they made their way down the steps to the catwalk. The sound of their movements on the metal steps seemed deafening to him. He didn't understand how they weren't already compromised. His skin was slick with sweat under the suit.

Harris reached the catwalk ahead of him and then froze. A moment later Tyler understood why. The facility had felt empty in the way that you instinctively know when you're alone in a room. They were, however, anything but alone. There were twelve Bio-Ts, nine males and three females, all naked, hairless, alabaster-skinned, perfect physical specimens, lying face down on the antiseptically clean concrete floor in a semi-circle around the huge stainless steel sphere of the 'bioreactor'.

Harris turned to look at him, as if she held him responsible for this. Tyler did not know what to make of it. It looked like some kind of pseudo-religious ritual of obeisance.

Harris pointed to one of the open-plan medical procedure areas. The same area where Tyler had met Fitzgerald earlier in the day. A thirteenth Bio-T was sat on a stool. Tyler couldn't quite make out what was going on. It looked as though the skin on her abdomen had been peeled open and pinned up in geometric flaps. Harris sighted on the Bio-T with the carbine's scope. She spent a few moments studying the thirteenth Bio-T. Tyler pulled a small ruggedized telescope from a pouch on his body armor and extended it, putting it to his eye.

It wasn't just the thirteenth Bio-T's skin that had been peeled back and pinned: it was her flesh as well. Her musculature looked different to how it should, but Tyler couldn't say why. Denser somehow? It was the exposed rib cage, however, that caught his attention. Tendrils of some dark material were growing through the bones themselves, like a time-lapsed film of a hemiparasitic plant growing through its host. As Tyler watched, appalled, the material grew into a kind of armored lattice. At first, Tyler assumed that that material had to be some kind of hardened carbon composite, but the more he watched the more he was convinced that the tendrils, as they moved, were showing the properties of some kind of silicone resin.

The Bio-T receiving the treatment betrayed no sign of discomfort at all. Her head was arched back. There was a drip containing blue liquid. The tube from the drip ended in a needle canula hooked into the Bio-Ts eye. It was the same blue liquid that Tyler had seen Fitzgerald inject earlier in the day. Tyler was pretty sure that whomever the Bio-Ts had been to begin with, they were now dealing with a different species.

Harris pulled the photoreactive veil back over her head and motioned Tyler to do the same. It felt like walking through cobwebs. She moved to a place on the catwalk where the main body of the crane provided the most amount of cover between her and the Bio-Ts, but where she could still observe them. Tyler followed suit.

It was a strange mixture of tension and boredom. There was a reason that Tyler had felt the genetics facility had been empty when he had entered. It wasn't so much the silence—there was noise in here from the various machines—but it was so still. Neither the twelve Bio-Ts, prostrate before the 'bioreactor', nor the thirteenth, undergoing her strange medical procedure, had so much as shifted. Tyler found himself speculating that the twelve Bio-Ts were engaged in some kind of communion. That was when he started to suspect that his imagination was getting the better of him.

Tyler was also wondering if Harris was going to scrub the mission. He ached from trying to remain still on the hard catwalk and he was exhausted from being constantly on edge. Every time he shifted, he felt like the metal shrieked and Harris's veiled head turned in his direction. He could feel her judgment through the photoreactive material.

Tyler didn't hear them move, they were so quiet. Instead he caught movement out of the corner of his eye and peeked around the crane. The twelve bioreactor devotees were on their feet, walking beneath the catwalk to disappear under the office mezzanine where Tyler knew the door to the hypersleep pod chamber was.

Tyler signaled that they should move. Harris signaled *not yet*. The thirteenth Bio-T was still undergoing her bizarre procedure, but Tyler didn't think that was what Harris was waiting for. Finally, Harris drew back behind the roof crane and flicked her veil up.

"With the Bio-T in the room I'm going to have to move more stealthily than you can manage," she whispered. "You need to go back."

Tyler shook his head. He felt like a petulant child. He had nothing more to prove here, yet some instinct wouldn't let him withdraw.

Harris shrugged. The veil covered her face again. She stood up, reached up and pulled herself silently into the roof supports. Tyler watched as she crawled across a rafter like a spider. Her stealth suit obfuscating her form, it was only by following her movement that Tyler was even able to see her progress. He finally lost sight of her as she disappeared behind one of the floor-to-ceiling support pillars close to the mezzanine. Tyler could only imagine her fast-lining down the other side of the pillar.

He was on his own. The only reasonable solution was to go back the way they had come. Take the line over to the Stagecoach. At least this time he wouldn't have to go so slowly, but again for some reason he didn't. Once again, he became aware of movement in his periphery.

The thirteenth Bio-T was on her feet, skin and flesh tightly wrapped around her torso like a ragged shawl, the armored lattice of her ribs still exposed. She was looking around as though searching for something, but she wasn't looking up. It wasn't Tyler that she was looking for.

The Bio-T started moving. Stalking between workbenches and smoking freezers, her head shifting from side-to-side. Tyler had to draw her attention away from Harris. He moved as quietly as he could to the stairs leading from the maintenance catwalk to the mezzanine, and all but slithered down them. It was only when he reached the mezzanine that he realized that had he just made a run for it, got her to follow him, it would have achieved the same result and given him a better chance at escape.

The Bio-T was moving towards the mezzanine now, presumably still tracking an unseen Harris. Tyler could imagine Harris drawing a bead on the Bio-T with her carbine but Tyler doubted that the carbine was enough firepower for one of them.

The Bio-T was practically under him now. He crawled on his belly across the mezzanine to the first door and reached up for the handle. It turned in his hand. He pushed the door open and wriggled in. It was foolish. He understood the psychology of it, the need to have a barrier, any kind of barrier, between him and the predator hunting him, but it was too much movement, too much noise. As he closed the door behind him as quietly as he could, Tyler heard just the slightest sound of someone on the metal stairs to the mezzanine.

He was in a minimalist office space. A desk, an ergonomic chair and a modular AV/holographic port for a P-Dat were the only objects in the office. There was nothing in the furniture to suggest any kind of personality at work here.

Tyler scuttled to the far side of the office, behind the desk, away from the door, and drew his service weapon. That was when he saw it. Lying on the desk were several sheets of paper. They looked out of place in this spartan environment.

Tyler looked to the door. Nothing. He listened. No sound. He grabbed the papers, flipped up his photoreactive veil and read. What he was looking at didn't make any sense. First of all, it was a hard copy of a shipping manifest. Few processes, let alone supply chain, required hard copies these days. Second of all, it was a Chisholm Meats shipping manifest, for live cattle to be transported to New Kiev, a colony world belonging to the communist Union of Progressive Peoples in the demilitarized Borderline Region of the Frontier, set up in the wake of the Tientsin Campaign. He couldn't understand what it was doing here. If the day's events had proved nothing else, it was that Chisholm Meats and the church were two mutually antagonistic organizations.

A shadow fell across the office window. A figure out on the mezzanine, backlit by the faint ultraviolet light. Tyler put down the shipping manifest and aimed his service weapon at the door. He was surprised that whomsoever was outside couldn't hear his heart hammering in his chest. The figure was still for so long that Tyler almost convinced himself they had always been there. He was struggling to breathe, trying to will himself into not having a panic attack. He wondered if all the augmentations the Bio-T had undergone meant that she could actually smell his fear.

She moved.

Tyler felt his bowels loosen.

He saw the door handle start to turn slowly.

Crouched in the corner. His gun held outstretched. He had to decide if he was going to fire.

The door creaked open.

Gunplay would be a huge escalation.

The Bio-T was a grotesque shadow in the pale light. Even backlit Tyler was terribly aware that her torso was a peeled atrocity, like she was an undead creature from some commercial horror dream given form. She didn't say anything, but she was staring straight at him.

"I need you to move and then I am going to leave. That way nobody gets hurt," he said.

She didn't move.

"I don't want to shoot you." It didn't feel like much of a threat. "Please." It sounded like he was begging.

This time she did move. Reaching out with one hand, Tyler's finger tensing on the trigger of his weapon, she knocked once on the wall next to the door. Then she returned to her original position. Still standing in the doorway. Still blocking his escape.

Tyler felt his legs start to cramp. He stood up.

"Now I'm going to leave, so you will move, or I will have to shoot you."

There was no response. He tried to take a step forward but couldn't make himself do it.

His heart sank as he heard a nearby door open and close.

"Step aside please."

Now the Bio-T moved out of the doorway. Dawkins was standing there in gray utilitarian shorts and a T-shirt.

"Special Agent Matterton," Dawkins said. His voice flat, devoid of emotion.

Dawkins moved into the office, keeping close to the external wall. Tyler had a choice, but he chose to keep his gun leveled at the Bio-T. She was the greater threat. Dawkins peered behind his desk and saw the shipping manifest on the floor where Tyler had left it. Dawkins looked back up at him; even in the dim light Tyler could make out the sympathy on Dawkins' face. That was when he knew he was dead.

"You kill a federal agent, they never stop coming after you," he told Dawkins. "People know where I am."

The church administrator said nothing.

Tyler swung the gun around so it was pointing at Dawkins.

"That's really not the threat you think it is," Dawkins told him. He sounded resigned, almost sad.

"Why don't I turn myself in?" Tyler asked. He took one hand away from his weapon and pulled his P-Dat from one of his pouches.

Now Dawkins' expression was almost apologetic. Tyler was running out of options. He wasn't sure it was even a conscious decision when he swung the pistol towards the office's window and fired a burst, started running, then fired another burst. The bullets fragmented the plexiglass but didn't break it: he did that himself when he threw himself at the window. The plexiglass shattered and he hit the metal of the mezzanine, hard, a mere few feet from Dawkins. The Bio-T was already pushing Dawkins out of the way. Tyler knew he only had moments before she caught him. Then he heard the screaming. Dawkins dived for cover as the Bio-T crouched down, still moving towards Tyler. Tyler had no idea what was happening, but holes were appearing in the mezzanine platform. He pushed his phone into its pouch and threw himself forwards, sliding under the mezzanine's railings and falling onto the stairway to the ground level. That was when he was able to work out what was happening. Someone, was firing up through the mezzanine. The screaming was the sound of thorn-like, hypersonic, penetrators chewing through metal.

Tyler slithered over the side of the steps, gripping

with one hand, almost losing his weapon as he swung under and dropped to the floor. He could see Harris standing by the open door to the hypersleep pod chamber, firing burst after burst up through the mezzanine. She shouted something at him. Tyler didn't even have to lipread the word: *Move*! He was already running.

Behind him a bulky figure leaped from the mezzanine. As Tyler ran past Harris, the extractor shifted her aim. Three sharp pops as Tyler jumped over the lip of the hypersleep pod chamber's door. He turned to cover Harris as the grenades the extractor had fired from her carbine's underslung grenade launcher exploded. Fire and force blossomed on the main floor of the genetics laboratory as the explosion tore through expensive equipment, throwing benches up into the air.

Harris moved quickly into the hypersleep pod chamber, ejecting the spent magazine from his carbine as she did so.

A figure leaped high through smoke and fire. The Bio-T, with her pinned open flesh, looked like a demon jumping through the flames of hell. Tyler opened his mouth to shout a warning, but Harris was already in and hitting the door mechanism. The door slid shut and immediately the metal frame started to glow red.

Something hit the door hard enough to dent the metal, making it bulge inwards.

Harris was about to slide another magazine into her

carbine when someone grabbed her from behind and lifted her into the air by her neck.

Tyler was bringing his service weapon up before he realized it was a Serena-model artificial person. He hesitated, then fired. A single shot to the head. Moving closer, firing again and then a third time. The Serena staggered and then finally collapsed, milky internal fluids running from the holes in her face. The artificial person pulled Harris to the floor, her neck still in the Serena's death grip.

Tyler moved to help, holstering his side arm. Harris's eyes went wide. Too late Tyler realized someone was moving towards him. He turned, another Serena sprinting silently at him. Then she staggered, and again, bullets tearing into her as Harris fired multiples bursts from her own, integrally suppressed sidearm, even as she was being throttled. The second Serena collapsed as the slide flew back on Harris's sidearm. She had almost reached them.

Tyler grabbed the extractor. It felt like desecration standing on the corpse of the first Serena to get the leverage to pull Harris free. Harris rubbed her neck, glaring at Tyler for a moment.

"Find Fitzgerald," she told Tyler.

Tyler was staring at the Serena he had killed. Her eyes lifeless. Seeing her bullet-exposed internals, it was clear that she wasn't human but also that she had been alive.

"Hey!" Harris snapped.

Tyler's head wrenched round to stare at the extractor as she reloaded her sidearm.

Tyler nodded. He was breathing heavily from exertion and panic, and he was drenched in sweat.

The door was smoking. Tyler was pretty sure that Harris had run a fuse-strip around the door frame before she had come to his aid. As soon as the metal door had slid shut, it had effectively welded itself to the frame.

Harris trotted towards what looked as though it used to be a fire exit. Reloading her carbine as she moved. The ex-fire exit had metal plates bolted over it.

Tyler felt eyes on him. He turned back to the internal door and saw Dawkins staring at him through the small window.

Reloading his sidearm, Tyler moved away from the door taking a moment to understand his surroundings. They were in a large, concrete-floored open space. The two walls without doors were lined with organic-looking hypersleep pods shaped like sleek eggs. There were five offset rows of ten pods on either wall. Most were open. Only about a dozen had their transparent lids down.

Tyler glanced in one of the empty pods. It was little more than an empty metal shell. The closed ones, however, were all fed by slick, faintly organic-looking cables that seemed to pulse with an inner life as Tyler watched.

Harris was attaching some kind of collapsible frame to the metal plates over the fire exit.

Tyler reached the first occupied hypersleep pod. It was filled with exactly the kind of freezing mist that he would expect from such a pod. The mist cleared enough for him to make out that the occupant was female. He gasped and almost threw himself away from the pod when he saw that she had some kind of biological mask covering the bottom part of her face. Pulsing bladders on the biotech device/creature breathed with her. The pod she was in was lined with a contoured resinous material that reminded Tyler of Snell's lair beneath the printers.

Then she opened her eyes. Pitiless black pools stared at him. Tyler let out an involuntarily yelp and staggered back.

"Wind your fucking neck in and find Fitzgerald!" Harris shouted at him.

Tyler moved to the next pod. It took a moment to check through the freezing mist, but it wasn't him. Then the next, and the next. Even if he found Fitzgerald, Tyler wasn't sure how he was going to get him out of the pod. Harris presumably had a brute force answer of some kind.

Then the pods started opening.

"Harris…" Tyler said before realizing he'd used the extractor's name.

"Fitzgerald!" Harris snapped.

The next pod. No. At least as they were opening, he could see their inhabitants more easily. The next. No. The next. Tyler had to climb up the pods to the third row: that was where he found Fitzgerald. Their target was still unconscious. He had one of the living bladder masks covering the bottom part of his face and then something similar over his groin. He was lying in a shallow bath of pearlescent liquid.

A moment's indecision, but Tyler knew he just had to get on with it. He grabbed the bladder mask and pulled. He tore the thing off Fitzgerald, ripping an oesophageal intubation tube out of his throat. He did the same with the living groin covering, ripping out organic penile and anal catheters. Tyler didn't want to think too much about that.

He struggled to get a grip on the unconscious Fitzgerald's flesh because he was so slippery from the liquid inside the pod. Then Harris was at the other end of the hypersleep pod.

"Hold on tight," the extractor told him, "Fire in the hole." She squeezed the radio detonator she was holding three times in quick succession. Despite the frame charge being shaped to direct the energy against the metal plate and the wall, the overpressure almost tore Tyler off the pod. He just managed to hold on. He lost hearing in one ear and heard ringing in the other. The chamber was full of choking dust, though little in the way of smoke.

It was the first time Tyler had seen Harris smile, though it was more of a grin. She clambered into the pod and started pushing Fitzgerald's bulk, trying to curl under him and use her leg muscles to push him out. They managed to get him to a tipping point where they could lower him to the floor, but he slipped through their fingers and half slid, half fell to the concrete.

Tyler jumped down, grabbed Fitzgerald under his armpits and started dragging him through the dust towards where he thought the wall was. Harris was following, her carbine sweeping left and right. Tyler wasn't sure if it was his overactive imagination or he was actually catching glimpses of movement in the dust. Harris reached out for him, correcting his direction. She turned around when they reached the hole, covering the inside of the chamber.

Tyler managed to drag Fitzgerald's not-insignificant bulk out into the mud and falling, gritty snow. A rental prairie rover was waiting for them. The tailgate open as was the passenger door. Lace was in the driver seat.

The hypersonic screams made Tyler jump as Harris fired back into the hypersleep pod chamber. It was the burst of adrenaline that Tyler needed to manhandle Fitzgerald's bulk into the back of the rover, dragging him roughly into the covered cargo bed.

Moments later Harris threw herself into the back of the rover.

"Go! Go! Go!" she shouted.

Lace put his foot down. Wheels spun in the mud before achieving traction and surging forward. The hole in the bolted-over emergency exit was still bleeding powdered concrete, the cloud illuminated from within by the facility's internal lighting.

Harris pulled her legs up into the rover and pulled the bottom part of the tailgate up.

A sprinting, naked, figure emerged from the dust cloud. Mud splattered his chalk-white legs as he powered after the rover.

Harris levelled her carbine at the Bio-T.

"Faster, faster, faster!" Tyler shouted unhelpfully at Lace.

The figure was gaining on them.

"Lace, I'm gonna' drop the hammer on this prick if you don't hurry the fuck up," Harris said.

Lace didn't answer. His foot was down as far as it went: as the buildings shot by, Tyler realized that they were running out of town.

He looked back. The Bio-T was no longer gaining on them. Then they were being thrown around as Lace took them onto the prairie and cut south-west, making for the highway.

Tyler looked down at Fitzgerald. He had maybe fifty pounds on Tyler, probably more. He had no idea how he'd managed to drag him, let alone manhandle him into the rover. Adrenaline was a wonder.

When they reached the highway, Harris popped

the cap off a syrette full of sedative and stabbed it into Fitzgerald's thigh. Then she held up the syrette, looking at the bent needle. She sighed and started pulling smart restraints from her load-carrying vest and used them to bind Fitzgerald's arms and legs, doubling up on each pair of limbs.

"Well, that was a little hairy, wasn't it?" Harris said. She was grinning again.

13

This was a mistake, but Cass figured it didn't matter that much. Between being the instigator of the greatest loss of life in a law enforcement shooting incident in the colony's existence, the pistol-whipping of a subordinate, and her attempt at defying the judge, her marshal career was effectively over. It had been a busy day. So, she decided to end it by aiding and abetting a kidnapping.

She had been surprised to receive Agent Matterton's text and was looking forward to having it read back to her in court during her inevitable trial. As she sat at her desk in the marshal's station, waiting, leaning on the Trayler shotgun, she half suspected that Fitzgerald would just crush Harris and Matterton's head himself. After all, Snell had seemed a broken man, only to turn serial killer. The Fitzgerald family didn't know what they were getting into, and she couldn't see two mercenaries like Harris and Lace warning them. They would take the money and run. Still, arranging a place to lay low until they could be snuck off world seemed like the least Cass could do for Matterton.

The explosion still took her by surprise. It caused her to spill the coffee she had been sipping, scolding herself. Sorgram and Deputy Romane were both looking at her.

"What was that?" Sorgram asked. He still hadn't gone off duty, which made Cass suspicious. She wished he'd just go home.

"It sounded like a breaching charge," Cass said. She wasn't an explosives expert by any stretch of the imagination but she'd heard her fair share of breaching detonations. It had sounded like a pretty significant one as well. She cursed Harris and Lace. Explosives was a little over the top.

Cass was on her feet, as was Sorgram. She wanted to tell him to stay but couldn't really justify it.

"Where?" Sorgram asked.

"Guess," Cass told him. "Check the cameras on Jersey Street," she told Romane, who was working through the town's screens.

"Got it," Romane said. "It's the back of the old genetics facility."

Sorgram was looking at her.

"How'd you know it was the church?" he demanded.

"Because it's always the church," Cass snapped, and

then to Romane: "We're in the prairie rover." She was sick of trying to slog through thick mud. "Get Michaels and Rodriguez over there, now." The other two town nightshift deputies had been on patrol, though she'd sent them far from the church. "Amsa and Williams are on call, get them over there as well."

Romane nodded.

Sorgram was already making for the door.

"Sorgram," Cass called. She threw him one of their aging AR-150s. The deputy caught the assault carbine as Cass collected four magazines for the weapon and followed Sorgram out.

Sorgram was driving, making for the high-rise lights of the shuttle port. It would still be faster to drive to the center of the spokes formed by the town's roads and then turn down onto Jersey Street than run through the alleys. Cass had just finished loading the carbine for Sorgram and secured the magazines for the weapon in easy reach as the deputy slewed the prairie rover onto the asphalt that surrounded the shuttle.

She heard the screaming as the rover lurched into the muddy slush of Jersey Street, the falling snow was picked out in the glare of their vehicle's headlights.

"What was that?" Sorgram asked. He sounded spooked. It took a moment for Cass to work it through.

"Hypersonic rounds, automatic fire," she told her

deputy. She hoped it was Harris doing the firing because the body armor Cass and her deputies were wearing wouldn't stop penetrator projectiles flying at that velocity.

People were appearing out on the boardwalk, most in their bedclothes, looking south towards the sound of the explosion and gunfire. Many held guns.

"Put on the lights," Cass told Sorgram. The bar of lights mounted atop the rover's roll bar started flashing red and blue. She needed people off the streets if there was going to be a firefight.

"This a hostage situation?" Sorgram asked, the rover's revolving lights making grotesque shadows from the armed bystanders.

"Unknown—leave the talking to me. If there's going to be shooting, I'll initiate unless you've come under fire yourself. Clear?"

Sorgram nodded, but the worst of it was that Cass couldn't trust him to have her back.

In the headlights they could see the back of the genetics facility building. The source of the explosion was clear. There was a door-shaped hole where there had previously been a welded-shut fire exit. The fire exit in question was embedded in the wall of the store on the other side of the street. Someone, presumably Harris, had overcooked the breaching charge by the looks of it. Three of the Bio-Ts were standing in the mud around the hole, gazing out impassively at the slowly advancing crowd.

The flashing red lights gave their pale skin a hellish cast.

Sorgram slewed the prairie rover to a halt in the muddy slush. Cass was out of the rover, chamber checking the shotgun again. Sorgram spent a moment storing the magazines for the carbine in the pouches of his body armor and then he climbed out as well. Moving to one side, for a clear shot, carbine at his shoulder but muzzle down. Sorgram or not, Cass was glad for the cover.

"Move aside," Cass told the Bio-Ts, knowing they wouldn't. They didn't. "You're obstructing a marshal in the execution of her duties, so either start talking or get out of the fucking way."

No response. She didn't relish getting close enough to one of them to try and push past. Not after what she'd seen today.

"I know you guys can talk. We spoke to Fitzgerald… Brother Dak yesterday."

Nothing.

Just as Cass made to move forwards, more spinning lights lit up Jersey Street, accompanied by the sound of engines.

"It's Bobbie and Ray," Sorgram called. Bobbie Sykes was the drone-jockey, the one-woman fire service for Steer City. Ray Velazquez was one of the town's two paramedics.

"Keep them back," Cass told him.

Sorgram moved back, keeping his carbine trained on

the Bio-Ts. Cass heard him speaking with the other two first responders.

"Marshal, you okay?" Velazquez called.

"I'm good, Ray," the marshal lied.

"Just so you know, I've got a shotgun in the cab." Velazquez was a good guy but a little given to macho behavior. As an ex-marine she didn't think the Marshal Service provided nearly enough firearms training for this kind of situation, never mind adding a civilian to the mix.

Sorgram was back.

"We've heard gunfire and we can see the results of an explosion," the marshal told the Bio-Ts, "under Colonial Law that gives us exigent circumstances to enter your premises. We need to check to see if anyone is hurt, make any appropriate arrests and gather evidence." Tension crept into her voice as she tried not to grip the shotgun too hard. "So, we're coming in there if—"

"We are?" Sorgram said. He sounded shit-scared.

"If you interfere with us in any way, we will defend ourselves. Is that clear?"

The Bio-Ts didn't respond, didn't move and showed no sign that Cass's words had even registered.

"Ready?" Cass asked Sorgram.

"You don't want to wait for a few more deputies?" he asked after a moment or two's hesitation. He didn't sound ready.

Cass shouldered the shotgun. She did want to wait,

but she had no idea what was happening in there and couldn't take the risk of losing more time. For all she knew Harris and/or Matterton were still inside. Though the explosive exit suggested someone had gotten away.

As she moved closer to the breached doorway, she could see that there were at least four other Bio-Ts on the other side of the hole. She knew this was going to get messy. She heard running from within the genetics facility.

"Marshal, wait!" She recognized Dawkins, out-of-breath voice from within.

Cass stopped moving and Sorgram followed suit.

The Bio-Ts parted and a sweaty Dawkins appeared, wearing what Cass assumed he slept in. He was trying to catch his breath.

Michaels, one of the nightshift deputies, arrived on the scene, grabbing his AR-150 from its saddle sheath as he slid off the hover ATV. A moment later Rodriguez turned up as well. Both of them took up positions with their weapons leveled at the Bio-Ts. Cass wasn't sure she'd ever been so happy to see anyone.

"Dawkins, stand your people down. We're entering your premises to investigate this explosion," Cass told the huffing-and-puffing Dawkins.

"Marshal, a moment," Dawkins said.

"No!" Cass snapped. "Now!"

Dawkins looked up at her more surprised than anything else.

"One of our people has been kidnapped," Dawkins told her, "Agent Matterton was involved. The explosion was them escaping."

This was good. It sounded as though Matterton had made it out and they had managed to extract Fitzgerald.

"Fine, I'll arrest Matterton and we can get on with finding your missing guy, but at the moment you're acting against your own best interests," Cass said.

"Marshal, I'm afraid given your association with Special Agent Matterton you're compromised in this matter. Also, we don't know that this wasn't done at the behest of federal authorities. No, I'm afraid I cannot provide you access to our facilities until we can sort this out legally."

She found herself wondering when people had decided that magical thinking superseded the law.

Something made Cass glance to the edge of the boardwalk on her left. Serena was standing there, watching the Bio-Ts. She had clearly positioned herself as close as she could without putting herself in anybody's field of fire.

"Here's how it gets handled legally. I arrest you for obstruction of justice and anyone resisting gets dealt with."

Dawkins stared at her.

"Move! Move!" It was Williams running along the boardwalk ordering the bystanders out of her way, Amsa with her. Both women wearing their uniform pants, but under their body armor they wore their PJs. They joined the other deputies, adding another venerable AR-150 and a shotgun to the weapons leveled at the Bio-Ts.

"I am not going to take any risks with the safety of my people," Cass told Dawkins, knowing that he was shrewd enough to understand her meaning.

Dawkins stared at her.

Cass was aware of Williams and Sorgram glancing her way. There was a general shifting of position amongst the deputies.

"Marshal, you are truly out of control," Dawkins said. He seemed very calm in the face of having so many weapons pointed at him.

The silence stretched out.

Cass found the tension bleeding out of her. She knew what this silence was. A gunfight was inevitable now, so there was no point in worrying about it. It was like a switch in her head. She had a bead on her first target. She would go for head shots. They just needed to take the Bio-Ts down before they were able to close with the deputies.

"Boss," it was Amsa, "they're unarmed."

Cass knew her deputy was right but having watched a Bio-T smash a cowboy's head in she knew they weren't wrestling one of these transhuman nightmares into the back of a prairie rover. She didn't want any of her people within arms' reach of them. Well, maybe Sorgram. The thing of it was, firing on them was almost certainly proactive self-defense but that could get very difficult to prove at her murder trial. It was optics. She couldn't do her job because of optics.

"I'm afraid I no longer have sufficient faith in the Steer City Marshal Service to allow you entry to the facility. If you want in you will have to shoot your way through us," Dawkins told her.

"Suits me," Deputy Michaels muttered. He had never been a fan of the church.

"Are we arresting these guys?" Sorgram asked.

She didn't like how any of this was playing out. She was aware of more and more people edging towards the facility. The increasingly angry-sounding murmurs coming from the crowd. She needed to de-escalate.

"Stand down," she muttered and then repeated it more loudly so everyone could hear.

The Bio-Ts remained impassive, red-lit ghouls in the spinning lights. Dawkins at least had the courtesy to look relieved.

"You're kidding," Michaels said.

"Enough," Sorgram said.

"Dissension in the ranks?" Dawkins asked.

"Yeah, it happens when your ranks aren't mentally spayed meat puppets," Cass told him, lowering her shotgun, the other deputies relaxed as well. Though all were keeping a wary eye on the Bio-Ts.

"Rodriguez, Michaels, disperse this crowd," Sorgram said.

"Sorgram, I want you here as well," Cass told her 'second-in-command'.

"You want me on crowd control?" Sorgram demanded, insolence returning to his tone.

Cass walked over to Sorgram.

"Look, I get that we don't like each other and I shouldn't've pistol-whipped you—"

"You think?"

"I'll pay for that, and that's just the right of it, but for now we've got bigger problems to worry about. I need people here out back. I need people round the front watching the entrance to the slaughterhouse. And I want someone watching the roof."

"There's five of us," Sorgram pointed out. "Six, we include Romane."

"We need Romane on the cameras," Cass said. Sorgram nodded. Something else they'd managed to agree on. "You watch the roof from the Stagecoach, coordinate the others."

Sorgram was just looking at her, his expression one of open suspicion.

"And you'll be?" he asked.

"I'm going to find Matterton," she told him.

"Know where he is?" He tried to make it sound casual but it just didn't sound casual enough.

"I know where to start looking," she told him.

"Dawkins is right, you're compromised. Why don't I go and find him?"

Cass was quiet. She didn't just want to come out and say that she didn't trust him. That he was in Chisholm's pocket, Charter's creature. She'd said it before but now she needed his cooperation. Instead, she pointed to the breach.

"You'll get your day, but this is nothing to do with you and me."

He considered this for a moment and then nodded. It was clear that it cost him.

"Tell everyone to keep their distance," she added. "And we err on the side of caution. Anyone thinks they're in danger they respond with force, yeah?"

"Agreed," Sorgam told her.

Cass turned away from the senior deputy and waded through the muddy slush back towards the prairie rover. A figured appeared next to the vehicle. Cass brought the shotgun to bear, before realizing it was Serena.

"May I accompany you?" Serena asked.

"Nope," Cass told her as she climbed into the vehicle.

"Are you going to arrest Special Agent Matterton?" Serena asked.

Cass just closed the door and pressed the ignition. She turned the prairie ranger around as her deputies cleared the thinning crowd out of the muddy street. In the rear-view mirror, she could see Serena standing in the mud watching the rover. Cass headed north towards the lights of the shuttle port. She took a left turning off

Port Street and onto Longhorn Street, which linked to the highway, that would take her south into the plains.

Cass disabled the rover's transponder and switched off her P-Dat's location finder. Her career in law enforcement had been on life support anyway. Now it was dead. Her pension would be a significant prison term. At best.

A light dust blew up off the prairies, flurries forming in the Rover's lights across the empty highway. Ahead Cass could make out the glare of Coldstream Station.

She wondered just how hard they would come after her. Sorgram was a stuffed shirt, and as far as she could tell she wasn't much of a threat to Charters, who was really calling the shots. The church, on the other hand, assuming they had sacrificed two of their own by sending them to Alexandria after Snell, could come after her pretty hard. Or rather they would come after Matterton, Lace, Harris and most-importantly Fitzgerald. Unless something changed in the very near future, she would be standing next to them when that happened.

She had some moves she could make. She had friends out on the prairies, particularly amongst the independent ranchers. If they wanted her, they were going to have to work for it. The unknown here was how much influence the church could bring to bear. She had not expected Judge Khan to turn on her the way he had.

In terms of tracking her there was little in the way of satellite coverage on GL3, but any of Coldstream Station's perimeter cameras and drones would've noticed her passing, as well as, Matterton and the other kidnappers before her.

Ahead of her the highway disappeared into the darkness as snowflakes and dust threw themselves at the windscreen.

Cass turned the prairie rover onto the Jermaine property in the early hours of the morning, taking the long, meandering dust track up towards the three-story, cut-stone ranch house.

A masked Harvey was waiting for her as she pulled up in front of the house, carrying a magazine-fed, semi-automatic hunting rifle. He gestured for her to put the rover in the barn, out of sight.

Cass pulled up next to the rental that Harris, Lace and Matterton had presumably arrived in with Fitz-gerald. Even in the barn Cass could hear the screaming as soon as she climbed out of the rover. While there were a few noises in the mix that could have charitably been considered words, the screaming sounded inhuman. It reminded Cass of marines and enemy combatants that had been injured beyond their ability to cope with the pain during the Dog War.

She slid the Traylor Model 15 shotgun and her own rifle, still in its bag, out of the rack in the rover's cab and headed back towards the house.

"This isn't what we agreed," Harvey said by way of greeting, falling in with her as she crossed the yard towards the house. The dust was blowing stronger out here, making Cass cough.

She wasn't sure what to tell the old farmer.

"I'm sorry," she said in the end. It felt like she'd said that a lot recently. "Where's your stock, still up on the high pasture?" Though she couldn't see him leaving them out there even in a light dust blow like this.

Ahead of them Matterton was a shadow on the stone and wood porch, backlit in the open doorway. A sniper's dream.

"Sold them," he said looking down at the ground as they reached the porch.

"Oh Harvey, I'm sorry," Cass told him. They stopped; she threw Matterton the shotgun and a caddy of shells. He was still wearing stealth clothing. She turned back to Harvey.

"The Steer City Cattle Company gave me what they could," he told her.

She suspected it was little comfort but at least he hadn't been forced to sell them to Chisholm.

Cass almost didn't see Harris leaning against the stone work. She was dressed in gray as well, wearing load-bearing body armor, a compact, Belgian-made

EM carbine slung horizontally across her chest, one hand resting on the grip. The carbine was presumably the source of the hyper-velocity rounds she'd heard earlier in the day.

"A bomb, in my town?" Cass asked. Except it wasn't her town anymore.

Harris just shrugged. She didn't give a shit about anything except payday. Cass had suspected that she didn't like Harris. Now her suspicions were confirmed.

"What's going on?" Cass said turning to Matterton as he was attaching the shotgun-cartridge caddy to his body armor. "And don't silhouette yourself in the doorway."

"I've been telling him," Harris said.

Fitzgerald's screams rang out across the prairie. Cass could see Harvey's point. Someone hiding out, even for a couple of weeks, was one thing. This was another.

"He suffering separation anxiety?" Cass finally asked as nobody seemed forthcoming. She made her way into the house. Harvey, closing the door after them, leaving Harris outside.

"We took Fitzgerald out of one of the pods," Matterton told her. He had to raise his voice to be heard. The ex-special agent looked like shit. "The pods were disconcerting," he continued. "It was biotechnology. His face was covered by some kind of living bladder, with an intubation-like tube down his throat. It was connected to the pod by what looked like a concertinaed intestine."

Cass just stared at Matterton. Even with everything she knew about the church they somehow just kept getting weirder.

"Similar catheter set-up, and we were not gentle when we dragged him out," Matterton added.

Cass didn't really want to think too much about a living biotech catheter being torn out.

"The interior of the whole pod was biological. Like the inside of a shellfish or something." The distaste only crept into Matterton's voice towards the end. It was clear that he was exhausted.

"What have you gotten me into?" Harvey asked. He was right. Cass shouldn't have brought this trouble to his door. Just another mistake in a long line of fuck-ups.

"I'll get them out of here as quickly as I can," she told the old farmer.

Harvey pointed up the stairs towards the sound of the screaming.

"That right there is why I don't go into town unless I have to," he told them and then walked into his lounge, his rifle over one shoulder.

"How are you holding up?" Cass asked Matterton. He looked as pale as a Bio-T, his features drawn.

"The screaming's grating on me," he told her.

Cass turned and followed the screaming up the stairs to the second floor, she found herself struggling to work through what Matterton had told them. She got that the church was working with some cutting-edge bio-tech, but she'd never heard of anything remotely like a living hypersleep pod.

Fitzgerald was securely strapped to a now-broken bed in one of Harvey's spare rooms. The Bio-T screamed and thrashed around. His pale skin was covered in flop sweat. Lace was standing over him. The heavy-set, bearded cult specialist looked at his wit's end.

"I can't even sedate him!" Lace shouted at him. "His skin's armored, doesn't even feel like skin! The needles keep breaking!"

"Try the eye," Cass suggested.

Lace just stared at her.

Cass sighed and moved to the open field medic kit atop a rough-hewn chest of drawers and took out one of the auto-syrettes.

"Hold him down," she told them.

Lace moved to help Matterton. Between them, they managed to hold Fitzgerald's head steady enough for Cass to push the needle of the auto-syrette into the black pool of one of Fitzgerald's eyes. There was enough sedative in the syrette to knock out a buffalo but Cass figured that it was better to be safe than sorry. Slowly Fitzgerald stopped struggling and finally was still.

Lace put a stethepad on the Bio-T's chest.

"He still with us?" Cass asked.

"I think so. I get that he looks mostly human, only

cosmetic changes, but that guy's physiology is really fucking different." Clearly Lace was also struggling with the situation.

"Any idea what's up with him? Why the screaming?" Cass asked.

Lace shrugged.

"Withdrawal," Matterton suggested.

Lace and Cass both looked at the FBI agent.

"Could be," Lace finally agreed.

Cass had seen withdrawal before. It looked like a miserable experience but nothing like this.

"Look, I can't help this guy." Lace admitted. "He needs medical support well beyond my capabilities before I even attempt to speak with him."

Cass was pretty sure that they had all worked hard together to discover the perfect nexus point of cluster and fuck.

The three of them looked at the unconscious Fitzgerald.

"Serena," Matterton finally said.

"Well, you're full of bright ideas today," Cass muttered, but she had been thinking the same thing. Serena was the only one with the skill set to help here. The marshal was very much looking forward to her time in prison, she decided. It would be a welcome respite.

"Won't she just arrest us all?" Lace asked.

"Probably," Matterton admitted.

14

Tyler practically had to beg Serena to come. She had a degree of latitude in how she interpreted her programming to follow the law. He knew that he had made a decent argument that the rule of law had broken down on Gamma Leporis 3. Even allowing for that, there was no question that his actions had taken him well beyond anything even remotely resembling his legal remit. Nevertheless, some hours later he found himself standing on the porch watching a rental hover ATV make its way down the dirt track towards the Jermaine farmhouse.

Masked, Serena climbed down from the ATV as the impellers stopped spinning, beating the dust from her clothes. She slung the cumbersome bags that contained the field forensic and medkits over her shoulders as though they weighed nothing, and walked towards him.

"Where is Matthew Fitzgerald?" she asked him. No greeting, nothing. In theory, artificial people were supposed to have little in the way of emotional responses to stimuli. In practice, she wasn't angry, just very disappointed. Though it was pathetic, Tyler found her disapproval somehow hopeful. It was an emotional response of a kind after all.

"Serena?" Stock said from the landing as Tyler and Serena reached the top of the stairs. The marshal had stationed herself in the master bedroom, overlooking the front of the house, on what she called overwatch.

"Marshal, can I assume that you were part of this conspiracy?" Serena asked, looking over at the marshal.

Stock didn't say anything.

"She found us after the fact and, like I said on the call, we have some concerns..." Tyler's explanation faltered. She had turned back to look at him. Even grimy with dust she was beautiful, and it was obvious that she knew he was lying.

"My only concern is with Fitzgerald," Serena told them.

Inside the spare bedroom, Lace was still with the kidnapped Bio-T.

"He's starting to come to," Lace told them.

Fitzgerald's head was rolling from side to side like a drunk.

"Did you tell anyone else you were coming here?" Lace asked.

Tyler didn't like the way Serena ignored the question.

"Serena?" Tyler said.

She turned to look at him.

"I did not tell anyone else I was coming here," Serena said. "Against my better judgment."

Lace looked between Serena and Tyler. He didn't seem convinced. Tyler wasn't either.

The Bio-T muttered something as Serena kneeled by him to take his vitals.

"He's been saying things. I can't make much out. Something about hollow people. Maybe hollow cattle, or the people are cattle, I don't know," Lace told them. "Chances are we're catching a glimpse of their inner belief structure. What they tell the true believers to alienate them from external influences."

Suddenly Fitzgerald tried to wrench himself upright against his restraints. Every muscle was taut, his face a rictus mask. It made Tyler jump and then his service weapon was in his hand. Lace had a sidearm drawn as well.

"Communion… the goddess." Each word sounded as though it was torn from Fitzgerald's throat.

Serena knelt on Fitzgerald's chest forcing him back down onto the mattress. One hand held his alabaster head still as she administered sedative with the other. The syrette's needle sank into the black orb of an eye.

Then she stepped away, giving the sedative time to take effect. She looked over at Tyler. *Goddess.* They had both heard it clear as day. The same word that Snell had used when talking to his mother.

"It does sound like he's begging for a fix," Lace said.

Tyler nodded, holstering his weapon as the sedative took effect and Fitzgerald sank back into the bed.

"I'm disappointed," Lace added. "I was hoping for a cult centered on the female divine for a change."

Tyler could see his point. 'Goddess', in this context, sounded like the street name of some kind of drug. While Tyler didn't have the anything like the expertise that Lace did, he was aware that many cults and other coercive organizations used narcotics as a means of control.

"Leave me with him," Serena said.

"I don't think that's a very good idea," Tyler said.

"I am not going to run off with him, Agent Matterton," Serena told him.

"I'll stay with her," Lace said.

Reluctantly Tyler left the room.

Harris was waiting for him outside in the hall. He hadn't heard her come up the stairs.

"We're going to have to run again," she whispered.

"Let her do her thing first," Tyler said.

"We're working an extraction, not trying to gather evidence, because I assure you that you're not an FBI agent anymore." He nodded towards Serena. "She's the enemy now."

Tyler stared at Harris. He knew that the extractor would have no compunction about killing Serena if she became a problem. He wanted to warn Harris off, but he knew it would do no good whatsoever. Tyler flashed back to the Serena-model artificial person he'd shot in the genetics facility. He should tell Serena to just leave. Sneak out when Harris's attention was elsewhere. He felt selfish. Doing what many of his colleagues did, using their artificial person partners as tools, as expendable resources. The problem was that Tyler had to know, had to understand what was happening here. He had to know how Snell had been created and what had happened to all the other church recruits.

Harris read it in his expression. There was an unpleasant smile on her face as she turned and headed back down the stairs.

"Asshole," Tyler muttered to himself.

Tyler awoke to find Serena standing over him. Even in the darkness of the farmhouse's lounge, Tyler could see that her features were expressionless and not the designer sympathy that normally greeted him when she woke him from a troubled sleep.

He looked over at the other sofa. Stock was asleep, snoring gently. Harris and the farmer, Harvey, were keeping watch, while Lace, presumably, remained with Fitzgerald.

Tyler pushed himself up. He was suddenly very awake but not in a good way, in the way he felt in his chest. A fight or flight response.

"What?' he managed.

"I've finished my preliminaries," she said.

"Where's Lace?" Tyler asked.

"Asleep. If you left Mr Jermaine on guard, he is also asleep."

Stock stirred.

Tyler checked that his P-Dat's earpiece was still in place. It was.

"Tyler to Harris, copy."

"Harris here," her voice soft over the line.

"Where are you?" Tyler asked.

"In the copse, down by the bend in the road," she told him.

"Okay, I've just woken up. I think Harvey has fallen asleep."

There was a pause. Tyler found himself looking at Serena. On the other couch, Stock was sitting up now.

"Understood, making my way back to the house," Harris finally said.

"What's going on?" the marshal asked, rubbing her face.

Tyler told her.

"Let him sleep. I'll take over," she said standing up reaching for her rifle.

"Serena's finished her preliminary examination of Fitzgerald."

Stock turned to look at her.

"I need some coffee," the marshal said.

The three of them sat around the kitchen table, Tyler and Stock both nursing cups of coffee.

"Before I begin it's important that you understand two things: the first is that the equipment I am using is rudimentary for the level of analysis we are striving for," Serena told them. "The second is that the cells that form your bodies have a far greater potential than their inevitable end use. They are biological problem-solving machines that can collaborate with other cells to solve even greater problems." Tyler knew that Serena was simplifying the explanation for the sake of expediency. "Within any given organism, such as a human body, your cells are restricted in the roles they perform by their interrelationships. This is necessary because it means a liver cell does the job it has to do for a liver to function."

"So, something has changed Fitzgerald at a cellular level?" Stock asked.

"I have found a protein that has triggered a morphogenesis: in effect a wide-reaching cellular redevelopment of Fitzgerald's physiology. Increased muscle mass, more efficient nerve connections. In addition, the protein, a by-product thereof, or an additive is either artificially stimulating opioid neuropeptides, or delivering an endorphin hit to provide a euphoric quality to the experience."

"We think 'Goddess' may be a drug," Tyler told her. "Or perhaps this protein."

"Have you ever seen anything like this protein before?" Stock asked.

Serena gave the question some thought.

"I have not, though the closest analogy I can think of is to that of the royal jelly that was secreted by the now-extinct *Apis Mellifera* and fed to larvae to trigger the morphological development of a hive queen."

"Except honey bees were a much simpler form of life than humans are, and royal jelly didn't have a morphological effect on other species," Tyler said. He did not like where this was going.

Stock looked horrified. Tyler suspected that the marshal was sorely missing breaking up barfights.

"It is reductive to describe the honey bee as a simpler organism. After all, humans shared forty-four percent of their genes with the species." Serena explained.

"Is something secreting this protein?" Stock asked.

"It is perhaps best not to speculate," Serena told the marshal. "This protein could have been developed in a laboratory."

"There's a group of people in my town who believe that humans were engineered by alien gods. It's kind of difficult not to speculate," Stock pointed out.

Tyler found himself in complete agreement with the marshal. The analogy with royal jelly was exactly the kind of thing that encouraged speculation—and some pretty wild speculation at that.

"In addition—" Serena started.

"Addition?" Stock demanded.

"—Fitzgerald's skin and bones have both been reinforced with some kind of hardened, polarized silicon material."

"So, he's stronger, faster, and more durable?" Stock said.

"And effectively armored," Serena added.

It got better and better.

"All biotech?" Tyler asked.

Serena nodded.

"Whatever Fitzgerald has become—" Tyler started.

"Becoming," Serena interjected. "I do not believe the process is complete."

"It's what Snell was trying to turn hims—"

"We have movement out here," Harris said over the P-Dat group call they were using for comms.

"Serena, with Lace—look after Fitzgerald," Stock said. "Matterton, second-floor landing, make sure you can see the front door but be aware they may not come through the door. I'll get Harvey." Then over comms: "Any more info, Harris?"

Serena didn't hesitate, Tyler followed her up the stairs.

"Three, no, four at least. They're low, trying to keep it stealthy. Making for the house," Harris said quietly.

"Okay, I want you to keep quiet. Don't let them see you. You're going to call my targets, clear?" Stock said. She was coming up the stairs readying her huge, scoped, lever-action rifle. "If you have to fire, watch your shots. Your EM-driven penetrators will go straight through these walls. We're all on the second floor."

"Just to check," Harris whispered, "the first floor is on the ground, where the doors are."

It was an odd question, Tyler thought, but Stock didn't hesitate to answer in the affirmative anyway.

Matterton took up position in the doorway to the room where Fitzgerald, Lace and Serena were. He had a good view down the stairs and to the front door. Cass was pleased to see that he switched off the lights so as not to silhouette himself again. Lace had moved behind the chest of drawers, his sidearm leveled at the window. Serena was in the process of sedating Fitzgerald again, which was almost certainly for the best.

Cass moved into the already dark back bedroom. Harvey was asleep in a chair in front of the window. By moving the scoped, semi-automatic hunting rifle out of his hands, in case she startled him, he woke up.

"I'm sorry," he said immediately.

Cass gestured for him to be quiet.

"We've got trouble," she told him and was gratified that, age notwithstanding, he became immediately alert. She handed the rifle back. "I need you to watch the rear of the house. Stay back from the window but make sure you've got a good view. You see anyone you call me, you don't fire, 'less I tell you to." It was no way to talk to a man in his own house, but Harvey just nodded.

"Speak to me, Harris," she said over comms as she made her way carefully into the darkened front bedroom. She regretted not setting the room up better earlier in the day, making more of a nest. She'd been too dog tired.

She stood between the bed and the window deathly still. Her chest still ached from the shot her body armor had absorbed earlier in the day, the side of her face throbbing.

"We've two making for the front door. Then one going either side of the house. "I'm by the barn."

The barn was just to the north of the house. Cass's right.

"Harris, I'm going to need you to take out the one on the north side of the house closest to you, on my go," Cass said over comms.

"Understood, the two approaching the house have just emerged from the copse, half way down the drive. They've got a lot of open ground to cover."

The words every sniper liked to hear. She brought the Marlin 12-81 Magnum up to her shoulder. Searching for movement with the naked eye. She saw it. Two of them sprinting towards the house. *Jesus, they're fast,* Cass thought as she brought the rifle up. The scope adjusting for the range and amplifying the ambient light. She could see the Bio-T's face bright as day. They may have been moving quickly, but at least they were coming straight on to Cass. She took a deep breath.

"Go," she said over comms and squeezed the trigger.

The big game rifle going off in the enclosed space sounded like the end of the world. Cass didn't even hear the pane in the window explode, raining glass, as the sizeable muzzle flash lit up the room. The butt slammed back into her shoulder despite the recoil absorbers. She refocused as she worked the lever, ejecting one of the big spent cartridges and chambering another. The Bio-T was on the ground. There was smoke rising from all around him. Cass didn't understand why and had no time to figure it out.

She switched target to the other Bio-T but he had changed direction and was running at an angle for the southern corner of the house. Cass forced herself to take her time to inhale, to lead him, doing ballistic calculations by instinct. Only then was she aware of the hypersonic scream of Harris's carbine as the extractor fired burst after burst from the weapon. Cass could feel the rounds tearing through the house below, hear Harvey's belongings being turned to shrapnel on the first floor beneath her.

Another inhalation. She squeezed. The thunder of another round, the recoil against her shoulder. She got the scope back on target in time to see the Bio-T stagger but not go down, then he disappeared around the south side of the house.

She moved the rifle back to her original target as she worked the lever again. Astonishingly the Bio-T she'd shot was getting up. He was wreathed in the smoke rising from the earth all around him. She fired again, the powerful round all but disintegrating the Bio-T's head.

"One X-Ray down, south of the house," Harris said over comms. "Be aware they take some killing."

Cass guessed an X-Ray was what the Brits called a tango. She was about to report her own kill when she heard Harvey firing his rifle rapidly from the back of the house.

Fuck! I told him to call me.

"Harris, if you don't have a target sweep east around the back of the house," Cass said.

"Moving," from Harris.

"Harvey, what have you got?" Cass said, when the firing stopped, presumably because he'd emptied the hunting rifle's magazine.

"I saw two of them," Harvey shouted to her from the back bedroom, voice full of nervous excitement.

"Use the comms, Harvey," Cass said. "Be aware two have gone south around the side of the house. One tango down out front."

Cass couldn't shake the feeling that the fight was going to be somewhere else now but she knew that someone needed to watch the front of the house as well. She took the time to reload, keeping watch as she did so.

The marshal's first shot had made Tyler jump but not her second or third. Looking down the stairs and seeing the EM-driven penetrators fired from Harris's carbine tear through walls, furniture, the stairs themselves, it was difficult not to feel as though he was in the line of fire. He felt his breath quicken, the violent beat of his heart, his hands slick on the shotgun, but he was holding it together. After all it was his third gunfight of the day.

"Harvey," Stock said over comms. "Take your time. Aim. Harris is going to call out the targets."

"Yeah. Sorry, Marshal, got carried away," the old man replied.

"Harvey," Harris said over comms, "do not fire until I've finished. There's one just come round the south side of the house, making for the back door. Right under you, he's mine. There's another behind those three trees. He's yours, Harvey, on my go."

"Understood," Harvey said.

"Go," Harris said.

Tyler didn't even hear Harvey's shots as Harris's carbine started screaming again.

Tyler almost started firing as he saw movement at the front door. Then one of the Bio-Ts ran straight through it, turning the door to so much kindling. Tyler shouted a warning over comms and then started firing the shotgun. He was sure he was hitting, but the Bio-T was still charging up the stairs towards him, filling his vision. He pulled the trigger again and again. Saw it stagger. Everything seemed to slow down. Panic clawed at his brain. They couldn't be killed. The marshal shouted something at him. They were almost on him.

He stopped. Shifted his aim. Breathed in. Alabaster hands reached for him. He squeezed the trigger. The Bio-T's head turned to bone and smoking yellow pus as they flopped backwards down the stairs. Tyler kept firing as the nearly headless body of the Bio-T slid down the stairs and then fell through them, the wood smoking. Then he realized that he was just dry firing the shotgun.

"Jesus fuck, Matterton!" Cass screamed at him from across the landing in the front bedroom. "You are a law enforcement professional. Aim, then fucking fire. Get that shotgun reloaded!"

Harris was trying to say something over comms.

Tyler felt numb as he tried to remember his firearms training.

"Say again, Harris," Stock said over comms.

"The tango by the back door is down, but I can't confirm the kill, I think Harvey winged the other but

I'm going after him. Harvey, I will go wide. Do not under any circumstances point your weapon at me. Look for movement. Call it out, shoot only if you're sure of your shot."

"Understood," Harvey said over comms, his voice still a little shaky.

Tyler had the butt of the shotgun on his shoulder, the weapon turned on its side as he double-loaded it from the caddy. Sliding two cartridges home at time.

Glass shattered at his back. Two shots from a pistol. Tyler swung around, working the charging handle to chamber a round as he did so. It was the same female Bio-T that had almost had him at the genetics facility earlier in the night. She had lifted Lace off the floor by his head. A dark-colored and very inhuman secondary mouth, lubricated by some kind of viscous fluid, shot out of the Bio-T's mouth and bit through the flesh and skull of Lace's face like it was an apple.

Tyler almost fired but then Serena was in the way.

There was an explosion out the back that shook the house.

Serena tore the Bio-T away from Lace, who left a smear as he slid down the wall into a pile on the floor.

There was an exchange of blows. Then the Bio-T lifted Serena off her feet and threw her into the corner where the ceiling met the external wall. She bounced off and hit the floor upside down in a tangle of limbs.

Tyler risked a shot but missed as the Bio-T leaped

through the air and landed on Fitzgerald. The mouth shot out again and again and again, leaving a bloody crater where a face should have been. Tyler couldn't bring the shotgun to bear quickly enough. Then Serena was on her feet. She grabbed Fitzgerald's attacker with synthetic strength and swung around, tearing the Bio-T off her victim and flinging her back at the window. The Bio-T bounced off the frame and hit the floor. She quickly got to her feet, framed in the smashed window, and Tyler emptied the three remaining rounds from the shotgun into her. She half flew, half fell through the window.

There was more firing from the back window, quickly drowned out by hypersonic screaming from Harris's carbine.

Serena crossed the spare bedroom to Lace. She picked up his sidearm. The parameters that allowed her to arm herself in defense of her colleagues and innocents had well and truly been met. She chamber-checked the sidearm and then used it to cover the window. She didn't even bother checking Lace. There was a hole clean through his skull.

Tyler had the shotgun back in the reloading position and was double-loading it again. Taking his time. All firing had stopped, but his ears were still ringing. The shotgun loaded, a round chambered, Serena covered him as he moved to the smashed window and glanced out. Nothing.

"Sitrep?" the marshal said over comms. "Harris, did you fire a grenade?"

The explosion out back. Tyler knew that Harris's carbine had an underslung grenade launcher.

"That was me. Second tango down, moving to the one at the back door to confirm kill but he's not moving."

"Matterton?" Stock asked.

"Lace is dead," he glanced the red concave mess that used to be Fitzgerald's skull. "So's Fitzgerald. I hit one of the Bio-Ts, blew her out the window, but she's gone." Glancing at the window he noticed that parts of the frame were smoking, but he couldn't process that now. He couldn't process anything other than the simple task that the marshal had given him.

"You got the window?" he asked Serena. She nodded. He read something in her expression, but he wasn't sure what.

He turned back to looking down the partially collapsed stairs to the broken-in front door. He wondered how much more punishment the old house could take.

"That was a real gunfight, like a regular Western, huh?" Harvey called from the back bedroom.

It took a moment for the words to sink in. Tyler started turning. He could see into the bedroom from his position. Harvey was standing a little way from the broken window but looking at Tyler. Tyler opened his mouth.

"Movement, movement!" Harris shouted over comms.

A shadow swung through the window behind the old rancher as he opened his mouth to say something. There was a wet, sickening crunch: another inhuman mouth tore through Harvey's own, splintering teeth and tearing flesh. Twitching, Harvey was lifted into the air. The Bio-T wearing his corpse like a beard.

Tyler was moving to the side, firing. He knew the rancher was already dead.

Hypersonic screaming, EM-driven penetrators flew through the Bio-T and Harvey's corpse from behind as Harris fired up from the ground. The wounds smoked. Tyler threw himself to the floor. Something hot and wet brushed his face, down his side and he was screaming in agony. He tried to bring the shotgun up but it was smoking as well. It came apart in his hands. The pain was too much. Blackness swam up to consume his vision and he was still.

15

The Marlin at her shoulder, Cass was out of the front bedroom and moving across the landing towards the back. Serena appeared from the spare bedroom in front of her, making for the back bedroom as well.

"Down!" Cass snapped.

Serena crouched and scurried toward an unmoving Matterton lying on the floor. Cass got a glimpse of smoke rising from the FBI agent's raw red wounds as she moved into the room, sweeping her weapon left and right before moving to the bodies.

"Aww shit!" She could see through Harvey's head. At first Cass couldn't figure why the old rancher's wounds were smoking. Then she looked at the dead Bio-T. She was lying half out of the window, the floor, wall and frame all smoking, yellow pus dripping from her wounds. Harris had fired up from the ground at a sharp angle. The EM penetrators fired by the assault carbine had torn through the Bio-T and then Harvey. Cass was pretty sure that the rancher had already been dead. She glanced up at the ceiling. She could see more holes where the thorn-like projectiles had continued on their hypersonic way. Harvey's wounds were smoking because of transfer from the penetrators. "Oh, old man," she said quietly. There was not a single doubt in her mind that she had gotten him killed.

There was a creaking noise, and the floor and window frame gave way. Cass had to back off as the Bio-T's body flopped through the window frame, landing outside, and Harvey's body fell through the floor of his own house.

"They have acid for blood," Cass said to herself. Then to Serena: "Is he alive?" She nodded. "Get him out of here," Cass told her.

Serena scooped Matterton up into her arms as though he weighed nothing.

"Harris, are we clear? Do you have eyes on any other tangos?" Cass asked over comms.

"We're clear, they're all down," Harris told them. "But we may have another problem."

The house was falling down around them as Cass and Serena, carrying Matterton, walked out into the front yard. Cass could see the spinning blue and red lights from the small convoy as they turned off the highway.

The two other marshal prairie rovers from town and an eight-wheeled Daihotai, all-terrain cargo truck, with a Chisholm Meats logo emblazoned on the side. Cass coughed as the dust blew across the yard, momentarily obscuring the vehicles except for the spinning lights.

So this is how it ends, she thought. She found herself laughing at the thought of going out like Butch and Sundance.

"Marshal," a pain-soaked voice said. She turned around to look at Matterton. She hadn't even realized that he was conscious. Serena was applying some kind of salve to his wounds and then binding them. "Follow my lead. We're going to need someone on the outside." By 'outside', Cass guessed that the now presumably-former FBI agent meant not incarcerated.

Cass raised an eyebrow. In the few days she'd known Matterton he'd earned her trust. She wasn't sure the opposite was true. Even so he'd backed her play during the gunfight on Guernsey Street. She nodded at him.

The rovers and the big Daihotai came to a halt. Part of Harvey's house collapsed behind her.

Sorgram jumped out of the flatbed of the first rover. He wore his duster and mask, AR-150 in hand as Rodriguez and Michaels climbed out of the cab as well. Deputies Amsa and Williams climbed out of the other rover. Armed Chisholm Meats ranch hands were piling out of the Daihotai. Cass just stood there watching.

"I'm out. It's been fun," Harris said over comms. Cass was half convinced she could hear something in the extractor's voice. Harris and Lace had been close, after all. Compadres.

Sorgram was striding towards her looking all around at the carnage.

The Chisholm ranch hands were spreading out in front of Cass and the others. Cass's own deputies were standing in a semi-circle around her. Their weapons at the ready.

Jeez, how many guns for an old woman? she wondered.

"You slaughtered all these people?" Sorgram asked. She could hear the incredulity in his voice. This wasn't something that fitted into the narrow parameters of his experience. Nor her own for that matter, Cass decided, but she'd had little choice but to play the hand she'd been dealt.

Cass pointed at the ranch hands with a gloved finger.

"So, after I told you to watch the church, to prevent something like this happening, you instead thought you'd go and round up this posse?" she asked. She coughed again from the dust and raised her neckerchief to cover her mouth and nose.

"You're under arrest," Sorgram told her.

Cass just laughed at him.

"How'd you find us?" Cass asked.

"Put your weapons down, put your hands behind

your heads and lace your fingers together, and get down on your knees."

Cass pointed at Serena.

"She told you where we were when Agent Matterton called her for help, because her programming gives her no choice but to accept you as the most senior peace officer in town in my absence, right? Even though I think she knows that you're a corrupt sonovabitch." Cass practically spat this last.

"Michaels, Velazquez, disarm the suspect and get her in restraints."

Cass turned to look at the two deputies that she'd trained and worked with ever since they had joined the service. Even with their features obscured by their dust-masks, their body language suggested that neither of them was in a hurry to comply.

"Yeah, that's not going to happen," Cass said, turning back to Sorgram.

The ranch hands were getting uneasy; there was a lot of muttering. After all, she'd gunned down a number of their friends in the street earlier in the day.

"You went running to your sugar-mama, Charters, because that's what you always do. She gave you your extra guns—"

"They're all deputized," Sorgram said, like it meant a damn thing.

"But who told the church where to find us?"

"Stock, this is your last chance," Sorgram said.

Cass had a good look around.

"Or what?" she asked. She knew she was being dangerously bloody-minded, but she was through with this bullshit.

"I'll put you down." A voice from behind the mask of one of the ranch hands.

"Yeah?" Stock said looking in the direction she hoped the voice had come from. "Your friends'll get me—a few of them'll go down as well but that won't be your concern. You'll never have to worry about a thing ever again." She took her time looking them all over. "Who's first?" She really wished that Harris had stuck around to cover her. Even so, none of the ranch hands seemed to be in a great hurry to step forward.

Matterton nearly got shot by nervous deputy marshals as he staggered to his feet. The left side of his face and his left arm were now covered in gauze and bandages.

"What are you charging the marshal with?" Matterton managed.

There was a moment of quiet, as though Sorgram considered the question too dumb to dignify with an answer.

"Aiding and abetting a kidnapping," Sorgram finally said.

"She came here to arrest us, Deputy," Matterton told him.

"Marshal," Sorgram corrected, making Cass raise an eyebrow.

"Sorry, Marshal. She was in the process of taking myself and my co-conspirators into custody when we were attacked."

"Where's Fitzgerald?" Amsa asked. Cass thought it was nice that somebody was concerned for the kidnappee.

"Dead," Serena told her. "Killed by one of the church adherents."

"How do we know that Matterton and his friends didn't kill him?" Sorgram demanded.

"You could go and look, maybe a little light investigation if you've got the inclination," Cass suggested. "He's up there in the spare bedroom, his face pecked out by a telescoping secondary mouth, which neither myself, Agent Matterton, or any of the other kidnappers have, as far as I'm aware." There was another crash as part of the house collapsed. "Best do it quick though."

"They have acid for blood," Serena told Sorgram.

"Bullshit!" Sorgram snapped. To Cass's ears it didn't sound like he wasn't coping terribly well.

"Where's Old Man Jermaine?" Williams asked.

"Dead," Cass said, working to keep the strain out of her voice. She pointed at Sorgram again. "Which his bosses'll be pleased to hear."

"Enough of this bullshit, arrest her!" Sorgram snapped.

"For what? Doing my job?" Cass demanded. It

felt cowardly to hide behind Matterton's lie and she couldn't see it working, anyway. Serena would have no choice but to tell the truth. That said, Matterton was right, she couldn't do any good in a cell next to him.

"I don't believe a word of it," Sorgram said. Now he was pointing at Cass. "She was in on it."

Cass smiled. He was overplaying his hand.

"You got anything? Anything at all, other than our mutual dislike and your need to keep your real employer sweet?" Cass asked.

Sorgram turned to Serena.

Here we go, Cass thought. It was all over now.

"You're pretty quiet," Sorgram said.

"I have nothing to add," Serena told. She was standing now as well.

"I'm asking you a direct question: is Stock telling the truth?" Sorgram demanded.

"I'm sorry, Deputy—"

"Marshal!" He all but screamed it at her.

"I am afraid that I have enough data to suggest that you are compromised and will no longer to be able to cooperate with you until such a time as these informed suspicions can be laid to rest," she said.

Cass stared at Serena.

Sorgram did as well. Even with his mask on, Cass could tell he was livid.

"Okay, enough," Cass pointed at Matterton, "let's get him in the rover. Show some respect, he was one of us." Weasel words but she had to do what she could for Matterton. "We need to start processing this mess. Serena, much of it is a biohazard..."

"I have the requisite skills to help you process the scene," Serena said. Velazquez and Michaels walked over to Matterton and started searching him, removing his remaining weapons.

"We need to see to the dead but first we have to handle the church. I'm going to give Colonel Thakore a call at Camp Rodriguez—"

"Stop!" It was practically a screech from Sorgram.

"You have a choice here, Deputy. Either you're part of the solution or part of the problem. You don't get to work, and I mean right now, you can consider yourself suspended. Any more of your nonsense and you're going back to the station on an obstruction charge."

"Check your P-Dat, you stupid bitch." His voice seethed.

Cass had a sinking sensation. Despite herself she pulled out her P-Dat. She saw the message form the GL3 office of the Colonial Administration. She didn't have to open it to know what it said. It was inevitable, but it couldn't have come at a worse time. Removed as Marshal. Effective immediately. Sorgram to replace her. It would have been copied to the deputies.

"Give me your star and your guns, bitch," Sorgram snapped.

"Hey, c'mon now," Michaels said from where he

stood by Matterton. The agent wasn't cuffed, but Velazquez had a firm hold on him. Sorgram shot the deputy a look.

Cass unhooked the marshal's badge from her body armor and threw it to him.

"The guns belong to me," she told him.

"I said give me—"

"Come and take them!" she hissed.

Sorgram took a step back. A number of the ranch hands shifted, readying weapons.

The moment stretched out. Nobody moved.

Then Sorgram walked over to the rental hover ATV that Serena had arrived on and put three rounds from his AR-150 into the engine block.

Cass closed her eyes. She saw where this was going.

Then Sorgram took his time walking over to the barn. Another three rounds. Harvey's prairie rover.

Cass shifted position as she heard Harvey's horses whinnying in distress. There was a three-stall stable attached to the barn. If Sorgram tried to do anything to them she was just going to shoot him, consequences be damned. You didn't mess with someone's horses, even if they were dead. Thankfully Sorgram was at least cowboy enough to leave the horses be. He emerged from the barn. Cass could feel him smiling through the dust mask. He made for Cass's rover.

"You petty asshole," Matterton said as Sorgram passed him.

Sorgram stopped, turned, rushed the few steps to him and back-handed Matterton.

"Hey!" Michaels snapped.

Velazquez put himself between Matterton and his new boss.

"He's a prisoner and he's wounded," the deputy said.

"Get some goddamned respect around here," Sorgram muttered.

"Deputy—" Serena started.

"Marshal! Marshal! I'm the fucking Marshal!" Sorgram screamed in her face.

"Temporary Acting Marshal Sorgram, under Colonial Code 537A, Paragraph-"

"Take the synth as well," he told Amsa and Williams. "Doubtless the FBI will want to dismantle this malfunctioning piece of uppity office equipment."

Neither of the deputies moved.

"Fucking now!" he screamed.

"On what grounds am I being detained?" Serena asked.

"You're not being detained, you're being fucking confiscated," Sorgram told her, speaking to her as though she were stupid.

Amsa and Williams clearly did not know what to do. Sorgram in full flow was something to behold, Cass decided. Clearly, she'd been holding him back.

Williams looked over at Cass for guidance. Cass just

nodded to her. Williams motioned to Amsa for them to do as they had been asked.

"Get both of them in restraints," Sorgram snapped.

Cass just stood there and watched as Serena allowed herself to be put in the backseat cage of one of the rovers. Sorgram marched Matterton to the other rover himself. The temporary acting marshal had a tight grip on the FBI agent's wounded arm. Matterton's legs buckled under him as they reached the vehicle. Sorgram sent Velazquez for Cass's rover, before climbing into the passenger seat of the vehicle transporting Matterton. Michaels got into the passenger seat beside his new boss.

The Chisholm ranch hands clambered back up into the Daihotai, glaring in Cass' direction before they did so. They seemed disappointed. Sogram had come with enough people to start a range war. Cass guessed he had been expecting to find more of them hunkered down in the ranch house. She noted that he hadn't given a shit about Lace and Harris, nor the Bio-T attack.

Vehicles drove around her, kicking up dirt, making her duster flap in the wind. Then the convoy, with one more prairie rover, headed up the drive and re-joined the highway. Cass had never felt every second of her fifty-some years more than she did at that moment. She was so tired that she suspected she had actually died and been reanimated. Every muscle ached, even the slightest movement was painful, she'd picked up all the bruises and abrasions that you seemed to get during a gunfight, and her chest still hurt from the previous gunfight.

Still, she was alive. Neither Lace or Harvey had been that lucky. It had been a mistake to come here. She knew people up in the mountains. They should've gone there.

Cass would've liked to have been angry at Serena but she just wasn't. She was angry at herself. She'd brought death to her friend's door and while she hadn't, couldn't, have expected this, she had known that something was going to happen.

She wanted to sit down. Wanted to lie down. Let the dust blow over her, but she knew if she laid down, she wasn't getting back up again.

It had been a damnable long day, and it wasn't over yet. She turned and headed for the stables.

If Tyler had been in worse pain in his life he couldn't remember when. The left side of his face and his left arm all felt as though they were on fire. Serena had time to dress and bind the acid burns but not to give him any painkillers. Every jolt sent lightning-like flashes of pain coursing through him.

To take his mind off the pain Tyler found himself focusing on the back of Sorgram's head. He was struggling to think of anyone he'd ever had more contempt for. Despite his work, or more likely because of it, Tyler was not a violent man. He still would've quite liked to punch Sorgram in the face, even after all the carnage he'd seen and experienced today.

Nursing his loathing for Sorgram also kept his mind off Serena. Well, for the most part. He understood why she had done what she had done. He still felt betrayed.

Tyler didn't want to think about the fight. He wasn't ready to process. Despite the modifications Snell had made to himself, the bizarre physiology of the Bio-Ts had still come as a surprise. Now he understood why they didn't speak. It was unlikely they could. Fitzgerald had still been in the process of transforming. He guessed all the missing church recruits had been part of the trial-and-error process. Those whose bodies had rejected the protein, for some reason, had probably ended up in the medical incinerator. What he didn't understand was why it was all happening. What were the church up to? Nor did he understand why there had been a shipping manifest in Dawkins' office.

"Acting Marshal," Michaels said from the driver's seat.

Tyler saw Sorgram seethe at the 'acting', but it would be technically correct until his position was confirmed. Tyler moved a little to look out the windscreen, wincing, movement was just pain now. The acting marshal's rover was at the head of the convoy, because of course it was. Coming towards them on the other side of the road was another Daihotai. Its headlights were off but by the light of the dashboard in the cab Tyler could make out a Bio-T driving. Dawkins was sat next to him.

"Should we stop them while we have the manpower?" Michaels asked as the Daihotai passed them by.

Sorgram said nothing.

"Pull them over," Tyler said.

The acting marshal ignored Tyler. Whatever happened between Stock and Sorgram, it had never occurred to Tyler that the acting marshal wouldn't act against the church. The attack on the ranch house had been a hit on Fitzgerald, presumably to prevent him from talking. Almost certainly the same reason Snell had been killed.

"What are you doing?" Tyler demanded. "There's evidence back there."

Sorgram just ignored him.

"Do your fucking job! Pull them the fuck over!" Tyler screamed at the acting marshal.

"There's no evidence back there, only proprietary tech," Sorgram said. "You kidnapped a member of the church. Some of the church went to negotiate their return, you opened fire."

Tyler was just staring at Sorgram. His words sounded rehearsed.

Michaels was looking rapidly between the road and

his new boss as though he couldn't quite believe what he was hearing, either.

"Stock was right about you, you're just a sock puppet." Tyler said.

"Stop the vehicle," Sorgram told Michaels.

"Boss?" Michaels asked.

"Now!"

Michaels brought the prairie rover to a halt on the side of the road. Sorgram was out of the passenger seat in a moment, coughing in the dust, having not taken the time to mask up. Tyler watched him open the door to the backseat cage. He didn't fight. It would've just been more painful. Sorgram hit him again and again with the shock-stick. Tyler collapsed, his face hitting the caged window, drooling as he watched Amsa and Williams' rover pass them. He saw Serena in the back of the other vehicle, staring at him.

PART III

16

Cass had been lucky enough to hear the throaty roar of the Daihotai's engine during a moment's respite in the screaming winds. Through the dust she was just about able to make out the silhouette of the eight-wheeled vehicle as it turned off the highway onto the ranch's drive. The vehicle's headlights were off.

The marshal had saddled and dust-masked Harvey's horses. She had taken both horses—King and a mare—so she could switch between them to allow them to rest on the long ride, but also because without anyone to look after them they would die in the approaching dust blow.

It took some coaxing, but Cass managed to get both horses to lie down among the prairie tussock. She lay across the mare, the more skittish of the two animals, having slid the big Marlin rifle out of its carry-bag and laid it across the horse's flanks, looking through the scope. She saw Bio-Ts moving from the now parked-up truck into the partially collapsed ranch house.

She scanned the truck's cab. The scope's image intensification properties allowed her to pick out Dawkins in the passenger seat. He was just sitting there, clear as day, saying nothing, presumably overseeing the Bio-Ts. Cass moved her finger from the guard to the trigger. With the range, the high wind, the reduced visibility from the dust, the glass in the cab and not knowing if the Daihotai's windscreen was armored or not, she could not be sure of a clean kill. Plus, it would be cold-blooded murder. She had been a sniper: it wouldn't be the first time.

More importantly, she wasn't sure that it would do any good. She couldn't shake the feeling that there was somebody behind Dawkins. She had a suspicion as to who, but it didn't line up with the current facts. It wouldn't do any good to speak to the Bio-Ts. Whatever they may have once been, they certainly weren't human now. She needed to interrogate Dawkins, properly. At least that was the reason she gave herself for not firing. She didn't want to analyze it too closely. Dawkins had at least six Bio-Ts with him. Possibly all the others from the church. It had taken Cass and five others, including an artificial person and an ex-special forces operator, to kill six Bio-Ts—and in doing so they had lost two of their number. She didn't like her odds. She told herself that it was practicality rather than cowardice that stayed her trigger finger, that made her watch as the Bio-Ts removed their dead from the ranch house and then set fire to the structure.

Cass waited until the departing truck had been swallowed by the dust and she couldn't hear its engine anymore. Then she coaxed both the masked horses to their feet and put the glow of the burning ranch house to her back, before heading north towards Steer City.

The sensation of starting to slide out of the saddle jerked Cass awake, startling the horse. She calmed the mare down, looking around, wondering how long she had been asleep for. Judging by the red glow of the dust that teased the double sunrise somewhere through the murk, it had been longer than she had previously thought possible in the saddle. It was a good thing that she had tied off King's reins to the horn of her own saddle.

She could see the steel blue of Coldstream Station's perimeter lights. She patted the horse's neck, rubbing it affectionately. The mare was a good horse to have stayed on the highway while Cass slept. The last time she had felt this tired had been during the war. She just wished that she could remember the animal's name. The mare had been Harvey's wife's horse before she had passed. Steadying herself she reached into her duster and pulled out her ruggedized P-Dat.

With some difficulty she managed to run a search

on the marshal database. Sorgram hadn't pulled her access yet, because he was sloppy. She found the contact details she was looking for. While fighting the urge to just slide off the horse, to lie in the dust and succumb to sleep, she managed to compose and send a text.

Cass almost fell asleep again at Coldstream Station's gate. Despite being brightly lit, the facility looked deserted. She guessed that all the cattle were in their dust shelters—though it was unusual not to see at least one of the land trains that they used to transport livestock parked up in the yard.

As she looked through the dust into the station's vast courtyard, at the sheds, empty pens, the bunk room, and admin block, she saw a hover ATV making its way towards the gate. Its headlight illuminated the dust particles in the air. The wind blew it sideways as the bulky cowboy riding it wrestled with the controls. Finally, the ATV made it to the gate: Teddy climbed down off it and stepped out through the much smaller personnel gate. Cass found herself wondering where the station's security personnel were.

"Marshal!" Teddy shouted up at her over the wind.

"Wasn't sure if you were going to come," Cass said, raising her voice as she bent forwards in the saddle, the horse moving a little under her.

"You killed some of my friends yesterday," Teddy

told her, leaning closer. He was masked against the dust and Cass was too tired to even try and read his body language. For all she knew the big cowboy was getting ready to drag her off her horse, beat her and shoot her. Was this a good idea? No, but it was her only one.

"I tried real hard not to, Teddy. They gave me no choice."

Nothing. He just stood there completely still as the wind and dust blew around them. Finally, he nodded.

"Is Charters in there?" Cass asked nodding towards the station.

"No, she took the VToL into town."

"In this?" Cas was surprised despite herself. Teddy just shrugged. "Where is everyone?" she asked.

"Took both the land trains into town as well."

That did not make sense at all. It was Halfday today and under normal circumstances that meant the arrival of the midweek shuttle. It should, however, have been cancelled because of the dust storm. The shuttles were large, powerful and sturdy enough to fly through anything but a category four or higher storm. The problem was their engines tended to superheat the dust particles, turning them to raining glass.

Then she remembered the shipping manifest that Tyler had seen.

"Teddy, anything weird about this delivery?"

"They're transporting live. I've never known them to do that before," he said.

Whatever was happening was happening today.

"Why are you still here?"

"I'm on Charters' shit list. No overtime for Teddy."

Cass nodded. Charters struck her as a deeply vindictive person.

"Did you bring what I asked?"

This time the hesitation in Teddy's body language was obvious.

"It's not a bust, Teddy. I'm not even the marshal anymore and even if I was it'd be entrapment. I just need something to help me stay awake."

Still clearly reluctant he handed over a crumpled and folded paper bag. Even through her gloves, Cass could feel the pills inside.

"Why don't you leave the horses here?" Teddy asked. "I can look after them, you can take the ATV."

Cass just shook her head. In this wind all she would be doing was fighting the ATV and not going any faster than she would be on horseback.

Two Neversleep pills allowed Cass to make good time after leaving Coldstream Station. She hadn't seen another soul on the highway. The dust formed drifts on the asphalt in front of her as she made her way towards town. She somewhat regretted disabling the location device on her P-Dat in a dust fall this heavy but she hadn't wanted Sorgram, or anyone else, tracking her movements. It did, however, mean that her best bet for not getting lost in the storm was to stick to the highway. She had, however, set a bearing for town on her P-Dat compass and her mechanical backup.

Two of the three suns were up now. It hadn't made that much difference to visibility, though it did infect the blowing dust with a deep red tinge. Like anyone who had lived on GL3 for a while, Cass knew how to protect herself from dust. The clothing that she wore was designed to allow the wearer to survive in a storm until they were able to find more permanent shelter. It wasn't designed for this kind of prolonged exposure. The dust had worked its way through her layers and she could feel it abrading her skin. Some had worked its way under the seal of her mask and she was starting to cough a little. She was concerned about the filters clogging up. There was only so much she could do to clear them out while she was riding through the middle of it all. Cass found herself fighting the claustrophobic feeling of being stuck in a failing mask with nowhere to run to.

King, and the mare, who Cass had now named Queen, were getting more and more skittish as well. They had the same issues as Cass: tired, irritated by the dust, particularly under the saddle, and their masks would be struggling to cope. It was a tribute to both horses that they were as calm as they were. Both had presumably had been out looking for cattle in the past when the wind rolled in off the mountains and kicked up the dry plains dust.

Cass almost rode into the parked-up land trains. Only a brief respite in the dust allowed her to see their hazard flashers. Beyond she could just about make out the street lights on the edge of town. The two multi-trailer vehicles were parked end-to-end, taking up more than half the width of the highway. The only thing protecting the lowing beasts in the open cattle trucks from the storm was a flimsy dust cover. The cattle did not sound happy. Cass checked the time. The shuttle wouldn't have landed yet but she couldn't work out why they hadn't parked up closer to the port.

She thought about giving the parked-up convoy a wide berth, riding across the prairie, using her compasses to guide her back into town. Cass knew, however, that if she made just one mistake she was lost. Instead, she pushed herself upright in the saddle and made her way forwards. She was riding King now, Queen's reins wrapped around the saddle pommel.

There were Chisholm Meat ranch hands out on the highway, in their dusters and hats, most carrying rifles. As she rode by them, she felt their suspicious glances through their masks. Did they know who she was? Had they been part of the posse from the previous night? If so, none of them made a move. She still kept one hand on the reins and the other close to her Hancock .357.

Cass noticed a number of saddled and masked

horses had been tethered to the land trains. If she hadn't known better, it would have looked like they were intending on driving the cattle through town but she couldn't work out why. Chisholm Meats kept a number of different kinds of cattle, but their mainstay was a Scottish Highland and Aberdeen Angus hybrid. The hybrids had been genetically modified to increase the hardiness of the cattle and make them more resistant to the harsh conditions of GL3. They would be able to survive a short drive through the town, but it wouldn't do them any good and it needlessly risked losing some of them. It made no sense.

Cass made it level with the tractor cab of the lead land train. She could make out the lights at the edge of town much better now. Two of the ranch hands were standing just ahead of the tractor, looking towards the town. One held a rifle, the butt against her hip. The other's rifle was leaning against one of the huge tires of the front tractor unit.

It was a spur of the moment decision.

Cass steered the horses towards the two ranch hands. The one without a rifle looked up at her approach. Cass noted that he still had a sidearm in a dust-flapped holster riding his hip. She got as close to him as she could and then leaned forward in the saddle.

"Are you about to drive cattle through the town?" she asked, having to shout over the wind.

"What's it to you?" he shouted back. Cass found

herself wondering why people just couldn't be nice. "Wait a minute! It's the marshal!"

Cass grabbed the man's mask and tore it from his face, the storm winds sending his hat spinning off to be swallowed by the dust. He tried to grab for it but Cass kicked him away. He went down immediately, choking and coughing. The other cattle hand was bringing her rifle up to her shoulder but Cass already had the .357 drawn and levelled at her face. Cass took a moment to calm King. There was a reason why she used a revolver but even she wasn't sure the .357 would fire after this much exposure to dust.

"He's got maybe a minute to live," Cass said. "Put the rifle down, answer my questions and I'll give him his mask back."

The other ranch hand didn't move, she just kept the rifle leveled at Cass whilst her friend tried and failed to breathe dust. Maybe she didn't like the guy.

"Take your time," Cass told her.

The ranch hand put the rifle down and raised her hands.

"Give him the mask back," she shouted over the screaming wind.

"Why are you about to drive cattle through the town?" Cass demanded.

"We don't know! None of us like it, all of us have said so!"

"Whose orders?"

"Hargreaves."

Hargreaves was the foreman: like Sorgram, he was very much Charters' creature.

"Where's Charters?"

"How the fuck would I know?" the ranch hand demanded.

Cass just looked down at the ranch hand's choking friend.

"She'll be staying at the nicest, most expensive, place in town!" The ranch hand was practically pleading with her now.

Cass threw the choking ranch hand his mask back and put her heels to King's flanks, sending him galloping into the dust and pulling Queen behind them.

Cass was almost bent over double as she made her way along the boardwalk on Port Street. She had to hold on to her hat. The wind was catching the heavy rifle bag slung over her back and threatening to push her too fast up the street, taking her legs out from underneath her. The storm was getting stronger. She had dropped off the horses at Murcheson's Stables. Serafina Murcheson had promised to look after them both.

The town was buttoned up against the storm. Some light leaked out from under dust shutters but for the most part the only light came from those street lights that hadn't already been knocked out by the high winds. Through the occasional breaks in the dust, she could make out the lights of the shuttle cradle in the port at the end of the street.

Cass managed to make it to the Stagecoach's dust-lock. A shouted and somewhat heated discussion over the intercom meant that Cass was eventually allowed in. The fans and suction in the dust-lock felt like a blessed relief after the storm. She took another one of the Neversleeps. She was still a grimy mess, despite having brushed herself down while waiting for the dust-lock to cycle. When she was admitted into the hotel's lobby Cass took her mask off and glared at the receptionist, who blanched a little.

"Just going to leave a gal out there in the storm?" Cass demanded. The receptionist's mouth flapped open and closed. "Where's Regina Charters?"

"In here, Marshal." Charters' cut-glass English accent came from the dining room. Cass followed the voice, leaving a trail of dust in her wake.

The dining room seemed to be trying for a degree of elegance while sticking with the general Western décor. Cass had no idea if it worked or not and didn't really care. She was wearing the false amphetamine energy of the Neversleep pills over the top of her exhaustion. She only had the vaguest idea of the time and her surroundings were swimming a little.

There were only a few other guests at the tables in the

dining room. They had the look of off-world tourists. They took one look at the marshal's craggy, dust-and-grime-encrusted features and decided to make themselves scarce. Cass suspected she must look like some spirit of the storm, a plains dust specter, a prairie ghost.

Regina was sat at a table near the dust-shuttered window. Her bodyguard, was on his feet, standing to one side of the table, ready to interpose himself if need be. He held a compact personal defense weapon in his hands. The Serena-model secretary was just pulling off a multidigit glove, the additional micro-gesture controlled, artificial digits sliding back into the fingers of the glove as she lay it on top of her P-Dat.

"Tea, Marshal?" Regina asked, pouring orange-colored tea from a teapot into a third cup on the table. They had been expecting her. The ranch hands with the land trains must have called ahead. "Except I understand that it's not Marshal anymore, is it?"

"That your doing?" Cass asked, she remained standing.

Charters added a splash of milk and then took her time stirring her tea before placing the spoon on the saucer and taking a sip. Her face wrinkled into an expression of distaste.

"Well, it's not Fortum and Mason but one does what one must when amongst savages." Then finally she looked up at Cass. "I rather suspect your loss of position was your own doing, Ms. Stock."

Cass found herself actually grinding her teeth. She had always thought of Charters as an arrogant, entitled annoyance. She'd underestimated her.

"Why are your people getting ready to run cattle through the streets of my town?" Cass demanded.

"Your town?" Charters said, her voice cold. "Do you mean our town? As in the town that we built and continue to pay for, one way or another? That town? This is the problem with people like you: your sense of entitlement is such that it completely overwhelms where a sense of gratitude would be in a normal person. You tell yourself myths of the big bad corporation. Never mind that without the corporation in question you wouldn't be here and this place wouldn't exist. Our employees literally pay the taxes that keep, sorry, *kept* you in a job, and you still have the temerity to bite the hand that feeds. Your selfishness, your disregard for the wellbeing of the people of this town, and your refusal to accept that our people also deserve the protection of the law, quite frankly disgusts me."

Cass was struggling to keep her temper. Neither the amphetamines flaring through her nervous system nor her fatigue were helping in this regard. If nothing else, it was clear that she and Charters saw things very differently, almost to the point that they lived in different worlds.

"I'm going to ask you one more time—" Cass started.

"Or what?" Regina demanded, not even bothering to

hide her scorn. "You'll force Shane here to kill you in self defense? Ms. Stock, it should be patently obvious to the meanest of intelligences that as general counsel to Chisholm Meats I have absolutely no part in the movement of cattle. I'm not a fucking ranch hand. My shoes alone should tell you that. I have no idea why, or even if, the cattle are about to be run through the town. It doesn't sound right to me, but then I studied economics and then law at LSE and Georgetown. Not fucking animal husbandry. Now do you wish to leave me in peace, or should we call Marshal Sorgram?"

Their discussion wasn't going well.

"Did you lean on Khan to release the Bio-T after he killed one of your ranch hands?" Cass persisted.

"Did I… 'lean'?" Charters actually looked pained. "Leaving aside your adolescent vernacular, no I didn't 'lean' on Khan. I made a legal argument to the judge that persuaded both him and the colonial attorney that attempting to prosecute one of the church adherents would be a waste of time and could very easily result in an expensive civil suit brought against the Colonial Administration."

Despite the delivery, this didn't ring true to Cass. There was too much prosecutorial evidence but Charters was professional enough to not deviate from the party line without sufficient incentive. Cass had no leverage here. She was starting to feel foolish, like a scolded school child, which she guessed was Charters' intent. She also had the feeling that the bodyguard was competent. Harris levels of competence. Still, Charters had admitted to working for the church.

"Why?" Cass asked.

"Why what? Why get the adherent released? You are aware what I do for a living?"

"You work for Chisholm Meats," Cass said.

Now Charters looked at Cass as though she was studying an exotic animal.

"You really are a simple creature, aren't you? Everything in black and white."

Cass had grown up in a place where you couldn't speak to someone like that with impunity. She took a step towards Regina. Regina didn't so much as flinch, but the bodyguard, Shane, stepped forwards.

"Easy," he said.

Cass, seething, looked between Shane and Regina. Regina smiled with such mock-saccharine glee that Cass wanted to wring her chicken neck.

"I am general counsel to Chisholm Meat on GL3 and a non-executive board member. I still have a private legal practice and the church is one of the few organizations on the planet that can actually afford my services. Where there's no conflict of interest with my main client, I am free to represent the church."

Cass stared at Regina. At least she now understood the chain of events. Matterton had contacted Serena, Serena had told Sorgram where they were holding

Fitzgerald and Sorgram had run to Charters who had informed the church.

"No conflict of..." Cass started. "That Bio-T killed one of your people in cold blood!"

Regina took another sip of her tea and grimaced.

"If one of CM's employees commits a felony they can be dismissed summarily and even retrospectively. When they chose to attack what was at the time a representative of local law enforcement, however corrupt she may have been, they effectively dismissed themselves. It's in their contract."

Cass pointed in the general direction of the church.

"They've brought dozens of people here under false pretenses! Experimented on them! And something like a hundred of their recruits are unaccounted for!"

It was the first time Regina had looked genuinely irritated throughout the entire conversation.

"No."

Cass stared at her.

"What do you mean, 'no'?"

"I mean that you are incorrect and that I will not have you slander my clients. Is that clear, Ms. Stock?"

Cass took another step forward, not quite able to understand what she was hearing. Shane didn't move to intercept. Instead, he took a step or two backwards, raised his weapon and put a hand on Regina's shoulder as though readying her to move if it kicked off.

"I need you to back up a bit there, Marshal," Shane

said. "Let's not do anything we'll all regret." Now she could hear his Australian accent.

Cass swallowed but took a few steps back.

Shane relaxed a little.

Cass glanced at the Serena. Regina's secretary's expression was blank but she was definitely keeping an eye on Cass.

"The recruits are made completely aware of the risks, risks that they are prepared to take for the rewards that are offered. They have signed waivers; everything that has happened within those walls has been perfectly legal."

Cass couldn't believe what she was hearing.

"You can't kill a hundred people in biotech experiments whether they've signed a waiver or not!" she shouted at Regina.

"I oversaw the waivers, and I'm here to tell you that on this planet, with its lax laws on genetic engineering, you can. It's why the church settled here. It's not without its cost but those people are bold explorers on the very frontier of biotechnology and one day all of humanity will thank them. You see things only in terms of your own arrogance, your need to be important. As a result of this malignant narcissism you have convinced yourself that you have discovered some sinister conspiracy. When in fact all you've done is try to set back progress and created a minor PR difficulty for the church."

"A minor PR…" Cass managed. She thought about all the recruits, little more than kids, who'd met their ends in a medical incinerator.

"It's the Frontier, Ms. Stock, nobody cares. Nobody of import, anyway. Oh, there is another consequence of your actions: you have destroyed yourself."

And somehow Cass knew it was all true.

"You alright, miss?" Shane asked and Cass realized that she must have been swaying.

At this Regina stood up. The Serena was already on her feet, helping Regina on with her heavy dust coat.

"They attacked us," Cass said quietly. "Killed Harvey and…"

Regina slid her arms into her coat and then turned to face Cass again.

"And what? Killed Herbert Lace, perhaps? A known kidnapper and brainwasher? Tell me, who fired the first shot? Were any of my clients even armed?" Regina demanded. What little patience she'd had was now well and truly gone.

"They're not human!" Cass screamed at the lawyer.

Regina's face became a cold mask.

"Your bigotry notwithstanding, my clients will continue to be treated as humans under the law."

Regina allowed herself to be steered around Cass by Shane, the bodyguard giving the ex-marshal quite a wide berth.

"There's a long line of dead stretching out behind

you," Cass said as Regina passed. She wasn't sure why she said it.

"We all have our ghosts, Marshal," Regina replied. Cass thought she detected a hint of weariness in the lawyer's tone, just for a moment.

Cass was such a bad mix of exhausted and completely wired that she didn't even question why Regina and her two subordinates were heading back out into the dust storm.

17

Tyler ached from head to foot. There was nothing like having fifty thousand volts repeatedly slammed through your body, causing every muscle to contract, to make you really feel like crap. Particularly when the application of the shock stick came on top of acid burns. He would have quite liked some medical attention, but Sorgram wasn't that kind of marshal.

Tyler forced his eyes open, cursing his existence as he did so. He was lying on a hard bench in one of the cells under the marshal's station on Port Street. He cried out as he forced himself to sit up. Pain from the burns boiled through him, bringing water to his eyes. The Naproleve that Serena had managed to sneak him had worn off.

Serena.

"Tyler?" She was in the next cell. It seemed needlessly cruel that, despite the cells being fronted with bars, there was a solid wall between them.

He cried out again and moved to the bars, gripping them as though he needed their support to stand. Outside the line of cells was a corridor with a line drawn on the floor that if the deputies crossed, they knew any prisoners could reach them through the bars. Opposite his cell were the stairs up to the station's offices. He could hear Sorgram screaming at one of the deputies. It appeared the strain was bringing out the worst in the acting marshal.

"Serena," Tyler managed. There was a coppery taste in his otherwise dry mouth.

"Could you please check your dressings?" Her voice told him that she had changed position, that she too was close to the bars in her cell.

He looked at the dressings. They looked soiled. They needed changing, but there was nothing he could do about it right now.

"They're fine," he said. He was still struggling with Serena's 'betrayal' despite understanding that she'd had no choice. He'd brought this on himself by involving her. That just made it worse.

"Tyler," Serena said, "I am sorry."

Suddenly he was very still. Gripping the bars. His eyes squeezed shut.

"It's not your fault," he forced himself to say, and he knew it was true. He just didn't feel it right now.

"I had significant reason to doubt Acting Marshal Sorgram but still chose to follow protocol. While I cannot condone your actions, and they will need to be reviewed by the Office of Professional Responsibility, I was wrong to take Sorgram into my confidence."

OPR? Tyler was pretty sure he was just going to prison. Assuming the acting marshal, or whomever he was working for, didn't just decide to tie up loose ends, have them taken out onto the prairie and put two in the back of their heads.

"Do you wish to discuss how you feel?" Serena asked.

He couldn't help but laugh.

"No," he said, "no, I don't." *Pretty fucking despondent*, he decided. "Did you find out anything more?"

"I am no closer to tracing the origin of the slush fund," she told him, which made sense: that was the whole point of slush funds. "It is a matter of public record, however, that Chisholm Meats is owned by Lasalle Bionational."

"The biotech megacorp?" Tyler said. It wasn't as strange as it sounded. Most frontier agricultural endeavors required a degree of genetic engineering of the crops and/or the livestock, even post terraforming. Except… "Any connection to our biotech church?"

"None that I could find, but if they were behind the slush fund, I would not necessarily be able to make the connection with the resources I have available."

Particularly while locked in a cell, Tyler added mentally.

"Anything else?" Tyler asked. The lack of information wasn't helping with his mounting sense of despondency.

They had screwed up here. He personally had made some very bad decisions.

"I'm not sure how relevant it is but the General Counsel for Chisholm Meats has a very colorful resume," Serena told him. "Economics at the London School of Economics, before graduating summa cum laude from Georgetown Law."

"Then let me guess, some high-flying job with one of the megacorps?" Tyler asked.

"A minor legal clerk with the State Department," Serena said.

Tyler frowned. While State definitely had employees in its own right, whenever he heard mention of the department, particularly as a member of an alphabet agency himself, one thing came immediately to mind.

"Was she CIA?" he asked.

"There is not enough information to definitively say," Serena said, "her educational background would definitely make her an attractive recruit."

"Is she not a British national? A subject of the 3WE?" he asked, meaning the Three World Empire.

"Joint citizen," Serena told him.

"So, from either State or the CIA to Lasalle?"

"She runs an independent legal practice but sits on the board of Chisholm Meats. Before that she worked as legal counsel for the biotech arm of Weyland-Yutani."

This was getting weirder and weirder. WY's roots ran deep into both the United Americas and 3WE governments, with extensive links to the military. He had heard ex-marines who had joined HRT claim that Weyland-Yutani all but used the Colonial Marines as an extension of their own corporate security forces. Legal counsel was pretty impressive. Weyland-Yutani's biotech arm was one of the most prestigious and valuable parts of their business.

"Board member or not, isn't Chisholm Meats something of a step down in terms of prestige from WY? Particularly all the way out here? Did she do something wrong?" Tyler asked.

"If she did, I was unable to discover it. Just to be clear, I found nothing that connects Charters to the Church of Biological Transcendence."

"Except that someone got to Judge Khan and you told Sorgram where we were. Stock was convinced that Sorgram was in Charters' pocket—"

"Though no proof of this assertion was ever provided," Serena pointed out.

"But someone told the Bio-Ts where we were."

Suddenly it went very quiet.

"I regret that a great deal," Serena said. Where others wouldn't, Tyler thought he could hear regret in her voice. "As I believe it caused the death of Herbert Lace, Harvey Jermaine and Matthew Fitzgerald, not to mention the other church adherents whose identity we have yet to learn."

Tyler wanted to tell her it was alright but it wasn't,

none of it was. He rested his head against the cool metal of the bars. He had nothing for her. He felt cold as he went back to business.

"Speculate with me for a moment. Let's imagine that Charters was, or possibly still is, an operations officer. What if her job was to recruit a network, to corrupt and suborn people, find the correct leverage and then bend them to her will."

"Judge Khan's micro-expressions were consistent with someone frightened of more than a public corruption investigation by an FBI agent," Serena pointed out.

"Sorgram wouldn't stand a chance," Tyler said. "Dawkins?"

"Tyler, I have to stress that there is still no evidence of any of this and we are in danger of manipulating the facts to fit the theory."

By 'we' Serena of course meant 'you.' On the other hand, there wasn't much else they could do down here. Except wait.

Cass didn't want to drink in the Stagecoach. It was too expensive and too pretentious and they were definitely looking down their noses at her filthy appearance. On the other hand, she couldn't quite face the walk back to her apartment just yet. That was assuming she hadn't already been evicted: she wouldn't put such petty spite past Sorgram.

Cass was sat at a table in the hotel's saloon bar, her back to the wall, staring down into her whisky. Her rifle bag leaning against the wall next to her. She could feel the bar staff's judgmental eyes on her, sense their muttered conversation. She just wanted sleep but was still too wired, despite her fatigue.

She was done. She knew that. Regina's explanation had been fucked up but had a ring of truth to it, or rather Regina had the resources and power to make it true. What else mattered at the end of the day? The one thing she couldn't figure, that Regina hadn't explained, was why Chisholm was about to run cattle through the streets. It didn't make a damned lick of sense. Not that there was anything she could do about it now. She was, however, near ornery enough to pick a fight with the barman if he didn't stop giving her the hairy eyeball.

"Feeling sorry for yourself, Marshal?"

Cass was too tired to be particularly surprised when she looked up and saw Harris standing in front of her table. The extractor was wearing a dust poncho, the EM carbine hanging down under the flap, on its sling, mostly concealed. Her mask was pushed down, but she didn't look nearly as grimy as Cass felt. There was just enough of a suggestion of a smile on Harris's face to further piss Cass off.

"Y'know, I've had just about had as much shit from sarcastic English bitches as I'm going to take for one day."

"Shame, just as we were starting to get on. Good shooting back at the farm."

Cass just looked at Harris. She could see the extractor valuing people based on their ability to shoot, but Cass suspected it was more than that. Harris valued useful people. Cass couldn't see her having much time for self-pity.

"You too," she finally said.

"Sorry about the old man. I liked him. He didn't have to do what he did for us."

"Sorry about Lace."

Just a trace of something on Harris's face, almost an emotion, then a hardening.

"I liked him a lot," she said.

She turned away and went to the bar. Cass couldn't make out the initial exchange but whatever the barman said it seemed to piss off Harris.

"Stop fucking around and give me the bottle!" the extractor snapped. Cass looked up to see that Harris had half dragged the barman across his own polished bar. She would have had to intervene once, but she wasn't the marshal anymore.

Moments later, a bottle of single malt scotch thumped down on the table, along with two crystal tumblers, both now smeared with dust.

"Would've preferred bourbon," Cass pointed out.

"Like I give a shit," Harris said as she poured some of the amber liquid into the two tumblers before sitting down and sliding one of the drinks towards Cass. She looked down at it and then back up at Harris.

"How'd you get here?" Cass asked.

"I'm a guest here. Got a card for the door," Harris said. Cass did not enjoy the talent that the English seemed to have of making you sound stupid for asking reasonable questions. She spat the dust out of her mouth onto the wooden boards close to Harris's feet. Harris just looked at her. "You mean from the farm? I just climbed into the back of your rover, pulled some kit over me and waited for them to drive me back. Had my short in my hand the entire way."

Cass guessed that short was British military slang for a sidearm. There wasn't a doubt in Cass's mind that Harris would have shot any one of her deputies if they had discovered her.

Except they're not your deputies anymore, she told herself.

"I'm guessing you did something ridiculous, like walking back," Harris said.

"Rode back."

"Very fucking cowgirl. Your ancestors would be proud."

"So, what are we doing?" Cass asked lifting the tumbler of whisky off the table but not raising it to her mouth.

"Well, we've got a choice, haven't we? We can sit here and get wankered, which is a solid option," Harris said. Cass guessed that 'wankered' was another British term, probably for being drunk. The British had more words for that than the Inuit had words for snow. "Or we drink to dead friends and then we go and put the band back together."

"Your subject's dead, you're not getting paid," Cass pointed out, still holding the glass. Harris didn't reply. "Charters is behind it all. You just missed her."

"Some idiot just took off in an executive VToL," Harris told her.

"That sounds like her," Cass said, too tired to be surprised that anyone could fly through the worsening storm. "She explained it all to me. Everything she's done, the dead Bio-Ts, all legal and above board."

"I couldn't give a fuck," Harris said. "I'm a criminal. I was a criminal before I joined the Commandos and frankly, when I was special forces, I was doing criminal things for the pleasure of Their Majesties. When I left, criminal again. I mean I don't like to make excuses, but I look at all these corporate cunts and I can't see a difference in my behavior and theirs. Except magically what they do is legal. I say magically; I mean because they're rich and powerful."

It was spurious self-justification and Cass had heard the like from many petty criminals before. Except Harris wasn't that petty a criminal and after having listened to Regina, Harris's logic sounded a lot less tortured.

"To Lace," Cass said raising her glass and knocking the single malt back in a way she suspected you weren't supposed to. It hit the back of her throat like smooth liquid fire, lighting her up inside.

"To the old man," Harris said lifting the tumbler to her lips.

"His name was Harvey," Cass said.

Harris lowered the tumbler again.

"To Harvey," she said raising the glass again before knocking the contents back. She stood up. "Fucking loving this cowboy shit."

She turned and made for the reception area and the dust lock, pointing at the barman as she passed.

"Don't play the arsehole next time," she warned him.

Cass stood up, grabbed her rifle bag and followed.

Outside it was raining glass.

"Fuck!" Harris spat. It seemed the wind-blown glass particles had found exposed skin.

Cass looked up to see the lights of the heavy lift shuttle sinking through the dust towards the shuttle port. Its main engine, along with all its stabilization and directional boosters were burning hard as it bled off velocity and tried to remain steady in the high winds. The shuttles only flew in a category three storm if they absolutely had to. The current dust storm was on the border of a cat four. The shuttle's torch was superheating the dust, turning the particles to glass, which was then being caught by the wind.

"Head down!" Cass shouted through the mask, grabbing Harris and leading her along the boardwalk.

Glass rain notwithstanding, Harris had overridden the dust-lock to the marshal station before the shuttle had even settled in its cradle at the port. They stepped into the dust-lock, which was crowded with both of them in there. Harris adjusted her carbine on its straps, readying it. Cass's rifle was slung across her back in its sealed bag, too bulky to even think about taking out. Instead, she drew the Hancock .357 and waited for the dust-lock to finish cycling. It felt like forever. Anyone in the station's office would know they were coming and that the lock had been hacked.

The office's artificial light flooded into the dust-lock as the door clicked open.

Harris was through first, the carbine pointed at Deputy Amsa who, along with Deputy Williams, had their sidearms levelled at the extractor.

There were a number of demands from both the deputies for Harris and Cass to drop their weapons.

"Don't do anything silly, girls," Harris warned them.

Cass strode out of the dust-lock and made straight for Sorgram, who was just standing by his desk shaking. She wasn't sure if he was angry or frightened.

She couldn't be sure that Amsa or Williams wouldn't shoot her but was too tired to care.

Sorgram tried to draw his weapon. Too late. Cass grabbed his gun arm with her left hand and forced it away from his sidearm, pushing him onto his desk with the momentum of her movement. The sensation of his teeth breaking as she forced her revolver into his mouth was satisfying.

"Acting Marshal Sorgram, I'm hereby relieving you of command," she told him.

He made a squealing noise through a mouthful of blood, teeth, and stainless steel. It sounded like he wanted to know by what authority she was relieving him of command. She thumbed the hammer back on the revolver. Sorgram pissed himself. As satisfying as that was, she did get her boots wet.

She turned to look at Deputies Amsa and Williams.

"Lower the guns, ladies. We've got work to do."

Amsa and Williams exchanged a look and then holstered their weapons. Cass could have easily predicted that neither of the deputies would have been enjoying Sorgram's reign of error. Their actions seemed to confirm as much. Harris lowered her carbine as well and then yawned.

Tyler heard the commotion upstairs in the marshal's office. Then it went quiet. Moments later the reinforced door at the stop of the stairs was unlocked. He could just about make out the sound of movement on the stairs and then Harris was on the other side of the bars.

"Hey kids," she said. She seemed to be enjoying herself.

"Oh no," Serena said from the next cell.

Tyler found himself grinning and he wasn't sure why.

"So, I'm going to let you out," Harris told Tyler, tapping a P-Dat, that probably didn't belong to her, against the cell's locking mechanism. The door sprung open. "But we're not sure about her." She gestured with her thumb towards Serena's cell.

"Either you let her out or just lock me back up again," Tyler told Harris.

"… Others are all buttoned up for the storm," Deputy Williams was telling Cass as Tyler reached the top of the stairs. Glancing around he saw Deputy Amsa cycling through the town's camera feeds, though it looked as though the storm had knocked out more than a few of them.

Sorgram had been handcuffed to the leg of a desk that was bolted to the floor. He was sat in a puddle of urine, alternating between muttering that everyone was getting fired and sobbing. It was pitiable. Never a cruel man, Tyler resisted the urge to go over and kick him. He did wonder why Sorgram hadn't been taken to the cells. He guessed that Cass might want to interrogate her erstwhile senior deputy and usurper.

"Okay, I'd rather have Romane working the camera feeds, than Amsa, but I don't want him coming through the storm. Can he work the feeds at home without any further loss of fidelity?" Cass asked.

"I mean, there are multiple redundancies but the storm's chewing threw them, so yes unless the whole network goes down," Williams told her old/new boss.

"We're in the same position if the network goes down anyway. Tell Michaels and Rodriguez to shelter in place but to get their tac gear on and stay close to comms. Same for you and Amsa, full tac gear, but I want you here holding down the fort."

"Marshal, what's happening?" Williams asked.

Tyler was eager to hear the answer to this as well.

The marshal straightened up and winced, pushing her palm against her back.

"I don't know," she admitted. "But I want to know why the shuttle's risking flying through this and why Chisholm has two land trains full of livestock that they're about to run through the streets of my town."

Tyler frowned. None of it made any sense but then he was struggling to think through the pain.

"Is this the livestock they're sending to New Kiev?" he asked.

"It must be," Cass said but she looked too tired to think.

"So, they have to be carrying something," Tyler suggested.

"Goddamned patriot," Sorgram muttered.

"Like a disease?" Harris asked.

"Yeah," Tyler said. Biowarfare against the communist UPP made a degree of sense.

"Why would Chisholm or the church want to commit an act of bioterrorism against the UPP?" Cass asked.

"A fucking patriot!" Sorgram screamed.

"Shut up!" Serena snapped. Tyler turned to look at her, impressed with Sorgram's ability to even piss Serena off.

"Charters worked for the State Department, straight out of university," Tyler told the room. He saw Cass frown.

"She's a spook?" she asked.

"We don't know," Serena said as she found the station's first aid kit.

"We suspect," Tyler said.

"Even if it was a cattle-delivered bioweapon, there are much easier ways to infect cattle. It could be done embryonically and with a syringe," Serena said, searching through the first aid kit, "there would be no need to drive the cattle through the streets." She handed Tyler two Naproleve tablets, which he gratefully took.

"Marshal," Amsa said from where she was pouring over the camera feeds. "Is this what you're looking for?"

Tyler moved with the others to get a look at the feed. He could make out six, no eight, figures wearing armored environmental suits and carrying assault rifles with some kind of underslung weapons modules making their way south along Port Street. He watched as, outside in the storm-blown street, they moved past the marshal station, their weapons raised to cover the dust-lock as they did so.

Tyler saw his own sense of incredulity mirrored in the marshal's face.

"Who the fuck are these guys?" she muttered.

"They must have come off the shuttle," Williams said.

"They're wearing servo-assisted APE suits," Harris told them, "and those are NSG23s they're carrying."

"So?" Tyler all but demanded. He hoped that Harris had a point beyond simple gun fetishism.

"Both are standard issue for Weyland-Yutani security commandos," Serena explained. She was trying to change the dressings on his wounds.

"And their Dog Catcher units," Harris added.

"Dog Catcher?" Amsa asked.

"A unit within the security commandos responsible for the capture and containment of hostile organisms," Serena explained.

Nobody said anything for a moment or two.

"Are they here for the Bio-Ts?" Williams sounded almost hopeful.

"Ha-ha-ha-ha!" Sorgram shouted at them, making Tyler and both the deputies jump.

"Make another sound and I'll gag you!" Amsa told her erstwhile boss.

"Charters worked for WY after her time at State," Tyler told the room.

Stock turned to look at him.

A flare on one of the screens caught Tyler's eye. He turned back to the bank of monitors. The camera flared again, the image washing out as though suddenly flooded with light.

"That's the church," Serena said,

"Someone's opening the door to the old slaughter-house," Stock added.

"Marshal," Amsa said. She was pointing at another feed. Tyler didn't recognize the part of town the image showed, but he guessed it was from a camera on the southern edge, as it looked out over the prairies. It took Tyler a moment or two to work out what he was looking at through the billowing clouds of dust, but then he was able to make out the mass of cattle being driven towards town by masked cattle hands, riding masked horses.

Then all of them heard the unmistakable sound of automatic weapons fire.

18

They geared up, armor, weapons—except Serena—dusters or dust ponchos and masks, and then went out into the street. Cass left her rifle and instead took one of the Traylor Model 15 shotguns with her. She had advised Matterton to do the same because he couldn't shoot for shit: with the low visibility all of them were going to need every edge they could get. Cass had told Amsa and Williams to stay on the cameras and keep them updated but if anything happened to her, they should improvise, up to and including evacuating the town. Cass still didn't understand everything that was happening here but what she did understand, she didn't like.

She led the way. Tyler, who was running on painkillers and adrenaline as far as Cass could tell, was directly behind her. Serena was behind him and Harris brought up the rear. They were battered by the wind the moment they left the dust-lock. Cass felt like she could get blown off her feet at any moment. They had managed to make it half way across the dust-mud-clogged Port Street when she heard it. Faintly at first over the storm, distorted by the wind, Cass's fatigue and amphetamine-addled brain recognized the familiarity of the clamor but was unable to immediately place it. Then the first cattle emerged from the dust as they were driven down Port Street.

"Move!" Cass shouted, wading through the mud as fast as she could manage, the others following suit. She made it to the boardwalk on the other side of the street as the mass of cattle, packed in shoulder-to-shoulder, surged north towards the shuttle port. Serena was somehow already on the boardwalk ahead of them; both of them helped Harris up, who immediately covered south down the street. They pulled Tyler up onto the boardwalk moments before the herd surged through where he had been struggling.

Cass cried out as a horn tore through one of the boardwalk's wooden supports and ripped her duster and body armor through to the skin of her back. The force sent her staggering. Tyler caught her, steadying her. Serena was reaching for the medkit she was carrying. Cass waved her off: there was no point while they were out in the storm. She could already feel dust against her skin. If nothing else it would clot up the wound. Instead, they moved over to the wall and Cass handed Serena a dust patch. The artificial person used it to try and seal the tear in the duster as best she could as Cass watched the river of cattle pass.

She signaled for Harris to take point. Serena was more than capable of watching their six, even if she had chosen to go unarmed again. For the life of her, Cass couldn't see why. The artificial person had to be well within the parameters that allowed her to arm herself to defend the humans around her.

Harris leaned in close to Cass.

"Just so you know, boss," the extractor shouted over the storm, "I'm erring on the side of caution and just killing people today, yeah?"

Harris met her eyes. Even through the mask, Cass could see the resolve. She guessed everyone grieved differently. She just nodded. It wasn't like either of them would ever testify to this exchange.

Harris led them off. As Cass followed, she kept glancing at the flow of cattle.

Ahead of them she could see the light from the old slaughterhouse seeping out into the dust. The slaughterhouse's door had to be wide open.

"Amsa, what you have you got for me?" Cass asked over comms. "Any movement down by the church."

"Marshal, the door to the genet—" then the comms went completely dead.

Cass patted Harris's shoulder to signal her to stop and then held up her hand to stop the others.

Harris leaned back and the others closed in to hear her.

"Comms are down!" she told them, not just competing with the wind but with the noise of the cattle, which was getting louder and louder—as though they were becoming more agitated.

"It's what I'd do!" Harris shouted back. It made sense. Whether the gunmen and women in the APE suits were WY or not, they wouldn't want Cass or her deputies contacting the marine base.

There was nothing for them to do but continue. Harris led them off again.

Amongst the mass of cattle, Cass saw a number jump up, landing on the backs of others in the press. At first her addled mind wondered if they were trying to breed, but these were all cows—no bulls. She couldn't shake the feeling that something was agitating them but whatever it was, she couldn't see it. She knew well the devastation that a stampede could cause even in such tight quarters where they had no place to go. Especially in such tight quarters.

Turning away from the cattle there was a lull in the blowing dust. Cass could see the entrance to the old slaughterhouse, the cargo door wide open, bleeding light into the dust. She could make out two armored figures standing either side of the door. As soon as Cass saw them, they were turning, but Harris was already firing. The hypersonic scream of the EM-driven projectiles was torn away from them by the wind. Harris kept moving and firing. The armored figures were swallowed by the dust again.

Cass and the others emerged from the dust by the open door to the old slaughterhouse. The man and the woman in the APEsuits were both on the floor, unmoving. Harris still put two rounds in each of their heads even as she continued towards the opening. The extractor went wide around the doorway and then covered right; Cass followed her into the church covering left; Tyler followed her covering straight ahead.

"Clear!" Harris shouted.

"Clear!" Cass announced.

"Clear! I think!" Tyler's words were almost lost to the wind.

Only then did Cass take a moment to more fully look around at the strangely contoured, organic-looking space. Everything inside was now coated with dust: the floor looked like a beach. Despite the press of cattle outside, none of the cows seemed to want to take advantage of this empty space, probably due to the fleshy pods scattered throughout the chamber. They were roughly the shape of eggs and about the size of a trash-can. Unfolded leathery flaps hung down their sides.

"What the fuck?" Cass wondered.

Serena was edging closer to one of them, peering in.

"Careful!" Tyler called, the wind and cattle quieter inside, the strange architecture deadening the sound.

The titanic patrician face of an Engineer stared

malevolently down at them. That was when Cass noticed the dead body industrially bolted to the huge bust. Fitzgerald's arms were stretched across the Engineer's heavy brow, the murdered adherent's torso and legs running down the Engineer's prominent nose. There was a deep red cavity where Fitzgerald's face used to be. The Bio-Ts had brought his corpse here as a grisly decoration. It certainly didn't look out of place.

"It's empty!" Serena called.

Cass was close to shutting down. She didn't want to look into the moist insides of the strange, biological pods. She could hear more and more sounds of distress from the cattle outside.

"Seriously, any ideas?" Tyler asked.

"I think they might be eggs of some kind," Serena suggested.

A thought had been trying to push its way through the uppers and fatigue for a while now. There's something amongst the cattle. Cass turned to look out at the press of cattle surging past, seemingly trying to give the old slaughterhouse as wide a berth as possible.

She turned back to look at Tyler.

"This is why they're running cattle through town," he called.

Cass nodded, numb.

Harris looked mystified.

"There had to be a better way to do it, than this," Serena said.

"We need to find Dawkins," Cass said. She moved towards the hidden stairway, Tyler and Serena falling in behind her. Harris bringing up the rear again.

It had taken a moment to find a way to activate the fold-away spiral staircase. At the top Harris overrode the concealed door's lock mechanism and they were out onto the connecting bridge over Port Street. A never-ending tsunami of cattle flowed below them. Cass guessed the Chisholm ranch hands were feeding them in at the south end of Port Street and then staying well out of the way. Not that there was anything they could really do in this press anyway. The cattle were leaving a swathe of destruction in their wake.

They were halfway across the bridge when Cass registered something moving towards them at speed in the air outside. It hit the bridge hard. The window next to her cracked and shattered, the superstructure buckling. The bridge shook like it was going to collapse, as though the walkway under her had just bent. Cass brought her shotgun up but didn't fire. Tyler did. The shotgun blast was deafening. Cass flinched away from the noise, losing the hearing in one ear, feeling the heat from the muzzle flash that illuminated the smashed-up hover ATV that had just been thrown at the bridge. The wreckage fell amongst the press of cattle. Through the crack in the bridge, even over the storm, Cass could make out the noise of the herd and the sound of the accompanying destruction.

Then she heard the crack of bullets penetrating the glass of the bridge's windows. They were taking incoming fire.

"Move!" Harris shouted.

Cass scuttled after the extractor, trying to stay low. She could see the distant flicker of muzzle flashes from the north. Someone was firing at them over the heads of the moving herd, further confusing and frightening the cattle.

Cass found herself crouched by the hermetically sealed door to the genetics facility, covering back across the now bent bridge as Harris rapidly ran a lock bypass. It was only then that what had just happened really sank in.

"Someone threw an ATV at us."

Nobody said anything. Cass guessed, like her, they were struggling to work out how that had come about. Her ear was just about working again, though she could still hear ringing. Whomever had been shooting at them seemed to have stopped now.

The door hissed open. Harris packed away her intrusion kit and went through first, assault carbine at the ready. Cass followed. The facility's huge cargo door was open onto the yard that ran between Port and Jersey Street. Another dust beach was encroaching into the cavernous space through the opening. Isolated fires burned throughout the facility. Some kind of fight had taken place here. The top of the spherical 'bioreactor' was lying upturned on the floor, having crushed some benches and equipment. There was water all around the open 'bioreactor', presumably the result of some kind of now-inoperable cryogenic system. Inside the hemisphere formed by the bottom half of the 'bioreactor', was a spiral of some kind of segmented, membranous, very biological, liquid-filled tube, attached to the metal by a webwork of resinous material.

"Okay—" Harris said. Cass suspected it was the closest the extractor came to being surprised. Harris continued down the stairs and onto the floor of the facility, the others following.

They passed a still-smoking hole in the concrete floor, surrounded by limbs and part of a skull, tatters of an alabaster-pale face hanging from it. One of the Bio-Ts had died here, their body either destroyed by powerful munitions or perhaps by its own acidic blood. Was that possible? Cass could see holes from small arms fire, which she guessed must have come from the WY security commandos. She even saw what looked like the results of grenade detonations. They found the scattered limbs and a headless torso wearing an APEsuit.

What the fuck happened here? Cass wondered feeling at the edge of her calm.

"Serena!" Tyler shouted. Cass turned to see the artificial person move quickly and quietly up the ladder attached to the 'bioreactor' to get a closer look inside.

The three of them took up positions to cover as much of the facility as possible while Serena examined the biological material within the hemisphere.

"Can you hear that?" Tyler asked.

"No," Cass muttered, "because someone let off a shotgun right next to my ear." Though now she could hear something: sobbing, interspersed with coughing. Harris heard it as well. The extractor caught Serena's attention and signaled for her to come back.

"Well?" Tyler asked as she rejoined them.

"I have never seen anything like it," she told them. "My best guess is that it is some kind of external egg sac."

"Those pods we saw in the slaughterhouse?" Tyler asked.

"Again, it's a guess but yes," Serena said.

"So, whatever's laying them is pretty big then?" Cass asked. Serena nodded. "Big enough to throw an ATV at us?"

Nobody said anything. Cass was liking this less and less, especially as she was now very much aware that there was someone else in there with them.

"We need to find whoever that is and secure them," Harris said. She didn't exactly seem spooked, but she was definitely less than happy. "Serena, with me—watch my back. We'll cut right around this thing," she nodded at the bioreactor. "Marshal, you and Matterton cut left. Watch your shots—I don't want to be picking buckshot out of my armor, yeah? And keep a lookout above."

As Harris said it, Cass looked up at the crane that ran above them on rails connected to the reinforced rafters. There was no doubt about it, she was very much out of practice at all this tactical shit.

Then they were moving. Tyler followed as Cass went wide around the 'bioreactor', which seemed, in actuality, to be some kind of nest. She swept left and right, looking up, the barrel of her shotgun following her eyes. She could see a figure kneeling on the dust beach, close to the threshold of the open cargo door. The opening was leeward so the dusty wind was not as strong as it could have been. The storm was still howling outside, however. Cass could just about make out the sound of the unsettled herd on the other side of the facility on Port Street. She moved closer so she could better hear the figure sobbing and coughing.

"Stay where you are! Do not move!" she told the kneeling Dawkins. He ignored her. He wasn't wearing a mask.

Harris moved past the figure, her back to him, covering out into the yard, out into the storm.

"Dawkins?" Cass said, more quietly.

"She's gone," Dawkins said. His voice didn't sound right, changed somehow, full of loss.

"Who's gone?" Cass asked. Tyler had joined her, Serena was scanning the rest of the facility, watching their back, despite being unarmed.

"The Goddess," he told them.

"What was in the bioreactor?" Tyler asked. "What were those pod-things?"

"They didn't understand. They were trying to make it all tawdry. All their talk of enhanced soldiers and eggs for their insane scheme. They didn't understand what we were doing. The adherents were striving for the perfection of our weak and debased flesh. The eggs were vessels of the Goddess's children. We were engaged in holy communion and they called it science." Dawkins started laughing, snorting at the same time, spitting out bloodied dust. He still hadn't looked up.

Cass couldn't make sense of what he was saying, but it didn't sound good.

"The goddess was in the bioreactor, wasn't she?" Cass asked. "And you let her out."

Dawkins' head moved incrementally in what might have been a nod.

"They sent a clean-up crew. Could you imagine anything more inappropriate, anything more hubristic? They wanted to destroy her," he told them.

"Who did?" Tyler demanded with more emotion than Cass could muster.

Dawkins didn't answer for a moment.

"It's instinct not to answer, to keep their secrets because of the money and their threats, but I don't suppose it matters now, does it?" he said.

Cass was fairly sure it didn't, but she was also pretty

sure she knew the answer. The APEsuits and the NSG23s were a giveaway.

It was Matterton that said it out loud: "Weyland-Yutani. They were behind the slush fund."

Dawkins nodded.

Three things occurred to Cass as the wind screamed outside. The first had her wondering why the fuck some near-omnipotent megacorporation was messing with her town. The second was whether or not Charters was just infiltrating Chisholm, a subsidiary of Lasalle Bionational, WY's main competition in the biotech industry, for Weyland-Yutani, or if she was still CIA. After all, megacorporations had been heavily entangled in the military and intelligence industries since at least the twentieth century. Her third thought was that she should have been recording this.

"Snell?" Tyler all but demanded.

"When you're a dreamer, sensitive, you can hear her, feel her in here." Dawkins tapped the side of his head. "It's… a beautiful, a holy terror." Cass was pretty sure Dawkins was holding something in his curled-up fist. "Poor boy. I guess he was just a little too sensitive."

One thing, however, still didn't make sense to her.

"The cattle?" Cass asked.

"That was your fault," Dawkins told them.

Cass glanced over at Tyler to see if it made sense to him. He didn't look as confused as she felt but then he'd had some sleep since their last gunfight.

"You were forced to move your plans up," Serena said, her back to Dawkins as she scanned the genetics facility, still looking for further threats. "You hadn't intended for the shuttle to fly in the storm. You had not intended to drive the cattle through the dust."

"The adherents moved the ovomorphs to the Engineer Chamber," Dawkins said, still not looking up. Cass guessed that the ovomorphs were whatever the leathery pod things were in the old slaughterhouse. "They were going to cycle a few cattle in at a time and expose them to the *Manumala Noxhydria*."

"The what?" Cass demanded.

"Her children," Matterton said.

"The bearer of her children," Dawkins corrected.

"These *Manumala Noxhydria*, they are parasitical, yes? They lay something in the cattle?" Serena asked.

Cass wasn't following well enough to understand how Serena had arrived at that conclusion.

Dawkins' hacking laughter sounded bitter.

"Then you send the parasitized cattle to the UPP," Tyler added. "It's some kind of bioweapon."

"Bioweapons. Parasites. Cattle. Such small minds," Dawkins said. Personally, Cass thought Serena and Tyler were doing pretty well to keep up. "The *Noxhydria* are holy vessels. They should not be inseminating mere cattle."

Inseminating was an unsettling new word to be introduced into an already unpleasant conversation.

"What *should* they be inseminating?" Cass asked, sure she wasn't going to like the answer.

Dawkins finally looked up. Cass recoiled. At first, she thought he'd undergone the same process that the Bio-Ts had to turn their eyes black. Then she realized that where his eyes had been were now just two bloody cavities.

"We would be accepting a holy sacrament," he told them. "I made her an offering." He raised up both hands, turned them over, opening them. His two eyes stared up at her, unseeing, from the palm of his hands. "She didn't want them. Why didn't she want them?"

Cass took a step back, the butt of her shotgun a comfort against her shoulder. If she squeezed the trigger, it would be a mercy killing. She could barely look at him. It was the childlike expression of confusion on his face that bothered her the most. As though he'd done everything he was supposed to and still his goddess had rejected him.

"We still don't know what the goddess is, what her children are," Tyler said.

Dawkins' hands dropped to the dust-covered ground. He started laughing, then he was crying, his cheeks flecked with bloody tears.

"Is he good for anything else?" Harris asked.

Cass was watching him sob uncontrollably.

"I think he held it together for as long as he could," Cass told the extractor.

Harris let her carbine hang on its sling as she drew her sidearm and levelled it at Dawkins.

Serena moved in between Harris and her prospective victim.

"You can't do that," she said. "He needs to testify."

"In case you haven't noticed this isn't a fucking court; it's not even a crime scene, it's a warzone. Different rules apply. I'm not leaving anyone alive who doesn't very much wish us well," Harris told her, moved to the side and raised her sidearm again.

Serena struck out with lightning speed, capturing Harris's arm, twisting it and taking the sidearm.

Harris took several rapid steps back and raised her carbine.

"You don't get to manhandle me, love," she told Serena. It was the closest to sounding angry Cass had heard Harris.

Then Tyler was standing between Harris and Serena.

"Even in a warzone, you can't just shoot unarmed prisoners."

"So they keep telling me," Harris growled.

Cass noted that Tyler was very careful not to point his shotgun in Harris' direction.

"This is stupid. Harris, lower your weapon. He's no threat," Cass said.

Harris glanced at the eyeless, still weeping, Dawkins.

"He's not until he is," Harris said, lowering her carbine before taking her sidearm back from Serena and holstering it. “So, we need to get to the shuttle, get off this world, yeah?”

“We need to contain this,” Cass told them. “Deal with the threat, make sure none of the townsfolk get hurt.”

“And stop any inseminated cattle getting off world,” Matterton added.

Serena nodded in agreement.

Harris looked between the three of them and then down at Dawkins.

“Fucking Americans,” she muttered, then turned and stalked into the storm.

Cass and the others followed.

19

It was clear that nobody knew what they were doing. It was understandable—Tyler had certainly never experienced anything like this before. It seemed unlikely the others had either, even Harris. That said, he was pretty sure that the current plan was to go looking for something that had thrown an ATV at them earlier. In fairness that was still a better plan than trying to find inseminated cows amongst the hundreds that they were following, now they were back on Port Steet. The dust blow was so heavy that Tyler was only occasionally able to see the tail end of the herd and the wind-blown debris left in their wake.

He guessed they were supposed to be engaging in some kind of tactical movement but even Harris just had her head down against the howling wind and dust. There was a flash of red ahead of them and Tyler risked putting his head up as he saw a gout of flame lighting up the dust, bending against the harsh wind. The burst of fire enabled Tyler to see more of the herd milling around at the head of Port Street, spilling through the open gates of the shuttle port and into the loading bay.

Tyler could just make out the blinking lights of the heavy lift shuttle. It stood about five stories high in its docking cradle. The cradle grew out of the engine-blackened concrete of the loading bay. Concrete ramparts surrounded the loading bay, protecting the northern edge of the town from the shuttle's torch.

Ahead there was another gout of flame and Tyler caught a glimpse of its source. One of the APE suited WY clean-up crew was triggering his assault rifle's underslung incinerator unit. Cows clambered over each other in a bid to get away from the fire. They were herding cattle with flame throwers. It was a novel approach, he guessed.

Harris signaled a halt. Tyler almost missed the signal in the swirling dust. Serena put a hand on his shoulders and gestured towards the extractor. His partner was wearing a mask simply because it was easier to shout through the filter rather than a mouthful of dust.

Harris was looking through her carbine's scope.

They were joined by Stock, who put her back to Harris covering behind them. Tyler was trying not to think too much about the 'goddess' that was apparently stalking the streets of Steer City.

"Well?" Cass asked. Tyler guessed the marshal was

asking Harris if she could hit any of the WY clean-up crew from her position.

"Probably!" Harris shouted over the storm.

"Wish I'd brought my rifle!" Cass replied, glancing back towards the Marshal Station. "Let's keep moving!"

The marshal motioned for them to continue. They were out in the street, moving from one trampled or overturned vehicle to the next as cover. They couldn't use the boardwalk and stay close to the buildings because the boardwalk was just so many splinters now.

Harris, the only one of them with a longish-range weapon, covered them as they moved and then joined them. It was slow progress up the street. Tyler had to keep reminding himself to look around and make sure they were all together. With comms down and the wind drowning out even their loudest shouting, they risked losing contact with the others if they didn't stay close. Still, they were slowly closing with the back of the herd. Tyler felt his palms get sweaty, his heart rate increase. He didn't want to get in another gunfight, let alone instigate one. The only good thing about the situation was that between nerves, adrenaline and the pain killers, he was less aware of the pain from his burns.

They made it to within about a hundred feet of the rear of the roiling mass of cattle. Tyler joined Serena and Cass, crouching behind a partially flattened plains buggy. Moments later Harris appeared next to him, pointing her carbine around the edge of the vehicle.

"Got to get started some time!" she shouted to them.

Tyler looked to Cass, who had apparently ended up in command by default. Tyler was okay with that. He didn't want to be in charge, and he didn't trust Harris to do the job. In fairness the extractor seemed happy enough to follow Cass' lead. For the time being, anyway.

The marshal looked as though she was about to say something.

"Wait!" Serena shouted. All of them turned to look at her. She was pointing at a cow lying against the horn-scored frontage of a general store that had been buttoned up against the storm. At first Tyler thought the cow was dead, then he noticed it was breathing. There was something attached to the cow's head. Something very wrong.

Serena moved over to investigate. Tyler followed. He wasn't sure if he heard or had imagined the marshal telling them to stop.

He guessed the thing wrapped around the cow's head was the *Manumala Noxhydria* that Dawkins had been talking about before he fully succumbed to hysteria. Not for the first time today, Tyler was trying to make sense of what he was looking at. It looked like a pincer-less scorpion: eight long, multi-jointed, finger-like legs clasped the cow's head. A long segmented tail was wrapped around the cow's neck. External, leathery, lung-like organs inflated and deflated as though breathing for the cow. It was clear that the biotech he had seen inside the strange hypersleep pods in the church's genetics facility was somehow connected to or derived from, this creature. Tyler had never had such a singularly strong revulsion to another living thing before.

"Nope," he said and leveled his shotgun at it, stepping back from it as he did.

Serena moved away as well.

He squeezed the trigger. The parasitic nightmare ceased to exist. Smoke boiled into the air only to be whipped away by the howling wind. Yellow pus burned deep into the general store's external wall. These creatures had acid for blood as well.

A new hole appeared in the wall of the general store. Tyler heard a popping noise. Tyler turned towards the murk-obscured lights of the shuttle port. There were eddies in the dust. Serena threw herself at him, bearing him to the ground. Only then did it register with Tyler that he was being shot at. Again. It had all happened in a matter of moments. He half crawled, was half dragged by Serena back behind the wrecked ground buggy.

There was screaming. Tyler looked over to see Harris on one knee, firing her assault carbine around the edge of the buggy. Three-round-burst, shift target, three-round-burst, shift target again.

Next to him Cass peeked over the flattened roof of the ground buggy. Tyler heard metal hitting metal at speed. A bullet exploded through the side of the wrecked vehicle inches from his head, fragments tearing through the side of his mask.

Harris raised her carbine and there was a popping sound barely audible over the storm. She worked the pump-action mechanism on the carbine's underslung grenade launcher. Then the grenade she had just fired exploded. Harris rapidly reloaded the carbine.

Tyler could hear the herd sounding more and more distressed. Hear the thunder of their hoofbeats.

"Move!" Harris shouted.

Tyler wasn't sure where she meant them to move, but Cass was up on her feet, running around the ground buggy. Tyler forced himself up and after her, Serena following.

There was more screaming as Harris laid down covering fire.

Moving quickly, he wasn't even sure where the WY shooters were. He could hear gunfire but the bullets were zipping by, which suggested that they weren't shooting at him. Harris had to be drawing their fire.

Cass was moving towards the north-west corner of Port Street.

Between Tyler and the shuttle port was a mass of panicking cattle. They were stampeding in a circle, kicking up more dust as they tried to get into the shuttle port.

Glancing to his right, Tyler could see a smoking

crater. Presumably the result of Harris's grenade. He wondered if the extractor had taken out one of the shooters as well.

The sound of a shotgun being fired rapidly yanked Tyler's attention back to Cass, ahead of him. She was firing at the corner of the last building on Port Street, the one they were moving towards. Tyler increased his pace, passing Cass, going wide round the corner. Serena with him.

There were two shooters against the wall of the building. The first at the corner sheltering from Cass' incoming fire, the other trying to go wide around the first. Trying the same flanking maneuver that Tyler was performing.

Tyler felt Serena snatch his service weapon from his hip holster as he went down on one knee and started firing his shotgun at the flanking shooter. Squeezing the trigger again and again, sending the APEsuited shooter staggering. Over his head Serena was firing burst after burst into the head of the first shooter, the one at the corner. Serena's headshots knocked him into the wall but neither of the shooters went down. Their APEsuits protected them from the shotgun's combat loads and the 9mm bullets from his service weapon.

Cass came wide round the corner. Having transitioned to her .357.

Serena shifted her fire to the second shooter.

Tyler's shotgun ran dry. He let it fall on its sling. He

was on his feet passing two magazines for his sidearm to Serena as she moved past him towards the second shooter.

Cass fired three times at near point-blank range into the first shooter's faceplate. The heavier magnum rounds cracked and then penetrated the armored glass.

The slide on Serena's pistol locked back as it ran out of ammunition. Serena hit the magazine release and flicked it away before sliding a new one home.

Tyler was firing his backup weapon at the second shooter, flattening more 9mm bullets against his armor, just trying to keep him off-balance as the WY gunman tried to raise his weapon.

Then Serena was firing again, burst after burst.

The shooter was turning towards Cass, who'd just killed his partner.

Cass shot four times into the second shooter's faceplate and the second shooter went down as well.

Something whistled past Tyler's head.

A moment of panic as he saw Serena spin as though hit.

A sledgehammer blow hit his side: he couldn't breathe. He staggered forwards and went down on his knees.

A spray of red painted the wall behind Cass as she bounced off it and then slid to the ground as well.

Harris stalked out of the dust past Tyler, firing her carbine. Hypersonic penetrators screamed into the storm. Whomever had been shooting at them stopped.

"Can you walk?" Harris shouted at Tyler. Stupid question. "Can you fucking walk?!" she demanded.

Tyler patted his side. It hurt. His hand came away red. He still couldn't breathe. Then Serena was there.

"Move back to Stock!" Harris ordered. Gesturing to the wall.

Serena performed a cursory examination of Tyler's wound.

Tyler noticed white pearlescent fluid seeping through a hole in his partner's body armor. He opened his mouth to say something, but he couldn't speak, he couldn't breathe.

Serena pulled him to his feet.

Harris, down on one knee now, glanced back at them. As she did so a huge, inhuman shadow loomed out of the storm over her. Tyler, tried to shout a warning but there was no air. He flailed, trying to get Serena's, or even Harris' attention.

A black, serrated bone spike burst through Harris's back, severing her spine. She was yanked up into the air and disappeared into the dust.

Serena was aware now. She aimed her borrowed pistol at the place Harris had been as she pulled Tyler back towards Cass' position against the bloodied wall. The shadow was gone.

Serena deposited Tyler next to a bloodied Cass. The marshal still wasn't dead. Instead, she was screaming at herself in frustration as she shook the spent cartridges out of her revolver and tried to reload it with shaking hands. She was wounded in several places.

Serena was still covering the area where Harris had been, checking all around her. Tyler knew it was a waste of time. What he had just seen, as awful as it was, he was awestruck by it. There was no chance of stopping it.

The ability to breathe returned to Tyler like a hammer blow.

"Goddess!" he cried out almost involuntarily.

Cass stopped what she was doing to stare at him for a moment.

Tyler wasn't sure if he heard the wet, ripping, tearing noise or imagined it, but suddenly the three of them were covered in blood as the two bloodied halves of Harris's body hit the ground in front of them.

"Cover!" Serena said, dropping Tyler's own service weapon and a spare magazine in his lap. He'd lost his backup when he'd been hit. He picked up the weapon and did as he was bid.

Working quickly, Serena retrieved one of the dead WY shooters' assault rifles, and gave it and two spare magazines to Tyler. He handed his pistol back to her and forced himself up onto one knee, pain lancing through his side so he could provide cover. It didn't matter. He knew they couldn't fight the thing that had just murdered Harris.

Cass managed to flip the cylinder of her revolver

closed as Serena knelt by her. The marshal grunted in pain as Serena checked her wounds.

"Thigh, through-and-through, missed the femoral, looks like you took a fragment to the chest, penetrated your body armor, I think broke some ribs, might be pressing on your lung, you'll live if you don't move. Third one creased your skull. It may be fractured: it's bleeding a lot, but it looks worse than it is," Serena told the marshal.

"Lucky me," the marshal said. "I can't see."

"It's just blood," Serena said, "but it's under your mask."

Cass grabbed the front of Serena's body armor.

"This is a shit position. We're exposed. Our only cover is the storm. We need to take that shuttle."

Tyler was trying not to watch the exchange. He was supposed to be covering, or rather watching for their inevitable death.

Serena removed the medkit from her body armor and handed it to Cass.

"You're out of this fight, Marshal. You need to see to your own wounds and get as far from here as you can."

Tyler glanced back at Cass. He could tell that she wanted to argue, but she knew Serena was right. Cass nodded.

Then Serena was by his side. Examining his wound.

"It looks like your body armor significantly slowed the bullet, helped deflect it across the side of your rib.

I think the force of the blow caused your diaphragm to spasm. The wound is already packed with dust," Serena told him. He nodded. He could feel the grit in the wound. The dust inside his armor, against his skin, abrading it. He had calmed down now. He knew what they had to do.

He cupped a hand around her neck.

"We need to kill the herd and that thing," he said looking into her eyes through their masks.

She met his eyes and nodded.

Both of them looked to the shuttle.

Tyler and Serena were moving around the herd. The Naproleve allowed him to suppress the pain from his burns and from the grazed rib enough to function, but every movement was pain. The cattle were milling around in front of the shuttle, filling the loading bay and spilling out, past the ramparts and into the open area between the north end of the town and the shuttle port. The press of cow flesh was so much that some of the herd had been forced up the concrete slope and were wandering around the ramparts' flattened tops.

Tyler's shotgun was slung across his back and he was carrying one of the Weyland-Yutani assault rifles, having taken a few moments to familiarize himself with it and the underslung incinerator unit. Ahead of him Serena carried the other shooter's rifle; Tyler's service weapon now rode her hip. She had retrieved Tyler's backup pistol and returned it to him.

As they moved through the dust on the edge of the herd, the stench from the cattle was overwhelming, even through the dust mask's filters. Glancing behind him, he could still see Cass, her back against the bloodied wall of the of the corner building on Port Street. Serena had reloaded the marshal's shotgun for her. The weapon was laid across Cass' legs as the marshal saw to her own wounds as best she could.

Tyler tried not to think about the Goddess stalking through the storm. Stalking Serena and himself.

They clambered up the concrete rampart and dropped down into the loading bay. Now they were moving amongst the cattle at the edge of the herd.

The level of noise from the already nervous cattle picked up. Tyler glanced to his right into the press of beasts. He thought he saw one of them go down amongst the herd.

He almost ran into Serena's back. She had come to a halt and was looking down at another fallen cow. Tyler saw the *Noxhydria* clutching the cow's head with its long finger-like legs, the inflating and deflating lung-like organs, the tail tightening its grip on the still living cow's neck, as though the parasite sensed their presence.

Serena raised her weapon and shot the parasite twice. Acid splashed out of the wound. Serena lowered her weapon. There was something almost sad in the movement.

Then dust was being kicked up in the dirt around them and Tyler heard the pop and zip of incoming bullets. He hunkered down, trying to use the herd as cover. Trying to work out where the incoming fire was coming from. Serena was already returning fire, short, controlled bursts towards the shuttle. Tyler, still crouching, could see twin muzzle flashes from inside the shuttle's cavernous cargo bay. He forced himself to think. He could return fire, and he and Serena could try and maneuver around the herd, exchanging fire, burning through their ammunition. Or he could try something else.

He sent gouts of flame over the head of the herd, the wind catching the stream of fire, further unsettling them. He yelled and screamed at them as he sent more flame over their heads. Some of the nearest cows galloped away from him but not enough to make a difference. More incoming fire. He kneeled. Tyler aimed the assault rifle's underslung incinerator unit low and triggered it again. The flame shot along the edge of the herd, the wind blowing it towards them. The cows trying to push hard into the herd, to get away from the threat. Distress travelling through the press of cattle.

"Move!" he told Serena as he sent flame shooting in the other direction.

Serena stepped back, crouching down, reloading her assault rifle.

More gouts of flame and then he heard it, the thunder of hoofbeats as the herd tried to get away from the fire. Stampede.

"I am just the worst vegetarian," he whispered to himself as the herd pushed away from him in any way they could, many spilling into the heavy lift shuttle's cargo bay. He tried to convince himself it was the wind he heard screaming, not the shooters as they were gored and crushed under hoof. He was now pretty sure that he understood the full extent of Weyland-Yutani's plan. It wasn't going the way the clean-up crew and possibly Charters had hoped. Maybe they had expected more help from the ranch hands? The couldn't have planned for the Goddess stalking the storm either.

Now that the herd had moved, Tyler and Serena were exposed. Nobody shot at them as they moved through the cow-shit covered loading bay towards the shuttle.

Tyler sensed movement in his periphery. He swung around to see more *Noxhydria* than he could easily count scuttling towards him from out under the press of cattle.

"Serena!" he called through his mask. The wind whipped the word away from him. A quick glance saw her disappearing into a bank of fresh blown dust. He almost fired the assault rifle. Instead, he had the presence of mind to move his hand forwards and squeeze the incinerator unit's trigger again, holding it down, trying not shoot fire into the wind as he played the flame left and right. One of the creatures squealed like a punctured balloon as the flames engulfed it. Left and right, again and again. The parasitical creatures knew enough to fear the flames, scuttling away from it where they could, trying to flank him as he kept backing away from them. Slowly, however, they were encircled him even as he left a number blackened and sizzling amongst the flash-fried cow shit.

The incinerator unit guttered and died. The remaining *Noxhydria* surged towards him. He wasn't a good enough shot to pick them off with a rifle. He let the rifle drop on its sling. Crying out as the hot incinerator unit burned his leg. Getting the slings tangled as he tried to transition to the shotgun.

The gouts of flame were renewed as more of the creatures were cooked. Serena was by his side, firing her assault rifle's own underslung incinerator unit.

Tyler was exhausted, his breathing ragged, his whole body ached and his side was agony. The herd had calmed down but they were packed in tight on the wide ramp leading up into the shuttle's cavernous cargo bay. Now close up, Tyler could see the cattle-sized hypersleep pods, stacked up inside. The cows milling around Tyler and Serena were starting to press against them as they tried to make their way towards the shuttle. Had he not felt so hopeless, he would have taken some pride in knowing that their actions had so inconvenienced Weyland-Yutani's or Charters' plan that the black op had almost certainly failed. The problem was it had failed with the Goddess on the loose, something he would be far more terrified of if he still had the energy. There was also the matter of an unknown number of parasitically inseminated cows wandering around the shuttle port. Though inseminated with what, he still wasn't entirely sure.

"We can't get through that!" he told Serena. Trying to stampede them now would only increase the chance of them being crushed.

"We don't have a choice!" she shouted back.

He looked at her. He could see very little of her expression through her mask but he could see enough.

Tyler nodded. He was pretty sure he was dead anyway.

Following Serena, Tyler moved slowly through the mass of cow flesh. He slapped a cow's flanks to get it to move. He had read about this in a book once. The cow shifted as much as it could and he squeezed past, very aware of how easily he could be crushed. Even through the filter, the stench was so bad that he was close to filling his mask with vomit. He was pretty sure that real cowboys didn't do things like this because it was so stupid. He had the assault rifle in his left hand, holding it high above the press, his backup pistol in his right. Ahead of him Serena was doing something similar.

Tyler tried to move forward but couldn't. He felt something tug at him, dragging him backwards. He glanced behind him and saw that the sling of his shotgun was caught around the horn of one of the cows. He couldn't turn enough to unhook it. The cow, sensing the sling, shook its head, almost taking Tyler off his feet. He knew if he went down here, he wouldn't get back up. He pushed his backup pistol into the webbing on the front of his body armor and drew his knife, unfolding it with his thumb, and started to saw through the shotgun's sling.

The cow shook her head again. The force of the cow's movement pulled him back sharply. He almost dropped the knife and felt a horn pierce through his duster, the strap of his body armor and into his shoulder. He bit back on the scream trying to escape his throat. This wasn't the place to make sudden noises. He managed to get a better grip on the hilt of his knife and continued sawing. Finally, the sling gave and he pulled away from the shotgun, continuing after Serena.

Slowly but surely, they made it up the ramp but the cargo bay was packed with pressed in cattle as well. On the other side of the hold, he could see steps up to a door in the bulkhead, presumably opening into the shuttle's interior, but they were so far away that they may as well have been on another planet.

Tyler felt something crunch and squelch underfoot. He was pretty sure that he had just trodden on the rib cage of one of the Weyland-Yutani shooters. Their APE suits hadn't protected them from the sheer power of the stampede. He caught up to Serena, who was stood next to a rack of cow-sized hypersleep pods. It looked as though the racks worked on the same principle as a paternoster lift. A pod would be loaded with a cow and then revolved for the next empty pod to be loaded and so on. All of them were currently empty.

He saw the legs of the *Noxhydria* first, as they curled over the back of a cow pressed in tight against Serena. The finger-like legs pulled the parasite's lunging scorpion-like body over the cow's spine, tensing as though about to leap.

"Serena!" Tyler screamed as he pulled his backup pistol from the front of his armor, levelled it and fired without thinking. It was probably the best, or luckiest, shot he had ever made in his life. The bullet caught the creature center mass, blowing it off the cow's back. Acid sprayed amongst the nearby cattle who were already spooked by the close proximity gunshot.

Serena tried to whip her head away from the spray but some of it caught her, her face smoking as the panicking cattle battered her. She went down just before Tyler was pulled under.

20

Cass's world was pain. Everything fucking hurt and frankly life sucked. Fortunately, the Colonial Marines had taught her what to do with the suck.

"Stop fucking whining and get on your feet," she muttered to herself. It had been faint over the wind, which was blowing from the south, but she was sure she had heard gunfire from the general direction of the shuttle port. Without comms there was no way to know whether or not Tyler and Serena were still alive, but there was certainly active fuckery within the shuttle port.

She put the butt of her shotgun on the ground and used the weapon to help push herself up the wall that she'd made bloody with the help of a number of high-velocity rifle rounds. The irony of it was she had been very lucky. She had only been grazed but even that had taken her completely out of the fight. In the storm there was little she could do about her wounds, except pack them with dust to stop the bleeding. The medkit that Serena had given her was useful for painkillers and stimulants, both of which were taking the edge off. A bit. Besides, she didn't want to put off her first heart attack.

Using her shotgun as a walking stick in the way that would disgust any firearms professional, Cass managed to hobble around the corner and back onto Port Street. She moved to the middle of the debris and cow shit-strewn road to make it difficult for anyone or thing to sneak up on her. She had no plan beyond heading south, though going back to the marshal's station was starting to seem like a slightly better than shit idea. She casually thought about executing Sorgram to cheer herself up. She was about ninety percent sure it wasn't a serious thought. Well maybe eighty percent.

Other than a few stray cows there was nobody on the street. It was what she would expect during a storm. Everyone was buttoned up tight. The cattle drive and subsequent gunfight were even less of an incentive for the townsfolk to leave the vulnerable comfort of their own homes. She did find herself wondering where the Bio-Ts were. With the dead one in the genetics facility, presumably the handiwork of the Weyland-Yutani clean-up crew, that left at least six still alive by Cass's reckoning.

The scorpion-like parasite flew out of the dust

straight at her face. Too many, too-long fingers reaching for her face, the strangling tail whipping around behind it. Cass reacted without thinking. Bringing the shotgun to her hip and firing. Winging the thing in mid-air, sending it spinning, bleeding burning yellow pus. The loss of support and the shotgun's recoil knocked Cass off her feet. She hit the ground at the same time as the wounded parasite. It began skittering towards her, dragging several useless legs behind it, acid blood making the ground smoke in its wake. Cass rolled to one side and fired the shotgun, then again. The creature disintegrated in a cloud of yellow smoking pus.

Some instinct honed long ago in the island jungles of Tientsin sensed movement in front of her as another of the creature's leaped at her face. She just managed to get her shotgun between it and her. Its legs gripped the weapon with surprising strength. Its tail wrapped around her neck, constricting, cutting off air, dragging itself closer and closer to her face. Seeing the parasite's under side for the first time, she could make out some kind of fleshy tube flailing out of an unpleasant orificem reaching for her mouth. The word 'inseminate' suddenly flashed across her mind. It was enough. She cried out and, with a sudden burst of adrenaline, pushed against the shotgun for all she was worth. She flung the parasitical thing and the shotgun away from her and drew her .357.

You've got all the time in the w… *shit*! She fired twice

in quick succession, the revolver bucking in her hand. The first shot missed, the second didn't, largely because the thing was so close. The powerful bullet knocked the creature away from her. She howled in agony as acid burned into her leg. But the smoking creature was still moving, however. She blinked away tears of pain, steadied her grip on the revolver with both hands and fired again, two more times, this time taking her time. The creature lay still, the ground under it dissolving.

More movement to her left. A quick shot. A miss. Another of the skittering parasites was almost on her. Again, she forced herself to take her time. It leaped. The last two rounds in the revolver caught it center mass, the power of the bullets reversing the creature's direction in mid-air.

Cass slumped back onto the ground and screamed in pain and frustration.

Then she fell into shadow.

Something loomed out of the dust clouds above her. A wedge-shaped, blackened crown of bone wreathed an eyeless face; a long exoskeletal neck connected the head to a torso of armor-like bone. It stood on long, mantis-like legs with too many joints, its wickedly spurred arms ending in long, clawed fingers. A spiny, segmented tail flicked around behind it ending in a spike that would have shamed a medieval pike head. It towered over Cass.

It opened its slime-lubricated, steel-toothed maw

and a secondary mouth slid out as it hissed. Cass recoiled. This was the thing that had torn Harris in two. There was no question in Cass's mind that this was the Goddess. There was also no question in her mind that she was dead.

Tyler took a hoof to his already injured side as he curled up in a protective ball. Somewhere in the back of his mind he knew he had to try and stand up, but his sight was pinholing, the world getting further away, as he came close to blacking out. He was getting shoved around in the cow shit, repeatedly trod on. A hoof caught him in the head, skewing his mask, and he was coughing, breathing dust. He almost welcomed the panic threatening to overwhelm him.

The air turned orange above him. He felt heat, heard gunfire as the cattle kicked around his curled-up form some more. It had only been a matter of moments and already he felt like he'd received an extensive beating. He was only vaguely aware of strong fingers wrapping around his wrist and pulling him inexorably to his feet. He flinched away from the burst of automatic weapons fire as, one-handed, Serena fired her assault rifle into the air, the surrounding cows all but clambering over each other to get away from the noise. With her other hand she lifted Tyler back onto his feet.

One side of her face was covered in the white of her

internal fluids. The acid had eaten through her synthetic skin and pitted her metal, ceramic and hardened-plastic skull. She also bore the marks of an extensive trampling. The sight of her was enough for Tyler, however. He forced himself to calm down, to straighten his mask, to perform a dust clearance procedure.

She nodded to him. He nodded back.

Serena had made them some room but they needed to clear space to the raised doorway on the bulkhead wall. Serena raised her weapon again, fired another burst into the air, then moved. Then did it again and moved again. Tyler checked his assault rifle but one or more cows had stepped on it and bent the weapon. He removed the magazine and discarded the rifle.

Cattle were fleeing before them, more and more of them deciding that the shuttle hold wasn't for them, pushing their way down the broad ramp, and back out into the blackened concrete of the loading bay. Any that didn't get out of Serena's way were given some incentive via her underslung incinerator.

They had almost reached the steps up to the bulkhead door. Serena had stopped firing to save ammunition as there were now far fewer cows in the shuttle's hold than there had been. Then they heard the shotgun blast, carried to them on the prevailing wind. Moments later, another two more shotgun blasts in quick succession. Then there was only the sound of the screaming wind. They looked at each other.

"I have to go," she told him.

Tyler nodded, though he was starting to wonder if Serena was somehow programmed with a series of actions to take in just such a situation as this. She handed him the assault rifle. He checked the magazine. It was almost empty. He reloaded the weapon with one of the full magazines he was carrying.

"You should go now. Help the marshal," she said.

This was goodbye.

Two rapid shots from a .357 distracted him. Then another two shots. When Tyler turned back, Serena was already at the top of the steps, opening the bulkhead door.

He limped as fast as he could towards the ramp. Another three shots from the .357 and Tyler knew the revolver was now empty.

He reached the top of the ramp and looked back towards the corner of Port Street, where they had left Cass. He couldn't see it for the dust. Then the dust cleared. He saw something huge standing at the top of the street. He raised the rifle to his shoulder.

Take your time, he heard Cass' voice telling him. *Use the scope, the intelligent targeting,* his voice now. He knew how to do this. It didn't matter that he was an investigator. He was a fucking FBI agent, a gang buster. The huge alien creature filled the scope. He knew it for what it was, but it wasn't his goddess. It was just another murderer.

Tyler squeezed the trigger, firing over the loading bay, over the ramparts and into the mouth of Port Street four hundred meters away.

The dust was kicked up all around her by the incoming fire. Cass just couldn't shake the feeling that it was adding injury to insult. Not only was she about to be torn apart by this demonic monstrosity but somebody was shooting at her as well, someone with absolutely no trigger control. Cass curled up in a ball, making herself as small a target as possible. Whomever was shooting seemed to have found a measure of control and was just about managing to fire shorter, more controlled bursts. With her eyes tightly squeezed shut Cass heard a hissing, inhuman scream and heard the earth sizzle as it was splashed in acid. She risked opening an eye. The Goddess was gone.

Tyler fired again and again. Dust drifted across the Goddess and made her a shadow as she lifted her head in an unheard scream. Then the Goddess was swallowed by the dust again. Tyler stopped firing and lowered his weapon. He looked around and glanced towards the door that Serena had just used. He looked back to see if he had a clear shot.

The Goddess exploded out of a dust cloud much

closer to the shuttle, leaping up the ramparts, loping at speed straight towards the ramp.

The shuttle's engines roared into life and everything became flame.

"Shit!" Tyler turned and ran, all his pain forgotten in a sudden burst of adrenaline. He made for the bulkhead door as fire licked into the shuttle's still open cargo hold. He ran up the steps and hit the door release. He glanced behind him and saw the Goddess emerge from the flame, heading straight towards him. The door slid open. Tyler was through the doorway and ran down the short corridor, to the cage elevator that was only just now coming back down to this level, Serena presumably having taken it up to the cockpit.

Something hit the bulkhead behind him with a resounding clang. He heard the scream of reinforced steel being ripped open.

Tyler threw himself into the elevator's open cage and mashed the *up* button. The Goddess was tearing her way through door and bulkhead behind him. Tyler started laying down fire, burst after burst, as the elevator started to rise.

The Goddess forced her way through the rip she'd made. The metal smoking as she bled acid. Her wounds weren't slowing her down. The whole elevator structure shook as the Goddess launched herself at it and starting clambering after Tyler. The assault rifle's magazine ran dry. He ejected the magazine and clumsily wrestled another, his last, into place. Tyler leaned back over the edge of the elevator cage. She was much closer now, having gained ground while he'd reloaded. He triggered the incinerator, spraying her with flame. It only seemed to anger her.

He almost soiled himself when the lift juddered to a halt, thinking it had broken down. Then he realized that he was at the top and that was what the lift was actually supposed to do. He hit the button on the bulkhead door, feeling the whole lift mechanism shake as the unkillable Goddess clambered up after him. The door took forever to slide open. He squeezed through the narrowest gap he could fit through and hit the door control to close it on the other side. The door continued to slide open, apparently having to go through the entire cycle before it could close again.

Tyler turned around. He saw long dagger-tipped, skeletal fingers grab the edge of the elevator cage, her weight bending the metal. Tyler squeezed the trigger on his assault rifle and held it down. Acrid yellow smoke filled the air and the hand disappeared. The door started to close. Tyler fired and fired until the gap was too narrow. Then he turned and ran. Behind him he heard something hit hard against the bulkhead door.

Ahead of him the door to the cockpit was sliding open. He hurdled the bodies of two dead shuttle crew. Behind him, thick metal was being shredded.

Tyler made it into the shuttle's cockpit and slumped into the co-pilot's seat. He found himself looking out over a dust-shrouded Steer City from five stories up as the cockpit door slid shut behind him.

Serena was sat in the pilot's seat, flicking switches and tapping at a keyboard. The display told Tyler that she was disabling failsafes that had some pretty stridently worded warnings.

She finished what she was doing and sat up straight. Turned to look at Tyler.

The creature hit the heavy door behind them, denting it. Then again.

Serena took his hand. He gripped hers tightly. Words were pointless now.

Then she pressed the release and dumped the entirety of the shuttle's fuel into the fire of its own engines.

Cass had given a lot of thought to just staying where she had fallen. Instead, she'd reloaded her revolver and the shotgun, and forced herself to her feet. She liked to think that it was her dauntless frontier spirit responsible for her actions, but really, she'd promised herself a lot of bourbon if she could make it back to the marshal's station.

That said, the sound of the shuttle's engines starting some moments ago had forced her to pick up her hobbling pace: she was still using the shotgun as a walking stick.

She didn't even hear the explosion. The wave of force took her off her feet and then nothing.

Cass came to, to find herself further down Port Street. The shuttle port was a crater. Much of the town north of her position was a smoking ruin. The street and many of the surrounding buildings were covered in blackened cow carcasses.

Cass couldn't feel anything, but she had faith that the pain would return and remind her that she still yet lived. For now, she would stay exactly where she was. She laid her head in the dust. Ash and embers rained down on her.

She rolled her head to one side and saw a cow lying on the ground close by. Unblackened, the cow must have been outside the blast radius of the exploding shuttle. It had one of the parasite things wrapped around its head, except the lung-like organs weren't inflating and deflating. The parasite fell off. The tube-like organ slid from the cow's mouth in a way that made Cass nauseous. The cow shook its head and then it stood up.

ACKNOWLEDGEMENTS

I would like to thank the following:

At Titan: Daquan Cadogan, Steve Saffel and George Sandison. Also Kevin Eddy for an excellent proofread.

At Fox/Disney: Nicole Spiegel and Jeremy Huling.

My agent John Baker at Bell-Lomax.

To Mark Stay (one of the nicest and most supportive people in the SFFH community), and Andrew and Hannah from the *Authorized Podcast* (a must listen if you like films, books and films-about-books) and our fellow enthusiasts at AVP Galaxy.

For their support, both in terms of writing and general contribution to my wellbeing, particularly as it pertains to adventures in publishing: Ed, Tade and RJ (the Brain Trust), James, Brendan, Gillian, Joe and Sarah (the Punjab Irregulars), Allen, Karen, Chris, Marcus and Stew (Worldcon Adventurers).

And of course, Yvonne for not strangling me yet (I'll probably have to change this bit).

ABOUT THE AUTHOR

Gavin G. Smith is the author and co-author of 14 books, a couple of novellas and multiple short stories. His books include (but are not limited to) *Veteran* and its sequel *War in Heaven*, the Age of Scorpio Trilogy, the Bastard Legion Series and *Spec Ops Z*. As well as having written for Black Library, Gavin wrote the novelisation of the Sony Pictures *Bloodshot* movie and Marvel's Original Sin series.

Within the games industry he has worked with Yoozoo, Ubisoft, DPS Games and CCP. In addition, he has optioned several film scripts.

In his free time, he enjoys walking, travel, film, reading, studying for his PhD and is a very keen TTRPG and board gamer.

For more fantastic fiction, author events,
exclusive excerpts, competitions, limited editions and more

VISIT OUR WEBSITE
titanbooks.com

LIKE US ON FACEBOOK
facebook.com/titanbooks

FOLLOW US ON TWITTER AND INSTAGRAM
@TitanBooks

EMAIL US
readerfeedback@titanemail.com